# JANE ASHFORD

Cover art by Alan Ayers



Published by Sourcebooks Casablanca, an imprint of Sourcebooks, Inc.
P.O. Box 4410, Naperville, Illinois 60567-4410
(630) 961-3900
Fax: (630) 961-2168
sourcebooks.com

Printed and bound in United States of America.
OPM 10 9 8 7 6 5 4 3 2 1

# *One*

Lord Randolph Gresham attracted more than one admiring glance as he walked along Grosvenor Square toward Bond Street on a Tuesday morning. And indeed he felt unusually dapper. His dark-blue coat had arrived from the tailor only yesterday. His dove-gray pantaloons outlined a muscular leg. His hat sat at a jaunty angle. He'd often been told that he was the best looking of the six sons of the Duke of Langford—tall, handsome, broad-shouldered men with auburn hair and blue eyes—and today he thought he almost deserved the accolade.

He breathed in the early April air, invigorating with a tang of spring, and listened to the birds calling in the trees. For the next four months, in the interval between parishes, he was not a vicar or a model for proper behavior. He had no special position to uphold and no clerical duties. He was free to enjoy the London season, and he fully intended to do so.

A familiar shape caught his eye in passing. He turned, then went quite still. His feet had taken him automatically into Carlos Place. How odd. His body had somehow remembered what his brain had passed over. He would not have come here consciously, although in an earlier season, six years ago, he'd walked this route nearly every day.

Randolph went a bit further and stopped again to gaze up at a narrow brick house. Behind those tall, narrow windows he'd wooed Rosalie Delacourt, asked for her hand, and been delightfully accepted.

A vision of her laughing face assailed him. She'd so often been laughing, her lips curved in the most enticing way. Her hazel eyes had sparkled like sunshine on water. She'd been elfin slender, with chestnut-brown hair and a few hated freckles on her nose. She was always trying to eradicate those freckles with one nostrum or another.

From the moment they met, introduced by a friend of his mother's at a concert, he'd thought of no one but Rosalie. The fact that she was eminently suitable—by birth and upbringing and fortune—was pleasant, but irrelevant. He would have married her if she'd been a pauper. She said the same. It had all been decided between them in a matter of weeks. Life had seemed perfect to a young man freshly ordained, with a parish, and ready to set off on his chosen path.

Gazing at the unresponsive house, Randolph felt a reminiscent brush of devastation. Why had he come here? His grief was muted by time. He didn't think of Rosalie often now. The Delacourts no longer lived in town. Indeed, he'd heard that they rarely came to London. And who could blame them?

Not for the first time, Randolph was glad that only his mother had known about his engagement to

Rosalie. Randolph had enjoyed keeping his courtship private, away from the eyes of the *haut ton*. His brothers had been busy with their own affairs. And so, in the aftermath, he'd been able to stumble quietly off to Northumberland and what he'd sometimes thought of as exile, though of course it wasn't. He'd found solace in his work and the good he could do, and gradually his pain had eased.

Randolph took a moment to acknowledge the past with a bowed head and then walked on. He wouldn't come this way again.

A few minutes later, Randolph reached his original goal, another place he hadn't been in years, Angelo's Academy on Bond Street, next to Gentleman Jackson's boxing saloon. Entering, he heard the familiar sound of ringing steel and murmured commentary. Pairs of men fenced with blunted foils, guided and corrected by the famed proprietor and his helpers. Others worked on their stance or observed. Randolph joined the latter until he was noticed and the owner of the place hurried over. "It's been far too long since we've seen you, Lord Randolph," said Henry Angelo, scion of the dynasty of fencing masters.

"And I've probably forgotten most of what you taught me," replied Randolph. "But I thought I'd try a match if it could be arranged." The clash of blades filled him with pleasant nostalgia. He'd spent many a satisfying hour surrounded by that sound. Angelo's was a fashionable gathering place where gentlemen socialized as well as learned the art of swordsmanship.

"Of course. I'd like to see how one of my best pupils has kept up his skills."

"You mustn't be too harsh," replied Randolph with a smile. "I had no opportunities to fence in Northumberland." He had practiced the moves now and then, but he'd found no partners in the North.

A young man nearby stepped forward. "I'd be happy to oblige."

Henry's smile went slightly stiff. "Unnecessary, Mr. Wrentham," he said. "I'll take on Lord Randolph myself."

"Oh, but I'd like to try my chances against one of your *best pupils*."

The newcomer spoke with a belligerent edge, as if Henry had angered him somehow. Randolph eyed him. A well-set-up fellow in his twenties with dark hair and eyes, he looked familiar. "We've met, haven't we?"

"At Salbridge," the younger man agreed. "Charles Wrentham."

"Of course. You acted in the play."

Wrentham grimaced as if he'd been criticized. "So, shall we have at it then?"

Randolph understood from Henry's stance and expression that he would prefer otherwise. But Wrentham's face told him there was no way to refuse without giving offense. Randolph agreed with a bow.

Donning fencing gear brought back more memories. Randolph relished the feel of the canvas vest and wire mask. He took down a foil and swished it through the air, feeling old reflexes surface. It was said that physical skills learned as a youth stayed with you, and he didn't think he'd lost his touch. He tried a lunge and parry. Fencing had fascinated him from the moment he'd picked up a sword. The combination of concentration, precision, endurance, and strength exactly suited his temperament, and he'd picked up the skill quickly. Faster than any of his brothers, which added to his enthusiasm, he acknowledged. Here was one area where he outshone them all. Well, except Sebastian, who had a cavalryman's fine slashing style with a saber from horseback. That was quite a different thing, however. No one fought to the death at Angelo's.

Randolph moved to an open space on the floor. Wrentham faced him, raising his foil in a salute. Noting that Henry was hovering, and wondering why, Randolph matched Wrentham's gesture and took his stance. Muscle and mind meshed in the old way. He smiled behind his mask.

Randolph let Wrentham make the first move, to get a sense of his style and skill. The young man came in with a lunge. He overextended, and Randolph parried the thrust. Wrentham pulled back and slashed downward. Randolph blocked the blow. And so it went for some minutes, Wrentham attacking and Randolph easily fending him off. The younger man had some ability, Randolph noted, but he lacked control. And he didn't seem to pay much heed to his opponent. Divining an adversary's next move was half of winning.

Satisfied, Randolph went on the offensive. He knocked Wrentham's blade aside with a ringing clang and scored a hit on the younger man's chest with a clever riposte. Wrentham sprang back, then surged forward again. Randolph feinted left. Wrentham reacted. Randolph struck through the resulting gap in the young man's defenses, scoring another hit.

Wrentham reacted with a flying lunge, a move usually reserved for saber matches, leaping and thrusting at the same time in an effort at surprise.

Randolph dropped low, touching the floor with his free hand for balance. Straightening his sword arm, he stabbed upward and scored a third hit to Wrentham's ribs before drawing back under his opponent's blade.

Something seemed to snap in Wrentham at this clever exhibition of superior skill. He went wild, beating the air with his foil like a windmill. Randolph met each slashing blow—above, left, right—with a clang of metal that he felt all the way down his arm. He could hear Henry commanding them to stop, but he couldn't spare an instant's attention. The blunted foil wouldn't stab him, but a great whack to head or shoulder would nonetheless hurt. He'd seen men knocked silly by flailing like this. Nothing for it but to fight Wrentham off. Randolph blocked and parried over and over again, waiting for a chance to end it.

At last, he found an opening and used a move Henry had taught him, twisting and flicking his sword to disarm Wrentham. The younger man's foil went flying across the room. It hit, bounced, and skittered over the floorboards to a stop.

With a curse, Wrentham jerked off his wire mask and hurled it against the wall. A flake of plaster came loose and dropped with it. He stalked out, chest pumping, teeth bared.

Silence filled the academy. All the other fencers

had stopped to watch this unusual bout. "Well done," called several of them.

Randolph removed his own mask. He was breathing fast but not panting, he was happy to see.

Henry took his foil. "Very well done," he said quietly. "You're as skilled as ever, my lord."

"What the deuce is wrong with Wrentham?" Randolph asked.

"He's an overly dramatic young man with a tendency to lose his temper at the least obstacle," said Henry. "I've been trying to teach him there's more to fencing than the win."

"Can you teach that?"

Henry shrugged. "Sometimes. Mr. Wrentham was doing much better before he went out of town in the autumn."

Randolph unbuckled the straps of his fencing vest and pulled it off. "I can see why you tried to discourage that bout."

Henry bowed. "Discernment was always one of your greatest strengths, my lord."

The remark came back to Randolph later that day as he sat in his room at Langford House and contemplated a bleeding fingertip. Again. He was beginning to see why no one had played the lute for hundreds of years, and to doubt his supposed discernment. The archaic instrument was proving difficult to master despite his musical talent. Learning to play the pianoforte had not been nearly so slow.

He set the lute aside, careful not to touch his

clothing or the fabric covering the armchair, then blotted his finger on a bit of toweling he'd procured for the purpose. He didn't want to bloody another handkerchief for the servants to launder. It wasn't fair to them. And a bloody cloth roused unwarranted concern. His former housekeeper, back in Northumberland, had concocted a whole tragic tale, imagining that he was leaving his clerical post in the North to go off alone and die of consumption.

He'd had to show her the lute and demonstrate its perils to keep her from rallying the entire village of Hexham to nurse him. He wouldn't miss that lady's constant presence in his new posting in Derbyshire. Though kindly intentioned for the most part, she'd made privacy nearly impossible in his parsonage.

The bleeding stanched, Randolph put the lute in its case and set it in the bottom of the wardrobe that had held his possessions throughout his youth. He'd chosen to stay in Langford House for the season. Why take a couple of rooms when he could enjoy the luxury and convenience of his old home? He *liked* his parents, after all. He was looking forward to their company and their help.

He might have stayed with his older brother Sebastian, who'd taken a house not far away. But Sebastian's new wife was bringing out her next-younger sister this season, and her youngest sister, Hilda, was with them as well. Randolph wouldn't have dared to practice his lute around her. Young Hilda would nag until she pried the whole odd story out of him, and then store the knowledge away for her own purposes. She was not above a spot of genial blackmail.

Randolph would also have been welcomed by his younger brother Robert and *his* new wife in Russell Square. Their household held out the lure of intellectual stimulation. But Randolph admitted, silently, that he relished a more fashionable address. He wasn't a snob. Far from it! But he was here for a particular purpose, and first impressions were important.

He was in London, in fact, to acquire a wife. A churchman was expected to have a partner in his parish work, and it was past time for him to find one. He'd waited long enough for another love. He was reconciled to the idea that he'd had his chance with Rosalie and lost it. There would be no other grand passion for him.

This was no huge hardship, Randolph told himself, not for the first time. Or the twentieth. He would find a young lady who shared his values, and they would come to an agreement. During a London season, he'd be surrounded by eligible girls eager to find husbands, a plethora of choices. What more could a man ask?

He rose and went over to the cheval glass, meeting his own blue eyes in the mirror. He was said to be handsome. Noting others' opinions wasn't vanity. So that was an advantage. He was wellborn. He was making some progress in his profession at last. He had a moderate income, though it would be well to have a bit more. He wasn't shy. He was quietly confident of his own strengths and talents.

Randolph exchanged a wry glance with his reflection. On the negative side, he'd never quite gotten the hang of flirting. It seemed to be the art of talking about nothing, and he vastly preferred to talk about *something.* But then, he had a tendency to go on and on about a topic if not curbed. He could easily imagine some girls poking fun at him for that. And what *about* fun? Randolph had noticed that his finely honed sense of humor was too dry for some. They missed his point and stared as if he was mad. Of course he was looking for an intelligent wife, so perhaps that didn't matter.

He liked helping people. It was one of the delights of being a clergyman. He'd had the great pleasure of aiding Sebastian and Robert, just a bit, as they won their brides last year. At the same time, he'd learned that strangers didn't always wish to be helped.

Randolph took a last look in the mirror. Surely those character points added up to a good chance of success? He gave himself an encouraging nod. He'd test it out tonight. He'd been invited to an informal evening party, a mere nothing before the season truly began, the hostess had claimed. It sounded like an ideal opportunity to ease his way into the *haut ton.*

Verity Sinclair looked around the opulent drawing room, drinking in every detail of the decor and the fashionable crowd. She had to resist an urge to pinch herself to prove she was actually here and not dreaming. It had taken her five endless years to convince her parents that she should have a London season. They hadn't been able to see the point of it, no matter what advantages she brought forward. Papa and Mama were quietly happy living in a cathedral close and being held up as models of decorum for the whole bishopric. Verity, on the other hand, often thought she'd go mad within those staid confines.

She sighed. She loved her parents dearly, but for most of her life she'd felt like a grasshopper reared by ants. Indeed, at age eight, she'd shocked her parents by asking if she was adopted. She hadn't meant to hurt their feelings or to imply any lack of affection. Their differences had just seemed so marked. Mama and Papa relished routine; Verity yearned for adventure. They read scholarly tomes; she pored over *Robinson Crusoe* and accounts of the voyages of Captain Cook. They preferred solitude or the company of a few friends; she liked a large, lively company. They took sedate strolls; she tried to teach herself knife throwing, which would come in handy if and when she required food in the wilderness.

Her mother was watching her with an expression that gently suggested skepticism. Verity smiled at her and turned toward the chattering crowd. She was in the capital at last, in position to carry out her plan. Surely this room was full of men who were *not* clergymen and who were, or were acquainted with, far more intrepid types. Indeed, from some news she'd picked up recently, 1819 might be the perfect year for her purposes, even if she was twenty-four and seen by some as practically on the shelf.

She *would* succeed, despite the misfortune of possessing hair the color of a beetroot and milky skin that freckled at the least touch of sun. Despite the fact that nature had chosen to endow her with a bosom that seemed to positively drag men's eyes from her face and her arguments. Which was not her fault, as her father sometimes seemed to think. It was a reasonably pretty face, she thought. Her features were regular, and she'd been told her blue-green eyes were striking.

"Miss Sinclair."

Verity turned to find her hostess beside her, along with a tall, exceedingly handsome man. He had wonderful shoulders and intense blue eyes. Compared to the fellows she knew, he looked polished and sophisticated. More than that, he met her gaze, with only the briefest straying to other regions of her anatomy. Verity smiled. This was promising.

"May I present Lord Randolph Gresham," the woman continued. "Lord Randolph, Miss Verity Sinclair."

A lord, Verity thought. Not a requirement from her list, but nothing to sneeze at either.

"I think you will have much in common," their hostess added. Addressing each of them in turn, she said, "Lord Randolph is vicar of a parish in Northumberland. Miss Sinclair is the daughter of the dean of Chester Cathedral."

When the woman left them together, Verity's budding elation collapsed. It could not be that the first man she met in London—and such an attractive man—was a clergyman. Were there so many in the world that she couldn't be spared another? Possessed by an oddly urgent sense of danger, Verity blurted, "I could never abide life in a country parish."

He blinked, clearly startled.

"I would find the limited society unendurable." Her comment came out sounding like an accusation. Verity bit her lower lip. There was no reason to be *this* keenly disappointed. What was the matter with her?

"I don't recall asking for your opinion," he said.

"The isolation makes people narrow-minded."

"I beg your pardon?"

He looked offended. Verity couldn't blame him. She was right, of course; she'd observed the tendency often enough, but there was no need to say it aloud. Or to continue this conversation. She should move away, find a more promising prospect. Instead, she said, "And quite behind the times. Antiquated, even."

"Indeed?"

His blue eyes had gone cool. What had come over her? She was never rude. She ought to apologize.

"If you will excuse me, I see that some friends have arrived," he said.

Lord Randolph gave her a small bow and walked away. Which didn't matter, Verity thought. She'd meant to stop talking to him. And yet a pang of regret shook her. *Stop it at once*, she told herself. That was not the sort of man who searched for the wellspring of the Blue Nile, or discovered unknown species or peoples. Silently, she repeated her talisman phrase—Twelve Waterloo Place—and turned to find other town dwellers to meet.

Randolph crossed the room to join his brother Sebastian's party. They'd come in at just the right moment to cover his escape from the opinionated young lady. Who had asked what she thought? Who did she think she was? "I've just met the most fearsome girl," he said.

"Really?" His military brother looked sleepily formidable, as usual.

"Which one?" asked Sebastian's lovely blond wife Georgina, resplendent in pale-green silk. Her sister Emma stood just behind her, a younger, less self-assured version of Stane beauty.

"The one over there, with the extremely vivid hair."

"And the generous…endowment?" Sebastian said. When Georgina elbowed him, he added, "I was only making an observation. It's nothing to me."

The pair exchanged a lazy smile that told anyone with eyes of their marital bliss. Randolph envied both the fact and the ease of it. "That's the one. Miss Verity Sinclair. Daughter of the dean of Chester Cathedral, if you please." Which had seemed promising. Until it turned out that it wasn't.

"Cathedral? I would have thought that was right up your alley," his brother replied. "What's so fearsome about her? She looks harmless enough."

"She imagines that I am narrow-minded. And antiquated."

"What? Why would she think that?" Sebastian frowned.

"Whatever did you say to her?" Georgina wondered.

"I had no opportunity to say anything. She…graced me with her opinions all unasked."

"Will there be any dancing?" Emma asked.

Georgina turned to her sister, shaking her head. "Not tonight. This is a small party, a chance for you to make some acquaintances before the big squeezes later in the season."

Emma scanned the crowd. "Everyone looks old."

"Not everyone. You'll meet plenty of young people."

"Georgina's been studying up," said Sebastian proudly. "She means to give Emma a bang-up launch into society."

"You make me sound like some sort of ship," Emma replied. But she smiled.

Scanning the crowd, Georgina did look rather like a canny navigator plotting a course. "Come along," she said to Emma, ready to plunge in. Then she paused. "Sinclair," Georgina said. "Wouldn't she be a connection of the Archbishop of Canterbury?"

"Would she?" It needed only that, Randolph thought. Given his unfortunate…incident with the archbishop, the chit was a walking recipe for disaster. It was fortunate that she'd put him off. Who knew what trouble he might have fallen into otherwise! Now he could make a point of avoiding her.

The ladies went off to begin Emma's introduction into the *ton*. The Gresham brothers snagged glasses of wine and stood back to observe.

"Did you meet Georgina at an evening like this?" Randolph asked after a while.

"At a ball," replied Sebastian.

"Dancing is a good way to become acquainted."

"I had to fight my way through a crowd of fellows to snag one." Watching his wife, Sebastian smiled. "Say, Georgina could give you a few pointers." He offered Randolph a sly grin. "Bring you out along with Emma."

"I'm no bashful eighteen-year-old," replied Randolph, revolted.

"Or you could marry Emma. Two birds with one stone and all that."

"No!" The word escaped Randolph without thought. "I mean, she's a nice enough girl, but—"

"Only joking," Sebastian assured him. "You'll want a serious, brainy female. Likes poetry and that sort of thing. Emma's more along my line, a bit dim."

"You aren't dim," said Randolph. Unwillingly, he found his gaze straying back to Verity Sinclair. At first glance, she'd seemed so beguiling, her eyes brimming with interest and…a crackle of spirit.

She turned, and he looked away before he could be caught staring at the archbishop's relative, for goodness' sake. It was a sign, he concluded, a warning to be careful on his hunt. One spent one's whole life with a wife. A mistaken choice would be disastrous. He returned his attention to his brother.

Toward the end of the evening, Verity found herself briefly alone. Even though this had been called a small party, her mind whirled with names. It seemed as if she'd been introduced to scores of people, more than she met in a month at home. The buzz of conversation was positively thrilling.

Verity ran her eyes over the crowd. She noted the colors in their clothes, particularly the ladies' dresses, the sparkle of jewels and candlelight. She breathed in the mingled scents of perfumes and pomades and hot wax. She absorbed the oceanic rhythm of talk. The taste of lemonade lingered on her lips. She gathered all these details into one impression and fixed it firmly in her mind. Then she added this moment to a string of such memories stored in a special place in her mind—a string of vivid scenes that punctuated her life. She'd been creating moments since she was quite young. She could move down the string and revisit each epoch of her life. And before long, she'd be adding far more dramatic, exotic moments to her collection. She was absolutely resolved on that.

Verity looked about her. The blond girl nearby was Lady Emma Stane. Verity remembered her not only because Emma was one of the few here near her own age, but also because she was part of the group Lord Randolph had joined when he abandoned her. Not abandoned, Verity thought. What a poor choice of words. She'd wanted him to go away. Indeed, she'd repelled him. On purpose. A country clergyman! Still, she drifted toward Emma. They'd been introduced as cohorts, both at their first *ton* party. Emma was obviously younger, but Verity had as little experience of high society. "Have you enjoyed the evening?" she asked.

"Oh yes," Emma replied. "I've waited so long to be in London!"

"I, too. I had such a time convincing my parents to give me a season."

"Mine just refuse to come to town," said Emma with an incredulous smile. "They are absolutely fixed in Herefordshire."

"And so you are here with—?"

"My sister Georgina." Emma indicated the beautiful blond woman Verity had noticed earlier. "She married Lord Sebastian last summer."

Following Emma's gesture, Verity eyed the two handsome men in the corner of the room. Lord

Sebastian and Lord Randolph then. They were clearly brothers.

"And now she's brought me to London just as she promised. I intend to have a *splendid* time. The duchess has promised me an invitation to her ball."

"Duchess?"

"Lord Sebastian's mother. She's positively the height of fashion."

The man was a duke's son? As well as handsome and obviously self-assured? Why bury himself in a country parish? Not that she cared. It had nothing to do with her. Verity turned her back on the impossible Lord Randolph. Her mother was beckoning. It was already time to go.

# Two

The Duke and Duchess of Langford arrived in London three days later, in the early evening, trailing a cavalcade of carriages bearing a small mountain of baggage. With a clatter and bustle, Langford House came to life around Randolph. "There you are!" he exclaimed from the stairs as his parents strolled inside, arm in arm.

They stopped to smile up at him—a tall woman, rather angular, with arching brows and an aquiline nose, and a taller, distinguished man of sixty, with a lazy assurance that made him formidable. He could hardly have been more fortunate in his progenitors, Randolph thought. He'd inherited Mama's hair, a rich, deep color between chestnut and strawberry, and Papa's intense blue eyes and rangy frame. But it was so much more than that. These two people had taught him, by example, nearly everything he knew about being a worthwhile human being.

Mama had shown him that an inability to tolerate fools did not prevent one from being kind. Papa had demonstrated that immense dignity and presence could coexist with compassion and a wicked sense of humor.

And the two of them together embodied the reality of enduring love. Randolph had admired his parents' marriage since he was old enough to notice such things. He'd had hopes of finding a similar combination of passion and companionship, tenderness and support through life's challenges. Must he really abandon the idea?

"How lovely this is," said his mother as she kissed his cheek in greeting. "It's been so long since I've had a son living in the house. You look well."

Randolph met her discerning gaze. As children, he and his brothers had decided she could see through walls. "And you are as beautiful as ever, Mama."

"Flatterer."

"The truth is not flattery," said the duke as they walked together up the stairs to the drawing room.

The duchess's eyes danced. Decades of laughter crinkled the skin around them, but this mark of age suited her. "So you've come to London in search of a wife," she said.

"I have," Randolph replied. "And I will be glad of your help."

"None of your brothers wanted any," said his father.

"Ah, but I have always been the wisest of your sons."

Smiling, the duke raised an eyebrow. "The most earnest certainly. I seem to remember that you once tried to reform a cat."

Randolph burst out laughing. "Ruff! I'd forgotten about him."

"A disturbed animal," said his father.

"Ruff was taken from his mother too early," said the duchess. "He suckled people's fingers as a form of comfort." She didn't sound entirely convinced.

"That was his excuse," Randolph replied. "Or your excuse for him. Robert thought that cat knew quite well what he was doing. Ruff always chose people who hated cats, you know."

The duke nodded. "Old Dalby leapt from his chair with a shriek like a steam whistle. Not long after that, I found you trying to make Ruff see the error of his ways."

"I used pictures," Randolph recalled. "Since words never had the least effect on him. James helped me draw them. But Ruff couldn't seem to grasp their significance, no matter how many times I sat him down and took him through my demonstration. Finally, I put his front paw into my mouth." Randolph smiled at the memory. What a ridiculous little boy he'd been.

"You what?" said the duchess.

"To show him, literally, how he made his victims uncomfortable."

"And did he, er, get the point?" asked the duke.

"He clawed several furrows into my tongue, which bled copiously, all down my chin," Randolph recalled. "James nearly choked me with his handkerchief. I wonder if he remembers? My tongue hurt for days."

"You never said a word." His mother shook her head.

"I didn't want to admit my…miscalculation. And watch Sebastian laugh himself sick. You'd have laughed, too."

"I would not," declared the duchess.

"Oh, not out loud," Randolph said. "But your lips would've twitched. And Papa's eyes would have twinkled as he said something…dry. It's a terrible trial to be amusing at seven years of age."

"Humor was a…bastion against the antics of six boys," observed his father.

"I'm sure it was," Randolph replied, remembering some of his brothers' wilder pranks.

They enjoyed a mutual laugh, and Randolph savored the moment. With two older brothers and three younger ones, he'd seldom had his parents to himself. He was going to enjoy spending time in their company. "In any case, I learned a useful lesson," he added. "Cats are not good candidates for reformation."

Amid more laughter, they settled in the drawing room. The duke poured small glasses of Madeira from a decanter awaiting them. "So how are we to help in your quest for a wife?" he asked as they sipped. "Introductions, I suppose?"

"Indeed. I hope Mama will make them. Judiciously. Not the pert London misses." Miss Verity Sinclair would fit right into that group, Randolph thought. But Miss Sinclair had made herself irrelevant to this conversation. "I intend to take a systematic approach," he added.

"Systematic?" his father repeated.

"Yes. I mean to meet all the eligible young ladies currently available. I shall make my choice from among them."

"Do they have anything to say about this?" asked his mother.

"Of course. Finding me charming is the chief criterion." Randolph smiled wryly. "Which has already eliminated one candidate." The duchess looked inquiring, but he didn't elaborate.

"That sounds rather clinical," said the duke.

Randolph felt a trace of impatience. "I can't wait

any longer, Papa. I'm thirty years old. I have to take a hand in my future."

"Yes, but Randolph..." began his mother.

He evaded her understanding gaze; he didn't wish to think of Rosalie again. "The thing is, Mama..." He hesitated over how to put it. "I've waited for years. No girl has...wandered into my life in Northumberland." He smiled and shrugged. "Perhaps I'm just not as lucky as my brothers. I've become quite lonely." His voice wavered slightly on the last word, and he tightened his jaw. Couldn't have that!

"Oh, Randolph." His mother's expression was suddenly all sympathy.

He cleared his throat and frowned to show that this was no great matter. "And so I have determined to use all my...faculties to remedy the matter. Systematic thought is merely one of them." Randolph pulled a sheet of paper from the inner pocket of his coat. "A quite effective tool. I've begun a list."

"Of eligible young ladies?" his father asked.

"That's it. Georgina was a great help. She's going at it from the other direction, you see."

"The other direction?"

"Likely husbands for her sister. But she noted the daughters as well when she was looking over the families."

"So she is also being systematic?" asked the duke.

"You may laugh, Papa, but you will see that it works."

"I shall enjoy that very much."

"Let me look," declared the duchess, holding out an imperious hand. Randolph gave her his list, and she scanned it. "Good Lord."

The duke raised an eyebrow.

"He's made a chart." She showed her husband the page, with its lined grid. Some boxes held notations; others were empty.

"I shall fill it in as I gather more information," Randolph said. His clever organizational methods, of which he'd been so proud, suddenly seemed less appropriate.

His mother read the labels in the top line. "Family, fortune, appearance, temperament, reputation. Randolph! Young women are not commodities."

"I know that, Mama."

"Do you?" She tapped the page. "This implies otherwise."

"It is just a…a mnemonic of sorts. To keep track."

"Will you also give them high or low marks, like a schoolmaster?" asked the duke.

Randolph wilted a bit under their combined gaze. He'd meant to do so, to decide where to concentrate his wooing. It wasn't designed to be an insult. But it seemed that he'd carried a subject too far once again.

"You are not some godlike being, looking down on mere mortals and passing judgment," said his mother.

"Of course I'm not!" It was a revolting idea.

"Well, someone seeing this might conclude that you thought you *were*." She tapped his grid again.

"I wouldn't show it to anyone else," he said defensively.

"I should hope not."

Randolph writhed a little as he retrieved the chart. Perspicacious as his mother was, she didn't seem to understand. He wasn't some romantic youngster. He needed a clear-eyed goal and a plan. He folded the page and returned it to his pocket. "If you don't wish to help me—" he began.

"Oh, of course we will help you," said his mother.

Randolph felt a spurt of optimism. Surely he couldn't fail with the Duchess of Langford solidly on his side.

❧

It was very pleasant, Verity Sinclair thought as she walked into her second *ton* party, to see someone she knew, and liked, at once. She went to join Lady Emma Stane, standing with a group of young ladies near the center of the crowded reception room. Emma—they had already agreed to abandon formality between them—introduced the others, and Verity committed their names to memory. Her mother claimed that an intelligent person had no excuse for forgetting such things. Verity had refrained from pointing out that Mama had lived her life in a small social circle.

"Ooh," said the small, slender girl in the center of the group. "There's Rochford."

Since Verity was facing in the opposite direction, she couldn't see the object of this remark. However, she could appreciate, and envy, the speaker's perfectly cut silk gown, cropped and crimped brown hair, and air of careless sophistication. Verity sighed, feeling slightly dowdy despite her new dress. Miss Olivia Townsend had the elfin figure best suited for current fashions. Verity could never wear such a low-cut bodice, even if Mama would allow it. With her ample bosom, there was too much risk of mortifying accidents.

"He's an out-and-out Corinthian," Miss Townsend

added. "And a terrible rake." Startled murmurs greeted this piece of information. "I overheard my older brother say that two slatterns fought over Rochford in the street. Like shrieking, snarling alley cats," she said, clearly relishing the phrase.

Gasps of delicious horror went 'round the circle—at the picture she painted and her use of the word *slattern*.

"They say he fought a duel when he was nineteen," Miss Townsend added. "Imagine, just our age."

Well, their age, Verity thought. But five years was not so very much older.

"With swords, not pistols. Like in a novel."

Verity edged around. "Which one?" she murmured to Emma.

"The light-haired man." Emma's eyes flicked right.

Verity followed the line of her glance to a tall, blond gentleman in impeccable evening dress. He moved across the room with careless grace, a mocking half smile on his face. He looked as if he knew people were talking about him. And enjoyed it.

"But what's he doing here, if he's so wicked?" murmured one of the other girls.

"Oh, wicked." Miss Townsend was dismissive. "He amuses the *ton*. Everyone loves gossip."

"Which we never get to hear," complained another girl.

"Not *officially*," replied Miss Townsend with a sly smile. "I can usually pry the best stories out of somebody."

Mr. Rochford wasn't as handsome as Lord Randolph Gresham, Verity thought. But he drew the eye. The people around him seemed to become background.

"Girls swoon over him," Miss Townsend continued.

"And he doesn't care in the least. He leaves a wake of broken hearts." She mimed ocean waves with one hand.

Here was the very opposite of a worthy clergyman, Verity thought. Though not precisely what she was looking for, he might know all sorts of bold people.

"That sounds rather wicked to me," said Emma.

Olivia Townsend shrugged. "It's not as if he encourages them."

"Will we meet him?" Verity asked. What did one say to a rake? It must be a very different sort of conversation than what she was used to. She wouldn't mind trying it out.

"Oh, no one will introduce him to *us*." Miss Townsend sounded disappointed. "We're meant to find husbands, not...adventure."

Expressions around the circle showed varying reactions to this truth—from regret to satisfaction. For her part, Verity was transfixed by Miss Townsend's final word. Here was a fellow seeker, it seemed. She decided that she wished to become better acquainted with Olivia Townsend.

There was a stir at the entrance. Verity turned to watch Lord Randolph enter, in the company of a striking older couple. Overhearing murmurs of *duchess*, she concluded that they were his parents. She saw a resemblance to the poised, patrician duke.

Candlelight glinted in Lord Randolph's auburn hair. He had the shoulders and torso and muscular legs of an athlete, not a country clergyman. Verity bit her lower lip. The bishop back home would be shocked if he knew Verity was admiring a man's leg.

Lord Randolph bent his head to catch some

remark, and smiled in response. Verity caught her breath. She hadn't seen him smile during their ill-fated conversation. Well, of course she hadn't. Not with the way she'd spoken to him. His smile transformed his coolly classical features. His face lit with warmth and sympathy and humorous intelligence. Verity's heart exhibited a disturbing tendency to yearn toward him.

Lord Randolph looked around the room and caught her staring. Their eyes locked for a riveting moment before Verity flushed and turned away. All right. He was…beguiling. That was too bad. If she'd wanted to settle in a country parish, she needn't have come to London at all. She could have accepted one of the extremely worthy offers she'd received in her father's house. In which case she wouldn't have met Lord Randolph. And it wouldn't matter either way, and she was getting tangled up in useless conjecture. *I have a plan*, Verity insisted silently. She was determined to lead an expansive, exciting life. Lord Randolph's bewitching smile was a distraction that she simply couldn't afford.

"Everyone. Your attention, please." Their hostess stood at the center of the crowded room, her hands raised to catch her guests' eyes. "I have a treat for you tonight."

Verity knew that London hostesses competed to offer novel entertainment. Mrs. Baines's triumphant smile suggested that she had scored some sort of coup. Verity moved closer, wondering what was coming.

"We have a very special guest with us," Mrs. Baines continued, candlelight reflecting off her jewels. "Herr Doktor Grossmann." She moved aside, like a magician pulling back a curtain. A plump gentleman of medium height stepped up beside her. He wore an old-fashioned frock coat and narrow trousers. Curly brown hair and a bushy beard wreathed his round face. Some here would dismiss him as foreign-looking and unfashionable, Verity thought. She found the look in his blue eyes shrewd and tolerant. He offered the crowd a crisp bow, not quite clicking his heels. "Herr Grossmann has the most fascinating system for judging character," said their hostess.

"Not judging, dear madam," said the man. His voice was deep, tinged with a German accent. "I discover propensities only."

Puzzled murmurs suggested that others shared Verity's uncertainty about this word.

Mrs. Baines waved it aside. "He's going to explain it all to us. Come along." Beckoning, she led her guests down the room. Footmen opened a pair of sliding doors, revealing rows of gilt chairs facing a small podium.

Dismay on a number of faces made Verity smile. Clearly they hadn't come here for a lecture. Several young gentlemen hung back and slipped away; others appeared resigned, or resentful. Lord Randolph, on the other hand, strode eagerly to a seat near the front.

Herr Grossmann took his place on the podium with an understanding smile and waited for the crowd to settle. When it had, he pulled a cloth from an easel at his side, exposing a large, complicated diagram.

Randolph leaned forward. The image showed a man's bare head in profile. All over the dome of the skull, sections were marked out and labeled with words like *hope, combativeness, self-esteem, parental love, acquisitiveness*, and *benevolence*. Too many to take in all at once.

"This is a map we use in the practice of phrenology," said Herr Grossmann. He picked up a wooden pointer.

Randolph analyzed the unfamiliar word. From the Greek, it meant "study of the mind."

Herr Grossmann gestured with the stick. "I am sure all of us have observed that human beings have various tendencies. To be greedy, say, or proud or unusually kind. Each person possesses a different, ah, constellation of propensities. It has recently been discovered that each one of these is situated in a different area of the brain." He tapped the pointer on the diagram. "For example, as you see here, the love of offspring is located centrally at the back of the head."

The crowd murmured, peering over one another's shoulders at the diagram. Randolph leaned forward to read more of the labels.

Herr Grossmann appeared gratified at the reaction. He moved the pointer around the pictured head. "Now, the cranium, the skull, reflects the relative sizes of these areas of the brain, revealing the potential influence of a given trait."

"You mean the shape of the head defines character?" Randolph asked.

"Rather the other way about, sir," responded the German. "The relative strength of propensities is reflected in the bone." He tapped on the diagram again.

"Herr Grossmann can lay bare the truth of our inner selves for all to see," put in Mrs. Baines. She gave a delighted shiver at the idea.

The gentleman in question frowned and shook his

head. "By careful measurement and assessment, an expert can deduce a great deal about an individual's *propensities*. This does not necessarily predict behavior. Each of us can control our impulses, can we not?"

From the buzz around him, Randolph concluded that no one had really heard this caveat. "I take it that you are such an expert, Herr Grossmann," he said. "How is the assessment made?"

Seemingly grateful for a sign of serious interest, Grossmann spoke directly to Randolph. "The phrenologist palpates the skull, feeling for the pattern of enlargements or indentations. He can then compile a report on the person's natural tendencies." He raised his voice a bit to add, "Not, I must emphasize, on any absolute limitations or strengths of character."

"So phrenology is not destiny?" Randolph asked with a smile.

"Precisely," the German replied. He offered a small bow at this evidence of understanding.

It was quite an interesting idea, Randolph thought. Up to now, the only way to study the mind had been through introspection. A rather circular process, he'd found. If there was an effective scientific alternative, that would be a step forward.

Their hostess clapped her hands to regain the crowd's attention. "Who will volunteer to be examined by Herr Grossmann?" She gave her guests an arch glance. "Who dares to reveal their innermost secrets?"

The German's objections to this phrase were lost in her guests' response. Everyone seemed to have a comment, but no one appeared ready to volunteer.

"I will." The murmurs intensified as Thomas

Rochford strolled forward, a wicked smile on his handsome face.

Herr Grossmann held up his hands. "I had not planned to do an assessment here and now. This is not really a proper venue. I do not have my calipers. And I require—"

"Oh, but you must." Mrs. Baines gave him a glittering smile, her narrowed eyes promising vengeance if he spoiled her party. "We are all so interested."

Grossmann grimaced. "Well, perhaps a partial..." His deep voice trailed off under the battery of eyes focused upon him.

Rochford stepped up beside him. "What shall I do?"

One could hardly have arranged a greater contrast, Randolph thought. The tall, exquisitely dressed Corinthian loomed over the plump, unfashionable foreigner with his untidy beard. And yet Herr Grossmann retained a curious dignity. "We will need a chair," he said.

One was thrust up from the front row. The German gestured Rochford into it. He sat with careless grace.

"I shall have to touch your head, sir."

Rochford nodded permission.

Herr Grossmann stood straighter. Delicately, he placed spread fingertips on Rochford's skull. People crowded forward to see. Randolph watched with interest as the German traced the contours of Rochford's head, mussing his artfully arranged blond hair. The room grew silent, Rochford increasingly bland.

"Strong predispositions to self-esteem and firmness," Grossmann said after a while. His deep voice was clear and confident.

You could look at the man and deduce that, Randolph thought.

"The amative bump is pronounced."

A titter circulated through the room. Perhaps the German knew Rochford's rakish reputation?

"A deficit in mechanical ability," Grossmann added. "Only moderately acquisitive."

"You have not seen me at the gaming tables, Herr Grossmann," said Rochford. Onlookers laughed.

The German simply continued his examination. "A decided bent toward mirth," he said, making Randolph suspect a sly commentary. "Overbalanced by secretive tendencies and the urge toward self-preservation."

Randolph caught a flash of surprise on Rochford's face, quickly masked. The man shifted out from under Grossmann's fingers and rose. "Fascinating. But I mustn't monopolize the Herr Doktor's attentions."

Others surged forward, eager to hear about themselves. Randolph watched Rochford fade back into the crowd. He looked unsettled, which was the most interesting thing about the whole incident.

"Please," Grossmann protested. "I have consulting rooms in Harley Street. A much better…situation for a thorough examination."

No one listened. The German was engulfed in a sea of waving arms and escalating demands.

"Aren't you going to try it?" asked a female voice at Randolph's elbow.

He turned to find Miss Verity Sinclair beside him. "Not just now." He'd visit Grossmann's premises if he decided to test out the procedure, Randolph thought.

"Afraid?" she asked.

Randolph gazed down at her. What was the matter with this girl? Why was she talking to him? Had she decided, for some unfathomable reason, to make a hobby of taunting him? "Discretion rather than fear," he answered.

She nodded as if she'd expected this response. "A timid and parochial attitude."

"I beg your… I don't see you rushing up to have your character dissected."

Miss Sinclair shrugged. "I don't care to call attention to my hair. Any more than usual."

Randolph glanced at her deep-red curls, then down into eyes the color of tropical seas. She was making no sense. She looked vivid and beguiling in white muslin.

"Are you acquainted with Mr. Rochford?" she went on, with a glint in those extraordinary eyes. "He was quite courageous."

Randolph experienced a surge of irritation quite out of proportion to the inquiry. He practically bit off his reply. "No."

"That's right, you live buried in the country. I don't suppose you know many interesting people."

For perhaps the first time in his life, Randolph was struck speechless. It wasn't due to a lack of arguments. In fact, words crowded forward so thickly that they immobilized his tongue. Not know interesting people? His parents epitomized that phrase. His brother Robert set fashions. Sebastian was a convivial favorite of the *haut ton*. With these and other family connections, Randolph knew, or knew of, everyone who was anyone. Which did not include Miss Verity Sinclair.

He glared at her. She gazed back with the oddest

look. Confused? Frightened? Her expression was at odds with her impertinent remark. Randolph puzzled over this, and realized that the pause had saved him from sounding like a perfect coxcomb. A coldly courteous bow would be much more effective. He offered her one. "Excuse me," he said, and walked away.

Randolph left the knot of people still besieging Herr Grossmann, paying little attention to where he was going. Near the doorway, his mother caught up with him. "Randolph, there's a young lady here I think you would like. Come and I'll introduce you."

"Not just now, Mama."

She raised her eyebrows at his sharp tone. Randolph didn't blame her. She was doing as he'd asked, and he'd practically snapped at her.

"Is something wrong?"

"No." He'd simply had enough conversation for now.

"Was that Miss Sinclair you were talking with?"

"If you want to call it that."

"What would you call it?" the duchess asked, with an inquisitive tilt of her head.

Randolph gathered his faculties. "I beg your pardon, Mama. I'm just…thirsty. I need a glass of wine. Would you like something?"

She shook her head, releasing him with a wave of her hand. As he walked away, Randolph thought he heard her murmur, "Thirsty? Is that the term for it these days?"

# Three

The following morning, Verity finally had the chance to make her expedition. Her mother was occupied with some important letters and wouldn't notice a short absence. Indeed, she was so engrossed that she didn't even acknowledge Verity's departure from their rented drawing room. The landlady, always interested in their doings, was out. Verity knew how the hackney coaches worked, and she had money. She was aware that young ladies didn't customarily wander about London without a maid or footman, but as she had neither, she'd have to do without. Such a small thing couldn't intimidate her. Wearing her most severely cut pelisse and plainest bonnet, she set out.

It wasn't difficult to find a cab. She flagged one down and climbed in, giving the address with an anticipatory thrill.

"Are you sure about that, miss?" the driver said. "It's down amongst the clubs."

"Quite sure," she replied.

He slapped the reins, and they moved off. Two

turns later, the hack was driving down a busy street clogged with vehicles and riders. The clop of so many hooves was very loud. At the sides, hawkers cried their wares and tried to thrust products upon pedestrians who pushed along in both directions. There was a smell of fish and horses and drains. Verity stared out at the frenetic scene. It was probably like this in the marvelous bazaars of the East, she decided, only more so. She gathered all her sensations together and recorded them in her customary way, adding this moment to her collection. One became used to the clamor, no doubt. After a few days, one wouldn't feel assaulted by it at all.

The driver maneuvered past a large construction works. The pounding of hammers and shouts of the workers added to the noise. "Piccadilly Circus, that's to be," the driver called down. "If they ever finish, and stop blocking the road."

Beyond was a wide gracious avenue, a little less crowded, with large stone buildings on either side. The driver turned down it and pulled up before an imposing gray edifice. "Here you are, miss," he said.

Heart thudding, Verity paid her fare and got down at Twelve Waterloo Place. Great arched windows on the ground floor looked back at her. Above, a pillared portico loomed. The door stood under a round window with an ornately carved surround.

The cab clattered off. Verity gathered her resolve and went inside.

She was greeted—or rather halted—in the entry by a liveried man with grizzled hair and a sour expression. "You must have the wrong address, miss."

"Isn't this Twelve Waterloo Place?" She said it aloud, as she'd said it to herself since she read the news.

"Yes, miss." The man glowered at her.

"The Travellers Club?"

"Yes, miss, but—"

"I understand there are lectures planned, by those who have explored the…the far reaches of the globe. I hoped to obtain a schedule."

"No ladies are allowed inside," he replied. "Particularly young ladies."

"Not even for the talks?"

"Never, miss."

"Are you sure?" He was only a servant after all, not a member of the newly established club.

"Heard Lord Aberdeen say so" was the smug reply.

This was a setback. Verity had looked forward to the travelers' tales, as well as the chance to meet a kindred spirit. "Perhaps I could leave a note—"

The guardian frowned. "This is a gentlemen's club, not a post office."

Verity peered past him to the inner doors. She'd read about the club's recent establishment "for gentlemen who had traveled out of the British Isles to a distance of at least five hundred miles from London in a direct line." Foreign visitors and diplomats posted to London were also invited. Lord Castlereagh was one of the founders, along with the Earl of Aberdeen and Lord Auckland, whose name graced a town on the other side of the world. These men had chosen the head of Ulysses as their device. Verity knew that *his* epic voyage was fictional, the marvels he'd seen unreal, but the choice had fired her imagination. She'd so often dreamed of sailing to unknown shores.

"I've read all of Cook's journals," she tried. "I'm an admirer of Alexander von Humboldt. I know a great deal about—"

"No ladies," the door warden interrupted, hostilely uninterested. "Particularly not the sort looking to write to gentlemen they don't know. You'll have to get out now." His expression was stiff and closed.

Verity gritted her teeth and turned away. Clearly, this fellow was no use. He knew nothing but orders. And insults; those seemed to come easily to him.

Outside, she considered loitering by the entrance and trying to speak to a member going in or out. Immediately, she rejected the idea. She wasn't some feeble petitioner. She wasn't going to be brushed off in the street. She'd have to find another way to meet the sort of man she wanted. Why must they make it so difficult?

Angry, she turned right and strode off. She wanted to dissipate some of her irritation before she found another cab, and movement generally made her feel better. That was the point of life, wasn't it? To move, to act. Not to sit with folded hands waiting for what came.

Randolph lengthened his stride and drew in a deep breath. He'd had a fine early match at Angelo's, learning a cunning new form of riposte from the fencing master. Invigorated, he'd taken a turn through St. James Square and down to Pall Mall. Now, as he headed for home, he felt splendid. Until, that is, he saw a familiar figure rushing toward him. What the deuce was she doing in this part of town? She could have no business here. But there was no avoiding the girl, even though she didn't seem to see him. He raised his hat. Did she always look annoyed? "Miss Sinclair," he said.

She stopped and looked up at him with a last-straw sort of expression. "You," she said.

Randolph felt the same. He would have walked on, but she must have lost her way to be in this neighborhood, seemingly alone. "Are you on your own?"

"Yes, I am. And you needn't tell me it isn't the thing. I know! And I'm not in the mood." She turned to leave.

He'd had quite enough of Miss Verity Sinclair, but still he had to say, "You shouldn't go that way."

"I beg your pardon?" was the icy response.

"That's Pall Mall." Randolph pointed down the hill.

"And so?"

"No respectable lady walks down Pall Mall."

She was the picture of exasperation. "Are you saying I can't even walk down a wretched street?"

"I'm not the one who says—"

"Whyever not?" she interrupted.

"Lots of clubs along there. It's sort of…male territory." It sounded a bit ridiculous when he said it aloud. He didn't wish to add that she'd be ogled through the windows and very likely mistaken for a lightskirt.

"Clubs," she echoed in tones of deep revulsion. "No ladies allowed. Particularly young ladies."

Randolph made no reply to this odd remark. Thankfully, Miss Sinclair turned about and started walking away from the offending street. He fell in beside her.

"Where are you going?" she asked.

"I'll escort you home," he said. He knew his duty, no matter how onerous.

"No."

"You can't—"

"I am so deathly tired of being told what I cannot do!"

Randolph bit back a sharp retort. "*I* can't just leave you here," he answered instead.

"Find me a cab then. I won't be walked home like a child."

He did so. An inner voice argued that he should go along, but he let her dissuade him, because he didn't wish to.

As she sat beside her mother in their hired carriage that evening, Verity was still fuming. The Travellers Club had seemed a heaven-sent opportunity to find the sort of person she wanted—all those explorers gathered in one place. And diplomats…an active diplomat might do in a pinch. She'd planned to go to their talks and…browse. Like a canny shopper in a well-stocked market. It had *not* been stupid to assume the lectures would be public.

When she was younger and less aware of the world's realities, she'd meant to be the intrepid adventurer herself, of course. She'd traced out routes on the globe in her father's study and read about the places she would visit. She'd assembled a cache of useful items and made long treks around her placid home, in dreadful weather as well as fine, to build hardiness. Eventually, though, she'd had to admit that solitary expeditions as a female would require more effrontery than she possessed *and* a vast amount of money, which she didn't have.

Learned institutions wouldn't sponsor trips by a woman. Wealthy patrons wouldn't fund them. And so, slowly, she'd changed her goal to finding a companion who would accept her as an exploring partner, and not leave her behind while he sailed off for years at a time. She acknowledged that this wouldn't be easy, but there must be at least one such man in the world. Verity was prepared to impress him as soon as he could be found.

She'd studied exotic botany and how to bind up wounds. She could speak French and Spanish. The knife throwing hadn't worked out in the end, but she could shoot a pistol with tolerable accuracy. She would have been a crack shot if finding a practice range hadn't been so…complicated. There was no point in sulking over the Travellers Club, even though she had no other idea half as good. She'd just have to work harder. The *ton* was crammed full of rich men; some of them would have connections to the sort of person she wanted.

The carriage set them down outside Lady Tolland's town house, and of course the first person Verity saw when they went in was Lord Randolph Gresham. He stood in the center of the large reception room as if the great crystal chandelier had been placed specifically to illuminate him. His auburn hair gleamed in the candlelight. His broad-shouldered figure seemed made for evening dress, and his face was a chiseled classic. Yes, all right, he was terribly handsome,

Verity thought. That didn't make him suitable for her purposes.

She vowed not to speak to him at all tonight. Why would he wish her to? She'd been positively rag-mannered the last time they met! He must think she was a shrew. Not that she cared. So it didn't matter. Except that she wasn't a shrew. Ask anyone in Chester, and they would tell you that the dean's daughter was poised and amiable. The word *sweet* was often used. Too often.

"Can people talk of nothing but this German fellow?" asked Verity's mother at her side.

It was true that everyone nearby was chattering about phrenology. Those who had managed a session with Herr Grossmann lorded it over those who hadn't yet seen him. Remarkably, the former all seemed to possess exceptional skulls that revealed a host of admirable traits.

"It's tedious," Mama added.

Verity took in her mother's bored expression and impatient gaze. Mama didn't like London. She preferred small gatherings of neighbors to large parties—and a weighty book to either. She missed Papa. But she'd promised Verity a season, and she was keeping her word. She'd made use of her family connection to the Duke of Rutland, which she didn't really like to do, to get invitations. She soldiered along to all the resulting events. And she didn't complain. It was practically heroic. "There's Mrs. Doran," Verity said.

Her mother brightened. Mrs. Doran was an old friend from her school days, and they never seemed to tire of rehashing those bygone years. Their reminiscences painted a picture of deep erudition and nunlike dedication. Verity had sent up more than one silent thanks that her parents hadn't sent her to that august institution.

As they moved toward the sofa where Mrs. Doran sat, Verity's gaze strayed. Lord Randolph was surrounded by a striking group of people. She spotted Emma with her sister and Lord Sebastian. Verity would find her later. A third tall gentleman looked like another brother. Verity had discovered that there were six of them. What a sight that would be—a half-dozen of these striking men. A pretty dark-haired woman stood beside this man, along with a younger blond girl. When she found herself wondering how the latter might be connected to Lord Randolph, Verity reined in her errant thoughts. It didn't matter. It was nothing to her. She turned away.

"This is a friend of ours from the Salbridge house party," Flora, the dark-haired woman, was saying to Sebastian. "Miss Frances Reynolds."

"Good to see you again," said Randolph, shooting Robert a sly glance. His next younger brother had won Flora's hand at Salbridge, and his wooing had been more difficult than anyone had expected for the most polished and fashionable Gresham. Robert pretended not to notice his look, and Randolph enjoyed it.

He turned his attention to Miss Reynolds. He'd always thought her rather pretty, with fair hair, blue-gray eyes, and a neat figure. She was scanning the crowd as if she'd lost someone. "Are you enjoying the season so far, Miss Reynolds?" he asked.

She turned to him. "Have you seen Mr. Wrentham in London?"

Startled by her abruptness, Randolph said, "As a matter of fact I have."

"Here?" Miss Reynolds looked around eagerly.

"No, we were fencing."

"Fencing? With swords? Was it a duel?"

"Of course it wasn't a duel." He frowned at her. "We met at Angelo's Academy."

Although she showed no sign of recognizing the name, she leaned a little toward him in her eagerness. "So you're good friends?"

"Acquaintances, barely." Randolph didn't intend to pursue a connection with the hotheaded Mr. Wrentham.

"Oh." Miss Reynolds resumed her survey of the other guests, appearing to lose all interest in Randolph.

Chagrined, Randolph examined her profile. Had he developed some inadvertent tone that made girls rude? "Are you a friend of Miss Verity Sinclair?"

"What?" Miss Reynolds looked mystified.

"Never mind."

"Who is Miss Sinclair?" murmured Robert.

Randolph turned to face his brother's raised eyebrow. "Someone I should know?"

"No," Randolph said.

"Ah."

"Don't give me your 'ahs.' She's nobody. Forget I mentioned her."

"Oh, I don't think I can do that. You were so

helpful to me at the Salbridges', you know. I intend to return the favor."

Randolph was considering this mixed blessing when Lady Tolland signaled that the entertainment was about to begin. Their hostess had arranged a somewhat unusual musicale. Instead of professionals, her daughter and a number of her friends were to play and sing in a formal program. It was a way for the girls to present themselves to the *ton* in a flattering light. If they had any skill, Randolph thought. If they didn't, the guests were in for an excruciating couple of hours.

Thankfully it turned out that Lady Tolland had chosen well. Randolph enjoyed the pieces right up until the moment when the hostess said, "A little bird has told me that we have some other talented singers among us tonight." She marched up to Randolph and took his arm, then pulled him over to Miss Sinclair and did the same with her. Ignoring their protests, she hustled them over to the pianoforte. "Now, now, no false modesty. I'm told that both of you are quite out of the ordinary."

Randolph was proud of his musical skills. He even enjoyed showing them off, on certain occasions. This was not one of them. He glared at his brothers. Robert and Sebastian shook their heads, disavowing any hand in this development.

"We must have a duet," Lady Tolland said, maintaining her grip on her captives. She turned to her guests. "Don't you think?"

The answering applause was more curious than enthusiastic.

Recognizing inevitability when it stared him in

the face, Randolph responded with a slight bow. On Lady Tolland's other side, Miss Sinclair bobbed a tiny curtsy. Their hostess released them and stepped aside.

Meeting Miss Sinclair's blue-green eyes, Randolph found his own emotions mirrored there. They were trapped together. He addressed the room. "Give us a moment to find some music."

The concentrated attention focused on them lessened.

Randolph reached for the pile of sheet music lying on top of the pianoforte. His hand bumped Miss Sinclair's, on the same mission. They both drew back, reached again, drew back again. With an exasperated sigh, Miss Sinclair took a step forward and spread the pages across the top of the instrument.

They looked together at a ballad. "Maudlin," said Randolph.

"Saccharine," said Miss Sinclair at the same moment.

They exchanged a brief, startled glance.

"Trite," she judged the next piece in line.

"Tired," Randolph said simultaneously.

Their eyes swiftly met and parted again. Unconsciously, they moved closer together as they considered a third choice. "Overly complex," said Miss Sinclair.

"Pretentious," said Randolph. "'The more notes the better' is not a wise rule of thumb for a composer."

Miss Sinclair giggled. It was an engaging sound, low and throaty. He rather liked it. Randolph leafed through more sheet music and finally glimpsed something he liked. "Ah," he said.

"Oh," said Miss Sinclair at the same instant.

Randolph tugged at the page and found that she

was pulling at the other side. They unearthed the music together. "One of my favorites," he said.

"Mine, too," she said.

They looked at each other, equally surprised, speculative.

"No need to be too scrupulous," called Lady Tolland from the crowd. "I'm sure we will enjoy whatever you sing."

Verity started. She'd been quite...lost for a moment there. She let go of the sheet music and took a step back. "Will you play?" she said.

Lord Randolph gestured toward the keyboard. "I defer to you."

"I'd rather you did." When it seemed he would protest, she added, "I've never sung before such a large group. I suppose you have."

He gave in at once and sat down at the pianoforte. He had beautiful hands, Verity noticed. He touched the keys with delicate authority. But they'd had no chance to discuss how they would harmonize.

Lord Randolph played the opening notes. Verity took a breath, set aside her nerves, and began to sing. She'd performed in other drawing rooms. She knew her voice was good. She'd had fine teachers. The melody belled out and filled the room.

At the perfect juncture, Lord Randolph joined in. He had a lovely resonant baritone, a perfect counterpoint to her soprano. His voice was full and rich, obviously well trained. It wove around hers as if they'd sung together a thousand times.

The song dipped and soared. He shifted into a more complex harmony. Verity followed. She tried a small flourish. He extended it without hesitation. The chiming sound vibrated in her body, an amazing sensation.

She embellished a sequence. He elaborated on her embroidery. With a smile and a little nod, he varied the tempo. She swooped in effortlessly to answer the change. It was a glorious, intimate call and response. As if they could read each other's minds. As if their bodies pulsed to the same rhythms. This was music she could never make alone.

Verity was swept away. She was always moved by music, but this was beyond anything she'd ever experienced. The room, the crowd, disappeared from her consciousness. Only their twined voices existed. Meeting Lord Randolph's intense blue eyes, she saw that he felt the same. It was as if their souls communed. She couldn't look away.

The song came to an end. The harmony died. Verity's careful breath control evaporated. Her hands shook. Lord Randolph blinked. He looked down at the keys of the pianoforte.

The burst of applause was a stunning intrusion. They both started. Verity felt the pounding palms as an intolerable sound. She wanted to put her hands over her ears. Lord Randolph recovered more quickly. He rose, took her hand, and led her in a bow. Verity clung to his fingers.

People rushed over, full of chattering praise. They were like a surging mob. Lord Randolph let go of her hand, and Verity felt bereft. Clearly she'd judged this man too hastily. She wished she could take back some of the things she'd said to him. All of the things, really.

As Randolph acknowledged the barrage of

compliments, he struggled to gather his scattered faculties, and to comprehend that...extraordinary experience. He was astonished and unsettled and aroused. He'd never imagined such an instant, automatic link. And yet it had happened. He couldn't deny that. With a rude girl who didn't even like him, an inner voice warned. Who scorned his *countrified* position. Who thought him, in a word, a failure.

"Oh, Miss Sinclair, the archbishop must be so proud of you," simpered a turbaned lady at his elbow.

And there was that, Randolph thought. He mustn't forget that complication. This was all as unfortunate as it was unexpected. He struggled to control his expression. Feeling uncomfortably exposed, he turned.

As if he'd spoken his need aloud, he found Sebastian beside him. "All right, there, Ran?" he said.

His hulking military brother could be remarkably like a sheltering wall, Randolph thought. "Need a moment," he said.

Sebastian nodded. "You don't like noise after you've been playing. Noticed that. Come along."

Gratefully allowing himself to be guided, Randolph noted that Sebastian could be quite sensitive. People didn't know that about him. Miss Sinclair was staring as if he'd abandoned her to ravening hordes. No, she wasn't. Couldn't be. He wasn't thinking straight.

In a far corner of the room, Randolph's family closed around him, a comforting bastion.

"That was splendid," said Flora.

Robert nodded agreement with his wife. "I haven't heard you play in a while. Vastly improved."

Randolph appreciated the praise. His most *tonnish*

brother was more likely to twit than compliment. But he knew it was undeserved in this case. His talent had been...amplified, exalted by his partner.

"Plenty of time to practice, I suppose, up there in the wilds of Northumberland."

That was more like the Robert he knew, and cut a bit too close after Miss Sinclair's remarks.

"It was absolutely beautiful," said Georgina.

"Top-notch," agreed Sebastian.

The pair exchanged one of their warm marital glances. Which were endearing, not annoying, Randolph told himself. He gathered more of his scattered wits. Miss Sinclair sang very well. So did he. They'd performed a successful duet, nothing more. He'd heard musicians wax enthusiastic about collaboration. None had ever mentioned being aroused, however.

Randolph looked over Robert's shoulder at Miss Sinclair. She was still surrounded by an admiring circle. Bright hair, gown of angelic white so tantalizingly filled by a shapely figure. Those blue-green eyes had threatened to drown him as they sang. It was unfair. He wasn't looking for an enigma. He had a plan.

"Yes, of course I'm going," said Robert. "Tomorrow afternoon."

Randolph reined in his wandering attention. "Going where?"

"To see that German fellow," replied Sebastian. "The one who runs his fingers over your head and then cuts up your character." He shook his head.

"He'll muss your hair," Georgina told Robert with a teasing smile.

Robert smiled back. “I shall, of course, take a comb to the appointment.”

“You think there’s something in it?” Randolph asked. “This phrenology?”

“It’s become the fashion,” Robert replied. “I must keep up.”

“I thought you set fashions.”

“I set them. I shift them. I critique them.”

“From the wilds of Russell Square?” Randolph asked, getting his own back for the remark about Northumberland. Immediately, he worried that he’d insulted Flora’s family home.

“It’s not where you live,” said Robert airily. “It’s how.” Flora gave him a warm smile. He took her hand and kissed it.

All at once Randolph remembered a remark Robert had made after Sebastian’s wedding, wondering how many happy marriages there could be among six brothers. Considering the matches of people they knew, he’d thought the odds must be against six.

Randolph looked at him now, gazing into the fiery blue eyes of his lovely wife. There was no doubt Robert was happy. Just as Sebastian was with his beautiful, blond Georgina. James, too, and Nathaniel and Alan, about to become fathers. They seemed as happy and contented as men could be. “I suppose the luck has run out,” Randolph muttered. He wasn’t to have what his brothers had found. He’d missed his chance.

“What luck?” asked Robert.

“Nothing.” His younger brother had always had the ears of a bat. They used to station Robert as lookout during midnight raids on the pantry at

Langford. Robert could catch the creak of a floorboard at fifty paces.

"Your luck is certainly good," Robert replied. "Unless you don't care to sing again. Lady Tolland is bearing down on us. A guinea says she asks you."

"Deuce take it," said Randolph. He slipped behind Sebastian and then along the wall, scattering smiles and nods through several chattering groups. The experience with Miss Sinclair had been too...confusing. He didn't wish to repeat it. Not now. Perhaps another time? Elsewhere. No, she didn't like him. Hadn't. What did she think now?

Lady Tolland was craning her neck, searching for him. He wasn't going to spend the remaining hours of this party playing hide-and-seek with his hostess. That would be rude, not to mention ridiculous. Best to go now and let everyone forget about the song, as they inevitably would when the next interesting tidbit came along. He made his way to the door and departed.

# Four

It was a perfect day for a walk, Verity thought. The sky was bright blue, without a hint of clouds. Hyde Park's rafts of daffodils dipped and nodded in the balmy breeze. Birds trilled in the trees. Fashionable Londoners strolled and rode and drove all around them. And she had two lively companions to talk with. Verity paused to record the moment. She already thought of Lady Emma Stane as a true friend, and Miss Olivia Townsend was fast becoming one. Olivia knew so many people. Thanks to her presence, their progress was marked by smiles and bows and blithe greetings. Verity appreciated that, because—it was an odd thing—here in London she felt younger than her twenty-four years.

Back home in Chester, she was a familiar figure and, she thought, respected. After several years of attending assemblies, making calls with her mother, and undertaking various charitable works, she'd seen herself as an assured fixture in society. But London was so much larger, and grander. She felt as if she was starting all over again, which made her search for the perfect explorer more daunting.

For example, nothing like that astonishing duet would have happened in Chester. She was acquainted with the musical circle there and couldn't have been ambushed in that way. And so she wouldn't be haunted by it now. Verity stood still, frowning. What an odd word to choose. Quite silly. She wasn't in the least *haunted.* It was true that people still spoke of the performance four days later. And some women combined their compliments with sly glances, as if she'd done something clever. Their air of amused complicity made her uncomfortable. But haunted—no. Nonsense.

"What is it?" asked Emma. The others were several steps ahead.

Verity hurried to catch up. "Looking at the flowers," she said.

They walked on, following a path that curved toward Rotten Row, with its press of carriages and riders. The wind gusted, whipping their skirts around their ankles. They laughed as they caught the cloth with one hand and held on to their bonnets with the other. "Don't you wish we could just let go and run with the wind?" asked Olivia.

Emma shook her head. Verity had noticed that her blond friend was wary of any suggestion that was the least bit unconventional. She, on the other hand, relished the sentiment.

"Oh look, there's Mr. Rochford," Olivia added. She walked faster.

Keeping pace, Verity saw the interesting gentleman who'd been pointed out at her first *ton* party.

He looked handsome and polished and perfectly at home on a magnificent black gelding. The horse tossed his head, clearly spirited. Mr. Rochford controlled him without visible effort. Verity could imagine this man heading into the wilds on such a mount. He came nearer. He was going to pass right by them. They wouldn't speak, of course, not having been introduced.

Olivia put a hand to her chest, and in the next moment the celestial-blue scarf that had been draped around her neck billowed in the breeze. The filmy cloth took flight. It floated up, writhed and twisted, and veered right under the nose of Mr. Rochford's mount.

The horse took instant exception to this mysterious attack. He snorted, half reared, and kicked out with his forelegs, then danced sideways as the scarf blew on. Mr. Rochford used knees and reins to contend with his mount as they nearly collided with another rider and threatened a barouche full of ladies just behind. With consummate skill, the man got the horse under control, bringing the gelding to a trembling standstill at the edge of the path.

"Oh dear, I'm so sorry," said Olivia, stepping right up to him. "I can't imagine how that happened."

"Carelessness, I expect," Mr. Rochford replied curtly.

"Utterly shatterbrained," she agreed. "I'm Olivia Townsend, you know. I expect you're acquainted with my father."

Verity stared at her. Emma's mouth hung open at their friend's blatant disregard for propriety.

Mr. Rochford looked surprised, then amused. "I

am." He bowed from the saddle and tipped his hat. "Thomas Rochford, at your service."

"These are my friends," Olivia added. "Lady Emma Stane and Miss Verity Sinclair."

Emma, who had been shaking her head emphatically, went still and stared as if confronted with a poisonous snake. Verity suppressed what she very much feared was a nervous giggle. She sketched a curtsy.

"Ladies," said Mr. Rochford, acknowledging them as he had Olivia.

Another rider came up with the escaped scarf. Olivia took it with a cordial nod. She did not introduce herself to the newcomer, Verity noticed. Instead, she smiled at Rochford and said, "We mustn't keep you. I expect your horse is *longing* for a wild gallop."

A tiny sound escaped Emma—something like "Erp." Verity didn't dare look at her.

"He may be," Mr. Rochford replied. "He's not likely to get one here in the park, of course."

"Such a stuffy place."

"I had thought so, Miss Townsend. Now, I'm not so sure." With another tip of his hat and a glint in his blue eyes, Mr. Rochford rode on.

"Olivia!" hissed Emma.

The other girl shrugged off her glare. "We wanted to meet Mr. Rochford. Now we have."

"I didn't want to," Emma declared. "Not in the least. Oh, you're just like Hilda."

"Who is Hilda?" Olivia asked with a smile. "It sounds as if I'd like her."

Emma plumped down on a nearby bench in a flurry of sprigged muslin. She let out a great sigh.

"Her younger sister," Verity supplied. "Prone to pranks, I believe." Emma had shared a story or two during their conversations.

"This wasn't a prank," said Olivia. "It was a plan."

"But how could you know that Mr. Rochford would ride by?"

"I didn't." The smaller girl shrugged. "The scarf was just one idea. I had others, for other contingencies."

"Contingencies," repeated Verity, enjoying the workings of Olivia's mind.

"Come, Miss Sinclair, you wanted to meet him, didn't you?"

Verity couldn't deny it.

"So now you have."

"Georgina will be annoyed," said Emma from the bench. "Even though it was not my fault." She sighed again. "She will say I must take responsibility for my life. But how can I when people just keep... springing things on me?" She gave Olivia another reproachful glance.

"Don't tell her," came the prompt reply.

Verity had been thinking something similar. She didn't intend to mention this incident to her mother.

"She'll find out," said Emma. "There were people all around, Olivia. They saw us talking to him. That other man heard what you said about galloping. Which sounded quite improper. Somehow."

"Oh, pish." Olivia waved her friend's concerns aside.

"Indeed?" Emma rose and rejoined them. "What will *your* mama say?"

The other girl grinned. "She'll scold me, all the while trying not to laugh. She'll say I must behave myself. And then she'll give me a load of unnecessary advice about rakes and libertines."

"Really?" Verity asked. She couldn't imagine such a conversation. The word *libertine* would never pass her mother's lips. The Townsend household must be very different from her home.

"As if I would ever do more than flirt," Olivia added, tossing her head.

Verity gazed at her. From her crimped brown hair under a stylish bonnet to her shining half boots, Olivia Townsend was the image of London sophistication. Verity wanted to know her better. And meet her mother.

"Oh no!" said Emma. "There's Flora. I wonder if she saw. What will I say?"

"Say nothing," replied Olivia. "Pretend you don't know what she's talking about."

"How can I—"

She broke off as the lady in question drew within earshot. She was accompanied by the young blond girl Verity had noticed at the musicale. "Hello, Emma."

Emma murmured a nervous response.

The newcomer waited, then added, "Perhaps you would introduce us to your friend?"

"Oh!" Emma hastily presented Verity.

"How are you, Miss Townsend?" asked the pale-haired girl, who turned out to be Miss Frances Reynolds. "We met at a house party last autumn," she told Verity.

"Isn't it pleasant to have friends in London," put in her companion. "I'm sure you'll want to catch up."

Miss Reynolds looked hopeful. Olivia said nothing, which surprised Verity.

They exchanged a few more remarks before the two parties went off in different directions.

"I don't think Flora noticed anything," Emma said when they were gone.

"Very likely not," replied Olivia. "And if she thinks she's going to foist that milksop miss off on me, she's mightily mistaken."

Verity and Emma stared. "Do you mean Miss Reynolds?" Verity asked.

"None other. She's the most priggish girl."

"She didn't seem so to me," Emma ventured.

"You didn't see her at Salbridge, constantly putting her oar in when no one wanted her opinion. She snaffled a major role in the play we put on, when she should have had the sense to efface herself and let her betters have the spotlight."

"She wasn't any good?" Verity asked, a little shocked at her new friend's sharpness.

"What is *snaffled*?" Emma asked. "Slang, I suppose." She sounded resigned.

Olivia made a dismissive gesture. "Miss Reynolds was adequate, when she wasn't using the opportunity to make sheep's eyes at Charles Wrentham. Which was nearly always."

"She spoiled the play?" Verity asked, attempting to understand Olivia's attitude.

Surprisingly, Olivia giggled. "No. *She* didn't."

Verity remained puzzled.

"She'll find it harder to push herself forward here in London," Olivia continued. "*I* certainly won't be helping her. I wonder..."

"What?" asked Verity when Olivia said no more.

"We shall see" was the mysterious reply.

"People are looking at us," said Emma.

"Isn't that why we're here?" asked Olivia. But she led them along the path toward the gates.

~

Randolph plucked out a run of notes on his lute. He could play parts of the melody now, but the sound was still far from the golden song he'd *heard* during that strange interlude last summer when an Indian gentleman had chanted in Sanskrit and tapped a drum. The combination had somehow evoked a vivid daydream in which Randolph saw himself in archaic surroundings playing a ballad that still haunted him. On a lute.

By an impulse both inexplicable and irresistible—an uncomfortable duo—he was driven to reproduce those notes exactly. No substitute would do. Not picking the tune out on the pianoforte, or trying to reproduce it with his voice. The whole thing was very odd, and so he kept his practice to the privacy of his bedchamber.

Randolph set the instrument aside with a strange mixture of regret and relief and went down to join his parents for dinner.

"I've had letters from Nathaniel and Violet," said the duchess as they began the meal. "Violet is feeling much better. Nathaniel says she's blooming."

"That's good," said Randolph. His eldest brother's wife had been ill at the beginning of her pregnancy, causing the family some worry. Randolph spooned up soup, savoring the complexity of the flavor. His mother's cook was another attraction of

Langford House. He wouldn't get a meal like this in rented rooms.

One of the footmen appeared in the doorway. He hovered a moment, looking reluctant. "I beg your pardon for interrupting, Your Grace," he said to the duchess. "A messenger brought this. He said it wasn't to wait even a moment." He held up an envelope with the crest of the Prince Regent on the flap.

The duke held out a hand. "Patience isn't one of the prince's virtues."

"I beg your pardon, Your Grace," repeated the footman. "It's for Lord Randolph."

"Me?" said Randolph, mirroring his parents' surprised looks. "Why would he be writing to me? I don't know him."

"I introduced you at court when you were eighteen," said his father.

"I made my bow. We didn't speak."

"What could be so urgent?" wondered the duchess.

"There's one way to find out." The duke gestured, and the footman stepped over to hand Randolph the envelope.

Setting down his spoon, Randolph opened it. Inside was a longish handwritten note. "The deuce!" he exclaimed when he'd scanned it.

"What is it?" asked his mother.

"The prince wants me to sing at a party."

"Sing?" said the duke, suddenly haughty. "As if you were some sort of hired entertainer?"

"Oh, the request is wreathed in all sorts of polite phrases and fulsome compliments. He abjectly requests it as a favor."

"Let me see that." His father read the note with a frown. "He really will say anything to get what he wants. Who is Miss Verity Sinclair?"

Randolph did not miss his mother's raised eyebrows. "A young lady. We sang an impromptu duet at Lady Tolland's musicale. It was...well received."

"Apparently, it was stunning," the duchess said. "I'm so sorry to have missed it. Robert said you were wonderful."

Despite his ambivalence, Randolph once again appreciated the praise from his most discerning brother.

"The prince hates to miss anything of note," commented the duke.

"Must I do it?" asked Randolph.

"Awkward to refuse a direct royal request couched in these terms," his father replied. "You can hope the young lady's parents object."

Randolph perked up. "Right. Not the thing for her to sing in public."

The duke considered the letter again. "He makes a great point of it being a private party, quite exclusive. Her parents will probably agree to it, unless they're remarkably straitlaced."

Randolph sighed. He hadn't gotten that impression from his encounters with Miss Sinclair. Hidebound parents couldn't have produced such a...forthright girl. It seemed he was doomed to perform with her. He'd have to call and discuss the matter. He wondered what new insult she'd find for the occasion.

"Miss Sinclair is the one related to the Archbishop of Canterbury, isn't she?" said his mother.

"Not one of his daughters?" asked the duke. "Doesn't he have ten? But no, not with the surname Sinclair."

"It's not as bad as that," Randolph replied.

"What do you mean 'as bad'? Is there something wrong with the girl? She must be related to the Duke of Rutland, too."

"Perhaps a good connection for you, Randolph?" said the duchess.

Randolph knew that look. She was intrigued. There was no stopping Mama when her curiosity was aroused. "Nothing's wrong with Miss Sinclair," he replied. Except the way she treated him. "I just need to stay out of the archbishop's way for a while. A while longer. Not too much longer now, perhaps. I hope."

"Why? What did you do to the archbishop?"

"I didn't *do* anything to him, Mama."

She waited, rather like Ruff at a mousehole. Papa waited as well, with the amused expression he assumed when his mate was extracting information from one of their progeny. The picture—and the conviction that there was no way out—was as familiar as childhood. Thinking he might as well get it over with, Randolph spoke quickly.

"It's ridiculous really. Three years ago, I organized a Christmas pageant at my church. The archbishop happened to be near Hexham at the time, so he paid a visit. Everyone was quite excited. It was a great occasion. But a young...humorist had put a ram in the manger instead of a proper sheep. The archbishop was leaning over to compliment one of the children who played an angel, and the ram, er..."

"Knocked him down?" said his mother when he hesitated.

"Bit off one of his coattails?" offered the duke when Randolph still didn't speak.

"No." Randolph sighed. The scene was engraved on his memory. Unfortunately. "The archbishop had on white vestments, from an earlier rite. When he bent down, the ram…seemingly…mistook him for a ewe."

His father's snort was not unexpected.

"Mistook…?" His mother's mouth fell open. "Oh. Oh dear."

"Two burly parishioners had to help me get the creature off him," Randolph continued. "The archbishop was thoroughly shaken up and not… understanding." The prelate's glare had been searing; his secretary's even more so. "Since then, I've been lying low in church circles."

"I daresay," said the duke. Only his blue eyes laughed, but they did it very well.

"It wasn't your fault," said the duchess.

"I was in charge," said Randolph. "I should have noticed the ram." The youngster who'd smuggled it in had been contrite—when he could stop laughing. But the damage had been done. "Time has passed," said Randolph. "The memory must be fading. I have a new parish, a fresh start. But I don't think a close association with a relative of the archbishop's is—"

"Advisable," supplied his father.

"Precisely."

The duchess's expression was hard to read. Randolph had seen her look that way when she was planning to canvas her country neighbors for contributions to her educational schemes, and when she was choosing jewels to match a ball gown.

"We'll sing a few songs for the prince's guests, and that will be that," he declared. "No need for concern, Mama. Or...intervention."

"I would never do anything you didn't like," she answered.

"Unless you thought it was good for me?"

"Don't be silly. You're a grown man."

Which wasn't exactly an answer, Randolph noted.

"So, that's settled," said the duke. "Nothing much to it after all."

Not being musical himself, his father had no idea, Randolph thought.

# Five

WITH THE DUCHESS'S AID, RANDOLPH DISCOVERED that Miss Sinclair and her mother were staying near Cavendish Square. He sent a note ahead rather than simply turning up on their doorstep. Thus, when he arrived the following day, he was admitted at once by an unexpectedly stately butler. He found the ladies sitting alone in a pretty drawing room upstairs. They rose to greet him, but Mrs. Sinclair sank back onto the sofa as soon as her daughter had made the introductions. "I never dreamt of anything like this when I agreed to come to London," she said. "Of course I had no idea that Verity would make a spectacle of herself."

"Mama! I have done no such thing."

It sounded like a much-repeated exchange. Taking in Miss Sinclair's pained expression, Randolph was certain it was.

"The Prince Regent!" continued the older woman. "My husband does not approve of his…way of life. Mr. Sinclair is dean of Chester Cathedral, you know, and very conscious of his responsibilities."

Randolph sat down beside the older woman. Thin

and wren-like, she didn't much resemble her daughter. He debated whether to encourage her doubts or try to assuage them. But a period of reflection had convinced him that refusing the prince's request would be far more troublesome than acceding to it. The Regent went to great lengths to satisfy his whims. "I believe you are overly concerned, ma'am. The prince is proposing a private party, with a select guest list."

"But his reputation is so very bad!" argued Mrs. Sinclair. "I am sad to say that about a member of our royal family. But the tales one hears!" Glancing at her daughter, she bit off a word.

"There's none of that at his *ton* parties," Randolph replied, mostly truthfully. He had an inspiration. "And certainly not with his mother present."

Mrs. Sinclair turned to look at him. "The queen will be there?"

"You admire her," murmured Miss Sinclair.

Randolph was sure, from the tone of the prince's letter, that he could make this a condition. His father was well acquainted with the prince and could add his voice as well. "It will be no different than entertaining guests at your own home," he added.

Mrs. Sinclair looked doubtful. "Our small circle in Chester can scarcely be compared. Who knows whom the prince might invite? Quite unsuitable people."

"They'll be on their best behavior. Perhaps you'd care to join my mother's party for the evening?"

"The Duchess of Langford," murmured Miss Sinclair.

"I don't know."

"Did I mention that Lord Randolph is a

clergyman?" said Miss Sinclair. She was becoming positively antiphonal.

"Really?" Her mother perked up.

"He has a parish up North. Somewhere."

Here was a change, Randolph thought. Suddenly the girl appreciated a country clergyman? And had she been inquiring about him? "In Derbyshire, actually," he said. "I have a new post beginning in the summer. Quite a pleasant town, not the least bit countrified." He had the satisfaction of seeing Miss Sinclair look self-conscious.

Her mother fixed her pale-blue eyes on him. "As a man of the cloth, you are not concerned about performing at Carleton House?"

"As a favor for the prince, no. I wouldn't make a habit of it, of course."

"Well—"

Randolph knew not to push. He'd had years of dealing with recalcitrant committees and quarreling parishioners.

"I suppose we can't refuse royalty," said the older woman with a sigh. "Perhaps you might write to my husband, Lord Randolph? You set forth the arguments very well."

Randolph hesitated, wondering if the dean had heard about the incident with the Archbishop of Canterbury. It was more than likely that he had. Naturally, there'd been gossip among the clergy. Nor was Randolph eager to become further embroiled with Miss Sinclair's family. "I'm not acquainted with the dean," he pointed out.

"Oh, I shall enclose your letter in one of my own," said Mrs. Sinclair.

She gazed at him expectantly. Randolph gave in with a nod.

"And perhaps you will reply to the prince for us, and make all the arrangements."

She said it as if it was a foregone conclusion, giving Randolph some insight into the workings of the Sinclair household. Her daughter did not look pleased, but made no objection. He nodded again.

A maid came in with a tray. "There you are at last," said Mrs. Sinclair. When the girl had set down the tray and gone, Verity's mother added, "We've hired only part of this house, you know, with use of the landlady's servants. It's not like having our own staff who know what we like. But I couldn't see taking a whole house and finding servants just for one season. Would you care for some marzipan, Lord Randolph?"

Randolph refused without visibly shuddering. He couldn't bear the sweetness of the confection. Turning, he found Miss Sinclair's blue-green eyes fixed upon him. "I feel we must make some preparations for this concert," he told her. "It can't be impromptu, even though our first…collaboration was successful." He saw his vivid recollection of that occasion mirrored in her gaze, and he couldn't look away.

Lord Randolph had managed her mother in a truly masterful manner, Verity thought. The subtlety of it might have been lost on some, but she was impressed.

"Do you agree?" he said.

"What?"

"Do pay attention, Verity," said her mother, nibbling on her sweet.

Which was quite unfair. But Verity couldn't

complain. She'd gotten what she wanted; she was going to Carleton House. The prince's fete would be stuffed with interesting people, perhaps the very ones she'd have found at the Travellers Club. And as the central attraction, she'd be in a position to meet whoever she pleased. Lord Randolph had done her a service by getting her mother to agree, and very neatly, too. "Yes," Verity said firmly. "We should plan and rehearse."

"Shall I tell the prince the performance must be, say, two weeks from now?"

That wasn't a great deal of time, but probably enough. Verity nodded. "I have no pianoforte here."

"We can work at Langford House," Randolph answered. "There's a fine instrument in the music room." He smiled at her mother. "You must both come, of course."

Verity watched that enchanting smile take effect. She'd never seen Mama flutter and dither in quite that way before.

"My mother will be delighted to welcome you," Lord Randolph added.

Verity didn't understand the wry expression that accompanied this assurance. Was he amused or concerned?

"Tomorrow afternoon perhaps? I could send a carriage for you."

"We'll get ourselves there," Verity replied before her mother could accept. She was grateful to him, but she wouldn't be managed. The coming duet was enough. She wasn't going to be taken over by a handsome parson.

"A charming man," said her mother when Lord Randolph had taken his leave.

"Umm," said Verity noncommittally.

"So very handsome, too. And the son of a duke. I daresay he'll go far in the church."

Verity ignored her mother's sidelong glances. If she became engaged, Mama would pack up and drag her back to Chester the following day. Not that Lord Randolph and engagements had anything to do with each other. The point was: she meant to accomplish her goals, and she wouldn't let her London season be cut short.

When Randolph returned to Langford House, he found Flora deep in conversation with his mother. To no one's surprise, these two had taken to each other at once, finding common ground in their charitable works. The duchess had established several schools for poor girls over the years. Robert's new wife oversaw a refuge for street children in rather the same vein. Plans were already in motion to funnel some of Flora's charges into the schools.

"But we shouldn't neglect the boys," Flora was saying when Randolph entered the drawing room.

"Life is not quite so hard for them," said the duchess.

"I don't agree. They may not be dragged into prostitution, but they often see no choice but crime and drink."

Another thing these two had in common, Randolph thought. They didn't mince words.

"There are charity schools for boys..." his mother began.

"Not enough. At the least I would like to be able

to offer the same opportunities to the boys at my refuge as to the girls." Flora's fiery blue eyes glowed with conviction. She showed no consciousness of their difference in rank.

Smiling in appreciation, the duchess nodded. "We must see what we can do then. Hello, Randolph."

"Mama. Flora. Don't let me interrupt your plotting."

"We are down to matters of detail," said Flora.

"Which I intend to leave to you, my dear, because I know you will be thorough and relentless," the duchess said.

Flora gave her mother-in-law a wry glance. "Is that how you see me?"

"It was a compliment," said the duchess.

The younger woman laughed. "Thank you. I believe I do know how to organize that effort," she said. "There's something else, however, on which I'd like your advice."

"Of course."

"I'm trying to help a young lady I met at Salbridge."

"Miss Reynolds?" said Randolph.

"Yes. She's here for the season," Flora told the duchess. "Staying with a relative who isn't much interested in her. I've gotten her into one or two parties."

"Shall I drum up a few more invitations?"

"Thank you. That would be very kind." Flora sighed. "The trouble is, Miss Reynolds isn't really... enlivened unless there's a chance of meeting one particular man. Are you friendly with Mr. Charles Wrentham, Randolph?"

"I've met him. No more than that." A very odd

fencing match didn't constitute an acquaintance. And he wasn't going to be dragged into matchmaking.

"Robert says the same," Flora said. "I don't know just what to do. I could try speaking to Mr. Wrentham again, but if he wished to see Frances, wouldn't he call on her?"

Randolph wondered what she meant by *again*. He wasn't going to ask, however. His mother had no such qualms. "Again?" she said.

Flora grimaced. "I tried to…intercede at Salbridge. It did not go well."

The man who'd flailed at him at Angelo's wouldn't appreciate interference, Randolph thought.

"I can't just shove him at her," Flora concluded.

"Perhaps she'll be diverted if she meets more young men," said the duchess.

"I hope so."

Robert strolled in, dress immaculate, air assured. "Has my wife cajoled a pile of money out of you for her orphans?" he asked his mother.

"You all talk about me as if I was some sort of despot," Flora objected. "I only want to see justice done."

"And we all love you for it," said Robert, dropping a kiss on her dark hair. "A thing I am very good at, I might add."

"Did Herr Grossmann tell you so?" Flora replied with a shake of her head.

"That and more." Robert pulled a sheet of paper from his pocket and showed them a smaller version of the cranial diagram Herr Grossmann had exhibited at the *ton* party. Handwritten notations had been made upon it. Randolph couldn't read them from his place by the hearth. "You will be interested, but hardly surprised, to learn," his brother continued, "that our esteemed phrenologist considers my skull fascinating."

"I would be surprised to learn that he expresses any other opinion in his sessions," said Flora dryly.

"Nonsense. My head is extraordinary," Robert insisted. Randolph noted that his blue eyes were dancing with laughter. "For example, my bump of comparison, which is to say intelligence—"

"How is it to say that?"

"One demonstrates intelligence by making comparisons."

"I would argue with that definition," said Flora.

"Of course you would, my love."

Randolph exchanged an amused glance with his mother. Robert and his wife couldn't seem to talk without bickering. They appeared to relish the jousting.

"I have little propensity to remain permanently in the same place or residence," Robert went on, reading from the page.

"You're nomadic?" replied Flora. "You never said so."

"Say flexible, rather. The most amiable fellow in the world."

Flora laughed.

"My *alimentiveness* is not pronounced, which seems to mean that I am not greedy for food."

"It's true. You never were," said the duchess.

"Not like Sebastian," said Robert.

"I wouldn't use the word *greedy*."

"No, that would be snatch-pastry."

"Active boys need fuel," replied the duchess with a smile. "And Sebastian was more active than the rest of you."

"Bigger, too. With a longer reach."

"Did Herr Grossmann call you a jokesmith?" asked Randolph.

"He said I have a bent toward mirth."

"That was certainly on the mark," said Flora.

"As well as strong self-esteem."

"Or vanity," teased his wife.

"Quite different. A healthy understanding of my own merits. And finally, I have a strong tendency to hope." He gazed at Flora.

Their eyes held for a lingering moment, then Flora bent to look at the chart. "Look here. Combativeness and conjugality are placed right next to each other in the brain."

"They are indeed." Robert's smile was tender. "In a cluster with friendship and parental love and amativeness. Perhaps there's something to this new science, eh?"

Randolph watched his mother gazing at them, reveling in their marital harmony. He felt a pang. He would probably never see that pleased expression directed at him. The thought was surprisingly painful.

"Herr Grossmann is putting on an exhibition tomorrow, if any of you would care to see him at work," said Robert.

"I can't," Randolph replied somewhat curtly. "I have to rehearse."

"Rehearse what?"

His brother's bright, inquisitive gaze made Randolph wish he'd kept mum. Everyone would know soon enough though. He might as well get the telling over with. "The Prince Regent has ordered me to sing at one of his parties," he said. "With Miss Sinclair."

"Ordered you?" exclaimed Flora. "How outrageous."

"And typical," said Robert. "Prinny has to get his paws on any new thing. Mark my word, he'll be telling his guests that *he* discovered your extraordinary talents."

"I hoped we might use the music room for our preparations, Mama."

"Of course."

Robert gave him one raised brow. "Assignations behind the harp strings?"

"Miss Sinclair's mother will be present," answered Randolph stiffly. Usually, he didn't mind Robert's teasing. But somehow, just now, it grated.

"How disappointing."

"Really?" said Flora. "Is that the sort of tryst you used to arrange?"

"I can't sing," said Robert.

"And that is not what I asked you."

"I studied Akkadian in secluded libraries," he said with a smile.

"Our library is not secluded," Flora replied. "That is an exaggeration."

They could go on like this for hours. At the moment, Randolph had no patience for it. "We agreed on one o'clock," he told his mother.

"I'll be happy to welcome them," said the duchess.

"I have an appointment at the dressmaker's at two, but I could change it."

"No need. We have to choose pieces to perform and try them out. This isn't a social visit."

"Very well. But I wouldn't want Mrs. Sinclair to feel slighted."

"I'm sure she won't." He rose. "I should look over the music you have, to see if I need to add to it." Not waiting for a reply, he walked out, conscious of eyes on his back.

The music room was a gracious space at the back of the house, overlooking the small walled garden. As he closed the door behind him, Randolph immediately felt better. He'd spent many happy hours here as a youth, and these surroundings soothed him. The walls hung with blue damask; the cello on a stand in the corner had occupied his youngest brother, Alan, for a while and then bored him; the antique instruments decorating the walls, none as old as his lute.

Randolph took the cover off the harp by the window and ran his fingers over the strings. The glissando lilted through the room. Miss Sinclair hadn't mentioned playing, and they wouldn't want to lug the instrument to Carleton House in any case. Or the prince would no doubt provide one. But no, they should keep to what they'd done before. Their royal host would expect that. Randolph replaced the cover and went to sit at the pianoforte. It was perfectly in tune, as he'd known it would be.

His fingers moved automatically into a favorite passage from a Mozart sonata. He gave himself up to it, falling into a heady harmony of body and senses as the movements of his hands and arms produced exquisite sound. This meshing had seemed a form of magic to him since he was five years old.

The music took over. It revitalized him. He rode the rhythms of the notes through the piece to the end. Then he sat back and let out a long breath. There was no solace like music, and he needed to remember that there were many pleasures in the world beyond the connubial.

# *Six*

Looking around the front hall of Langford House, with its soaring stair and rich marble floor, Verity judged it the grandest house she'd ever entered. Light poured down from high windows, glittered in a huge crystal chandelier, and gleamed in the gold stripes of the wallpaper. A hint of potpourri scented the air, along with beeswax and lemon. The clatter of the London streets didn't penetrate the gracious silence. "Goodness," murmured her mother. Verity was determined not to be intimidated.

A liveried footman led them through two beautiful reception rooms to the back of the house. He opened a door and stood back. Verity and her mother stepped over the threshold into a perfectly splendid music room. For a moment Verity forgot everything else as she took in the fine instruments waiting to be played, the older ones adorning the walls, and the piles of expensive sheet music. She could spend hours in a place like this and be blissfully happy, she thought.

And then a tall, stately woman came forward to greet them, and Verity was making her curtsy to the duchess, as well as wondering where Lord Randolph could be.

He hurried in on the heels of that thought. "I beg your pardon," he said. "I was just... Mama, this is Mrs. Sinclair and Miss Verity Sinclair. Ladies, my mother."

"Your Grace," they murmured.

The duchess said, "Welcome to Langford House." And with the warmth in her blue eyes and the ease of her smile, Verity felt the atmosphere in the room change from grandiose to relaxed. Or perhaps it was simply her own mood that had shifted. As they sat down and exchanged remarks about the weather and the season, she found she could talk to Lord Randolph's mother with surprising ease.

"I know you have musical matters to discuss," said the duchess after a while. She rose. "I will leave you to it. But I wanted to make sure you have all you need, Mrs. Sinclair."

"You're very kind."

"I've seen to the arrangements, Mama," said Lord Randolph.

"Sponge cakes and macaroons?" she asked.

"What else?"

The humorous look they exchanged gave Verity a glimpse into the Gresham family, which seemed a pleasant place. The door opened, and a maid came in with several sturdy working candles. "You said you'd bring some embroidery," said Lord Randolph to Verity's mother. "I wanted to make certain you had good light."

The duchess gave him an approving nod and went out. Lord Randolph made a great production of getting Verity's mother settled with the candles set just so and a cushion for her back and offers of tea or other refreshment. "So kind," she murmured as she was settled in the front corner of the room.

Verity noticed that it was the corner farthest from the pianoforte. And that the special candles and cushions—which a less observant person might dismiss as finicky items for a man to consider—effectively rooted Mama at a distance. It was unlikely that she would overhear much of what they said, unless they started shouting. Which she might, if Lord Randolph tried to maneuver her in a similar way. And where had he acquired such skill at diverting chaperones?

"I've pulled out piles of music," he said when they were at last free to begin. He led the way over to the table where the sheets were displayed. "I was thinking we should choose popular pieces rather than anything too complicated. Perhaps even repeat the song we did at Lady Tolland's."

Their eyes met, mirroring memories of that astonishing experience. Verity's cheeks grew hot. A self-conscious silence stretched out. She could actually hear her mother's needle prick the embroidery canvas.

Lord Randolph cleared his throat. "Ah, our audience at Carleton House will be varied," he went on. "Not all will be particularly musical. But I'm eager to hear your opinion about the program, of course."

He stopped and waited for her to speak. He gazed at her as if he actually wanted to know her views, and wasn't just pausing to give the appearance of listening before telling her what to do. It was a point in his favor. "What about some Italian songs, varied with

Scots or Irish ballads?" she suggested. "How long need we sing, do you think?"

"Long enough to satisfy the prince's wounded vanity," he responded wryly.

Verity looked down to hide a smile. "That sounds rather difficult to measure. An hour?"

"No more, certainly. We are doing a favor, not putting on a full concert. Shall we say six pieces? With one in reserve in case they insist on more?"

Verity agreed, and they looked through Mozart's and Haydn's arrangements of popular tunes and sheets of songs by Robert Burns and Thomas Moore. Langford House appeared to possess any piece one could desire, and Verity envied the bounty. She had to ration her purchases of sheet music on her allowance. The money her grandfather had left her was in trust until she married. And why was she thinking of that now? "'Robin Adair' would make a lovely base for a set of variations," she said.

They bent over the music together. "It would indeed," said Lord Randolph. He sat at the pianoforte and began to play the simple melody, and then to embellish it. Verity hummed along, following his elaborations. "Just here," he said, playing intricate series of notes. She caught the idea at once. Spontaneously they sang a verse with the new adornments, their voices blending in a twining harmony. By the end they were staring at each other, mutually astonished.

"Very pretty," said Verity's mother from the corner.

It was as if he could predict exactly what she meant to sing, Verity thought. Or, perhaps, his musical impulses ran in precisely the same direction. The phrase *in tune* took on a whole new meaning as they ran through the entire song, consulted briefly, and then tried it again. The result was equally lovely and interesting, but different with the varying choices of the moment. This must be what it was like to be intoxicated, she thought, as she fell into the music and a give and take with this man she barely knew—except that somehow they vibrated to the same pitch.

They chose three other songs and experimented with variations and harmonies. Verity was aware that they were taking more trouble than was required for a simple evening's performance. But the process was so delightful. Lord Randolph obviously felt the same way. "What about a change of key here?" she said.

"Perfect," he replied. And when he smiled at her—that devastating smile—Verity thought he meant more than simply a musical variation.

The next time she surfaced, at her mother's behest, Verity discovered that two hours had passed. How was that possible?

"Verity," said her mother again.

She had put aside her fancywork, Verity saw. A maid was setting out tea and an array of cakes. It was time to stop. Her sharp pang of regret seemed to be echoed in Lord Randolph's intense blue gaze. He didn't have any trouble devouring several macaroons, however.

"We've made good progress," he said between confectionaries. "Don't you think so, Mrs. Sinclair?"

Watching the boredom on her mother's face shift, Verity understood why he addressed the question to her. Not that understanding always helped anything.

"It all sounded pretty," her mother replied. "I don't

know why you need to sing a tune over and over though, when it was fine the first time. But then I've never been musical. Verity gets that from her father."

"Indeed? The dean is a musician?"

"Oh yes. He selects all the music for cathedral services. The organist is so happy to have his guidance."

And if you believe that, Verity thought, you've never heard one of their planning sessions. Papa was more a manager of music than a musician, in her view. But of course she never said so. He thought of the two things as the same.

"It's too bad he won't be there to hear us," said their host.

"Oh, well..."

Verity met her mother's eyes. For once, they were in perfect sympathy. Beyond Papa's likely disapproval of the event, he had a tendency to exalt his taste over everyone else's. There had been a few testy moments with the bishop. Would he hesitate to correct the prince? Verity suppressed a shudder. "He's far too busy," she said. "Is your family coming?"

"All of them who are in town," Lord Randolph replied promptly. He turned to her mother. "Perhaps we could rehearse again on Thursday afternoon?"

It was all well and good to include Mama, Verity thought. But she was the one doing the singing. "I've promised to visit my friend Olivia Thursday afternoon," she declared.

"Olivia Townsend?"

He'd met Olivia in Northumberland. Verity had forgotten that. "Yes."

"Perhaps you might go another day?"

"Oh, no, it's a set thing." He might have a glorious voice, but she wouldn't be...herded.

"Friday then?"

Verity allowed her mother to consider and agree. They chatted for a bit longer. Verity resisted a second cake, and soon after, they took their leave.

"You seem a thousand miles away," said Sebastian that evening as they prepared to go in to dinner at his house.

"Not so far as that," Randolph responded. His thoughts had strayed only a few blocks away, in fact, to the music room of Langford House and the hours he'd spent there this afternoon. How did such harmony of taste come about, he wondered, in two people with quite different histories? He'd met any number of individuals with fine voices, but when he sang with Miss Verity Sinclair, an unseen hand seemed to pluck the strings of his being. He lost himself in the music they created together; he felt as if his spirit expanded. And this with a young lady whose first reaction had been to reject him out of hand! She still glanced at him, now and then, as if he seriously annoyed her. It made no sense.

"You look like someone has hit you with a rock," said Lady Hilda Stane. "Not too hard, just enough to muddle your senses."

The youngest Stane sister had probably calibrated blows to the head exactly, Randolph thought. She had enough effrontery for three girls. He gathered his wits and smiled at the smirking blond. He suspected he'd been invited tonight to help Hilda feel she was enjoying a taste of society while Emma was out with friends. Sebastian had mentioned rumblings in his household as Hilda watched her older sisters go off to party after party. The fact that she was only fifteen years old, and not nearly out, didn't weigh with Hilda, and Sebastian feared some revolution was brewing.

Randolph watched his brother settle his wife into her chair at the dinner table, full of tender solicitude. Randolph was reconciled to his fate, but it seemed unfair that he should be burdened with so many blissfully married brothers. Taking the seat at his hostess's right, he addressed himself to the soup.

"We were wondering," said Georgina quietly after a few spoonfuls, "if you might be able to take Hilda about a bit."

Randolph choked on a mouthful of broth. This was far worse than he'd expected. He shot Sebastian an indignant glance. Cannily, his brother wasn't looking at him. He was keeping Hilda occupied at the other end of the table.

"I'm so busy squiring Emma about that Hilda's being left to herself a good deal. And with Miss Byngham gone—"

"Where?" Randolph couldn't help asking. Hilda's former governess had revealed a deep vein of eccentricity during the summer.

Georgina shrugged. "I'm not sure. But Hilda's becoming rather lonely."

It was hard to see the girl that way, but Randolph supposed her sister was a better judge. "Sebastian knows London better than I do," Randolph tried. The girl was Sebastian's sister-in-law, after all.

"He has a stretch of duty coming up. He can't get away."

Randolph sometimes thought that Sebastian's cavalry regiment took his time when he wished it to and not when he didn't. But that was unjust.

"I know you're busy as well," added his brother's wife with her lovely smile. "But it would be so kind of you."

Had Sebastian coached her on just how to appeal to him? That seemed too subtle for his military brother.

"You could take her to visit in Russell Square," Georgina continued. "She likes Flora."

"Really?" Randolph gazed at Hilda, who was trying to persuade Sebastian to buy her a sword stick. "She hates books, and Flora nearly always has her head in one."

"I know. I think Hilda is interested in Flora's charitable work with street children."

Randolph was assailed by a vision of Hilda at the head of a gang of grubby urchins, careening through the streets of London bent on mischief. He said as much to Georgina.

She laughed uneasily. "Flora's charges aren't grubby. And she wouldn't let Hilda... The thing is, Hilda's already sneaked out of the house once, with one of the maids, to visit Astley's Amphitheatre. She won't be shut in."

Randolph couldn't resist the appeal in his sister-in-law's gaze. "Oh, very well. I'll escort her to Russell Square." Perhaps Robert could overawe the girl.

"And perhaps to the menagerie at the Exeter Exchange?"

"The—?"

But the phrase had caught Hilda's ear. She leaned forward eagerly. "Are you talking of the animals? They have a lion and a tiger. As well as monkeys, a hippopotamus, an elephant...oh, all sort of creatures. I simply *must* see them."

"Lord Randolph might take you there," said Georgina, evading his reproachful look. "If you behave with some degree of propriety."

That was how Randolph found himself in one of his father's carriages the following morning, shepherding Lady Hilda Stane and a young housemaid to his brother Robert's home in Russell Square. Hilda had argued forcefully that the menagerie should come first, but Randolph had not been moved.

When they were ushered into the drawing room, they found two callers already present. Robert and Flora seemed glad to welcome newcomers. "You remember Miss Olivia Townsend," Robert said.

"We met in Northumberland," said the slender young lady on the sofa. "Well, not precisely met. I don't believe we were introduced. But I know who you are, of course. This is my sister, Beatrice."

Randolph made his bow. Miss Townsend's wide cheeks and pointed chin reminded him of a fox, if one could envision a fox with crimped brown hair, stylish apparel, and shining half boots.

Her sister, who looked to be of an age with Hilda, had to resemble a different parent. She was already taller than Olivia, sturdy and square shouldered, with dark-brown hair and slightly protuberant hazel eyes. Randolph barely had time to introduce Hilda before Miss Beatrice Townsend was chattering.

"Mama was very sorry not to accompany us," she said. "But my brother Peter broke his arm falling from the chandelier in the front hall." At the others' exclamations, she added, "He was very fortunate to escape with only that small injury. He brought down the chandelier with him—a positive blizzard of crystal. We thought the house was collapsing around our ears."

"It was very expensive," Beatrice added.

Her older sister nodded. "We decided to take ourselves off until the shouting was over." The Townsend sisters exchanged a laughing look. "And Beatrice so wanted to meet you because of your success on the stage," Olivia said to Flora.

"My—" Robert's wife looked startled.

"I told her how everyone praised your performance as Mrs. Malaprop at our amateur theatricals at the house party last autumn."

Hilda gazed at Flora with new interest as she shook her head.

"I would be glad to hear any advice you could give me," said Beatrice. She was uncommonly assured for her age. "I am *dedicated* to the stage. Particularly the comic roles. I was named for a character in Shakespeare's *Much Ado about Nothing*, you know."

"Not Dante?" murmured Flora.

Only Robert and Randolph appeared to hear.

"Does your family let you act?" asked Hilda.

"However would they stop me?"

"Lock you in your room?"

Beatrice met Hilda's eyes. Randolph watched the two girls exchange a wealth of silent information. An instant alliance seemed to form, and Hilda went to sit beside Beatrice on the sofa. They soon had their heads together in an intense, inaudible conversation. Randolph was struck by an elusive resemblance between them. He couldn't put his finger on it at first. Hilda was blond and green-eyed and Beatrice dark, with the stockier figure. Then he got it. They had the same stubborn set to their chins.

Miss Townsend chattered on about Lady Victoria Moreton's December wedding, in which she had served as a bridesmaid. The topic appeared to amuse Robert and Flora more than Randolph would have expected. He barely listened, straining to overhear what Hilda and Beatrice were plotting. Because they clearly were plotting. They weren't sophisticated enough to disguise it.

"So Miss Reynolds is also in London," Olivia said. "Do you have her direction? I should call, of course."

Flora looked surprised, then pleased. She readily gave the address. A few minutes later, Olivia rose to go. The grins that Hilda and Beatrice exchanged as the Townsend sisters departed only confirmed Randolph's suspicions. Those two would bear watching.

"A pair of slightly...fatiguing young ladies," Robert said when they were gone. Hilda frowned at him.

"Their father's a nabob," Flora replied. "Positively dripping with oriental jewels."

At Robert's raised eyebrow, she looked self-conscious. Indeed, the remark wasn't like her, Randolph thought.

"I'm quoting an acquaintance," Flora added. "Their mother is a relation of the Duke of Devonshire."

"Cavendish or Boyle?"

"I don't know." Flora turned away, dismissing the topic with a turn of her shoulder. "Are you enjoying London, Hilda?" she asked.

"I think I shall," said Hilda, who'd obviously been filing this information away. "Even more than I expected. Miss Beatrice Townsend invited me to call on her."

"You must ask your sister for permission," Randolph said.

"Of course I will. But she'll be happy. She was saying just the other day that it was too bad I hadn't any friends of my own in London."

Perhaps he should drop a word about Miss Townsend in Georgina's ear, Randolph thought. He became certain of it when he mentioned the menagerie on their drive home, and Hilda said, "Oh, never mind."

# Seven

Verity waited while her landlady's footman knocked at the door of Olivia Townsend's home in Berkeley Street. The door opened. A tall gray-haired butler looked down at them. He would have been imposing if he hadn't been swaying visibly, with the two bottom buttons of his waistcoat undone. The scent of brandy wafted down to them.

Verity's escort looked at her, scandalized. Verity ignored him and mounted the step to the threshold. "Miss Verity Sinclair to see Miss Townsend," she said.

The butler moved back, allowing them to enter. Verity's shoe crunched on something as she walked in. There were bits of shattered crystal in the corners of the entry hall, she noticed. A chain dangled high above, where a chandelier would commonly hang.

"If you will follow me," said the butler, articulating carefully. Walking behind him up a curving staircase, Verity was glad that he held the handrail. If he tripped, he would undoubtedly take her tumbling down with him. The man opened a door on the upper floor, gestured her through, and said, "Miss, er, to see you."

He shut the door on Verity's heels, leaving her to face what seemed to be a crowded drawing room.

Olivia came forward, holding out her hands. "Verity!"

"'Why, what's the matter, that you have such a February face, so full of frost, of storm and cloudiness?'" declaimed a girl of fifteen or so who stood by the hearth. She held a book rather close to her eyes.

"Is that beastly stuff supposed to cheer me up?" interrupted a boy of perhaps ten, reclining on a sofa at the side. One of his arms was in a sling.

"You don't deserve cheering up," replied the reader. "Not after wreaking havoc." She savored the final words like a connoisseur sipping a fine wine. "And it's Shakespeare!"

A tall, square-shouldered woman rose from a chaise and moved languidly forward. "Mama, this is Miss Verity Sinclair," Olivia said. "I told you about her. Verity, my mother."

Verity bobbed a curtsy. "Very pleased to meet you, Mrs. Townsend."

Her hostess greeted her with a sweet, if lazy, smile.

"And that is my dramatic sister Beatrice," Olivia continued, indicating the girl holding the book. She pointed at the boy with the sling. "My reprehensible brother Peter." The boy made a dreadful face at her. "My sister Selina and brother Gerard."

Verity guessed that the latter two were about eight and five. They were bent over a board game and barely acknowledged her arrival.

"And that is the lot of us, except the oldest," Olivia finished. "Winthrop is away at school."

All of the Townsend brood resembled their

mother, sturdy and dark-haired, except Olivia. "I'm the image of my father," said the latter, seeming to read Verity's expression. "Everyone remarks on it. Winthrop is the same."

Mr. Townsend must be a rather small, slender man, Verity thought. She wondered if his wife dwarfed him.

"We don't stand on ceremony here," drawled Mrs. Townsend, returning to her chaise.

It seemed an understatement. In any household Verity had ever visited, children this age would be in the schoolroom.

Selina reared back and whacked Gerard over the head with a throw pillow. He retaliated by pelting her with game pieces.

Mrs. Townsend laughed. "Barbarians."

"Get a pillow of your own," Peter urged Gerard. "You'll soon run out of ammunition."

No one looked at all self-conscious, Verity noticed. She would have been mortified at such a scene in her own home. She couldn't even imagine a parallel at Dean Sinclair's staid residence. Of course, she had no brothers or sisters.

Selina and Gerard swatted at each other with pillows for a while. Peter cheered them on. Beatrice paged through her book. Mrs. Sinclair laughed at them. After a bit, as the shock wore off, it began to seem rather...refreshing.

"Come out of this bedlam," said Olivia then. "We'll go to my room, where we can hear ourselves speak."

Beatrice made a move as if to join them. Olivia put her off with a gesture, and the younger girl looked hurt. But only briefly. She returned immediately to her book.

"I suppose you think you've entered a madhouse," said Olivia as she led Verity up another flight of stairs.

"Oh, no."

"Of course you do. With my raucous brood of brothers and sisters. And Cranford off somewhere watering the wine and filching the brandy. We call him our bibulous butler. But this is how we are. Mama married my father to escape a direly strict family. She says she was never so happy as when they cast her off entirely. She teaches us the proprieties, of course, but she vowed to let her children do as they pleased at home, and generally we do." Olivia smiled down from an upper step. "Papa was raised without any manners at all in a dreadful slum. Instead of learning polite behavior, he became very, very rich. He says that caring what other people think is like locking on your own manacles."

Verity felt dazed at this spate of personal information. "You don't worry that people will...object?"

Olivia laughed, sounding remarkably like her mother. "Oh, I'm exaggerating for effect, as Beatrice would say. Generally I behave. Last fall in Northumberland I spent several weeks as chief toadeater to an earl's daughter."

Verity shook her head. "You did not." She couldn't imagine her unconventional new friend in such a role.

"I assure you, I did." Olivia opened a door off the upper corridor and led Verity into a bedchamber.

Verity stopped short, dazzled by a riot of multicolored silk. Long swaths of the fabric draped the ceiling and walls, the bed and the two long windows. Scarlet, cobalt blue, emerald, gold, too many hues to count. "Oh!"

"Do you like it?" asked Olivia. "They're saris—the things women wear in India. Papa brought them back. I think they're lush!"

"They're astonishing." Verity felt as if she'd stepped into a fairy tale.

"Would you like some? I can get all I want from Papa."

"Oh! Thank you. Yes." Not that she'd be allowed to drape her room in this way. Not yet. But when she had a house of her own, she'd do as she liked.

"Splendid," said Olivia. "You can leave your bonnet on the bed."

Inspired by the household's free spirit, Verity untied the ribbons and tossed her hat onto the silken coverlet. Her pelisse followed with a flourish.

"Come and sit." Olivia plopped down in a brocaded armchair beside the fireplace. Verity took its mate on the other side. "Now we will plot," she added. "I'm sick to death of being meek."

"No one would call you meek," replied Verity.

The other girl looked pleased. "I shall see that they don't. This is my London season. Well, my first, anyway. I intend to make it *epic.*"

Verity nodded. She felt just the same. She wanted to grasp every chance for some adventure.

"And I've decided that Thomas Rochford shall be my project."

"Your… What do you mean, project?"

"I'm going to make him fall in love with me. Only think what a triumph!"

"You want to marry him?" Verity asked.

Olivia laughed. "No, no. In due time I shall find an

extremely amiable husband with tub loads of money who wants to spoil me utterly. I only want to… enslave Rochford." Olivia nodded. "Yes, that's the word. *Enslave.*" She seemed to taste it on her tongue.

Verity was fascinated by the idea. Olivia was full of thoughts that Verity had never had.

"Even Emily Cowper will envy me if I have Rochford languishing at my feet. I'll be famous!"

"But how will you manage it?" Verity asked. "It's difficult even to speak to him." She frowned. "And he didn't seem the sort of person to languish."

"That's why I need a good plan. And your help."

"Mine?"

"Yes. I require a truly bold friend. Like you."

"You think I'm bold?" Verity was flattered.

"Of course you are. Look at the way you rallied 'round when I stopped Rochford in the park. While Emma drooped as if she might faint. She's far too timid."

"But what do you expect me to do?"

"We shall see. I wanted to be certain you were on my side first."

"Yes, but—"

"Splendid!" Olive leaned back with a pleased smile. "Is it true you're to sing at Carleton House? At one of the prince's receptions?"

"You heard about that?"

"It's the latest on-dit. So it's true?"

Verity nodded. "He… The invitation said it was a private party. Quite exclusive."

"You'll be famous," Olivia crowed. "How lucky you are."

"Do you think so?" Verity was happy to have her

opinion confirmed. Everyone else had seemed to have doubts.

"Of course. Every girl coming out this season is trying to distinguish herself somehow. You hardly had to lift a finger."

"It's not quite that easy. We have to prepare a program of songs."

"You and Lord Randolph Gresham." Olivia's eyebrows worked up and down. "So handsome. Hours alone bent over a steamy pianoforte?"

The phrase made Verity laugh. "Mama sits with us as we rehearse."

"Oh, pooh. No chance even to steal a kiss?"

Even as Verity shook her head, the thought took hold of her. The scene ignited her imagination—the music ending, him bending near, the touch of his lips—and a bolt of heat shot from her cheeks…downward. Her breath caught. She wasn't going to settle for a country clergyman, but surely she could flirt with one. He sang so beautifully. A stolen kiss was such a delicious idea.

"Aha!" said Olivia.

"What?"

"Oh, nothing in the world," her friend replied with a wicked grin.

Verity pretended not to know what she meant.

"Speaking of kisses, I've just played the funniest joke," Olivia added.

Her sparkling eyes and impish smile were infectious. "What?"

"I sent Miss Reynolds a *huge* bouquet."

"The girl in the park?" asked Verity, puzzled. She'd

thought Olivia disliked her. And why would she send another girl flowers?

"The same. And I put in a mooning note that hinted the flowers came from Charles Wrentham. If only I could be there when she reads it!"

Verity tried to work this out in her head. "But if she should speak to Mr. Wrentham..."

"I know," crowed Olivia. "I wonder if I can arrange it? Somewhere I could watch."

"He'll tell her she's mistaken."

"And assume she's hoping to entrap him, which she certainly *is*."

"Won't that would be rather humiliating for her?"

"Exactly," replied Olivia with a nod. "And Miss Frances Reynolds will be taken down a peg, as she richly deserves. You may take my word for that."

Since she didn't know anything about Miss Reynolds, Verity had no other option. But even if Olivia was right, the bouquet seemed a mean trick.

When Verity and Olivia came downstairs a little later, they found a new caller in the drawing room. She looked familiar, and when Lady Hilda Stane was introduced, Verity realized why. Emma's younger sister resembled her in many ways.

"We're going up to my bedchamber," said Beatrice, tugging the other girl's arm. "And you are not invited."

Olivia and her mother merely laughed.

Randolph was adjusting the angle of the drapery to exclude the sun when his mother entered the music room on Friday afternoon. "I thought I would sit with Mrs. Sinclair today," she said. "I don't want her to feel neglected."

He was torn. Conversation would divert the lady from her chaperone's duties. But he would feel more self-conscious under his mother's observant eye. She would notice, as he already had, that he'd been anticipating this rehearsal more than a glittering *ton* ball. "She seemed quite content with her embroidery the last time," he said.

The duchess merely smiled.

Randolph silently conceded. One didn't argue with that smile. Not after the age of seven or so, when the futility of it had sunk in.

Miss Sinclair and her mother arrived soon after, and Randolph felt an odd sort of shock when his singing partner entered. Of course he remembered her perfectly well—the bright hair, pretty face, and frankly delectable figure. But the impact of her presence was greater than the sum of those details. He felt as if the room had grown a little brighter, its outlines a bit sharper.

Mrs. Sinclair followed the duchess over to the sofa in the corner and sat down. Randolph led the younger woman over to the sheets of music laid out on the table between the windows. "I thought we should try the songs in the order we discussed," Randolph said.

"To see how the whole program works," she replied.

"And if we need to change the sequence."

"So that the whole makes the perfect impression."

Randolph nodded. They fell into this automatic harmony, he thought. Over music. If nothing else. He took up the sheets, went to sit at the pianoforte, and they began.

It was just as before. When they started to sing, they seemed to enter a different realm where all was in tune. Depending on the mood of the piece, they could be spritely, tossing harmonies back and forth like skilled lawn-tennis players; affecting, hovering together on a tremolo of tears; or searingly sensual, once again rousing Randolph to a pitch he'd never experienced before. He knew that singing was an intensely physical act—the control of the breath, the shaping of the notes, and the projection of sound. But he'd never been aware of it in this reciprocal way, with a partner who matched him at every turn. It set him afire.

The quiet conversation in the corner, the room, the city all dropped away. He lost himself in the depths of Verity Sinclair's blue-green eyes, the movements of her lips, the sway of her torso. As the last refrain of the final song died away, he started to reach for her.

The sound of applause recalled him. The duchess was clapping enthusiastically, leading Mrs. Sinclair to join her. "Bravo!" declared the former. "You really are very talented, both of you." She smiled at Randolph. "My artistic son."

The pride in her eyes warmed him and brought him back down to earth. The descent was jarring, and a relief. He'd nearly thrown propriety right out the window. It was also an intense frustration. He rose and managed a humorous bow.

Verity put a hand on top of the pianoforte, afraid she might lose her balance. It was hard to breathe, even though she'd had no trouble while she was singing. With the music gone, she was dizzy with... aftereffects. She'd thought, there at the end, that Lord Randolph was going to pull her into his arms and indulge in the kiss that she'd now pictured a hundred times. She'd been more than ready, longing for his touch, until the burst of applause reminded her that a kiss was impossible.

"How nice to be able to make music like that," said her mother.

Verity stared at her. Could she really not have noticed that her daughter had been practically ravished before her eyes? It seemed so. Mama looked...complacent, practically smug. She looked like a woman whose tedious job is nearly done. Ah, Verity thought. Mama saw these rehearsals as courtship and expected an offer momentarily. Followed by a post chaise home to Chester and resumption of her comfortable, provincial existence. Verity resolutely *didn't* glance at Lord Randolph. She didn't want her life signed, sealed, and wrapped up in cotton wool. She just wanted that kiss.

Refreshments arrived. The cakes were luscious, but Verity hardly noticed despite her weakness for sweets. She struggled to make light conversation when her mind was still elsewhere, until one of her mother's remarks called it back.

"With your interest in female education, perhaps you've seen the works of Mary Wollstonecraft?" Mrs. Sinclair asked the duchess.

"I believe I've heard the name," Lord Randolph's mother replied.

"As have I," he said. "A rather unusual woman, wasn't she?"

"Her life was unorthodox, as her detractors are all too ready to point out. And of course I cannot condone all her actions. But do we judge male philosophers on the basis of their private behavior?"

"It depends," said Lord Randolph.

"Some of *them* crow about their bastard children," Verity's mother declared.

"Mama!" Verity glanced at the duchess. She didn't look shocked.

"Females aren't to say these things," Mrs. Sinclair added thoughtfully. "At least not in company. And that is part of the problem. Mary Wollstonecraft believes, rather fiercely, that women should be educated and have the same fundamental rights as men."

"Men don't all have the same rights," replied Lord Randolph. "Many have very few. What does she consider *fundamental*?"

And with that, the two of them were off on a spirited discussion of the nature of rights and responsibilities and the necessity of set societal roles. They gestured; they interrupted each other; they frowned over complicated points. And they showed no signs of stopping any time soon. As the conversation surged back and forth, Verity was amazed by two things. First, here was another person who could be swept away by ideas as easily as Mama. And second that Lord Randolph debated her mother without condescension. He spoke, in fact, as if she had an equal right to an opinion, as long as it was well reasoned. Mrs. Wollstonecraft would have been immensely gratified.

Verity met the duchess's eyes. She seemed genuinely

amused. "Birds of a feather," the older woman murmured. "Your mother has been rather quiet up to now. One might have assumed, mistakenly, that she had little to say."

"Mama is a…not a wolf but more like a crow, or a cat, in sheep's clothing."

Before Verity could worry that their hostess would find this remark odd, the duchess laughed. "I like that," she said.

Then, at the same moment, Verity's mother and Lord Randolph stopped talking and looked self-conscious. "I tend to go on and on," said the latter.

"I beg your pardon," said Mrs. Sinclair.

"Not at all. It was very interesting."

"Well, *I* was interested, but my family says I often take a point too far."

"So does mine," declared Lord Randolph, with a droll glance at the duchess. He turned to smile at Verity's mother.

The comradely look they exchanged was touching, even as it increased the sense of danger Verity felt around Lord Randolph. This man kept throwing out new, beguiling facets. He was terribly difficult to resist. But resist she must. "Were you always musical?" she asked him, to change the subject.

"He certainly was," the duchess replied. "As soon as he learned to walk, he used to toddle off to the kitchens, demand a set of copper pans, and beat out rhythms with wooden spoons."

"Mama!"

The duchess laughed at him. "My cook finally protested. Not at the noise. He produced a fine *rat-a-tat*.

But he set the kitchen maids to dancing when there was work to be done."

"I've always thought this story apocryphal," said Lord Randolph. "I have no such memory."

"You were too young. I can produce eyewitnesses," teased the duchess.

"Verity used to sing to our dog at that age," said her mother, her society manner once again in place. "And to flowers in the garden, and sheep in the meadows. She once sneaked into the choir stalls in the cathedral and joined in during a service."

The subjects of these reminiscences exchanged a commiserating look. And then as quickly looked away.

"Kindred spirits, I think," added Verity's mother with a nod.

The duchess obviously understood where Mama's thoughts were trending, Verity thought. This wouldn't do at all.

"Character does seem to form at a young age," their hostess answered. "My son James, for example, was always mad to go to sea. And now he's living on his own ship and sailing the globe."

"Living on a ship?" In an instant, Verity forgot all else. "He travels all the time?"

"He puts in to port now and then," said Lord Randolph.

"Wherever he's drawn to explore," Verity said. "The farthest reaches of the Earth." A fabulous, perfect way of life unfolded in her mind.

"And for supplies, I suppose," Lord Randolph said. "Fresh water, that sort of thing."

Verity leaned forward. "Does he visit you here?"

"He was in England last spring," Lord Randolph said. "He mustered out of the navy, now that the war's well over."

"I missed him!" The words popped out before Verity could censor them. Her chagrin at this lost chance was too strong. Lord James sounded like just the sort of man she was seeking. If only her parents had given in to her persuasion sooner!

"He stayed in one place long enough to meet his wife," said the duchess. "And then they were off together."

Verity's imagined life as a rover fell about her ears. Some other girl had snapped up Lord James before she had the opportunity. It was cruelly unfair. "Oh." She came fully back to her mundane surroundings with a bump.

Lord Randolph looked irked, her mother perplexed. And it felt as if the duchess's acute blue eyes could see straight through her, into nooks and crannies that Verity didn't even understand herself. She needed a diversion. "Shall we see you at the Mellons' this evening?" she blurted out.

"No." Lord Randolph sounded a bit curt. "I promised to escort Sebastian's young sister-in-law, and her new friend, to a play."

"Beatrice and Hilda?"

"Yes. You're acquainted with them?"

"I met them at Olivia's house. I expect you'll have a…lively time."

"If I can keep Hilda from disrupting the action onstage, I'll be satisfied."

"Or Beatrice from joining it," Verity said. She'd heard about her friend's sister's ambitions.

"I hadn't thought of that."

Verity was aware of the older women watching them. "You'll miss Herr Grossmann. He's putting on another demonstration."

"I do not understand why anyone would allow a stranger to run his fingers over their skull," said Verity's mother.

"I think it's rather like going to a fortune-teller," replied the duchess. "With another form of divination."

Lord Randolph cocked his head. "An interesting idea, Mama."

"People love to hear about themselves. And to have their…foibles dissected. As long as the report is mainly favorable, of course."

"*I* do not," said Verity's mother. "I see it as pure flummery."

"I should have said *some* people," the duchess said. "I don't intend to submit to Herr Grossmann's attentions either."

"He told Robert all sorts of flattering things," said Lord Randolph.

"And I'm sure Robert enjoyed it. But even so."

"What about you, Miss Sinclair? Will you be volunteering?"

He smiled at her—that devastating smile. Verity's pulse jumped, and she found she was glad he seemed over his pique.

"Of course not!" said her mother. She put down her teacup with a click and consulted the mantel clock. "We should be going, Verity. It's nearly five."

"So late! I had no notion."

In the bustle of departure, Verity managed to avoid meeting Lord Randolph's eyes. She did not evade a searching gaze from his mother.

# Eight

The date of the Carleton House performance came all too soon for Randolph. Indeed, the last few days before it seemed to rush past in a blur. He wasn't worried about singing. He knew their program was well crafted. But after this, he would have no more excuses to spend hours practically alone with Verity Sinclair. He'd come to cherish those times, and to dream of their singular…harmonies at night. He'd even wondered if they could find more occasions to sing together. But he knew that was unlikely. To perform at a prince's command was one thing. It couldn't continue.

As agreed, Randolph arrived early to check on the arrangements and the pianoforte provided. There was no real question; the prince would have the best of everything. But ever since the ram, Randolph had made a point of being thorough.

"Mama is adjusting her hair," said Miss Sinclair when she entered the music room a few minutes later. She looked stunning in a gown of pale blue-green that echoed the color of her eyes and clung to her contours in a way that tantalized while remaining perfectly proper.

Randolph was shaken by the desire that surged in him at the sight of her. He hadn't realized how far his impulses had roamed. She gave him a questioning look. He turned and sat down at the instrument, his fingers on the keys. They tried a few refrains and smiled at each other at the quality of the sound. "We go so well together," said Randolph, gazing up at her.

His lovely companion, who had been leaning against the pianoforte at his side, bent forward and kissed him.

For an instant, Randolph was startled. But the feel of her lips, soft and tentative, ignited him. He stood and pulled her into his arms. She threw hers around his neck and pressed closer. He reveled in the feel of soft, pliant woman, and in the knowledge that her feelings had been moving in the same direction as his. He let the kiss wander into deeper territory.

A discreet cough at his back made him jerk away. A liveried footman stood in the doorway. "His Majesty is coming to welcome you," he said, giving no sign that he'd seen anything out of the ordinary.

Well, most likely it wasn't unusual for Carleton House, Randolph thought as he reluctantly stepped away from her. The fellow had probably witnessed far worse. Randolph wished Miss Sinclair hadn't been involved, however.

Their rotund royal host sailed in, resplendent. "All in order?" he asked.

"Yes, sir," replied Randolph.

The prince's gaze had paused and fixed on Miss

Sinclair's bosom. "Going to stay in here until the time, eh? Just the two of you?"

"Miss Sinclair's mother will be along in a moment." Randolph was thankful that she hadn't been the one to discover them.

"Oh, you don't want that," said the prince. "I'll fob her off, shall I?"

"That's not necessary, sir."

"Really?" The older man's tone was incredulous. "Ah, you're Langford's parson son, ain't you?" he said then. "I suppose you have to act the saint." His expression mixed pity and mild contempt.

That made Randolph angry, but he said nothing. Mrs. Sinclair rushed in then, distressed at having taken a wrong turn. She stopped short and curtsied at the sight of the prince. He offered a few cordial platitudes and departed. "Oh my." Mrs. Sinclair let out a long sigh. "There's such a crush of people already. All very grand, of course. Your mother kindly helped me find my way, Lord Randolph."

"Come and sit down, Mama," said Verity.

Randolph took Mrs. Sinclair's arm and led her over to a sofa by the wall. "You can be comfortable here. No need to move until it's over."

"I wish it was," Mrs. Sinclair said, plopping down and fanning herself with one hand. "I can't abide strangers pressing all around me. And it's very warm, isn't it?"

"The prince hates drafts," replied Randolph. "He keeps his windows shut tight."

"I daresay it will be stifling when all those people come in here."

"I'll find you a glass of lemonade."

"Oh, I don't wish to trouble you."

"No trouble." He'd find that footman to fetch it, Randolph thought as he went out. And he would overcome his desire to kiss Miss Sinclair again, and again, before they became the target of hundreds of curious eyes.

---

At the appointed time, the crowd surged into the music room and filled the rows of gilt chairs provided for them. The air filled with the rustle of silks and curious murmurs. As Randolph had predicted, most of them stared. Miss Sinclair looked uneasy, and he tried to encourage her with a smile.

The prince came to the front and raised a hand for silence. "We have quite a treat before us," he said. "A pair of very talented *amateur* musicians kindly agreed to entertain us tonight."

He emphasized *amateur* not to insult their skill but to show that he didn't consider them hirelings, Randolph realized.

"A son of my friend Langford," His Highness continued. "One of the many."

The crowd laughed politely.

"And the lovely Miss Verity Sinclair, daughter of the dean of Chester Cathedral."

A small sound from his companion let Randolph know that she didn't appreciate the label.

"People will write to Papa," she whispered. "I thought it would be a few days before they connected me with him."

The prince stepped back with a wave of his hand. Randolph sat at the pianoforte. And they began.

After a slight quaver from Miss Sinclair at the beginning, they fell into the harmony that seemed natural to them. The melodies and variations they'd rehearsed chimed out, with further embroideries that came in the moment. Randolph was soon lost in the music. They might have been singing alone in the music room at Langford House, for all that he noticed of his surroundings. The lingering feel of their kiss made the experience even more intense.

The applause at the end of their program was loud and prolonged, punctuated with bravos. It was exhilarating. Randolph took his partner's hand as they made their bows.

People surged forward to congratulate them. They were gradually driven apart by the press of the crowd, but Randolph tried to keep an eye on Verity. If she showed signs of being overwhelmed, he intended to go to the rescue. His parents approached, all smiles, flanked by the prince.

"Oh, Randolph, that was exquisite," said his mother.

"Very well done indeed," agreed his father.

"Far better than their previous outing, I daresay," gloated the prince. He beamed at the chattering crowd.

Randolph stepped to the side as he thanked them. He'd lost sight of Miss Sinclair, and he found he didn't want that. But there were so many people in the way.

"That was...extraordinary," said a deep voice at Verity's back. She turned to find Thomas Rochford gazing down at her, tall and blond and handsome. He looked utterly at home in evening dress. His blue eyes seemed...speculative. That was the word that came to her. As if she'd well and truly caught his interest.

Elation bubbled through Verity's veins. She'd sung before royalty, and people had cheered. She was wearing the most beautiful dress she'd ever possessed. She'd *kissed* Lord Randolph! And now here was an acknowledged rake at her disposal, just the sort of opportunity she'd hoped to find at Carleton House. He must be an adventurous man, to flout convention and do exactly as he pleased. And even if his exploits were only amorous, he would know all sorts of unconventional people. "You're very kind," she replied.

"Most people will tell you otherwise."

"I suppose I can judge for myself." She could spar with words. At this moment, she felt she could do anything.

"Do you?"

"You think women can't make judgments?"

"I think most people don't bother. And I know you have a beautiful...voice."

His gaze roamed to other parts of her anatomy, but she wasn't going to be flustered. "As does Lord Randolph," she said.

Mr. Rochford made a throwaway gesture. "The Greshams have all sorts of talents. And there are so many of them. Have you heard about Hightower's Brighton race?"

It took Verity a moment to place the name. Lord Randolph's oldest brother was Viscount Hightower. She shook her head.

"I put him up to it, I fear," said Rochford. He described a careening melee of high-perch phaetons, making her laugh more than once.

A rake would have to be charming, she told herself. It was no surprise that he was. But she was more interested in his taste for action. This race sounded promising. Aware that she had limited time, Verity asked, "Have you been to Africa?"

"What?"

"Or Egypt? Well, that is in Africa, I know, but I always think of it as a separate place. Imagine standing inside one of those ancient monuments."

He looked bemused. "Sketches in travel journals are enough for me."

"Do you like travel writing? I found Captain Cook's voyages riveting."

Mr. Rochford shrugged.

He wasn't being very helpful. And Verity knew her conversation would be interrupted soon. "Are you a member of the Travellers Club?"

"I don't know it." His tone suggested it couldn't be worth knowing, in that case.

"It's new," she told him. "For men who have journeyed five hundred miles from London. Or more, of course."

"Nothing worth visiting is five hundred miles from London," he declared. "Even Edinburgh is closer than that, for God's sake."

He obviously found this remark witty. To Verity it was merely disappointing. "Perhaps you have friends who have made great journeys?"

"My friends have good taste, Miss Sinclair."

She supposed that was a setdown. She was too impatient to care. "Well, that's useless."

Mr. Rochford was visibly nonplussed.

Her mother's friend Mrs. Doran appeared at Verity's left side. Mrs. Doran's boon companion, Fannie Furst, planted herself on the right. They stood close enough to brush Verity's shoulders and glared at Mr. Rochford as if he'd insulted them.

"Ladies," he said.

The defending duo stuck out their chins and said nothing.

Their outraged silence appeared to amuse him. "Did you enjoy the performance?"

Mrs. Doran grasped Verity's arm and tugged. Verity resisted.

Thomas Rochford laughed. "Of course you must have. All the world did." He gestured gracefully at the crowd around them.

"The infernal gall," muttered Mrs. Doran.

Mr. Rochford did not roll his eyes, but he gave the impression of doing so. Then it seemed his amusement, or his patience, was exhausted. He produced a bow rather like a shrug. "Your servant, Miss Sinclair," he said, and departed.

Verity's unwanted guardians vibrated with pent-up emotion. She stepped back and slipped from between them before they could begin to scold, or whatever they planned to do. Moving quickly out of reach, she looked for someone she knew, and spotted Lord Randolph moving toward her. He was practically pushing people out of his way in order to reach her, and Verity felt a thrill at the sight. He was better looking than Rochford, she thought, in a completely different style. She smiled at him.

"You should not speak to men unless you've been introduced," he said.

"What?"

"Rochford." He spat out the name.

"I have been introduced to Mr. Rochford."

This brought him up short. "Who dared do that?"

Verity didn't intend to expose Olivia by explaining the circumstances. And then have to justify them. She waved the question aside.

"You mustn't talk to him again."

He put a hand on her arm. It felt proprietary. Verity shook it off. "Why not?"

"He is not a proper person for you to know."

"Oh, don't talk like a fusty country parson." She'd been so happy, and now he was spoiling things. Did he imagine she didn't know what she was doing?

Lord Randolph looked angry. Dauntingly so. "You kissed me!" he hissed in her ear.

"Well, and so what if I did?"

"Are you in the habit of kissing random gentlemen?"

Now he was just offensive. "Do you call yourself random?"

"*Are* you?"

Verity longed to hit him. "Perhaps I shall be. What's in a kiss?" The last sentence came out tremulous. Because there had been a great deal in it. As she'd meant there to be. But she wouldn't be scolded when she hadn't done anything wrong. Except with him. And he wasn't talking about that. Blindly, she turned and moved away. People gave her curious glances.

He'd exposed her to the stares of the crowd, another mark against him.

Just when Verity thought herself lost, she saw a friend not far away. She hurried toward her, nodding and smiling at compliments from those she passed. "Oh, Olivia," she said when she reached her goal.

"What a night you're having," came the slightly mocking reply.

Her friend's light tone was a relief. Nothing tragic had happened, Verity told herself. She hadn't made a fool of herself, except in her own mind.

"What did Rochford say to you?" Olivia asked.

"He was just being polite. Praising the performance." If he'd intended anything else, Verity meant to ignore it.

"Which made Lord Randolph furious?" her friend asked with an arch glance.

"He wasn't… What makes you say so?"

"I think everyone with eyes saw that he was furious." Olivia looked around as if gauging opinions. "It was rather obvious."

"Oh."

"So, are we to expect an engagement?"

"No!"

Olivia examined her as if she was an unusual specimen.

"He's insufferable. If he thinks he can dictate to me…" Verity got hold of herself. "You can't sing your way through life," she added, which sounded cryptic even to her.

"You might want to speak more softly," Olivia suggested. "And *I'm* not trying to marry you off."

Verity bit her lip. She hadn't meant to be so dramatic. And she certainly did not feel despair. That was ridiculous. She was at Carleton House, and she had scored a palpable hit. She had *kissed*... Perhaps she shouldn't have. But she'd wanted to. So much that she'd forgotten to make a follow-up plan. Would Olivia know how to manage men one had kissed? Not accidentally, but...inevitably?

But Olivia had turned her mind to her own concerns. "I need something to catch Rochford's attention," she said. "I can't sing like you. And anyway, that's been done." She acknowledged Verity with a smile. "I've heard he prides himself on his skill at cards. Perhaps I'll challenge him to a game."

"Could you?"

"Why not? I'll just have to think of a wager he can't refuse." Her smile this time was impish.

"Where would you play?" Ladies were banned from clubs, as Verity knew all too well, and the card rooms at evening parties were always filled with the older generation.

"It would take some arranging. I'll have to think."

"You could get into trouble." Olivia couldn't play Rochford in public without rousing a minor scandal.

"I know what I'm doing."

Verity discovered that the teachings of her youth had made a strong impression on her. She worried that Olivia was making a disastrous mistake.

"Verity!" Her mother bustled up. Mrs. Doran had undoubtedly poured out the tale of Rochford, and Verity was in for a scold. Briefly, she envied Olivia her easygoing mother. But of course she wouldn't trade her family for any other.

There were times when a large, voluble family was a blessing, Randolph thought on the opposite side of the room, and others when it seemed he had a few too many brothers.

"What do you mean, now it's Randolph's turn?" asked Sebastian.

"To be the goat," replied Robert.

"The..." Sebastian frowned at Randolph as if he was taking the expression literally.

"He's lost his heart to his singing partner," Robert added.

"I have not," said Randolph.

"Have too," said Robert, mimicking rhythms established twenty years ago. "And she's making difficulties."

"You don't know anything about it."

"I know she made you mad as fire a few minutes ago."

He'd allowed his emotions to overcome him, Randolph admitted silently. And he regretted it. But seeing a man like Thomas Rochford flirting with Miss Sinclair—with Verity, such an unusual, pleasing name—had revolted him. Rochford treated women shabbily; shameful cases were known. Randolph would have warned any young lady about the fellow. That was all he'd been doing. He couldn't quite remember what he'd said. The encounter was all muddled up with her flippant dismissal of their kiss and being called a "fusty country parson." He was certain, however, that he had *not* lost his heart to Miss Sinclair.

This…turmoil was nothing like what he'd felt with Rosalie. Randolph's hands closed into fists at his sides. He saw Robert notice, and forced his hands to relax.

"Anyone in the room who was paying attention knows that," added Robert.

"Don't tease Randolph," said Sebastian, going elder brotherly.

"Why not? You all teased me about Flora."

"You have a thicker skin."

Randolph and Robert stared at him.

"He's sensitive. Chafing rolls off your back like water off a duck."

"Well, thank you very much," said Robert. But he looked amused.

One could drift into thinking that Sebastian was an amiable dolt, Randolph observed. Sebastian had often applied the label to himself. He wasn't anything of the kind though, and since his marriage, he seemed to realize it. "I didn't tease you about Flora," Randolph said to Robert. "I did my best to help you."

"It's true, you did. Shall I return the favor?"

"I'm not doing anything. I don't need any help."

"Don't you?"

"Says he doesn't," replied Sebastian. He nodded at Randolph. "But if you find you do, just say the word."

And they would rally 'round, Randolph thought. If he needed them, Nathaniel would come down from the country and Alan from Oxford. James would sail home from halfway across the globe if word somehow reached him. They'd join a phalanx of Gresham brothers against the world. The knowledge was touching, and a little daunting. Like owning Aladdin's magic lamp, a power to use sparingly. "I'm perfectly fine," he said. "No help required."

From another corner of the large, overheated chamber, the Duke and Duchess of Langford watched three of their offspring converse. "I'm worried about him," said the duchess.

After more than thirty years of marriage, they usually understood each other without much explanation. The duke merely said, "Randolph? Why?"

"All of them learned the veneer that's so useful in society. But underneath, Randolph takes things harder than the others."

"Things?"

"If his heart should be broken." The duchess shook her head. "Again."

"You're thinking of Miss Delacourt?" The duke had heard the story of Rosalie after the fact. The delay had rankled a little at the time, but he was resigned to the knowledge that his duchess received confidences from their sons that he was denied. He supposed he knew things she didn't as well.

"Her loss brought him very near despair. To lose your love right on the verge of marriage—"

They looked at each other, their eyes mirroring the knowledge of what it would have meant to them.

"He struggled back to a kind of happiness," she continued. "Indeed, I'm sure he'd say he's very happy. To me, he has never seemed the same."

"Have you been fretting all these years?" her husband asked with concern.

"I'd feared he'd never fall in love again. Now I'm worried that he will...unluckily."

"Miss Sinclair?" The duke looked and found the young lady with the bright hair and lovely voice. "Is music the key there?"

"As much as any one thing ever is in mysteries of love."

The duke nodded. "They seem very harmonious together."

Though she smiled at his word choice, the expression was fleeting. "I can't make out how she feels. We were talking of James at one of their rehearsals—"

"She knows James?" he asked, surprised.

"No. But she came alive all at once when we were speaking of him."

"I don't understand."

"Nor do I." The duchess shook her head. "I only know that I couldn't bear to see Randolph as he was after Rosalie Delacourt's death. I don't know what I'd do."

"We would step in."

She looked up. She couldn't count the times she'd been thankful to have a partner she could rely on absolutely. "We agreed not to interfere in our sons' private affairs."

"And we were right. Look at how well they've all settled."

"Except Randolph."

"The exception that proves the rule."

"But what would we do?"

"That will depend on circumstances."

One brief glance was enough to forge a silent agreement. The duchess immediately felt better, recalling all the occasions when her husband had known best.

# Nine

Walking through the London streets toward Olivia's house, accompanied by her borrowed footman, Verity was conscious of a slight...melancholy? No, that was ridiculous. Not the right word at all. She never brooded.

She admired a froth of pansies in the window box of a stone house they passed. The June morning was balmy. She was on her way to see a friend. She was to attend a soiree that evening and her first grand ball in a few days. Such events would provide a host of opportunities to further her plans. There was absolutely no reason to feel as if something was missing from her life. And so she wouldn't. She refused. Verity walked faster.

Olivia's tall, apparently always tipsy butler admitted them and took Verity upstairs to the drawing room. The youngest Townsends weren't present today. Mrs. Townsend lounged in her customary spot, while Olivia and Beatrice faced off in front of the hearth. "I don't see why you had to stick your nose in," Beatrice declared.

"You told me about it," Olivia replied.

"Not so that you could betray me!" was the dramatic reply. Beatrice struck a pose. She stamped on the hearthrug.

"Oh, take a damper," said her sister.

Their mother's calm, amused voice intervened. "If you wish to go—and you notice I am not forbidding the outing—Olivia must accompany you," said Mrs. Townsend.

Verity was interested to see that she did exercise some parental authority.

"And Miss Sinclair, of course," added Olivia's mother, as if offering a treat.

"Where are we going?" Olivia's note had practically demanded her presence. Now Verity was even more curious.

Before anyone could enlighten her, the drawing room door opened and two new guests were inserted by the butler. Lady Hilda Stane marched in with a sullen expression on her pretty face. "My sister made me bring him," she complained, indicating her escort with an improper jerk of her thumb.

Verity stared at Lord Randolph, only to find he was gazing fixedly at her. She turned away as Beatrice said, "I have to take Olivia."

The two girls lined up shoulder to shoulder and glowered at their elders.

Lord Randolph ignored the glares, and their impatient seething, as he offered polite greetings and bowed over Mrs. Townsend's hand when introduced. He did it all perfectly, yet Verity thought he was as conscious of her as she of him. Finally, he turned to

Hilda. "Now you'll tell us what you're up to," he said. "We're not going anywhere else until you do."

"I'm not up to anything!" Hilda said, crossing her arms and frowning.

"Emma says you are. She claims you've been going about with your smug, about-to-commit-mischief look."

"Emma is a spineless peagoose! And a snitch!"

"Snitch," echoed Beatrice, seeming delighted by the slang. "So is Olivia. Sisters!" She and Hilda exchanged a disgusted look.

"Beatrice has an appointment with that German head examiner," said Olivia, biting back a smile.

"Herr Grossmann?" replied Lord Randolph. "The phrenologist?"

"That's the name." Olivia nodded. "She wrote him, pretending to be much older than she is, I suspect."

"I didn't 'pretend' anything," said Beatrice. But she looked away as she spoke.

"Of course you didn't," said Hilda.

"Really? He knows you're only fourteen years old?"

Lord Randolph had drifted closer to Verity, which she'd noticed, if no one else had. "She seems older," he murmured. As the lively argument continued, he added, "I'd thought young Hilda unique. But here's another. It's like throwing brandy on a fire." He shook his head. "Or one of my brother Alan's chemical experiments, where two elements create a bigger effect when mixed together."

Apparently, he was going to act as if their last conversation hadn't happened, Verity thought. And the kiss. Splendid. She could do the same. She was relieved. No, annoyed. Or both. It was difficult to judge. With him right there beside her, she couldn't think of anything but kisses.

"Enough!" declared Mrs. Townsend.

She had the voice that mothers possessed, or learned, Verity observed. It brought silence.

"Do you wish to keep your appointment?" their hostess added. "Or would you prefer to rip at one another right through the time?"

The group dissolved in a flurry of preparations. Hilda went with Beatrice to fetch her bonnet. Olivia didn't suggest that Verity come with her. She was left with Lord Randolph, under Mrs. Townsend's tolerant eye. Verity tugged at a glove. Every remark that occurred to her led right back to those dizzying moments in his arms. Well, let him make conversation.

"I suppose..." he began.

Verity waited. The silence lengthened. "You suppose what?"

"There's no need to snap at me."

"I didn't."

"No, I'm not going to apologize," he said quietly.

"I haven't asked—"

"I maintain I was in the right."

"About?"

"And the...other thing. I didn't begin it."

"Thing?" He was calling their kiss a *thing*. And saying it was all her doing.

"One might argue that—"

"*One* is an idiot," Verity snapped. Yes, snapped this time. And welcome. "*I* offer no opinion, as you seem to be talking to yourself."

He looked startled.

From her chaise, Mrs. Townsend laughed. It was a lovely, lilting laugh. And it reduced them to stiff silence until the others came back.

Lord Randolph had brought a carriage. It had the Langford crest on the doors, and the grandness of it improved Beatrice's temper. Or perhaps it was just getting her way, Verity thought as they piled in. Acting the perfect gentleman, Lord Randolph took a rear-facing seat. Olivia hesitated as if to let Verity join him. She declined by plopping down beside Hilda and Beatrice opposite. With raised brows, Olivia sat.

The younger girls chattered during the drive to Herr Grossmann's address, with occasional contributions from Olivia. This allowed Verity to seethe in satisfying silence. She looked out the window at the passing scene, eliminating any chance of meeting Lord Randolph's riveting blue eyes.

They arrived, were admitted by a housemaid, and ushered upstairs to a sparely decorated reception room. Herr Grossmann bustled in a few minutes later, then stopped short, looking puzzled. "Mrs. Beatrice Townsend?" he asked in his accented English.

"Mrs.?" exclaimed Olivia.

Taking this as a reply, the German addressed her. "I'm pleased you have brought your husband."

Hilda dissolved in a fit of giggles.

Their host gave her a sidelong look as he continued. "I prefer that ladies be escorted. It is more proper."

"I'm afraid you're mistaken," said Olivia. "My sister made the appointment with you." She indicated

Beatrice. "*Miss* Beatrice Townsend. No husband as yet. The male sex has been spared that horror so far."

Beatrice made a face at her.

"Oh. Ah. Quite a…young lady." Herr Grossmann looked at Lord Randolph as if he was in charge. Men always made that irritating assumption, Verity thought.

"She has her mother's permission," Lord Randolph said.

"Yes? Well, I—"

"We will remain with her, of course."

He looked eager. It occurred to Verity that he cared less about the proprieties than having an opportunity to observe Herr Grossmann at work.

"Of course." The German seemed to make up his mind. "If you will all come with me?"

They processed into a room across the landing. It was empty except for a large wooden chair on a dais, two small gilt chairs below it, and a large version of the phrenology chart hanging on the wall. There was no carpet. Light streamed in through two uncurtained windows. Herr Grossmann went to pull a bell rope.

The summons was promptly answered by a lad of perhaps sixteen. Tall and gangly, with black hair and pale skin, he was not dressed as a footman. Beatrice and Hilda eyed him with interest.

"This is Michael, my assistant," said Grossmann. "Fetch more chairs, Michael."

"Yessir, right away," the young man answered. His accent was not German. More London tinged with Irish, Verity thought.

He returned with two more gilt chairs and set them out. Olivia, Verity, Hilda, and Lord Randolph sat in an interested row. Michael went to stand at the side of the dais. He took a notepad and pencil from his pocket.

For the first time, Beatrice looked uncertain. "The evaluation requires that you remove your bonnet," Herr Grossmann said. Beatrice hesitated. Verity wondered if she was regretting her arrangement.

"I'll hold it for you," said Olivia with sly humor. "Unless you've changed your mind?"

Beatrice set her chin, untied the ribbons, and removed her hat. Her dark-brown hair was loose beneath it. She tossed her bonnet into Olivia's lap and marched over to sit in the large chair.

"Michael is observing in order to learn," the German added.

"In training, are you?" asked Lord Randolph.

"Yessir." Michael held the pencil poised over the pad.

"Now, if you are ready, miss, I will place my fingertips on your head."

"I'm ready," Beatrice said rather loudly.

Delicately, Herr Grossmann touched her forehead. "Yes, I thought so," he said. "A strong area of eventuality, the desire to know and be informed." His tone was clinical, not the least intrusive. Beatrice blinked as Michael wrote busily.

"That would be nosiness?" said Olivia. "You're certainly right there."

"I wish you would go away," replied Beatrice. "I never wanted you to come."

"My papa says it's our duty to be well informed," said Hilda in defense of her friend.

"I expect Herr Grossmann concentrates better in silence," put in Lord Randolph.

"Indeed, sir, that is true," the other man replied.

Gentlemen united to keep the ladies quiet, Verity thought. Although in this case, it was probably better if Olivia didn't taunt her sister.

"A bent toward firmness," the phrenologist continued. "And hope. A marked tendency to imitation."

"Like an actress?" Beatrice asked, brightening. "A stage role is a kind of imitation, isn't it?"

"The term refers to 'copying the manners, gestures, and actions of others, and appearances in nature generally,'" said Michael, as if he'd memorized the phrases.

"Acting," declared Beatrice with smug satisfaction. "You see, Olivia, I am *destined* to be an actress."

"Destiny has no part in this," said the German. "If you will keep your head very still, miss."

She subsided.

Herr Grossmann moved his fingers. "Ideality is pronounced."

"A love of the beautiful, desire of excellence, poetic feeling," recited Michael. "Abuses include extravagant and absurd enthusiasm, preference for the showy over the solid and useful, a tendency to dwell in the regions of fancy and to neglect the duties of life."

"You have her character to a T!" exclaimed Olivia, laughing.

"Please do not recite your definitions aloud, Michael," said the German. He sounded annoyed. "It is meant to be done silently."

"Yessir."

"Are there lists of the traits?" asked Lord Randolph. "In books perhaps?"

"Great thick ones in German," Michael answered. "But Herr Grossmann copied the details out for me."

The look his employer gave him made Verity wonder if the relationship would last much longer.

"Might I have a copy?" Lord Randolph said.

"What else about my head?" Beatrice demanded. "We came here about me."

"Yes, miss," replied Grossmann, who didn't appear eager to fulfill Lord Randolph's request. "If we might have silence, please." When his audience obeyed, he went on with his examination. "A bent toward combativeness."

Verity wondered if this point was real, or a subtle dig at the interruptions.

"Fortunately not combined with destructiveness," he added. He stepped back and lowered his arms. "Those are the main points I discern."

"That's all?" said Beatrice. "What about my... animal appeal? You told Mrs. Saxon that she was 'exceedingly amative.'"

"Where did you hear such a thing?" asked Olivia.

"She was visiting Mama, and she said—"

"That is not the way I would have summarized my findings," interrupted Herr Grossman stiffly. "I am a scientist, not a gypsy fortune-teller." He stepped down from the dais, muttering something about words being twisted. "Michael will prepare a written report for you, approved by me, with the proper terminology."

Beatrice looked disgusted.

"Do you keep records of all your sessions?" Olivia asked.

"Of course. As I said, I am a scientist."

"Even the more informal ones? You examined Mr. Rochford at an evening party, for example."

Verity glanced sharply at her friend. She noticed that Lord Randolph was frowning.

"I made notes afterward, naturally. Thorough records are vital to the scientific process."

"So you have files."

"Of course."

Verity watched Olivia, thinking that her friend was more akin to Beatrice than she'd realized.

Beatrice stood. "Well, if that's it, we may as well go," she said. She stepped over to snatch her bonnet from Olivia's lap and pull it on. "I must say I thought this would be more exciting."

"I hope you will tell all your young friends about your mistaken assumptions," said Herr Grossmann.

Verity laughed, then turned it into a cough when Beatrice frowned at her.

"There is the matter of payment." Herr Grossmann looked at Lord Randolph. Which was the other side of the coin, Verity thought. If you were in charge, you paid. It wasn't fair in this case, but she still somehow felt that it served him right.

"I brought the money," said Beatrice pettishly. She took a banknote from her reticule. "It does seem like a lot for what you get." Herr Grossmann glowered. Michael stepped forward and took the money before Beatrice could change her mind. The girl turned her back on them. "We'll go to Gunter's now," she decreed. "I want an ice cream."

"Miss Hoity-Toity," said Olivia. But no one voiced any objections.

Beatrice flounced out, Hilda on her heels. As Verity followed, she saw Olivia pause beside Michael and speak to him while Lord Randolph had Herr Grossmann's attention. She couldn't hear what her friend said, but it wasn't difficult to guess.

Randolph followed the ladies out. Herr Grossmann hadn't wanted to give him the list of traits. Perhaps he viewed the details as secrets of his odd trade. Randolph suspected that young Michael would be susceptible to bribery, however, if he decided to pursue the matter. Verity Sinclair turned her head at that moment and smiled at something Miss Townsend said to her. Randolph forgot all about phrenology.

When they reached Gunter's in Berkeley Square, Randolph dismissed his father's coachman. There was no need to keep the horses. It was a fine day, and he and the girls could easily walk home from here. And it had occurred to him that if he plotted the route correctly, he could escort Verity home last and carve out a little time to redeem himself after his earlier incoherent conversation.

"I want to have my ice in the park," declared Beatrice. She sounded like a child who'd been deprived of a promised treat and must be given another to make up for it. Hilda was the same, Randolph thought—childish one moment and alarmingly mature the next.

He found seats for his party in the park and flagged down one of Gunter's waiters. The popularity of outdoor dining meant these servitors had to dodge carriages and horses in the street to take orders and deliver confections.

"A lemon ice," Beatrice demanded as soon as the man approached. "One of the ones shaped like a lemon." When Hilda looked inquiring, she added, "They freeze it in molds shaped like fruit. Or vegetables. Bread or meat even, though that seems odd to me. Why would you want to eat an ice that looks like a lamb chop?"

"How splendid," said Hilda. "Do you have anything shaped like asparagus?" she asked the waiter.

"A pistachio ice cream, miss," he answered.

"I'll have that. I loathe asparagus."

Randolph didn't follow her reasoning, but it didn't matter. The rest of them gave their orders, and the waiter rushed off.

They looked about, and Randolph's companions began to comment on the other people present. This park of maple trees across from Gunter's shop was quite a fashionable haunt, one of the few places a young lady could be seen alone with an unrelated man without being exposed to scandal. Although such a visit was a strong signal of an attachment, Randolph thought. He was far from alone with Miss Sinclair, of course. The two youngest members of their party fell into a fit of giggles over some whispered remark. Very far from alone.

"I wonder how she holds her head up," Miss Sinclair said to Miss Townsend, watching a lady with an enormous feathered hat.

She hadn't really looked at him since their stilted

conversation in the drawing room, and it rankled. They'd sung together in perfect harmony. They'd kissed—a moment and a sensation that were seared into his memory. And then everything had gone wrong between them because of Thomas Rochford. Randolph felt a flash of rage at the man—the sort of person who cared for no one but himself and flouted convention simply for the fun of it, it seemed. Randolph's eyes strayed back to Miss Sinclair as he tried to dismiss the anger. She seemed peculiarly able to unsettle him.

His connection with Rosalie Delacourt had been just the opposite, he thought. They'd been introduced in the most conventional way. They'd danced and strolled under her parents' benign scrutiny. They'd talked and talked and found they agreed on every important point. He'd never really talked to Miss Sinclair, Randolph acknowledged, except a bit about music. With Rosalie, he had proposed, and she had accepted. All had been smooth as silk. Had it not been for a malign fate, they'd be living happily together right now. And he wouldn't be sitting in a park puzzling over how to speak to a stubborn, forthright young lady with a habit of arguing.

Why was he comparing Miss Sinclair to Rosalie? Did he place them in the same category? And if he did—

The waiter brought their sweets and set them out. Hilda and Beatrice dug in.

"Are you still with us, Lord Randolph?" asked Miss Townsend as she picked up her spoon.

"Yes, of course."

"It seemed you were a thousand miles away. Pondering higher matters, I suppose."

Randolph wasn't surprised that she was one who'd poke fun at his profession. Miss Townsend seemed to be rather shallow and self-centered. She was patently prone to sarcasm, a hopeful rather than successful wit. But the same might be said for many young people of both sexes, he added silently. No doubt she would improve with age. "I was just calculating how many birds perished to create that hat," he said, nodding in the direction of the bonnet they'd been observing. "And deciding it wasn't worth the slaughter."

The ladies laughed. They ate their ices, exclaiming over the flavors. The breeze blew a strand of bright hair across Miss Sinclair's cheek. As she tucked it back, their gazes intersected, and Randolph felt shaken, like a man who misses a step in the darkness. He needed to discover what lay behind those blue-green eyes. "What did you think of Herr Grossmann?" he asked her.

"Think of him?"

"Did his system strike you as credible?" The topic wasn't scintillating, perhaps. But here in public he couldn't ask her what she thought about deceptively charming rakes or explore the issue of kissing.

"I suppose it makes sense that the body would reflect the brain," she said. "But I wonder how they established the map of traits."

"Some sort of tests, I suppose."

"What kind though?"

"They might have examined people whose proclivities were well known and collated the results."

"Collated… What does that mean?" asked Beatrice.

"Put them side by side and compared them," Randolph explained. A possibility occurred to him. "If you had detailed descriptions of a deceased person's character—"

"You could measure their skulls and note the shapes," said Miss Sinclair.

"Ugh," said Hilda as Randolph nodded.

"A grim prospect," said Miss Townsend.

Randolph could hear Robert guffawing at the notion that he was entertaining young ladies with talk of palpating corpses. Once again, he'd allowed his curiosity to meander too far. "The Greeks saw the brain as the major controlling center for the body," he said, somewhat at random. "The Egyptians thought it was the heart."

"That would seem to depend on what controls you're thinking of," said Miss Sinclair.

"A combination of the two is best," Randolph replied. "Should that occur."

"You think cooperation is unlikely?"

"I believe that agreement of mind and heart is rare."

Verity Sinclair gazed at him. "A rather sad picture of life."

The other ladies swiveled their heads back to him. They'd been shifting like observers at a tennis match. Randolph sincerely wished them gone. "Realistic, rather," he said. "And often very useful."

"How so?"

Lobbing ideas back and forth with her was exciting. Even more than debates with friends at university. Perhaps because none of them had been entrancing females whom he'd kissed, Randolph thought. "Much can be discovered, or revealed, through inner debate."

Miss Sinclair frowned over this. He waited, fascinated to hear her opinion. "Working out what is truly important to the individual, you mean?"

"Precisely." She looked interested. He found that curiously encouraging.

"Well, you're too deep for me," said Olivia Townsend. She pushed her empty ice cream dish away.

"And very tedious," added her younger sister.

"Beatrice." But Miss Townsend's reprimand had no force behind it.

"Lord Randolph has a tendency to run on and on," said Lady Hilda Stane.

"He must have a great bump for that somewhere on his head," Beatrice said, giggling.

Randolph tried to shrug off the teasing. His brothers had said worse. Not in front of Miss Sinclair, however.

"Once, in Herefordshire, he talked for half an hour about some fusty poet. With quotations," Hilda said.

"George Herbert," murmured Randolph. Miss Sinclair looked surprised.

"He's as bad as my father," Hilda continued, pleased to have captured the group's attention. "Papa once lectured me for *hours* on the differences between Celts and Picts."

"Picks?" said Beatrice. "The tools miners use?"

Hilda shook her head and pronounced the word more clearly. "They're ancient tribesmen. Painted themselves blue. Instead of clothes. They ran screaming into battle stark naked."

There was an instant's silence, as they all visualized

this scene, Randolph imagined. Catching Hilda's sly sidelong look, he pressed his lips together. Clearly, she had a trap laid for anyone unwise enough to correct her simplistic description. And she knew more about Picts than he did.

"But wouldn't that be—" Miss Sinclair broke off.

"Remarkably distracting?" said Olivia Townsend.

"I suppose the other soldiers were familiar..." Miss Sinclair hesitated.

"With such equipment?"

"Olivia!"

"Well, they would be," responded her friend with mock innocence.

This led all four ladies to look at Randolph and then quickly away. The situation was almost too absurd to be improper. But not quite. Although shielding the youthful ears of Lady Hilda Stane seemed like a lost cause, Randolph rose. "Perhaps we should be going?" he said.

Hilda looked thwarted. What had she expected him to do? Huff and puff like a parson in a farce? The ladies stood up and gathered their belongings.

"You're fond of George Herbert's poetry," Miss Sinclair murmured as they strolled out of the park.

"Exceedingly."

"I, too."

"Really? What is your favorite?"

"Are you coming, Verity?" called Miss Townsend.

"Yes. Of course."

She walked faster. Randolph could only follow.

# Ten

"You do realize that this is a dreadfully unfashionable thing to do," said Olivia.

"Why did you come with me?" Verity asked. She'd been wondering about this ever since Olivia declared her intention of tagging along. Her expedition didn't seem Olivia's sort of thing at all. On the other hand, Verity quite understood her mother's absence. The place might have drawn Mama, but she'd trade almost any outing for a period of solitude. And in this case there'd been two letters from Papa.

"You can't go haring around London alone," Olivia replied.

Apparently her long-suffering footman escort didn't count. "Suddenly you're a stickler for the proprieties? Do you think the British Museum is swarming with importunate swains?" Verity smiled, rather proud of that last phrase.

Olivia laughed. "Oh lud. I can just see it. Hordes of decrepit old sticks, snuff stained, stumping after you with their canes and urging you to come and view their antiquities."

Verity had to laugh as well. "You have an odd idea of museumgoers. Perhaps we'll meet a dashing young explorer, here to examine previous finds before he sets off on an expedition to the antipodes." Verity didn't really expect such luck, but one could hope. She was guaranteed a look at treasures from all over the world.

They walked across the broad courtyard between the wings of Montagu House and up a few steps to the main entrance. Inside, Verity paused to consult the thorough guide she'd purchased before even coming to London and had pored over since. "I want to begin with the collection of objects from the South Seas," she told Olivia, and incidentally the footman, who was looking about as if he expected footpads. "Can you believe they have the actual things Captain Cook found on his circumnavigation of the globe?"

"Circum… Verity, really, this place is turning your brain."

"There are also books, engraved gems, coins, prints, and drawings," Verity told her as they moved farther inside.

"I daresay," Olivia said. "They seem to have a bit of everything. What a cramped jumble."

"And then I want to see the Greek and Roman artifacts," Verity continued, ignoring her friend's comment. "And the Egyptian sculptures, of course."

"My lord, do you mean to spend the whole day? Isn't there a gigantic foot of… Apollo, wasn't it?"

Verity turned to her, surprised and pleased. "Yes. How do you know that?"

"I can read, you know," Olivia answered dryly. "I'm not a ninny."

"Of course not. I just didn't think you were interested."

"Many things interest me. Who could resist seeing a gigantic foot? Let us begin there."

"But I wanted to—"

"We can find your South Seas bits right after," Olivia interrupted. She looked around, spotted an official, and went to speak to him. "This way," she said when she returned.

Verity followed her through several rooms full of items she would have liked to examine. But Olivia was walking fast and disinclined to pause. "Aha," she said a few minutes later.

They'd entered a large chamber adorned with Greek sculpture, but the more surprising sight was Miss Frances Reynolds standing alone beside one of the pieces. It represented the toes of a huge foot, Verity saw.

"Miss Reynolds, how odd to meet you here," said Olivia.

Something in her tone bothered Verity. Olivia didn't sound surprised.

The fair-haired girl flushed. "I'm waiting for someone."

"Here? Whoever would you meet here?"

"A...a friend."

"Are you ashamed of them?" Olivia asked with suspicious airiness.

"What? No, I... Of course not."

"It's just that a place like this." Olivia gestured at the statuary. "Seems tailor-made to hide a connection you don't want known."

The younger girl looked stricken.

"Fanny," said Olivia. "May I call you Fanny?"

"I'd prefer not," said Miss Reynolds. "I dislike that diminutive of my name."

Olivia rolled her eyes at Verity, as if to say what else can you expect of such a ninnyhammer. She turned to the sculpture. "How disappointing. It isn't the whole foot. Just a few toes. An exhibit like this is practically guaranteed to convey disappointment."

"There are many other things to see," Verity said. She didn't trust this oblique conversation.

"The Rosetta Stone," said Miss Reynolds. "Which allowed scholars to decipher Egyptian hieroglyphs."

"Indeed." Verity nodded.

"And the Elgin Marbles," the younger girl added. "From the Parthenon. Byron called Lord Elgin 'a filthy jackal' who 'gnaws at the bone' of conquest for taking them away. In *The Curse of Minerva.*" She spoke distantly, as if thinking of something else. Something melancholy.

"Do you admire Byron?" Olivia said. "I wouldn't have thought it of you."

"I don't admire him. Not in the least. I acknowledge that he has a gift for poetic expression."

"How generous of you."

"We're going to see the South Seas materials," Verity put in. "I'm particularly interested in those. You're welcome to come along." She ignored the face Olivia made.

"I think I'll wait a bit longer," Miss Reynolds replied. She seemed more determined than happy with her choice.

"Is your friend late?" inquired Olivia sweetly.

"Yes."

"How thoughtless." She turned and started toward the archway that led to other rooms.

Verity hesitated, then followed. "What was that about?" she asked when they'd left Miss Reynolds well behind.

"What do you mean?"

"Don't try to bam me. Something odd was going on back there."

"Oh well." Olivia smirked. "I may have sent Miss Reynolds a note that mentioned a certain bouquet and suggested a meeting by Apollo's foot. A great touch, the foot, don't you think? My father says that true brilliance is in the details."

"That's rather cruel, isn't it? I should go back and tell her."

Olivia gave her a sour look. "Certainly, if you're the sort of person who would betray a friend's confidence. And you wish to humiliate me."

"I don't, of course, but—"

"She didn't have to come," Olivia interrupted. "Nobody is making her moon over a certain gentleman. Or pay attention to anonymous notes. She could simply invite him to call on her, couldn't she?"

"I suppose Miss Reynolds would see that as too forward."

"They're pretty well acquainted. They portrayed lovers in a play last autumn. And it would be much more sensible than lurking by an ancient god's foot, wouldn't it?"

They were fair points, but Verity remained

uncomfortable. "Promise you won't send her any more notes."

"Pah, you're no fun."

"Nevertheless."

"Oh very well, Miss Prim. I swear." Olivia put a hand over her heart.

Verity didn't like being thought stuffy, but Miss Reynolds had looked so forlorn. She still wondered about going back to tell her the truth, but just then they reached the rooms displaying items from Captain Cook's voyages. Immediately, Olivia was full of amusing comments and charming questions, reminding Verity of why she'd liked her in the first place. She also made no complaint as Verity examined every piece and imagined what it had been like to come upon them in a newfound landscape. Still, the rest of the tour was not quite as delightful as Verity had imagined it would be.

It was late afternoon before they returned to Olivia's home, and when they entered the drawing room, they found Lord Randolph there, inquiring after Hilda. "She slipped away from Sebastian's house," he told them. "And as he is on duty, I've been delegated to find her. I thought she might be visiting Miss Beatrice."

"Who is not here," said Olivia's mother. "She said she was going to practice dramatic speeches in her bedchamber." The lady sighed. "We appreciated her thoughtfulness in sparing us."

Olivia snorted.

"Perhaps she's been kidnapped by pirates," suggested Peter, who was once again lounging on the drawing room sofa, nursing his broken arm.

"Pirates wouldn't want her," replied his younger sister, Selina, looking up from her card game.

"They wouldn't want you!" exclaimed her opponent, five-year-old Gerard. "You're cheating again. I know you are."

"I'll search Beatrice's room," said Olivia above the noise of their dispute.

"Nurse looked," said her mother.

"She doesn't know Beatrice's hidey-holes." Olivia went out.

Randolph was relieved that the two girls were most likely together. Hilda thought she was up to anything, an opinion for which she had some justification. She was clever and fearless. But London held hazards beyond her experience.

"Did Olivia enjoy the museum?" asked Mrs. Townsend, amusement clear in her voice.

"She liked Apollo's toes," said Miss Sinclair in an oddly dry tone.

"You went to the British Museum?" asked Randolph. "Did you see Ramses?"

"No."

It seemed she hadn't liked the exhibits. Or perhaps she didn't know the name. "He was an Egyptian ruler many thousands of—"

"I know," interrupted Miss Sinclair. "It is impossible to see everything in the museum in one visit."

Her friend returned, waving a piece of notepaper. "I've got it. They've gone to visit Mrs. Siddons."

"The actress?" Randolph was startled.

"Ah," said Mrs. Townsend. "Beatrice saw her in *Douglas*. She found her suicide scene *utterly devastating.* People say this play may be Mrs. Siddons's last."

"But how did she come to know the lady?" Randolph asked. Mrs. Siddons was a respected figure, unlike some other women of the theater, but schoolgirls weren't likely to be acquainted with her.

"Wrote to her, apparently," Miss Townsend answered. "Multiple times, I would imagine. The poor lady finally gave in to the siege and invited her to call." She brandished the page as evidence. "What a poor conspirator Beatrice is. She left this in her 'secret' cache under a loose floorboard. Can she have forgotten that she showed me the place? I'll have to teach her proper plotting."

Randolph didn't understand the look Miss Sinclair gave her. "Does she give her address? I'll go and fetch them."

"I don't suppose we could just let Beatrice come home on her own," said Mrs. Townsend. She added, "No," just as Randolph said the same. "She really cannot go haring off without telling me," their hostess continued.

And something might have happened to them, Randolph thought but didn't say. Wasn't it getting rather late for visiting? "I'll return her to you." He held out his hand for the note. "May I see?"

"I'll keep this," replied Miss Townsend. "The address is Westbourne Green. Where will we find that, do you think?"

"I shall go alone," Randolph said. His parents' coachman would know how to find the place. He suspected it would be a goodly distance.

"If you think I'll miss meeting Mrs. Siddons, you're mad," said Miss Townsend.

"The journey could take a while," Randolph replied. And it would be all for nothing if he missed them. He suppressed irritation. He didn't want a long carriage ride in the company of Miss Townsend.

"I don't care. It will be an adventure. Verity will come, too. Won't you, Verity?"

"Yes," said Miss Sinclair.

Suddenly, the trip seemed less onerous. "About what time did she leave?" Randolph asked.

"She went up to her room hours ago," said Mrs. Townsend.

Which wasn't particularly helpful, Randolph thought.

"I must send word to my mother," said Miss Sinclair.

This note was quickly written, and other necessities attended to. A few minutes later, the trio was in the duke's carriage heading west around Hyde Park.

"You have to admire Beatrice's initiative," said Miss Townsend. "I wouldn't have thought of such a lark at her age."

"You didn't have a coconspirator like Hilda," Randolph pointed out.

"True. If only we had known each other then, Verity."

Miss Sinclair made no reply. She was gazing out the window at the passing scene as they veered away from the park. Randolph admired her profile, wondering what she was thinking.

"I've never been out this way before," Miss

Townsend commented after a while. "It's a bit dreary, isn't it?"

The houses seemed commonplace to Randolph. It wasn't Mayfair, but neither was it a slum.

Conversation became sporadic as they rattled on. The light grew more golden as afternoon turned to early evening. Randolph thought of requesting more speed, but his father's coachman knew his business and would be as eager as he was to get this over.

"Wait, stop!" cried Miss Sinclair some time later. "There they are."

The driver heard and pulled up. When Randolph looked, there indeed were the miscreants, heads down, trudging along the side of the road. The girls eyed the carriage warily, until Hilda perked up and shouted, "It's Randolph! Thank heaven."

Randolph jumped out and herded them into the backward-facing seat. The coach made the awkward turn to reverse their direction.

"There are *no* cabs to be found way out here," Hilda declared. "And Beatrice *wouldn't* go back and ask—" She bit off the sentence as she apparently remembered the clandestine nature of their outing.

"I don't care," said Beatrice. "I don't care if I get a thundering scold. I've met the greatest tragedienne of our time."

It sounded like a quote, Verity thought.

"And she told me I would do very well on the stage."

"She said you were a dramatic young lady," Hilda corrected. "Lud, my feet hurt! These new half boots fit dreadfully. And I'm starving. The *greatest tragedienne of our time* didn't give us as much as a biscuit with our tea."

"She is above food," Beatrice retorted.

More likely she hadn't wanted to prolong the visit, Verity thought.

Lord Randolph leaned forward and produced a packet of sandwiches from a cloth bag at his feet. "I've found that a bit of sustenance comes in handy on rescue missions."

Verity admired his foresight, as well as his calm assurance—just the sort of attitude one needed to weather the hardships of exploration. This was not, of course, a voyage to the far side of the globe. It barely qualified as a mild adventure. And Lord Randolph was unlikely to have true ones, she reminded herself. Ever. He was a country parson. She really must stop forgetting this crucial point.

"You *are* a trump," said Hilda, unwrapping the sandwiches and handing one to Beatrice. "And not ringing a peal over us either." She bit into her own.

"Not my job," said Lord Randolph. "You may be sure Georgina will. And Mrs. Townsend."

"Mama will laugh," said Beatrice. "And admire my panache." She made a sweeping gesture with her sandwich.

"No, she won't," said her older sister. "She's very cross with you." She rather spoiled the effect by adding, "I cannot believe I missed meeting Mrs. Siddons."

This set Beatrice off on a paean that lasted for the remainder of their journey and left her sandwich largely uneaten.

When Verity reached her lodgings later that

evening, her mother was sitting in the drawing room with a book. "Is all well with the girls?" she asked.

"Yes, we found them safely."

"Oh good. You have a letter from Papa. It was enclosed in one of mine. I didn't see it until I opened them."

Verity eyed the packet on the writing desk. "Is he angry about the singing?"

"A little concerned. We *told* him it was just the once."

Apprehensive, Verity went to unseal the letter. But when she began to read, she found he had another concern entirely. After the usual salutation, he wrote:

> *I was startled to receive a missive from Lord Randolph Gresham enclosed with your mother's last. And distressed to hear that you were to be paired with him for this ill-advised concert.*

Verity blinked. Lord Randolph seemed just the sort of man her father would like. She read on.

> *I have confirmed that this young man is the one who caused the Archbishop of Canterbury considerable embarrassment. I will not repeat the story. Unlike certain frivolous persons, I do not consider it amusing. And it is certainly not suitable for your ears. I will say only that Lord Randolph's carelessness undoubtedly damaged his prospects in the church. It would be best to avoid any further linking of your names.*

Her father finished with his dear love, and so on.

Verity contemplated the words. What could Lord Randolph have done to earn this warning? If frivolous persons—Papa privately referred to the Bishop of Chester that way at times—thought it amusing, it couldn't be so very bad. The Lord Randolph she knew seemed quite unlikely to embarrass the archbishop. Could Papa have mistaken him for someone else? Or perhaps Lord Randolph wasn't as staid and parochial as she'd thought.

# Eleven

Verity stood before the long mirror in her bedchamber and evaluated her appearance. Her dress for her first London ball was white. The dressmaker had advised that this was the most suitable color, even though Verity was well past eighteen. She had found a fabric with a silvery sheen in the dressmaker's shop, however, and Mama had agreed that it became her. Her hair was gathered in a knot on top of her head with a few wispy curls drawn forward, making its bright hue less noticeable, she thought. Her pearl drop earrings and necklace completed a picture that would definitely do. No one would call her a diamond of the first water, perhaps, but she looked well.

She couldn't count on throngs of dance partners. She didn't know enough young men for that. Olivia thought that Verity's small notoriety from singing would attract interest and lead some to ask the hostess for introductions. They would see about that.

Verity knew that Lord Randolph would be at the ball. Surely he would ask her to dance! He'd sent her some lines of George Herbert's poetry after their recent outing. Verity retrieved the folded page from her dressing table and read it again.

*Sweet day, so cool, so calm, so bright,*
*The bridal of the earth and sky;*
*The dew shall weep thy fall tonight.*

She smiled. She knew the poem, and the rest wasn't so sweet. Some people might call it grim, actually. She'd twit him about that. And perhaps about the archbishop as well. She looked forward to it. To a surprising degree. Gathering her gloves and wrap, she went to join her mother.

Sitting in the line of carriages waiting to discharge their passengers, Verity breathed in the smoky scent of the torches flaming beside the front door. She watched beautifully dressed guests step down from their vehicles and enter in a swirl of colors. She ran her fingers over the silky fabric of her gown and listened to the clop of hooves and jingle of harness. And she gathered these details into one of her moments. The scene was all she'd imagined back in her provincial home.

As she moved up the stairs to greet the hostess and pass into the ballroom, this seemed like the glittering center of the world.

"All these grand people," murmured her mother. "And scarcely one word of sensible conversation among them."

"Mrs. Doran will be here," Verity said.

"That's right. She'll help me look after you."

Verity hid a grimace. She'd endured an intrusive scold about Rochford from Mrs. Doran because she was Mama's friend. The line moved up two steps, and then another.

The wait seemed long, but at last they were exchanging greetings and moving on. Verity drew in an appreciative breath when they entered the ballroom. Swags of flowers adorned the walls, filling the air with scent. A trio of musicians tuned up on a small dais in the far corner. Everywhere, members of the *ton* chattered and flirted.

She scanned the rows of gilt chairs lining the walls, found Mrs. Doran, and settled her mother beside her. Before they could insist that Verity join them, she said, "There's Lady Emma. I must say hello."

Emma, lovely in rose pink, stood with her older sister by one of the long windows. "You look perfectly splendid," Verity told her when she reached them.

Emma looked down at her gown. "It *is* pretty, isn't it? Hilda said I looked like the top of a chocolate box."

"I expect she's jealous," said Verity.

"She could never bear to wait her turn," sighed Emma's older sister. "And now I've had to confine her to her room as punishment for sneaking off. Lud knows what revenge she's plotting. Oh. Wait here, Emma, I'm going to speak to someone." She moved off in a rustle of cobalt silk.

"Is the rest of your family here?" Verity asked Emma. She hadn't spotted Lord Randolph in the crowd.

"Sebastian escorted us." Emma heaved a great sigh. "I shan't be able to waltz," she said. "We haven't been to Almack's. I don't see why we must all wait to be approved there."

"We don't aspire to vouchers," Verity replied.

"I could see if Georgina would ask for you."

"I don't care about going." Verity spotted Olivia and gave a little wave. "What a beautiful dress," she said when that young lady joined them. Olivia wore a gown of pale-blue tissue over white satin with a rather daring neckline. A sapphire ornament sparkled in her brown hair, matching a lovely bracelet. The ensemble referenced her father's wealth without flaunting it, Verity thought.

Georgina came back with a young gentleman in tow. "Emma, this is Mr. Lionel Packenham. Mr. Packenham, may I present my sister, Lady Emma Stane?"

Verity felt a pang of envy over Georgina's social expertise. She sometimes felt she was guiding her mother through the season rather than vice versa. Although Mr. Packenham wasn't terribly handsome, he had an engaging smile. Emma seemed pleased, and that was the important thing.

The two went off to join the set forming in the center of the large room. Georgina was summoned by her husband to do the same.

"What a wet fish," said Olivia.

"Olivia!"

"Packenham," Olivia added. "Oh, Packenham. Impeccable pedigree and tub loads of money. He doesn't require a chin."

"Someone will hear you."

"In this din? Never. But I must tell you my great coup." She leaned a little closer. "I've gotten a copy of Herr Grossmann's notes about Mr. Rochford."

"Did you bribe his assistant?" Verity asked.

"You're too clever. You've spoiled my story. But

yes, I did. And now I know all of Mr. Rochford's innermost secrets."

"Really? Such as?"

Olivia made a face. "Unfortunately there wasn't much more than what Herr Grossmann said in public. But I can pretend there were desperate revelations."

"Mightn't that make Mr. Rochford angry?"

"I hope so. One strong emotion leads to another."

As Verity considered this dubious proposition, the musicians showed signs of beginning. Olivia surveyed the room. "We don't want to be labeled wallflowers. Ah." She summoned a tall young man with a gesture. "Aren't you going to ask me to dance, Ronald?"

"Naturally," he said with a bow.

"A crony of my older brother," Olivia told Verity. "Known him since I was seven. Do you have a friend with you for Miss Sinclair, Ronald?"

Verity would have preferred to find her own partner, had she known anyone.

"All engaged for this set, I'm afraid. I hope I may snag you for the next, Miss Sinclair."

Verity smiled and nodded. One of the few advantages of Chester was her broad acquaintance there, built up over a lifetime. She never lacked dance partners at the country assemblies. She'd resigned herself to going back to her mother when Olivia said, "Oh." She waved, discreetly, then more broadly, attracting a good deal of amused attention before she was noticed by the young man who seemed to be her target.

With what Verity thought was reluctance, an athletic-looking fellow with dark hair and eyes came over to them.

"Have you no partner for this set, Mr. Wrentham?" Olivia said. "May I present my friend Miss Verity Sinclair?"

Mr. Wrentham was attractive, but his expression was closed. Verity felt thrust upon him as he bowed and requested the honor. She wanted to dance, however. And it wasn't her fault that Olivia had dragged him over.

They moved onto the floor. Mr. Wrentham danced well and even smiled once or twice as they exchanged commonplaces. Half the set had passed before Verity made the connection. This was the man Miss Reynolds was mooning over, according to Olivia. She eyed him with greater interest and indulged her curiosity. "I believe I know a friend of yours," she said.

"Indeed?"

"Miss Frances Reynolds."

He looked down at her, true interest flickering in his brown eyes for the first time. His hand tightened on hers. "She spoke of me?"

Verity wasn't quite prepared for the strength of his reaction. She couldn't repeat what Olivia had said. "Your name was mentioned."

"Where? How?"

"At, er, an evening party, I believe."

"Miss Reynolds is in London? What is her direction?"

"I don't know."

He looked annoyed. He might as well have said, "What use are you to me then?"

An irritating man, Verity thought, doubting Miss Reynolds's taste. Still, the girl had seemed so melancholy. "Surely you have mutual acquaintances who could supply that information," she said.

"Hah. Yes. Probably." He said little else before the country dance ended, and then he left her with a cursory farewell.

"Good riddance," Verity murmured under her breath.

Ronald did not reappear. Her next partner requested an introduction from their hostess and said flattering things about her singing. His gaze kept sinking toward her bodice, however. And lingering. It was a nearly unredeemable black mark in Verity's book. She insisted upon conversing with a face, not a forehead.

And then the musicians were striking up a waltz, and Verity found Mr. Rochford bowing before her.

His tall, fair-haired figure defined elegance. Some men just seemed made for evening dress, she thought. No doubt he danced exquisitely. His brows were raised, his expression challenging. Of course he was aware that he'd presented her with a conundrum.

Verity hadn't determined in advance whether she would waltz tonight. Mama had doubts about the dance, though she admitted that it was accepted among the *ton*. Verity had decided to wait and see how she felt when the time came. And here it was. In an untenable form. Waltzing with Mr. Rochford was a step further, so to speak, than she was willing to go. She'd have to refuse.

She wasn't particularly sorry. Mr. Rochford had proved to be a disappointment. He might be handsome and polished, but he wasn't an adventurer. An acknowledged rake was actually a rather conventional creature, she thought. He simply turned conventions upside down. And his air of lazy impudence felt both dismissive and artificial. His eyes might twinkle, but they were hard. She opened her mouth to deny him the dance.

A broad-shouldered figure stepped between them. Lord Randolph Gresham grasped her hand. "I believe this dance is promised to me," he said.

"I suppose the lady would know best about that," replied Mr. Rochford, looking down his nose even though Lord Randolph was a hair taller. They shifted slightly, gazes locked, poised to jostle and posture like…men, Verity thought. Or dogs growling over a tidbit. "I am *not* a bone," she said.

The declaration startled them out of their pose. And then Olivia was beside Rochford, her fingertips brushing the sleeve of his coat. "This must be our dance," she said.

"Must it?"

"Oh yes, I think so."

"How did I miss all these arrangements, I wonder?" But he looked more amused than angry, and he led her onto the floor.

The music had started. Couples swayed and turned. Lord Randolph still held Verity's hand. She made no objection when he set the other at her waist and steered her into the waltz. Her free hand found his shoulder. Nearly as close as when they'd kissed, they moved down the floor in tandem. He pulled her into a twirl. Her skirt belled out. It was exhilarating.

"Miss Townsend's behavior is quite fast," he said.

"You'd be well advised not to pick up her habits. She's…unwise to dance with Thomas Rochford."

In the blink of an eye, Verity was incredulous with rage. She'd never felt like hitting a man until this moment. Did he ask if she'd intended to accept Rochford's invitation? Did he expect her to have the sense God gave a goose? No, he assumed she was a fool. He pushed in and tried to make a decision for her. And then he criticized her friend. "I believe I've mentioned that I don't require your advice," she said through clenched teeth.

Lord Randolph looked surprised, which only compounded his offense. If he said he knew better because of his position or wider experience, she'd…spit.

He did not. He danced. They turned at the end of the room and moved up the other side. Verity's temper cooled somewhat. "Did you like the lines of Herbert I sent?" he said finally.

"That poem is about death," Verity replied curtly.

"Yes. And the words are beautiful. 'The dew shall weep thy fall tonight.' I've always found that phrasing lovely."

"Recording the presence of beauty, even though death is inevitable."

"Precisely." Lord Randolph nodded. "I should have known when you said you liked Herbert that you're a thoughtful person. I can see why you don't require advice."

Mollified, Verity said, "I don't say I never do." She almost added that she'd been about to refuse Rochford. But he spoke first.

"Herbert was such a master. He finds the words

even when he acknowledges there are none." Softly, he recited: "'Verses, ye are too fine a thing, too wise for my rough sorrows; cease, be dumb and mute. Give up your feet and running to mine eyes, and keep your measures for some lover's lute, whose grief allows him music and a rhyme; for mine excludes both measure, tune, and time.'"

"Grief?" Verity repeated, wondering at the emotion in his voice.

Lord Randolph looked self-conscious. "Much-read lines come naturally to mind." He hesitated before adding, "Yes, that poem helped me through a mournful time."

Verity glimpsed shadows of pain in his eyes. He looked away, a clear signal not to probe further. As if she would in the middle of a ballroom. But perhaps, some other time, she'd discover the cause?

Olivia and Mr. Rochford twirled right into their path. Verity nearly stumbled as a humiliating dance-floor collision loomed. Then Lord Randolph's hand at her waist swung her around, strong and sure, as if she was light as a feather. She felt as if her feet almost left the floor. Mr. Rochford's eyes, inches away as they brushed past the other couple, twinkled with malicious enjoyment. Clearly, he'd done it on purpose.

Verity looked up at her partner. It was curious, she thought, how different two pairs of blue eyes could be. One might think that eyes were simply…eyes. But it wasn't true. Thomas Rochford's were brilliant, piercing, and opaque. Rather than windows to the soul, they were shutters obscuring it. Lord Randolph's, on the other hand, were wonderfully expressive.

"Oaf," muttered the latter.

Verity smiled.

"Rochford amuses you?" demanded Lord Randolph.

"Your characterization of him does. I don't think many here would agree."

"My opinions are not dictated by the chattering of the herd."

"Of course they're not."

"Are you laughing at me?" He raised auburn brows. "I'm willing to amuse, but I like to know the joke."

"Not a joke. More of a...fellow feeling."

He looked confused.

The violinist hit a sour note. They both winced, with identical pained expressions. The player immediately recovered and moved on through the tune. "It's a hard job playing for a ball," Lord Randolph observed. "Tiring. Hostesses expect hired musicians to go on for hours without a break."

"And pay them as little as they can manage," Verity replied.

"It's a precarious life, most times."

"And yet, they get to make music."

He nodded. "Often for unappreciative audiences, however."

"We should tell them that *we* appreciate their efforts."

He looked startled. "A fine idea."

And so when the set ended, they went to commend the musicians, surprising these gentlemen with knowledgeable compliments on their skills.

"The violinist has a fine instrument," said Verity as they walked away side by side.

"Italian like the man," Lord Randolph agreed.

"I never tried the violin."

"I can scrape out a simple tune. It's easier to learn than a lute."

"You play the lute?"

Randolph wondered why he had mentioned his archaic obsession. They'd been talking so easily that it had simply popped out. And now Miss Sinclair was intrigued, of course. Any musical person would be. No one played the lute any more. "I've been fooling about with one," he said.

"The fingering is rather like a guitar, I understand?"

"A bit trickier."

"Really? I'd like to see how."

A scene rose in Randolph's imagination—the two of them bent close together, his fingers adjusting hers on the stem of his lute, a turn of her head, a second searing kiss. Other considerations fled his brain. "I'd be happy to show you."

"Show her what?" said his brother Robert's voice. "Take care, Miss Sinclair. Randolph once spent three hours inspecting the Elgin Marbles. I had to flee the museum in self-defense."

He'd walked automatically back to his family, Randolph realized. He ought to have delivered Miss Sinclair to her mother, but he'd been distracted. Under the eyes of his parents and two brothers, he murmured, "I was eleven years old."

"Even worse," said Robert. "What sort of boy—"

"I'm better at cricket than you," Randolph interrupted. He couldn't help it, even though he knew they'd laugh.

"Why must you always pretend you care nothing for intellectual subjects?" said Robert's wife, Flora.

"To tweak you," Robert answered with a fond smile.

"The Elgin Marbles are fascinating," Verity found herself saying. "I spent *more than* three hours at the British Museum last Tuesday." Her assertion was greeted by an interesting variety of smiles, from speculative to grateful. Suddenly, she felt like an animal stepping into a foreign herd.

Their hostess announced supper. Doors at the end of the ballroom were thrown open to reveal laden buffet tables in an adjoining room. "Shall we go in together?" asked the duchess. She took Miss Sinclair's arm in a way that worried Randolph slightly and led the way. There was nothing to do but follow.

Robert moved faster and snagged a pair of tables that he and Sebastian pushed together to accommodate them all. The ladies sat down—Flora, Georgina, and Emma ranged around one end and Miss Sinclair next to his mother at the other.

At least Olivia Townsend was far away, Randolph noted. There was no sign of Rochford; she sat with a group of young people. Miss Sinclair's mother was on the far side of the supper room at a table full of older ladies. She was looking toward them, but didn't seem disapproving.

The gentlemen had remained on their feet. "Shall we do the honors?" asked Randolph's father.

"Cream cakes," replied the duchess.

"As if I don't know, after all these years?"

His parents exchanged a smile. They were kind

people, Randolph thought. There was no need for concern. Except he didn't like the glint in his mother's eye. She looked that way when she was ferreting out some transgression. Of which there was none in this case, he assured himself. All was well.

Randolph went off with his male relatives and a young man he didn't know, who was squiring Emma apparently, to procure food.

He made it back in record time, having filled two plates rather randomly. "What did you think of the place?" his mother was saying when he sat down and placed the second plate in front of Miss Sinclair.

"Which place?" asked Randolph.

"Miss Sinclair attended a school for the daughters of senior clergymen," answered his mother.

"Is there such a… Well, there must be."

"In Lincolnshire," said Miss Sinclair. "I thought it an admirable establishment."

"Admirable," echoed the duchess. "And congenial?"

"For the most part. Miss Brell, the founder, decreed that we should study only subjects related to the church or church work."

She wasn't looking at Randolph as she spoke, but he remembered her remarks about narrow-minded country clergymen. "That could cover almost any topic," he observed.

Miss Sinclair shrugged. "Miss Brell's motto was: resolution, rectitude, industry."

At the other end of the table, Emma made a face. Everyone was listening to this conversation, Randolph saw.

"Many of my fellow students became missionaries."

"It sounds absolutely dire," said Emma.

"Not that," Miss Sinclair replied. "No one was unkind. We weren't deprived. But we were expected to be serious, always. Which was all very well for Latin class—"

"You know Latin?" asked Flora from the other table.

Miss Sinclair nodded. "And ecclesiastical history and moral philosophy." She shifted in her chair as if uncomfortable.

His family could be overwhelming in such an unadulterated dose, Randolph thought. "It sounds like Oxford," he offered. He wondered what music she'd been allowed to play. Church music, no doubt.

"And how much better than an education limited to embroidery and sketching and a smattering of Italian," Flora declared. "Very few girls have such a chance."

"True," replied Miss Sinclair. "And yet, I think girls should have opportunities to be frivolous and…a bit wild. Isn't that why they have all those games at boys' schools?"

All the other ladies looked at Verity Sinclair. Randolph tried to catalog their expressions—Georgina amused, Emma bored, Flora arrested, his mother speculative. He felt an odd spurt of pride. Miss Sinclair was holding her own in this formidable group.

"I've established several schools for penniless girls, you know," said the duchess. "Perhaps you'd like to visit one with me."

"Oh." Abruptly, Miss Sinclair looked like a lamb thrust into a flock of goats. No, she didn't, Randolph immediately told himself. That analogy was wrong on any number of levels—not least that it made his mother inappropriately caprine.

"I'd welcome your opinion," the duchess added.

"I don't know that I would… Of course I'd be happy to—"

Before Randolph could intervene, his mother did. "Splendid. What about next Wednesday?"

As Miss Sinclair agreed, perforce, the other gentlemen returned with their spoils. Randolph's father had a footman in tow bearing a whole platter of cream cakes, with bottles of champagne under each of his arms.

Plates were distributed. Corks popped and glasses poured. The conversation became more general.

"What is this?" Miss Sinclair asked, poking at a brown mass on her plate.

"Oh, er…" Randolph had no idea.

"Pickled mushrooms," said his father.

Miss Sinclair drew back her fork. "I cannot eat mushrooms."

"You don't care for them?" asked the duke.

"They…disagree with me."

"Sorry," said Randolph. "I didn't know."

"How could you?"

He reached for the platter in the center of the table. "Have a cream cake?"

With a smile, she took one.

Verity escaped the Greshams when the dancing began again after supper. It was a considerable relief to move down the ballroom with a stranger introduced by the hostess and talk of commonplace things. Not that she disliked Lord Randolph's family. Quite the contrary. They were charming, interesting people. She'd been comfortable with them except for the part when she'd felt…interrogated? No, that wasn't right. It had been like interviewing for a position without knowing what it was. No, that was silly. Like taking an examination in a subject for which she hadn't prepared? Ridiculous. What was the matter with her? There was no reason to feel wrung out by the encounter. But she was. And she'd completely forgotten to ask Lord Randolph about the archbishop.

The set ended. Olivia's friend Ronald asked her for the next. He was cheerfully cordial, and Verity glided over the awkwardness of not knowing his last name. When the music ended, he delivered Verity to Olivia with a flourish, demonstrating his obedience, and left them together.

"I always feel I should pat Ronald on the head, like a good dog," Olivia said.

Verity laughed but said, "Don't foist any more partners on me, please."

"Wasn't Ronald polite to you?"

"He was charming, but Mr. Wrentham clearly didn't wish to dance with me."

"Oh, Wrentham." Olivia looked mischievous.

"He was much more interested to learn that Miss Reynolds is in London."

"You told him that?"

"Of course I did, when he asked me. He was quite put out when I didn't have her address in my pocket."

"Well, drat it. Now I'll have to—" She bit off the rest of her sentence.

"No more notes." Verity realized that she didn't trust her friend on this subject.

"I promised, didn't I?" Olivia grinned. "Never mind them. I challenged Mr. Rochford to play cards with me."

"You did not! What did he say?"

"He laughed."

"So he refused?"

Olivia shook her head.

"He accepted?"

"Not yet."

"I wish you'd forget this idea."

"Don't you ever get tired of being so infernally… circumscribed, when fellows our age can do pretty much whatever they please?"

"Yes, but not in the way you—"

"And married women, too, if they're discreet."

"My interests run in other areas." A card game was trivial, Verity thought. She wanted to travel the world. And what had become of her plans in that regard? She hadn't made any headway.

"You can't tell me you disapprove of cards," Olivia said. "You're not one of those canting dissenters."

"Of course not. I just don't think Mr. Rochford is worth the trouble of a scandal."

"Don't force me to point out that you're not the arbiter of my behavior."

Olivia's smile was pleasant, but Verity heard finality in her tone. They wouldn't remain friends if she persisted.

# Twelve

Randolph joined the expedition to his mother's charity school on Wednesday afternoon. As he told her, he was interested to see the place. It had been several years since he'd visited any of her projects. And since she was taking a party of ladies along, he was only too happy to act as escort. Only when he added that the school seemed to be in an iffy neighborhood did his mother comment, dryly pointing out that she often went there quite alone.

"Surely you take a footman as well as John Coachman?" he said.

"As I will on Wednesday," his mother replied.

Randolph had had the sense to drop the subject then, before she could ask if Miss Sinclair's presence had anything to do with his offer. Because he didn't want to admit that of course it did. This pert young lady was occupying a large portion of his thoughts lately. He couldn't resist a chance to spend more time in her company.

Flora came to Langford House early on the day, and they set out in the ducal carriage to pick up Miss

Sinclair and, as Randolph discovered only then, Lady Hilda Stane on the way. Hilda had been allowed out of her house arrest for this unexceptionable expedition. Randolph found himself seated beside her on the rear-facing seat, directly opposite Miss Sinclair, who looked exceedingly fetching in a dark-blue pelisse and straw hat with a curled feather. To look up was to meet her blue-green gaze. Their knees touched with each lurch of the vehicle.

"Beatrice refused to come," said Hilda. "She and Olivia are deep in some scheme. A great secret, it seems."

She sounded sulky at the idea. Miss Sinclair looked concerned.

They drove along streets that grew narrower and shabbier. The duchess related the history of this particular school, which had been in operation for ten years. Randolph half listened. His mind *would* drift away on memories of music and kisses.

At last, they drove into a dilapidated square surrounded by houses that had once been grand residences, perhaps a hundred years ago. Two ancient trees in the dirt of the center marked the remains of a garden. Refuse had accumulated around them.

The coachman pulled up before a large dwelling built of red brick, surrounded by a high wall. Unlike neighboring properties, its wall was in perfect repair, and the building hadn't been broken up into a warren of smaller units. The square wasn't too bad, Randolph thought as he stepped down from the carriage. But through the narrow cobbled alleyways leading out of it, he glimpsed moldering slums.

A troop of ragged little boys appeared as if by magic.

The coachman clearly knew them from previous visits. He deployed them around the carriage.

"It's not always easy to find a location for my schools," said the duchess in response to uncertain looks from Hilda and Miss Sinclair. "Some people seem to believe that poverty is contagious. Or make ridiculous complaints about morality."

"Despite the youth of the students," replied Flora acerbically. "It could hardly be a house for fallen women at their age."

Miss Sinclair blinked. Hilda grinned.

"One must choose one's battles," said Randolph's mother.

A hulking man appeared at the iron gate in the wall. The battered condition of his nose and ears suggested an earlier career as a prizefighter. He unlocked the gate and bowed them in with a *Yer Grace*. His voice was gravelly.

"All well, Hordle?" the duchess answered.

"Aye, Yer Grace. No problems." The man's grin revealed several missing teeth.

They walked across a narrow garden toward the house, where the door already stood open. "The locks are not so much to keep the girls in, as to shut dangers out," the duchess said as they went through.

Verity followed the others into a large front hall with a staircase at the back. The space was painted white. Light streamed in from high windows. There were some cracks in the floor tile, but the space was very clean.

On one side stood two rows of girls in identical blue dresses with white aprons tied over the top. They ranged in age from perhaps four to fourteen, as far as Verity could judge. She was surprised to see them jostle a bit and whisper and giggle without earning reprimands from the five women on the other side of the hall. These were presumably the teachers; they looked competent and good humored.

The eldest of them, a gray-haired woman of fifty or so, came forward and curtsied. "Welcome, Your Grace," she said.

The girls and their teachers echoed her words and movement.

"Miss Fletcher." The duchess shook the woman's hand and then introduced her companions. "I'm here to show off your school."

Miss Fletcher smiled at the phrasing, but didn't deny ownership. "And we're happy to show it off, ma'am."

The duchess walked over to the lines of students. "How are you getting on with the mathematics, Sally?" she asked one of the older students.

The girl, blond hair in neat braids, grinned up at her. "Better, Your Grace," she replied. "That book you gave me helped a deal."

"Very good." The duchess turned to another of the taller students. "And is your embroidery still going well, Kate?"

"I sold three pieces to that grand shop you set me onto," replied a brunette girl proudly. "I'm going to be rich, I am!"

"I can read," piped one of the smallest in the front row.

The duchess bent to smile at her. "That's splendid, Emily. What do you like to read?"

The child pulled back, suddenly shy. "Stories," she murmured.

This wasn't at all what Verity had anticipated. She'd imagined a far stiffer, more distant visit—all noblesse oblige. Perhaps influenced by her own solemn schooling, she'd expected subdued, unsmiling students. But Lord Randolph's mother chatted easily with these girls, and they responded in kind. It was clear the duchess knew all their names and histories.

"Emily came here a few months ago from my refuge," Flora murmured in Verity's ear. "We could all see how intelligent she is, and she's made remarkable progress already. I dream of sending her to one of the new women's colleges eventually."

"Really?" Verity couldn't hide her surprise.

Flora acknowledged it with a nod. "It's the way of things that most of these girls are destined for service or work in a shop," she said quietly. "Far better than they could have hoped for without the school, but… Still, when we spot particular talents, we can nurture them."

"You've joined in the duchess's work then?"

"With delight. It's marvelous to have the resources to really help."

The duchess turned back and rejoined her party. They set off on a tour of the place—classrooms and dining parlor, a large comfortable room where the students could work and socialize, and cozy bedchambers. Afterward, the visitors sat down with Miss Fletcher for tea and scones produced in the cookery class.

"What do you think of our program?" the duchess asked Verity then.

"I?" She felt overwhelmed at the question.

"Well, none of us attended school," the older woman replied, gesturing at her companions. "I had a governess."

"As did I," said Miss Fletcher, making Verity wonder about her history.

Hilda made a face. "I had several. This looks jollier, I must say."

"My father taught me," said Flora. "I never had schoolmates."

"I did," Lord Randolph pointed out. "Loads of 'em."

"We are speaking of girls," said his mother with refreshing finality. She turned back to Verity.

"This seems a fine place to me," she said. "I admire the…feel of it." She realized that she did have some opinions. "Do you ever take the girls out to the country? To walk in a forest perhaps. Or meet horses." The others gazed at her. Verity felt a thread of concern. Had she said "meet horses"?

Then they began to nod. "I don't suppose they've ever been out of London," said Hilda as if the idea shocked her.

"Even an expedition to Richmond would be 'educational,'" Flora said. She smiled at Verity. "They could look at the deer, run a bit wild."

The duchess nodded. "A splendid suggestion. What else?"

"Do the students learn music?" asked Verity, emboldened.

"No." The duchess looked thoughtful. "I suppose I think of it as a lady's accomplishment rather than a practical one."

"It can be far more than that."

"Yes. I heard you sing."

Verity relished the implied compliment. "Flora said you encourage talents when you discover them. You might have some natural musicians here."

"Indeed."

"Perhaps I could come and teach them?" Verity added.

Lord Randolph stared as if she'd said something odd. "I could, too," he said.

"We have no male teachers," replied his mother. "We want the girls to see women in positions of authority. Exemplars, if you will."

He subsided, and Verity enjoyed it just a little.

The duchess seemed to come to a decision. "No. Thank you for the offer, Miss Sinclair, but the task would take more time than you imagine. And your family might not approve." Verity was about to protest when she went on. "Also, you'll be returning home in a few weeks. If we begin a new subject, we want to be able to continue."

Verity had to acknowledge that point, even though home seemed like a different world to her right now.

"But perhaps you might visit again, however," the duchess added. "And suggest the best way to organize the topic."

"If we're hiring a music teacher Miss Sinclair could test her capabilities," Miss Fletcher said. "I'm no expert."

The duchess smiled and nodded. "Very good. May we call on you for that service, Miss Sinclair?"

Assuring her that they could, Verity felt a surge of

pride. She'd helped with charitable works before, of course, but she'd never been consulted with such respect.

Tea finished, they rose from the table, and the duchess said, "You've seen everything but the garden, Miss Sinclair. Come and take a turn with me."

They all went out through the back entrance. The space behind the house was surprisingly large and lush, with grass and flowers and even a few trees. Hilda wandered over to examine a chicken coop. Flora took Lord Randolph's arm and went to look at a vegetable patch, leaving Verity with the duchess. "The girls do most of the gardening," she said. "So they are outdoors, if not in the country."

"It's a pleasant place," replied Verity.

"Lacking only a stretch of water, my son James would say. Nowhere to sail even a toy boat."

"I suppose he has been to the South Seas," Verity said dreamily.

"He has. His wife comes from that part of the world."

"How I envy her!" The words burst out on a tide of emotion.

"Her origins?" the duchess asked. "Her husband?"

"Her travels," corrected Verity passionately. "We can't even imagine all she'll see, the unknown places she'll explore. Like Captain Cook and Magellan and the other adventurers."

"You'd like that yourself?"

"I've wanted it nearly all my life." Verity rarely admitted her aspirations aloud. Some people mocked them; others were bewildered. But somehow the words poured out now. "To leave the familiar behind.

To strike out and be bold. Every day some new sight or people or piece of knowledge."

"Life in England bores you?" the older woman asked.

"No! I'm not some sour critic. I know I'm fortunate to have a comfortable home and all that goes with it. But I can't help wanting more."

"Voyages of exploration can be uncomfortable, and hazardous, according to James's tales."

"I'd like to hear them," said Verity wistfully. She grew self-conscious as her surge of enthusiasm ebbed. "You must think me—"

"Rather like myself," the duchess put in.

Verity turned to stare at her.

"I've always had a longing to do great deeds. Cut a swath through the world." She smiled to herself. "That phrase makes me think of the boys playing pirate."

"You couldn't cut swaths once you had them to look after," Verity said.

The older woman met her gaze. "On the contrary. Very much on the contrary, Miss Sinclair. Despite some wrong turns early on, I discovered that adventures are all around me."

It was easy to believe that the duchess could see right through her. Verity looked away to hide her skepticism.

The others were approaching. "We should be going," said Flora. "It's nearly five."

Hilda, who'd been looking bored, perked up.

The group went back inside and gathered their things. Miss Fletcher saw them to the door, and the Langford footman who'd accompanied them stepped forward to open it.

Outside, they found the coachman walking his

team around the square. A few people had come out of the other houses to watch. One of the boys sat on the box beside him, beaming, while the others skipped and cavorted behind. "A moment, Your Grace," the man called.

"We'll come and meet you," the duchess replied, starting off. The footman hurried ahead of her. Randolph joined the other ladies in following her.

As his mother neared the end of a cramped alleyway, a skinny, raddled woman lurched out of it, heaved the large wooden bucket she held, and threw a stream of slops into the square.

The reeking liquid caught the duchess full on, splashing her fashionable bonnet, her face, the hands she raised in belated defense, her immaculate clothing. Bits of filth hit her with a splat and slid stickily to the ground. Hilda, just behind her, caught a glancing surge that drenched her skirts.

After an eye blink of consternation, Randolph lunged forward. But it was too late. The damage had been done. The perpetrator stood openmouthed and swaying. She was very drunk, Randolph concluded.

Denizens of the square—man, woman, and boy—descended with a torrent of abuse. Tossing slops into the square was forbidden, Randolph gathered, and this was not the woman's first offense. Only the most shocking one. The woman blinked, bared her teeth in a snarl, and began screaming curses back at them. The noise brought others to doors and windows. Hordle came barreling out of the school gate, ready to break heads. John Coachman and the footman were agape with horror. A full-fledged riot was brewing.

Randolph reached out to his mother. "My God, Mama."

"Don't touch me," she replied with remarkable calm. "I'm filthy."

The shocked look in her blue eyes belied her tone. The shouting mob pressed closer.

Miss Fletcher ran up, holding out a dampened towel. "Oh, Your Grace, I'm so sorry!"

"Not your fault," said Randolph's mother. She took the towel and wiped the dirt from her face.

"Come back," the teacher urged. "We'll run a bath and find you—"

"No," said Randolph. "We must get her home." She needed her own room and things, he thought. With a preemptory gesture, he got the coachman moving.

"I'll dirty the seats," said his mother. "They'll be ruined."

"No matter." The carriage drew up beside them. Randolph held out his hand again.

"No." She drew back. "Don't touch me. I can get in."

The footman had the carriage door open. Slowly, as if she suddenly felt her age, Randolph's mother climbed up.

"You must go, too, Hilda," Randolph said. "You need to get out of those clothes."

Lifting her odoriferous skirts with a grimace, the girl got in the vehicle.

"I'll go with them," said Flora, striding past Randolph. "They should have someone to help."

"I'll escort—"

"I'm going. I'm accustomed to the reek of the

streets. You stay and take Miss Sinclair back to her lodgings." Flora stepped up into the carriage, pulling the door closed after her. Her clear, cool voice rang from within. "Drive on."

Randolph pointed at the footman before he could hop on the back. "Find me a hack, Thomas."

The young man looked around uneasily, but he didn't balk. "Yes, sir." Pushing through the yelling crowd, he set off.

"I wanted to help," said Miss Fletcher, the soiled bit of toweling hanging from her hand.

"Could you send one of these boys to Langford House to prepare them?" Randolph said as they made their way back to Miss Sinclair. "A clever runner might be faster than the coach."

"Yes, of course." The teacher scanned the crowd. "Georgie! Georgie Finch." She pushed through the crowd, waving at one of the boys.

Miss Sinclair was gazing at the puddle of slops with what seemed to be fascinated revulsion when Randolph joined her. He took her hand and summoned Hordle with a jerk of his head. The huge man cleared a path for them, and in a few moments they were back inside the walls of the school. Two of the teachers stood on the doorstep, distressed. Wide-eyed faces filled the windows. Randolph relaxed a bit as the gate clanged shut behind them.

"Your mother is extraordinary," said Miss Sinclair.

"She is." There'd never been any doubt about that.

"So many grand ladies would have collapsed in hysterics." She gave an odd little laugh. "Adventures."

"Mama can get through anything," Randolph

agreed. He had no fear for his mother's state of mind. In a day or so, she'd be laughing about the incident. He was more concerned about the contents of that foul deluge.

"You did very well, too."

Something about her tone made him smile. "Thank you."

Miss Fletcher came through the outer gate. "Georgie swears he'll beat the coach to Langford House."

Randolph thanked her with a nod. He handed her a coin from his pocket. "For him when he returns."

"You will tell the duchess how very sorry we are for this unfortunate—"

"She would never blame you," he interrupted.

The formidable Miss Fletcher's eyes filled with tears. "No, she wouldn't. She's the most admirable woman."

"Isn't she?" agreed Miss Sinclair.

A few minutes later, Thomas the footman returned with a hack. The crowd in the square had thinned, Randolph saw as he handed Miss Sinclair into the vehicle. He gave the driver her address and stepped up to sit beside her. Thomas found a perch at the back, and they set off.

The cab was small, a bit shabby but clean. Randolph's knee touched Miss Sinclair's when they clattered over some loose cobbles. Their shoulders brushed. They hadn't been alone together since the kiss, he realized. And then all he could think of was that caress. The flowery scent she wore filled his senses.

"Your mother is quite unusual, isn't she?" his companion said.

"What?" He pulled his mind back to the present.

She looked at him, her expression thoughtful. "She's doing something important," she went on. "With her schools. But great ladies often have charitable interests. It's the way she does it."

"The way?"

"She knew all about those girls. Every one, I wager. And she was truly interested in how they were doing."

"She was," Randolph agreed. He saw her point. Many of the wealthy would give to a cause when asked; few became so involved with the consequences of their donations.

Miss Sinclair turned to look at him. Her blue-green eyes were very close. And her lips—such an enticing shape, full, just slightly parted.

"You don't find that unusual, do you?"

For an instant he thought she meant her lips. He blinked. "Ah—"

"That she should take such a personal interest. Find Sally a mathematics book, and Kate a place to sell her embroidery. I daresay she'll send little Emily some stories."

"*You* remembered their names and their circumstances," he pointed out.

"I suppose that's why your brothers have such striking wives," she answered.

Randolph had missed a connection. "That?"

"Your mother's influence."

"She never interferes," he said, puzzled.

Miss Sinclair seemed amused. "She doesn't have to."

Before Randolph could ask what she meant, the hack jerked to a stop, and they were thrown forward.

Randolph put out his arm to keep her from falling, catching Miss Sinclair across the chest. Her beautiful bosom was at once soft and firm and delectable. Heat flushed through him. Their eyes met across inches. He heard her breath catch. For one aching instant he thought she would kiss him again.

Then she sat back. She cleared her throat, gripped the strap beside her as if she required support. "Have we…hit something?"

Stifling disappointment, Randolph lowered his arm. He stuck his head out the window. Up ahead, a large wagon loaded with barrels of beer was trying to enter a narrow lane. The street was blocked, and a line of carriages had formed. They couldn't move backward or forward. A rising chorus of shouting and stamping hooves added to the usual din of the streets.

The driver looked down. "He'll make it in a bit," he said. "See how he backs his team? Won't be too long."

The turn looked impossible to Randolph, but he accepted the driver's expert judgment. He pulled back into the carriage, and a self-conscious silence. "Wagonload of beer maneuvering," he said.

"Ah." Miss Sinclair held on to the strap and gazed out at a shop next to the hack. Its window displayed coal scuttles.

He had to talk. When he would so much rather have been…not talking. So, pick up where they'd left off then. Which was where? "How do you know about my brothers' wives?"

She started but didn't turn. "I've met two of them."

"But you said 'your brothers have such striking

wives.' As if you meant all of them." Had she been asking about his family? He rather liked the idea.

"Olivia was telling me. She hears everything. Including a rumor that your brother James married a pirate. I liked that one."

"Of course he didn't—"

"I know. I don't suppose Lord Alan dabbles in alchemy up at Oxford either."

Randolph laughed. "He'd be livid at the very idea."

Miss Sinclair nodded. "Olivia said *his* wife was an actress."

"Her mother was." He knew Ariel wasn't ashamed of her lineage.

"Really?" Finally, she abandoned the coal scuttles to look at him.

"Yes."

"And Flora studies some obscure ancient language. That's what I meant."

"By interesting?"

"Unusual. What other duchess would welcome such...individual females?"

"Mama looks beyond the surface."

"I've seen that she does. She really listened to me."

This was all well and good. Hopeful, even. But Randolph was ready to talk about something besides his mother. "I thought I might look into getting some instruments for the school," he said. "They must have a pianoforte, I think. What else?"

They fell into a discussion of how best to begin musical instruction. Once again, their tastes and ideas jibed. They seemed to have a harmony of spirit in this area that matched the harmony they produced when they sang. If only it extended a bit farther, Randolph thought.

The hack jerked again and started moving. The way was clear at last, though they were moving slowly.

"I had the funniest letter from my father," said Miss Sinclair then. "About you and the Archbishop of Canterbury."

Randolph stifled an oath. It had been too much to hope that she wouldn't hear the story that made him appear so ridiculous, when her father was a senior churchman. "Shouldn't they, of all people, forgive and forget," he muttered.

"Forget that you—"

"If His Grace had changed out of his vestments, it would never have happened." Randolph had brooded over this a bit. The archbishop had been rushing. The ram wouldn't have mistaken his normal clothing for… something else.

"His vestments," said Miss Sinclair.

"He presented such a…considerable expanse of white cloth."

The hack slowed to a stop. "Here we are," called the driver. Thomas jumped down from the back and opened the door.

Miss Sinclair hesitated as if she wanted to say more. But the footman was offering his hand. She hopped down. "Do you go to Mrs. Trent's soiree this evening?" she asked Randolph.

"I'm promised to Sebastian," he replied regretfully.

"Ah. Goodbye then."

"Goodbye."

Verity took a breath, made certain her hat was

straight, and walked away. If only she'd had more time, she'd have gotten the whole story out of him. Although her father had said the tale wasn't for her supposedly delicate ears. So perhaps not. The archbishop had presented an expanse of white vestment to what? Or who? Walking up the stairs to her bedchamber, Verity tried to imagine an ending. But she didn't have enough information. Would Mama know? She'd ask, but she doubted it. Her mother never remembered juicy stories. It was one of the most incomprehensible things about her.

She had to discover what came next, Verity thought, taking off her bonnet and pelisse. Because she needed to know all about the man whose merest touch made her dizzy with longing. She'd very nearly kissed him again when he kept her from falling forward in the carriage. Right in public, in front of the coal scuttles.

Verity paced her room. She looked out the window, but of course the hack was gone. One topic her estimable school, and her kindly parents, had utterly neglected was physical passion. It had never been mentioned, let alone explained. Why, oh why had it come to her in the person of a country parson?

# Thirteen

"She was drunk as a wheelbarrow, and she threw a *disgusting* bucket of slops over us," said Lady Hilda Stane, demonstrating the action with vigorous gestures.

"Ugh," replied Beatrice Townsend, wrinkling her nose at the idea.

Verity and Olivia walked behind them along a path in Hyde Park. Roses nodded on either side.

"My pelisse *reeked*," Hilda added with relish. "And the hem of my gown has the most dreadful stains. Georgina says we will see what the laundress can do."

"I wouldn't ever wear them again," said Beatrice with a grimace.

"Well, I won't if they're not clean."

"Quite an adventure," said Olivia.

"Hilda was only splashed," Verity replied. "The duchess got the brunt of it. She was drenched."

"That must have been a sight."

"She took it extraordinarily well."

"Have you joined the ranks of Her Grace's admirers?" asked Olivia with one of her sly smiles.

Verity acknowledged her friend's familiar bantering tone. "Is there a regiment?"

"Oh yes. And troops on the other side, who find the Duchess of Langford insufferable."

That was difficult to imagine. "I suppose no strong character is universally liked."

"How philosophical of you."

Verity gave her a sidelong look. "Have I offended you somehow?"

She got an exasperated sigh in response. "No, Verity. Am I not allowed a bit of a joke? Among friends?"

"Of course." She hadn't sounded like she was joking, but Verity didn't want to quarrel. It was difficult to know how to take Olivia sometimes, and how to respond. When Verity had considered asking her about Lord Randolph and the archbishop, she'd realized that she didn't trust Olivia with the information. Olivia could probably find out the truth. She seemed to have inexhaustible sources. But then she'd spread whatever it was all over London, with satirical commentary. Verity didn't believe Lord Randolph had done anything so bad. The man she'd come to know simply wouldn't have. But he'd looked mortified when he spoke of the archbishop. She didn't want people laughing behind their hands at him.

Verity noticed something odd up ahead. "What is that man… Is that Mr. Wrentham?"

Olivia looked. She snorted, then loosed a peal of laughter. She walked faster, overtaking the younger pair. "Stop dawdling," she said as she passed them. "We came out for a bit of exercise."

She led the group closer to the bridle path, where

Mr. Wrentham was riding along with other equestrians. Unlike them, however, he sat facing his mount's tail rather than its head. His saddle had been put on backwards, his reins pulled along so he could still grasp them, though he couldn't see where he was heading. He bounced awkwardly in the unfamiliar position. His horse looked bewildered and uneasy, despite an extra padding of blankets over its back.

Carriages and riders stopped to watch. People laughed and pointed. Wrentham set his jaw and proceeded. He looked pained but determined.

Olivia was overcome with laughter.

"Do you think he's paying off a bet?" Hilda asked at Verity's side. "Men are always doing idiotic things for a wager." She sounded like she rather admired that fact.

"I don't know," Verity responded, though she suspected she did.

Mr. Wrentham bounced and teetered along the path and out the gate. When he disappeared around a corner, general movement resumed, to an accompaniment of animated chatter.

"Did you have anything to do with that?" Verity asked Olivia as their group moved on.

"Why would you think so?"

"Experience?" replied Verity dryly.

Olivia giggled. "I didn't send a note. I keep my word."

The letter rather than the spirit, Verity thought. "What *did* you do?"

"I was wonderfully devious."

Olivia didn't rub her hands together, but she gave

the impression of doing so. She wanted to tell this story, Verity thought.

"It was dead easy to find out where Wrentham is lodging. And there's a hall boy there who runs errands for the landlady."

"You went to his rooms?"

"Of course not. Would I be so foolish? I have… minions." Olivia laughed again. "With a bit of bribery, I discovered that Mr. Wrentham had sent Miss Reynolds a note—yes, a note—through this hall boy. So I had a message…conveyed to the lad, for him to memorize. From 'the lady.' Perfectly true, I am a lady."

Her friend's eyes were sparkling with enjoyment, Verity noted.

"The message was a gem, if I do say so," Olivia continued. "All about how a hero endures hardship and proves his regard through deeds, like the knights of old. Would he dare ride through the park backwards, for example?" Noticing Verity's frown, she said, "It's just the sort of thing Miss Reynolds *would* say. And Wrentham would eat up, obviously. No one made him do it, so you needn't glower at me."

"I just don't understand why you're taking so much trouble to…mislead them," Verity replied.

"Because it's so diverting! Did you see how he bounced?"

Olivia also liked to think of herself as a hub of plots and schemes, Verity thought, remembering the machinations over Mr. Rochford's phrenology report. She'd probably make an excellent spy, but her life offered no proper scope for her talents.

"Oh, for the lord's sake, don't look so Friday-faced," Olivia exclaimed. "There was no harm done. And don't think to read me a pious lecture. I won't hear it." She sped up. "Are we walking or dawdling?" she asked Hilda and Beatrice as she passed them. Olivia strode by another party of ladies, barely acknowledging their greetings, and began a vigorous sweep of the park.

After a while, Beatrice dropped back. Since Hilda seemed to be engaged in a competition with Olivia, Verity slowed with her. "I wouldn't have come if I'd known Olivia was going to run a race," said Beatrice, puffing a bit.

"She's certainly energetic."

"Oh, she's been an absolute bear since she received that invitation. And all because I won't tell a lie."

"Invitation?"

"I don't mind a little bit of deception," Beatrice complained, absorbed in her own concerns. "Obviously. But this is different. Mama would have a nervous spasm. And then probably lock me in the attic for the rest of my life—with Olivia." She shuddered dramatically. "Well, *you* can't think it's a good idea."

She obviously assumed that Verity knew all about whatever it was.

"You should tell her so," Beatrice went on before she could speak.

"She doesn't seem in a mood to listen," Verity ventured.

"No." Beatrice huffed and marched over to sit on a bench beside the path. "I refuse to go any farther. Let them come back for us. If they remember we exist."

Verity joined her. She was torn between concern for her friend and a reluctance to pry. The former won out. "I suppose the invitation made Olivia think," she ventured.

"Think? What is there to think about?"

"The implications?" Verity said.

The younger girl stared at her. "Implic… It's perfectly plain. If you tease a rake, you're going to get in trouble."

"Mr. Rochford," Verity concluded.

"She *would* keep on about playing cards with him. Olivia can be so annoying."

"She made him angry."

Beatrice shrugged. "Oh, angry. He wouldn't bother to be angry. Indeed, he probably laughed himself sick."

"Because it was amusing to—" Verity trailed off, leaving the sentence for Beatrice to finish.

"Dare Olivia to come to his house for a game," the girl obliged. "At nine in the evening! I'm sure he did it to be rid of her. He has no idea how *brazen* Olivia can be."

She'd forced an introduction to Mr. Rochford in this very park, Verity thought.

Beatrice stuck out her lower lip. "But I am *not* going to tell Mama we are visiting Hilda together. And even if I would, she'd never believe me. It's a ridiculous idea. Hilda wouldn't invite Olivia."

Verity was silent, wondering if Olivia really meant to accept such a scandalous invitation. She had to know she was courting ruin.

"Where *have* they gotten to?" Beatrice wondered. "I'm ready to go home."

"So you're going to visit Hilda?" Verity asked.

The younger girl brightened. "Tomorrow. We'll have a grand dinner and see a play, and then I will spend the night. You can see that Olivia wouldn't be asked."

Verity nodded.

Their companions appeared on the path, walking back toward them at a slower place. "There you are," said Olivia when they arrived. "Sluggards."

Beatrice jumped up and took Hilda's arm. "Let's go back," she said, pulling her along. "I want to show you a copy of the play we're to see."

Verity fell in beside Olivia and followed them. She felt uncertain. "Will you come with me to the Boyntons' tomorrow evening?"

"I can't. I have another engagement." Olivia's tone was discouraging.

"But I'd be so glad of your company."

"Mama wants me to accompany her on a…visit."

"Your mother does?"

"I just said so." Olivia turned to stare at her.

"Perhaps she'd change her plans if you asked."

"No, she wouldn't. Why do you press me so?" said Olivia. She sounded belligerent and looked annoyed.

Verity lost patience. "I thought the Boyntons' party would be more fun than a…stupid visit."

Her friend's eyes narrowed. "Why do you call it stupid?"

"Because it patently is!"

"Beatrice," said Olivia, her voice disgusted. "She's always been a tattlebox."

"You can't be considering—"

"Will you be quiet!" Olivia looked furious now. She glanced behind to make certain no one was listening.

"I should tell your mother," said Verity.

"If you do, I'll never speak to you again. Not only that, I'll tell everyone that you betrayed a confidence. And that you're a malicious, jealous cat. And worse!"

"Why do you speak this way when I'm trying to help you?"

"What I do is none of your affair! Why do you think you have the right to meddle? I won't be judged by a pious little simpleton." Olivia sped up, joining Hilda and Beatrice ahead. She avoided Verity for the rest of their walk and retired to her room when they reached her home, declaring that she was worn out and needed solitude.

The Countess of Frane's evening party spread from two large reception rooms on the ground floor of her house into the large back garden. Lanterns furnished with colored glass lit the landscape, splashing walls and vegetation with beams of crimson, blue, and gold. "You see?" Randolph said to Miss Sinclair. He'd been watching for her inside and swooped down with an offer to show her the display as soon as she and her mother entered.

"It looks like fairyland," she said.

He led her down two shallow steps to join others strolling around the illuminated space. "A pretty conceit," he agreed. "And it has another advantage."

She gave him a sidelong glance. "Oh?"

"An escape from the music."

As if on cue, someone began playing the pianoforte inside. The notes plodded one after the other, correct but fatally inexpressive.

"Ah."

He led her farther into the garden. "Ever since our duets, people ask my opinion on every young lady who sets her hands to the keys. I've run out of vague generalities."

"It's worse when they ask for themselves," Verity replied. "And won't be put off."

She sounded distracted, as if her mind was elsewhere. Randolph looked down at her. Golden light from a nearby lantern gilded her face and sparkled in the braided trim of her pale gown. He was very conscious of her hand on his arm, of the light scent she wore, and of a strong desire to have all her attention. "Of course, the garden has dim secluded corners, too."

Now she turned to him.

"When I said the garden had advantages, that's what you thought I meant," Randolph added.

"Is it?"

"I could tell from your expression."

"Really?" She smiled a little. "Are you so expert at reading faces?"

"Of course. I've spent years in the study."

He'd hoped for a laugh. Instead he got a long, thoughtful gaze. "People ask you for advice," she said.

It was a statement, not a question. A practiced part of Randolph came alert.

"Yes, I imagine they do," she added, as if absently answering herself. "They would consult you about moral dilemmas. And what action to take."

The idea that Miss Sinclair was grappling with a moral dilemma made him uneasy. What, or who, had created it?

"And if they tell you things in confidence, you keep their secrets."

This was even worse. "Miss Sinclair."

"Because if a friend insists that something is none of your affair, even when it might be…disastrous, do you think—" She pressed her lips together.

Nine times out of ten when people said a *friend* they were speaking of themselves, Randolph thought. He'd seen it over and over in his parsonage. And he didn't like the word *disastrous*. He steered toward one of those dim corners beyond the lantern beams and took her hands. "Miss Sinclair. If you have doubts about some action you are contemplating, I urge you to consult—"

"What?" she interrupted.

Out of nowhere came the image of his lovely companion talking to Thomas Rochford after their performance at Carleton House. She'd laughed so gaily at that fellow's sallies. She'd shaken off warnings about a man who was notoriously seductive. Years of knowledge and experience, of carefully cultivated patience and objectivity, deserted Randolph in an instant. "Disastrous how, precisely?" he growled.

She pulled her hands away. "You have misunderstood me."

"So speak more clearly."

A laughing couple ran into the pool of darkness around them. The gentleman careened into Miss Sinclair. She stumbled into Randolph's arms.

"Oops," said the intruder. "This spot's taken." He pulled his giggling consort away again.

Randolph held her. Her arms had gone around his waist. Now her cheek rested on his chest. She was soft and pliant against him. He wanted her most desperately. "Verity," he murmured. Her name meant truth.

She let out a sigh. He could feel it.

"Verity." He savored the syllables.

She looked up, her face a dim oval in the dark. He kissed her.

Her lips were sweet. Her arms tightened around him, and she pressed closer. A sense of rightness enveloped Randolph, nearly as strong as his desire. This was where she belonged. And he. It was as if their kiss drew the scattered pieces of existence into order, and all was well. He wanted it to go on forever.

Impossible, of course. The kiss ended. He was bereft, and yet joyfully complacent. She couldn't kiss him like that and not care. "Now tell me about this disastrous thing, and we will dispose of it," he said.

She pulled away. "My friend—"

"There's no need to pretend you're speaking of someone else."

"Pretend?" She pushed at his chest. With great reluctance Randolph let her go. "Why would I pretend?" she said as she stepped back.

"You needn't be shy with me." He groped for words to capture the certainty he'd felt moments ago. But they eluded him. Astonishing. He always had words.

"I'm not shy. I'm perplexed. About my duty and my *friend*."

She'd moved farther away. A shaft of golden lantern light caught her from the side, painting her half gilded, half dark. "You look like a renaissance masterpiece," he said.

"What?"

With a breathless bustle, the couple who'd interrupted them earlier returned. "If you're just going to stand about, you might leave this prime spot for those with…other plans," the gentleman said. His companion giggled. Didn't the constant giggling irritate him? Randolph wondered idiotically.

Miss Sinclair turned and walked away. The look she threw over her shoulder was bewildering.

Verity moved fast, her skirts frothing about her feet, scarcely seeing the other guests strolling in the garden. She was dizzy with the feel of him. She'd wanted to stay forever in his embrace. It had felt like home, and like the most thrilling place on Earth at the same time. And the kiss! She missed a step and nearly fell into a clump of shrubbery.

She moved into the shadow of the bushes and stood still, catching her breath. After a moment she put her hands to her flushed cheeks, as if she could push down the emotion that flooded her. Her fingers felt cold. What was she doing?

Verity had known so many churchmen in her life, from canting prudes to foxhunting parsons who hardly seemed clerical at all. She'd thought Lord Randolph Gresham was the best kind—serious without being condescending, kind without being wishy-washy, intelligent and educated and…so very attractive. Not that the latter was relevant.

But just now he'd seemed positively...cloth-headed, exactly as she'd predicted for a country clergyman.

Her breath caught on a sob, and she swallowed fiercely. This would not do. She wasn't some feeble twit to be found sniveling at a *ton* party.

Verity let her hands drop. She straightened and held her head high. She stepped smartly out of the shadows and rejoined the strolling guests, walking as if she had a definite goal in mind. And then she rounded a low tree lit by a crimson lantern and came face-to-face with the Duchess of Langford.

She recoiled and nearly tumbled over backward. The duchess caught her shoulders and held her steady. Verity felt like a clumsy child. "Are you all right?" the older woman asked.

Those blue eyes, so like her son's, which seemed to see much more than one might have wished, Verity thought. "Not looking where I was going," she replied. "Sorry." She pulled free. The duchess made no effort to hold her. "Have you recovered from your dreadful dowsing?" Verity asked. The red light made the other woman look feverish.

"It was rather dreadful, wasn't it?" The duchess laughed. "A gruesome greeting to the neighborhood for you. I hope you weren't put off. Nothing like that has ever happened to me before."

"No." Verity made a move toward the house. The duchess fell in beside her.

"Miss Fletcher is quite excited about the idea of a music teacher. She's found a candidate already."

"Oh, good." She heard footsteps coming up behind them. Probably, most likely, Lord Randolph.

"She'd be happy to have your opinion when you can find the time to call. Our carriage is at your disposal, of course. As am I."

The footsteps came closer. She simply couldn't chat with the man she'd just kissed—and his mother—just now, Verity thought. "Yes, I'll see when... If you'll excuse me, I need to speak to Mama." Feeling confused and young and rude, she hurried off. When she ventured a glance from the doorway, she saw she'd been right. Lord Randolph had joined his mother on the garden path. What was he saying to her? It was all a great muddle, and to top it off, she still didn't know what to do about Olivia.

"I've made a mistake," Randolph was, in fact, saying.

"A large one?"

"I hope not. I'm not certain, because I don't know precisely what I was mistaken *about*. Only that I was ham-handed, and tongue-tied."

"*You?*" His mother smiled up at him.

He had to smile back. "Difficult to believe, I know. The circumstances were...unusual." Or unprecedented, or revolutionary, Randolph thought. Now that it was too late, his mind teemed with words.

"Pleasantly so?"

"I think...I hope...perhaps." He sighed. "People say wisdom increases with age, but I never felt so at sea with Rosalie."

His mother looked him over. The acute assessment was as familiar as childhood. "Can I do anything?"

Could she? Randolph considered the idea. "I don't think so. I need to make some inquiries. I wonder if Hilda might—"

"Georgina's sister might help?" the duchess asked when he didn't go on. She sounded dubious.

He nodded. "There's no one better at ferreting out secrets. Could she be the friend? No."

"Must you be so mysterious, Randolph? It's quite irritating."

He laughed. "Sorry, Mama. Sometimes a thing isn't ready to be told."

"I'm familiar with the concept," she replied, a touch of asperity in her voice. "I've often heard it from you and your brothers. Though less so in recent years. I'm also familiar with a wide variety of results, from hilarity to catastrophe."

"I hope to avoid either of those." His mother sighed audibly. She seemed to sway slightly. "Are you well?" Randolph asked her.

"Of course."

"You look a bit peaked."

"It's this red light. Like a beam from the infernal regions."

Randolph laughed but said, "Shall I take you inside? Where is Papa?"

"Arguing politics with Lord Holland." She made a shooing motion. "Go on and dig into your secrets. I'm perfectly fine. I like the night air."

Randolph examined her. She made a face at him. He laughed again and went on his way.

The duchess stood alone in the illuminated garden, an oddly isolated figure. Then a friend came along, and the rhythm of the party overtook her again.

# Fourteen

The trouble was, she sympathized with Olivia's yearning for adventure, Verity thought the following afternoon. She knew so well how it felt to long for excitement, to want *something* to happen. And to be the one who took action—plunged into uncharted jungles or sailed around the world. She didn't care for the way her friend had responded to the impulse, but she didn't want Olivia stifled and confined. Or ruined, of course. That would be the stupid squandering of a lively, clever woman. By narrow-minded biddies who gave her no scope for her abilities. Manifestly unfair, as if society had set a trap precisely for females like them. Her. Olivia. It was infuriating.

And so Verity decided she'd deal with the matter herself. She would betray no confidences, and cause no uproar, if she simply handled the matter. No one else would know. It was easier. And also, she had to admit, much more satisfying. Why turn to others? What need for willfully obtuse, distractingly attractive young men? Now that she'd worked it out in her mind, Verity felt perfectly capable of managing the thing. She'd show Olivia how an adventure was done.

As a first step, Verity went to find her mother, pleading malaise, and asked for one of her powerful headache powders.

"I thought you didn't like them," Mama said, surprised.

It was true that Verity didn't care for the strong effect of the medicine. "I just have the most dreadful headache."

"Oh my dear." Her mother was all sympathy, as Verity had known she would be. Mama was afflicted by terrible headaches that laid her low for days. Verity felt a bit guilty as her mother jumped up. "I'll fetch it at once," she said. In moments, she returned with one of the paper packets the apothecary made up for her. "Is it very bad?" she asked.

"I'll be fine after a good sleep," Verity assured her.

"I'll sit with you and rub your temples."

This wouldn't do. "No, you go on to Mrs. Doran's. She's counting on you to make up her whist tables."

"Yes, but—"

Verity held up the paper packet. "I wouldn't even know you were there."

"I suppose."

The headache remedy induced heavy slumber. When Mama took it, she was dead to the world for hours. Verity was counting on this fact for later, in case anyone knocked at her bedroom door while she was gone. "Really, Mama, you should go. Don't worry."

"Well…I shan't be late."

Verity smiled and nodded and at last saw her

mother off. She told the housemaid the same story, and by seven she was alone in her bedchamber, pulling an old, drab cloak from the wardrobe. She'd never been so deceitful in her life. It was thrilling.

At first, Verity had thought she'd catch Olivia before she entered Mr. Rochford's lair. Pull her away before she could knock on the door, perhaps. But there were problems with that plan. Days ago, Olivia had taken Verity past the man's small, narrow house, and a number of people, all men, had walked by in the brief time they'd lingered there. Verity couldn't stand about in that street. Nor did she wish to argue with Olivia on the cobblestones. It would have to be inside. Olivia was always punctual. Verity would arrive at a quarter past nine.

The minutes ticked past. Verity wrote a note explaining where she was going and why, sealed it, and placed it in her jewelry box. Should anything go wrong...but it wouldn't.

At last it was time. With her cloak over her arm, she checked the corridor outside her room, found it empty, and slipped out. She locked the bedroom door and put the key in her reticule beside the front door key their landlady had provided. Mama never used it, preferring to ring and be let in, so she hadn't noticed its disappearance from the parlor.

Verity crept down the stairs. The front hall was empty as it always was at this time. The grandfather clock next to the stairs began to strike nine. Verity put on her cloak; the chiming covered the sound of her exit. Outside, she pulled up the hood and set off.

Some light still washed the sky on this long June day, so Verity was able to walk purposefully down the street, like a shopgirl or servant who had urgent business. No one accosted her. She followed a route she'd mapped out in her head and reached Mr. Rochford's house precisely as planned.

There were lights in the first-floor windows. A figure appeared at one, pulling the draperies closed. Verity set her jaw and knocked sharply on the door.

After a minute, it was opened by a solemn man in black. He looked like a valet. Poised to move, Verity pushed past him and headed for the stairs. "I will see Mr. Rochford," she said, picking up her skirts and hurrying up them.

"Miss. I beg your pardon. Miss!"

She didn't pause. She wouldn't be stopped. With footsteps thudding behind her, she reached the upper floor, turned toward the front of the house, calculated where she'd seen the light, and threw open a door on the left.

She'd judged correctly. Mr. Rochford was there, smoothly handsome in evening dress. He sat in an armchair, a glass of red wine and a deck of cards on the small table beside him.

Verity scanned the room. It was a masculine space, with dark wood paneling, comfortable furnishings, and crossed sabers hanging above the fireplace. It was also empty of other people. "Where is Olivia?" she demanded.

The valet burst in on her heels. "Sir, this…creature shoved right past me."

"Where is Olivia?" Verity repeated.

"It's all right, Pearson," said Mr. Rochford, waving the man off.

The servant departed, shutting the door with an irritated snap.

Verity was left facing Rochford. He didn't rise as politeness dictated. He simply looked at her, clearly amused. "Olivia?" Verity said. She'd lost her confident tone, she was unhappy to hear.

"Not here," said Rochford. "It appears that Miss Townsend lost her nerve." He shrugged. "Or never meant to come. She seems a chancy chit. So, no valiant rescue required."

He was laughing at her. Verity gritted her teeth.

"Perhaps you'd care for a hand or two?" Rochford tapped the cards with a mocking smile.

"No."

"A glass of wine then?" He picked up his wine and sipped.

Verity felt very foolish and very angry, chiefly at herself. There was nothing to do but sneak home again. She turned away.

He was suddenly behind her, his hands heavy on her shoulders. "Come, come. I deserve something for my trouble. I refused a very attractive invitation to hang about here like a mooncalf. A kiss at least, I think. Before I send you packing." He pivoted her on the polished wooden floor. He was very strong. He smiled as he bent toward her.

Given a new target, Verity's bad temper took control. With the side of her fist, she hit him as hard as she could, square on the nose. She knew from an unfortunate encounter with a cricket ball when she was six years old that this was a very sensitive spot.

"Ow!" Rochford jerked back, though he didn't

let her go. "You vixen." His blue eyes watered. He shook her. Verity twisted in his grasp and prepared to hit him again.

There was a resounding bang below, followed by pounding footsteps. The door burst open, revealing Lord Randolph Gresham. Verity felt her humiliation complete. Of all the people who might have found her here, he was the last she wished to see.

Rochford released her. "Really?" he said.

Lord Randolph bared his teeth. He hurtled in, plucked one of the sabers from the wall above the fireplace, and brandished it at Rochford.

"What the devil?" said their inadvertent host.

Lord Randolph lunged and slashed at him. Rochford jumped out of the way. "Have you lost your mind?"

The saber whistled through the air again. Rochford leaped aside. Hard pressed, he grabbed the second saber from the wall and defended himself. The clash of metal filled the room as they moved back and forth, striking and parrying. Verity was startled to realize that Lord Randolph was by far the better swordsman. He was astonishing. He moved around the room like a great predatory cat. He made Rochford look clumsy and oafish. This Lord Randolph was nothing like a boring country parson.

"You've pinked me, you lunatic!" cried Rochford after a clanging interval. He dropped the saber and gripped his upper arm.

"I'll do worse if you ever mention this night to a living soul," Lord Randolph replied.

"Good God, you should go on the stage," said Rochford. When Lord Randolph waved the saber under his nose, he added, "Yes, yes, I'm sworn to silence. Word of honor, et cetera. Now will you get out?"

Gripping Verity's upper arm, Lord Randolph pulled her from the room.

Pearson stood on the landing, gripping a fireplace poker. "Stand back," Lord Randolph said to him.

"Have you killed Mr. Rochford?"

"Of course not," replied Lord Randolph impatiently.

"Pearson!" the former called from inside.

The valet dropped the poker with a clang and shoved past Verity. Lord Randolph pulled her onto the staircase just as the servant's foot came down on the pooled cloth of her skirts. For a moment, Verity was suspended between the two points, then there was a ripping sound. Seams parted in her old cloak and the waist of her gown before Pearson moved on.

Lord Randolph hustled her down the stairs. "Let go," Verity said.

He didn't until they were out the door and across the street to a waiting hack. It was full dark now. The vehicle's lanterns offered the only light. Lord Randolph practically threw her into the seat. "Drive," he commanded as he jumped in after her.

He was breathing hard. Verity could hear it above the clop of the horse's hooves. She could also feel a stream of air along her side where her dress had torn. Her mind was awhirl.

Randolph panted. Not from exertion, but from the lingering effects of the…temporary insanity that had caused him to skewer Rochford in his own home, with one of his own sabers. "I'm a peaceable, reasonable man," he said. "Yet somehow you, uniquely, drive me to extraordinary excesses."

"I do?"

"How could you go to that man's house? If ever there was a bird-witted—"

"I went there to rescue Olivia," Verity interrupted.

"As did I. But she wasn't there. You were." Randolph shook his head, hoping the movement might reorder his scattered wits.

"How did you find out?"

"Hilda." He shook his head again. "If there's a secret within a mile of her, that girl discovers it. I thought that if anyone had heard about your friend—"

"Oh, now you admit that I *have* a friend in trouble. Had. I thought."

If he'd listened then, perhaps they wouldn't be here now, Randolph thought. And yet, in an odd way, his jealous thoughts of Rochford had turned out to be prescient, if skewed.

"Beatrice must have told her, too," Miss Sinclair went on. "She can't keep a secret."

Randolph's breath had returned to normal. He was beginning to feel a bit amused. "They held out through the first act of the play. Until I threatened to get Hilda sent back to Herefordshire unless she told me whatever they were, very obviously, concealing." Randolph snorted. "The things I do because of you."

"I do not make you behave badly," she said. "I'm not in control of your actions."

"I ran a bit mad, seeing Rochford's hands on you."

She gathered her cloak closer, a gesture that exposed

the long rents in its seams. Randolph glimpsed a flash of white through one of them. "I was just about to hit him again," she said.

"Did you hit him?" Randolph was sorry to have missed that part.

"Of course I hit him! I would have gotten away on my own, too."

"And walked home alone in the pitch-dark?"

"I thought Olivia would be with me."

"Two young ladies stumbling through the inky streets," Randolph replied. "Very wise."

Miss Sinclair made a soft sound like a hiss. But apparently she had no answer for his very good point.

The hack slowed. "Here we are, sir," called the driver.

Randolph looked out. "Where?"

"You didn't give me no address, so I brought you back to where you hailed me," the man replied.

They were near the theater where he'd left Georgina's party. That wouldn't do. "I must get you home," he said to his companion.

"I have to do something about my clothes first. I can't go in like this." She plucked at her torn cloak.

"No. Dash it."

"I wouldn't be in this state if not for you."

Her last sentence seemed to resound inside the carriage, the words acquiring more weight and scope with every passing moment. Randolph felt as if the air had thickened in his throat. She was very close to him in the small vehicle.

A link boy passed the hack, lighting the way for three gentlemen revelers. Torchlight washed Miss

Sinclair's face. She was gazing at him, her eyes dark pools. "What are we to do?" he murmured.

This remark also fell into the charged atmosphere like a stone tossed in a still pond. Ripples of implication resonated between them.

"What indeed?" she murmured. Her tone was odd; he couldn't decipher it.

"Sir?" called the driver. "We going on?"

Randolph straightened. A solution was required. Where to go? An idea came to him. He leaned out and gave the man an address. The driver slapped the reins and got the horse moving again.

"Where are we going?" Miss Sinclair asked.

"To see an old friend of mine. She has a place you can make repairs."

"She? What will she think?"

"The best of everyone, as always."

"It's late." Miss Sinclair sounded uncertain.

"Quinn's a night owl."

"Quinn?"

"She used to teach me and my brothers, when we were very small."

Randolph expected more questions, but none came. The hack left the lively streets around the theater and clopped into a quieter neighborhood. "It's nearby," he said to reassure her. "That's why I thought of her. Are you expected back at a certain hour? I should have asked that before." That, or done something sensible.

"No. Everyone thinks I took a headache powder and went to sleep in my room."

"They'll check on you though."

"The door's locked."

Did she sound rather pleased with herself? He couldn't see her face.

"Here we are then, sir," called the cabby.

Randolph leaned out and surveyed the small cottage at the edge of the street. Light showed in the front window.

He got out and handed Miss Sinclair down, then paid off the hack. He knew from past visits that there was a tea hut nearby where drivers congregated before beginning their nightly work. He'd easily find another.

The cab departed, the horse's hooves loud in the quiet street. Verity fingered her torn cloak as Lord Randolph knocked on a low wooden door. People would say she ought to be worried, or feel guilty about deceiving her mother, but what she felt was a wild thrill along all her nerves. A web of lies, a saber duel, a flight in the night. Verity called up every detail of the past hour—Rochford's room scented by woodsmoke, the red of his wine, his watering eyes after she'd hit him, Lord Randolph charging in and seizing the saber, his powerful, sinuous fencing. She concentrated and fixed all of it into a stellar moment to add to her collection.

The door remained shut. "Perhaps there's no one home?" she said.

"Quinn's a bit slow these days."

At last the panels opened, revealing first a candle and then a small, bent woman in a neat gray gown. White-haired and wrinkled, she looked very old.

"Quinn, you promised me you'd always ask who it is before you open the door," he said.

The old woman chuckled. "Bless you, Lord

Randolph. No one knocks here but friends." She reached up to pat him with a gnarled hand.

The candlelight reflected off her eyes, and Verity saw that they were clouded. She must be nearly blind.

It didn't seem to hamper her. "Who have you brought then?"

"A friend of mine."

The old woman peered into the street. "A young lady? What are you up to?"

"Nothing, Quinn. We just need a bit of help, and then we'll be on our way."

He didn't introduce them to each other. Verity realized that he didn't want her name known in these circumstances. The idea, which probably ought to have shocked her, made her want to laugh instead.

"If it was young Sebastian, I'd have my doubts," Quinn said. "But you were always a good boy."

Lord Randolph made a face as if he wasn't entirely pleased with this characterization.

"Well, come in, come in." The old woman moved back and gestured.

The door opened directly into a small parlor, uncluttered and comfortable. A fire burned low on the hearth. Their hostess moved unerringly to a chair before it, set the candle on a little table to the side, and sat down. "I don't sleep much these days," she said. "I often sit up here. It's more interesting than lying in the bed, isn't it? I do miss reading though." She said it without self-pity.

"Where's Dorothy?" asked Lord Randolph.

"Away visiting her sick sister. And the fuss she

made about going! You wouldn't credit it. She'll be back tomorrow."

He looked relieved, and Verity wondered who Dorothy might be. Probably a companion for the old lady.

"Sit down now. Will you take a drop of cider?" Her gnarled hand fell to an earthenware crock at the side of the fireplace. She obviously knew the place of each object in her home, Verity thought.

"No, thank you, Quinn." Lord Randolph sat on a straight chair, leaving Verity the seat opposite their hostess.

"Always a polite boy." The old woman smiled, teasing a little. "He writes me more than all the others put together, you know," she told Verity. "A lovely copperplate, too. I taught him that. I can still see it, even if Dorothy has to read the words to me."

"My brothers visit," he responded.

"So they do." She nodded. "Such a mob of lads. Six! Why Nanny—Hannah, that is—had three nursery maids working under her and a junior cook slaving away just to feed them. And I was practically running a dame school all on my own. If two of the boys were busy, two others would be up and racing about. Little Alan…purely amazing, he was. Knew more than I did by the time he was four years old."

Verity found the picture both endearing and daunting.

"He lives up at Oxford, you know. Lord only knows what he does there. He tried to tell me once, but I couldn't follow beyond a—" Quinn's nod deepened and slowed. Her eyelids drooped. And then she was asleep in her chair.

"She does sleep," said Lord Randolph quietly. "Like a log, actually. Just not in her bed."

Indeed, the old woman showed no signs of stirring. "How do you know?"

"Mama keeps track of her. Quinn began to lose her sight before Alan went off to school, and so we had to find a place for her."

Which was more than many families would do, Verity thought.

"Dorothy takes her over to Mama's school every week. She tells stories to the littlest girls." He stood. "Come."

Verity followed him through a doorway at the left of the fireplace and discovered that the cottage was larger than it looked from the outside. The building stretched back from the street. They walked through a small kitchen with another hearth at the end; a wide room with beds on either side, partitioned off by thick curtains; and finally into a spacious, well-equipped sewing room. Shelves held a selection of fabrics, a rainbow of color. There was a long cutting table down one side and a daybed in the far corner. A sumptuous silk gown, half finished, was draped over a dressmaker's dummy.

"Dorothy's a seamstress," said Lord Randolph. "Daughter of a Langford tenant. Very talented, I hear. Mama set her up in business with the condition that she look after Quinn. Well, they were friends already. It was no hardship. Dorothy could sew up your cloak in a trice. Only, she'd give me such a glare for bringing you here at this hour."

He was babbling. Verity rather liked it. She took off her cloak. Her sensible, practical part noted that the old thing had torn at both shoulders, and the cloth was frayed along the seams. It would take an age to fix it. Best to stitch up her dress and carry the cloak. There was no fire in here, and the chilly air drifted through the long rip at the waist.

"I knew you'd easily find needle and thread in Dorothy's workshop," Lord Randolph added.

It was very quiet. And clandestine. Verity savored the word. She'd never been clandestine in her life, and she might never be again. She felt as if she'd fallen into a fairy tale. She'd come to the good witch's cottage, and magic was imminent. She gazed at the hero of the story. That seemed to rattle him.

"So, I'll, ah, leave you to it." He backed toward the doorway.

"You must undo my dress," said Verity. "I can't reach the fastenings. And no maid to help."

"I can't do that."

"It's not difficult." She felt curiously powerful.

"I know, but—"

"I can't mend it while it's on me." She turned her back and waited.

"Verity."

Her name on his tongue excited her. "Just hooks and laces. You know how to undo hooks and laces, don't you?"

After a moment, she felt his fingers on her back, a light touch but it sent a jolt right through her. As when they'd kissed, he woke her body. No one else had ever done that. It demanded more caresses.

The bodice of her gown loosened and slid down a bit. She let it. She felt him undo another hook, and after a pause, another. The dress slipped off one shoulder. It was astonishing how such a feather touch could rouse her. And then it was gone. "Don't stop," she protested.

His reply was choked. "I'm not made of stone, Verity. I shouldn't have brought you—"

She turned and kissed him before he could say something fatal. How she loved kissing him! The more she did it, the more she wanted to. Each time she found that there was yet another dimension to kissing, some farther place to go in the realms of physical passion. She slipped her arms under his coat and pulled him closer.

He groaned. It was a marvelous sound. She wanted to make him do it again. And she ached for his touch. Perhaps he knew that?

He pulled away. "We can't—"

She kissed him again to stop his talking. If he kept talking, all would be lost. She wiggled her shoulders, her hips, and her dress slithered to the floor. She laughed and reached for him.

And then he was pushing her backward to the daybed, and they half fell onto it. His hands were on her, and they did seem to know precisely where to go. They roamed to just the places she wished them to be. "Oh yes," she gasped, arching up to him.

It felt wonderful. Riveting. Desperately urgent. She pulled at his shirt until she could touch his bare skin, exploring the lovely muscles of his back. She joined him in a flurry of kisses. She tried to match his marvelous caresses. Until she had to clutch him to ride out a storm of release.

As it shook her to the depths, he claimed her lips again and entered her. She held on through a bit of discomfort and into an intimacy greater than she'd shared with any other being. She felt the urgency claim his body and carry him away, delighting in their kiss as it shook him. When he came to rest, their pulses beat heart to heart.

Randolph rose above her, disheveled, murmuring her name. He dropped quick light kisses on her cheeks, her eyelids, her lips. Verity laughed softly, letting her fingertips drift along his ribs. And then they were separate once again. He shifted so that they were lying side by side on the narrow couch.

The house remained silent. They might have been alone in the world.

Lord Randolph groaned. But it was a different sort of sound, not one Verity wished to hear. He sat up, his back to her, and put his head in his hands. The fairy tale had ended, Verity thought. The real world came rushing back. And with it came a tumult of consequences she didn't wish to consider.

He ought to have resisted, Randolph thought. Once he'd brought Verity here—which he should *not* have done—he should have made Quinn assist her. But he hadn't thought, and then a point had come when he didn't want to. She'd been so endearingly eager. That she'd wanted him, trusted him… She'd been irresistible, and he'd given in to temptation.

There was nothing wrong with desire or physical passion, of course. In its place. But this shouldn't have happened in a stranger's workroom, in a tumble of clothes. He still had his boots on, for God's sake.

He'd do anything in the world rather than offer Verity Sinclair an insult. Randolph pulled at his clothes, did up buttons, and turned back to her. She was half naked and delicious, and all he could think of was doing everything all over again as soon as possible.

Well, that wasn't an insurmountable problem. As long as he was willing to take an irrevocable step into the future. Which he found that he was. *And* as long as he didn't say something stupid and muck it up.

Randolph slipped off the daybed and sank to one knee on the sewing room floor. He took Verity's hand. This time, the words flowed. "I was swept away when we first sang together," he said, realizing the truth of it as he spoke. "I'd never felt anything like that in my life. And since then I've thought of you constantly. Will you do me the honor of being my wife?"

Verity gazed into his fathomless blue eyes. As Lord…but surely they were beyond titles now? As Randolph had sat with his back turned, silent, her fairy-tale world had crumbled to dust. How, a dry inner voice had inquired, had she come out tonight to save Olivia from ruin and then tumbled straight into it herself? Gradually, she thought. Step by tantalizing step. And she'd enjoyed it thoroughly, right up to that sobering moment.

She knew that inner voice of old; it was a font of sensible, sometimes irritatingly sensible, advice. Now it added that there was a crucial difference between her case and Olivia's—besides the fact that Olivia hadn't stepped off the edge of propriety into uncharted waters, as she had. Randolph was no Thomas Rochford, as was manifest in his gaze.

From their first duet—that astonishing dive into harmony—she'd known the depths of him. She looked, and saw reflected in his blue eyes the soulful bond she'd felt then. They had deep instincts, impulses in common. She believed that. And down at the base of their kinship lay a sturdy moral code. One did the right thing. This was not a burden, but a privilege. A belief they shared. And because of all this, he hadn't spoken like a man forced to an offer. And she didn't feel like a victim, not the least little bit. He hadn't said he loved her, of course. But he'd touched her as if he… Randolph was waiting. "Yes," she said.

His breath sighed out on a word. "Splendid." He squeezed her hand and let it go. Rising from the floor, he sat beside her. He didn't look at her though, and Verity wondered why. "I'll call at your lodgings tomorrow and speak to your mother," he added. "Make it official."

"Yes," said Verity again. She sat up. Mama would never know that she'd been duped. Was this a poor start to a marriage?

Randolph rose. "I'll go to see that Quinn is still sleeping."

Everything had descended to the mundane. "I'll sew up my dress."

She sounded forlorn, and Randolph risked a glance. Sitting on the daybed with her underclothes in disarray, her hair in wild tendrils, she looked utterly delectable. And sad—was that right? Or was she simply thoughtful? He hated the idea that she might have regrets, but he wasn't certain. He wanted to sweep her into his arms, but he didn't trust himself. It was best to keep his eyes off her. He turned and went out.

Verity found a needle and thread among the sewing supplies. Conscious of the cold now, she pulled her torn cloak around her as she quickly stitched up her gown. Hooking up the back, she managed to slither into the garment, with a series of wriggles and contortions that she wouldn't have wanted to exhibit before anyone else. The dress felt twisted and crooked when she was done, but she simply pulled the ripped cloak back over it and went in search of Randolph.

He was sitting in the front parlor. Quinn snored softly in her chair. Randolph stood. "Ready?"

Verity nodded. Her fund of conversation seemed to be exhausted.

"I'll have to wake Quinn to bolt the door behind us," he said. "If you stay quiet, she probably won't even remember you were here."

Verity nodded again. She went to the front door and slipped out, leaving it open a crack. As she lurked in the dark street, some of the thrill of the clandestine returned.

"Quinn," she heard Randolph say.

There was a snort, and a cough. Then, as if picking up a conversation in the middle, the old woman said, "I don't sleep much these days. I often sit up here. It's more interesting than lying in the bed, isn't it?"

"I must go," Randolph replied. "Come and bolt the door behind me."

"Late, is it?"

"Very late. Let me help you up."

Shuffling footsteps approached. Verity moved into

deeper darkness. The door opened. Randolph stepped through and turned. "I shall stay until I hear you shoot the bolt," he said.

"Yes, yes. But you'll come and see me again and stay longer."

"Of course I will." He shut the door. After a moment, the bolt slid audibly across. Randolph waited a moment, then murmured, "Verity?"

His soft whisper of her name shook her. "Here." She stepped to his side.

"Take my arm."

She did. It was warm and solid. "How will we get back in the dark?"

"There's a place to get a cab not far from here. There should be some light around the corner."

He was right. A short stumbling walk took them to a spot where they could see firelight, and then to a rough hut with one wall open, where a small wiry man served tin mugs of tea to a cluster of cabbies. Randolph engaged one, and they were off.

It was very late when Verity used her key to enter the house where she was staying. She felt Randolph's eyes on her back as she turned it as quietly as possible and slipped inside. Closing the door quickly—this was no time to linger—she relocked it with a click that sounded loud in the silence.

There was no reaction. Everyone was sleeping.

Verity didn't chance a candle. She groped her way upstairs to her room, held her breath as she unlocked it, and whisked in. She leaned against the panels and listened; there was no sound.

Moving carefully, Verity found the tinderbox and

lit a candle. She wriggled her way out of her clothes, ripping her gown again in the same place. It wouldn't be the same without serious repairs, which she would think about some other time, she decided. She bundled cloak and dress together and tossed them on top of the wardrobe. Pulling on a nightdress, she got into bed. An engaged woman, she thought as she lay there. A surge of emotion shook her. She hadn't realized one could be happy and anxious and triumphant and sad all at the same time.

# Fifteen

Randolph stood before the door of the house where Verity Sinclair was lodging and raised his hand to knock. It occurred to him that things had been entirely different six years ago when he'd done this. His courtship of Rosalie had been so conventional, while his connection with Verity was peppered with...contradictions and extremes. About to offer for Rosalie, he'd been bursting with impatience. He'd wanted to rush inside, blurt out the words, and seize his prize.

Today he felt... Well, he wasn't certain exactly what he felt. Not sorry; he was clear on that. Wakeful in the night, he'd had no regrets. He'd thought instead that there were many sorts of happiness. He'd seen couples bound by respect and contentment. Common values, a commitment to service. These things wove strong bonds. Shared interests, like music, cemented a relationship. And physical passion—Randolph's pulse jumped at the memory of Verity en déshabillé on the daybed last night. They would certainly have that, an area he was exceedingly eager to explore.

No, he had no doubts. On the contrary, he was content with this choice.

He let his knuckles fall on the door panels. A maid answered, took his hat and gloves, and led him up the stairs to the drawing room.

Verity and her mother awaited him there. From the look of things, Verity had prepared her parent. Mrs. Sinclair greeted him with bright eyes and an eager smile. Randolph found he was glad to dispense with chitchat. He was, in fact, nervous, even though all had been settled in advance. Verity had surprised him more than once. What if she'd had second thoughts? What if she refused him now? He found the idea startlingly worrisome. "I'm glad to have caught you at home," he said. "I've come to speak to Miss Sinclair about a very particular matter."

Verity's mother sprang to her feet. "Oh yes. Verity said—That is, she surmised you might be—I'll just let you—" She left the room without completing her sentence.

Randolph took a breath. There was no reason to be anxious. Verity had already accepted him. This was a matter of form. But the steady gaze of her blue-green eyes shook him. Thus, instead of sitting beside her, he sank to one knee for the second time. "I'm even more certain than I was last night that I want you, most desperately, for my wife," he said. And as the words came out, he realized they were true. He was not as calm as he'd thought. "I hope you feel the same."

At the worried look on his handsome face, something inside Verity relaxed. She'd tossed and turned through the night, alternating between the certainty that she'd made the right decision and a melancholy sense of narrowing choices. An engagement settled a young lady's future; there were so many fewer questions to ask and answer after that. For her, it meant that the dream of setting off to the ends of the Earth was finished. But with that lowering thought had come an image of Randolph wielding the saber, as wild-eyed as any intrepid adventurer. He was rather extraordinary. And his family was far from run-of-the-mill. The duchess had suggested that adventures were to be found everywhere. Perhaps that could be true.

Verity *had* wondered if Randolph would show up this morning with the hangdog air of a man doing his duty, looking trapped. Despite everything, that would have been the end. She looked deep into his blue eyes and saw no hint of resignation, or hesitation. "Yes, I do." She gave him her hand.

He kissed it and rose to sit beside her. Two people limp with relief, Verity thought. For the same reasons? Or different ones? How could anyone tell?

Silence fell. Verity wasn't sure what to say in the aftermath of setting their mutual life course. Did one talk immediately of wedding arrangements? That didn't seem right. If they could just sing together, all would be well, she thought. Which gave her a whole new perspective on opera. She laughed.

"What is it?" Randolph asked with a smile. When she told him, he laughed, too. "There's a missed opportunity," he said. "Why didn't I think of making an offer in song?"

"I'm not sure which one you could use," she replied.

"I can think of a few candidates. I would have altered the lyrics to fit the case, of course." His eyes twinkled. "Or written a new one, just for you. If I could come up with some tender rhymes for *Verity*."

"*Charity*, *clarity*, *parity*, *severity*," she answered. "*Not* particularly romantic."

He laughed again. "I see you've considered this issue."

"I tried to compose a personal…dirge when I was fourteen and spent hours lamenting that I wasn't named Anne."

"*Plan*, *man*, *ran*, *ban*," he replied.

"Exactly. You can see the possibilities."

"I can indeed."

"But, alas, I am Verity Louise. The enemy of rhyme."

"But ever true," he replied with much more than laughter in his gaze.

It will be all right, Verity thought as they smiled at each other.

Her mother peeked around the edge of the door.

"Lord Randolph and I are engaged, Mama," Verity said. Beside her, he stood.

"Oh!" Her mother surged forward. "How delightful. I'm so happy for you." She thrust out her hands. Randolph took them with a cordial bow. Holding on for just the right amount of time, he maneuvered her into a comfortable chair. He was such a lovely combination of kind and polished, Verity thought.

"Ever since that first duet you sang, I suspected this might happen," said her mother. "You were the picture of harmony."

Verity nodded. It was perfectly true. And harmony was a fine thing. Not...pedestrian. How could she think so, when music depended upon it?

"You must be married at Chester Cathedral, of course," her mother continued. "The bishop will want to preside. He's very fond of Verity," she said to Randolph.

"As who would not be?" he replied. Yet he looked suddenly wooden.

"So prettily said."

Her mother's eyes filled with tears, and Verity was touched. Mama had been uncomfortable so far from her familiar haunts, and now she was happy.

"I beg your pardon," the older woman added, taking out her handkerchief. "Silly of me."

"Not at all," said Randolph. "I'm glad you're pleased." His tone had gone flat. In fact, he sounded like another man altogether. What was wrong?

"Oh, I am! And Papa will be, too, Verity. So happy."

Verity blinked, stunned by the realization that she'd forgotten her father's objections to Randolph until this very moment. How was that possible? Yes, there'd been a great deal happening. Including a rapturous interlude on a daybed. And it was true she hadn't taken Papa's warning seriously. He did fuss about small things sometimes, and she simply couldn't believe that Randolph had done anything very bad. An *embarrassment* wasn't a crime. Perhaps the Archbishop of Canterbury was very easily embarrassed? But she knew, with a sinking feeling in her midsection, that none of this would explain to Papa how she'd ended up engaged to the one man in London he'd told her to avoid.

Randolph rose. "I must, ah, give my family the news," he said. With the briefest of goodbyes, he went out, walking rather fast, Verity thought. Like a man running from something? But that was silly. *He* didn't have an unreasonable father.

The room seemed a great deal emptier when he was gone. He filled her…consciousness. She wanted *very much* to marry him, she realized as her mind darted from her father's letter to wild ideas about what might have prompted it. She had to set Papa straight. Categorically.

"So very polite," her mother was saying. "And handsome! Oh, Verity, a duke's son and a churchman. He's ideal. He has a bit of money, too. Lucy Doran told me so. Though how she knows these things, I can't imagine. Not a great fortune, but we don't care for that, do we? You have a bit also, so you'll be comfortable. And you sing so beautifully together. I know that's important to you. Of course the chief thing is that you like him." She fixed Verity with an earnest gaze.

"I do, Mama." She hadn't quite understood how much.

"Good. Good." The older woman let out a satisfied sigh. "I must write to your papa at once."

"No!"

Her mother started at the snap in Verity's tone.

"I'll write to Papa. Myself. I want to do it myself."

"Well, of course you will. Is something wrong?"

"No. I just want to share my own good news. Don't mention the engagement until I write him."

Looking perplexed, her mother said, "Very well." She brightened. "Better still, why don't we just go home and tell him? We'd have such a happy, peaceful time together."

Verity hid a wince. Would Papa try to forbid the match? She was twenty-four years old; he couldn't actually do that. But she didn't want to fight with him. She had to fix this. "You promised me a season," she replied.

"Well, yes, but now that your future is settled, why not go home and begin to plan your wedding? We could reach Chester almost as fast as a letter."

"I want to stay in London," Verity replied. Every instinct said to stay near Randolph. So much could go wrong if they were hundreds of miles apart. She had to talk to him, at once. And she wasn't panicking. No, she was not.

Her mother looked impatient, then resigned. "Very well."

"I want to become better acquainted with Lord Randolph's family," Verity added.

"Ah." Mama nodded as if this made sense. "Of course. I suppose the duchess will approve of the match?"

The concern in her voice surprised Verity. "We got on very well when we visited her school," she said.

"I'm sure she'll be glad then," was the reply. "Verity, is all well with you? You seem agitated. You *are* happy with this match? I mean, you've always known your own mind, and I don't suppose you would have—"

"I am." She nodded emphatically and tried to look

like her customary self as her mind intoned, "A plan, a plan, must have a plan."

Stop dithering, declared that dry inner voice that seemed to be specializing in tardy pronouncements just now. Are you not the woman who was ready to face down charging lions and ford jungle torrents? What is the matter with you?

Verity sat quite still and considered the question. Part of her felt as if she faced a threat as dangerous as those ravening lions, though the comparison was ridiculous. She would simply ask Randolph straight out about the archbishop, she thought. Verity let out a breath she'd been unaware of holding. He'd tell her what had happened. They were going to be married; they could talk about embarrassing matters. Should be able to. Well, they could start right here. She was no fainting flower. And once she had the facts she—they—would figure out what to do. An errant thought suggested that if the situation could be easily remedied, Randolph would have done so. She brushed it aside.

"Verity?" said her mother, looking concerned.

"I'm fine, Mama," she told both of them.

Some streets away, the duchess had responded to Randolph's news with a searching look. "So you're happy?" she asked.

"Yes, I am."

"This isn't the way you talked when you told me about Rosalie."

"That was years ago," he said. "The case is different."

"But Randolph—"

"My future is settled, Mama. Just as I wished it to be. Verity will be a fine wife."

"Fine isn't the same as—"

"And I shall endeavor to be an exemplary husband to her," Randolph interrupted again. Immediately, he regretted his choice of words. He was being stiff and pompous—the opposite of the way he wished to sound. But Mama was making him feel defensive. She didn't understand the circumstances, and he had no intention of explaining last night. In any case, that wasn't the point. Somehow, in the heady rush of events, he hadn't thought of Verity's connection to the Archbishop of Canterbury. Then her mother had proposed a cathedral wedding, and that uncomfortable fact had come rushing back.

Had he just made his precarious position much worse? Would the archbishop see his engagement as defiance? A metaphorical fist shaken in his face? *Ha, take that! Try to keep me down, and watch me marry into your very family. I don't care a snap of my fingers for your disapproval.*

Part of him rather liked the idea. Nothing, and no one, would keep him from his chosen mate this time! But he had more than himself to consider. His prospects for promotion depended on the head of his church. If the archbishop took offense, again, Randolph would never have more to offer Verity than the country parish she despised. Was he honor bound to go back, explain this to her, and offer her a chance to withdraw? His spirits sank further.

"Well, what's done is done, I suppose."

Were those tears in his mother's eyes? That wasn't like her at all. Randolph examined her face. She looked pale and tired. "Are you well, Mama?"

"I have a touch of something. I'm sure it will be gone tomorrow. But perhaps I'll lie down for a bit."

Randolph could count on one hand the number of times his mother had admitted physical weakness. "Shall I ring for Harris?"

"Of course not. Do you imagine me leaning on my maid's arm like a doddering invalid?"

This sounded more like his indomitable mother. "I could walk with you."

"Don't be ridiculous, Randolph." The duchess rose and moved toward the parlor door. "I do wish you very happy, of course. And so will Papa."

Randolph nodded. He resolved to have a word with his father as soon as he came home. It seemed Mama needed rest. If she required convincing, Papa was the person to do it.

Verity's mother flitted about Lady Sefton's ball that evening, sharing her good news with every acquaintance she came across. She looked happier than at any time since they'd arrived in London, and Verity was touched to see it. Mama really had pushed herself to give Verity the season she'd asked for, so she deserved a little crowing. For herself, Verity had recovered her equilibrium and was ready for action.

In the congratulations that followed, most people claimed to have known how it would be since the famous duets. Some seemed almost smug, as if they'd made the match themselves. She and Lord Randolph were obviously made for each other, these individuals told Verity. "Are you saying it was an inevitability of fate?" she replied to the fifth person who expressed this complacent opinion. "That my marriage has nothing to do with me?"

"Eh?" replied the matron whose name Verity couldn't immediately recall.

"I'm not simply a pretty voice," Verity added.

The older woman drew back. "I beg your pardon. I meant no offense."

"I make my own choices."

"Do you?" Her companion's smile grew condescending. "How fortunate you are." Gathering her air of irony like an enveloping cloak, she turned away.

"And act on them," Verity said quietly.

"And thereby hangs a tale," murmured a deep voice in her ear.

Verity turned to find Thomas Rochford passing behind her. "I shan't linger, for fear of your fierce fiancé," he added. "I shall say only that the reasons for his bellicosity are clearer now." With a graceful gesture, he moved on.

Watching him move through the press at the edge of the ballroom, Verity saw no sign of his wound. Perhaps he held his arm a bit stiffly. She felt a thrill of secret knowledge. And no remorse whatsoever.

Mr. Rochford paused to speak to Olivia. From the expression on her friend's face, Verity was sure that he received a saucy answer. He laughed, the picture of debonair assurance, and resumed his progress toward the card room.

Olivia surveyed the crowd, saw Verity, and came over to her. "I wish you very happy," she said.

Verity realized that she wanted to reproach her friend for *not* visiting Mr. Rochford's house. When Olivia had done exactly what she'd urged her to do—avoid a scandal.

"Is something wrong?" asked Olivia. "You aren't still angry about my Rochford scheme, are you? I didn't go."

Verity almost said, "I know."

"I was never going to," her friend continued. "Not really, I think."

"You think?" Verity had to smile.

"When it came down to it, of course not." Olivia shrugged. "But that *of course* is rather dreary. I like to imagine a different sort of life. Wilder…unfettered."

Verity did understand.

"Ah, here's the lucky man," Olivia said.

Randolph joined them with a graceful bow. "It's a waltz," he said to Verity. "May I have the honor?"

"If she'll marry you, I expect she'll dance with you," Olivia said.

Verity gave him her hand, and they stepped into the waltz. "I must talk to you," she said, not bothering with a preamble.

"And I you," he said.

"Privately." She didn't intend to hash out their dilemma before the bulk of the *haut ton*. "Will you call tomorrow morning?"

He looked at the people surrounding them and nodded. "Tomorrow morning," he echoed.

He seemed unusually serious, but having gained

her point, she was satisfied. All would be revealed tomorrow. "Everyone is being unbearably smug about our engagement."

"Well, they've known how it would be since we first sang together."

Verity looked up and caught the twinkle in his blue eyes. "They've been saying that to you, too?"

"A great many people."

"It's as if they're taking credit."

"Indeed. It had nothing to do with *us*."

She laughed, and with that, the complacent comments seemed far less annoying. What did they matter?

Verity became conscious of Randolph's hand, warm on her back, of the strength of his fingers holding hers. Dancing with him was like floating around the floor; they moved to the music with an identical impulse. He smiled down at her, as if he was thinking the same thing. She'd wanted wild adventures, Verity thought. Last night on a daybed in a secret cottage had been wild. This hand she held had done such delicious things. Hers had run over his bare skin. With impunity. She'd been intoxicated with kisses. None of these smug people knew anything about *that*. And they never would. She smiled back.

She was smiling like a cat who'd found the cream pot, Randolph thought. Sly and…salacious? In that moment, he knew she was thinking of last night. She was back at Quinn's, which took him there as well. Waltzing was pleasant, but he wished for so much more. Where their hands clasped, he ran his fingertips lightly over hers. Verity shivered in his arms, her blue-green eyes darkening with emotion. Without missing a step, Randolph pulled her closer. Her hand tightened on his shoulder. How he wanted her! To sweep her up and carry her off and let the archbishop go hang. But not to make her unhappy—that was the damnable crux of the matter.

Too soon, the dance ended, and he had to let her go. Worse, another fellow came up and claimed her for the next set, as if he had the right. It was all Randolph could do to watch her walk off with him.

He didn't care to find another partner. Instead, he went to join his brothers by the wall. "Georgina's always buzzing about like a dashed bee," Sebastian was complaining. "Taking Emma to some party or ball. Or seeing what Hilda's up to."

"Flora's as busy," Robert replied. "On top of all else, she's promoting a match between Wrentham and Miss Reynolds. Can't see it myself. Did you hear about his idiotic stunt?" He snorted. "Riding through the park backward. He's not a stripling just let loose on the town, for God's sake."

"Charles Wrentham?" asked Randolph, his attention diverted. "The fellow from Salbridge? Acted in the play?"

Robert nodded.

"He tried to run me through at Angelo's a few weeks ago," Randolph said.

"What?" Both his brothers stared at him.

"Why would he do that?" Sebastian asked.

"He just felt like skewering someone, I think. And anyone would do. That's how it seemed to me anyway. We hardly exchanged two words."

"Perhaps he's run mad," Robert said. "That would explain it. How did he do against you?"

Randolph gave him a sardonic look.

"Wretchedly, I daresay," said Sebastian. "It's hard to match Randolph with a foil."

Randolph gave him a bow.

"A saber now… That's another matter," added his large military brother with a grin.

"You might be surprised." Randolph wished he could tell them about pinking Rochford with his own saber.

"Wish you happy, by the way," said Sebastian. "Forgot to say."

"Yes, felicitations," said Robert. "Miss Sinclair will be an ornament to your new parish."

Randolph's problems descended upon him once more. He wondered if Verity wanted to talk about their future tomorrow. What else? The feeling of failure gnawed at him again. With his lineage and education and abilities, his advancement in the church should have been practically assured. Would have been, if not for that dratted ram.

He hid a sigh from his brothers. He'd worked hard in his parish, and he'd done a good job. He knew that. He deserved recognition. Verity deserved…all the happiness he could give her, if not the moon and the stars. He hated the idea that he was going to disappoint her. He had nothing to be ashamed of, and yet he felt somehow that he did.

After the supper interval, as she stood near her mother and Mrs. Doran, Verity was suddenly flanked by two taller women.

"Verity," said Lord Sebastian's elegant blond wife. "We must call you Verity now."

"And we are Flora and Georgina," said Lord Robert's keen-eyed spouse.

"Welcome to the ranks of Gresham daughters-in-law," said Georgina.

"Sixth and last," said Flora with a smile.

They took Verity's arms and led her to a cluster of gilt chairs in the corner. She felt slightly hustled. "Is there an examination?" she asked as she sat down.

Georgina looked startled, but Flora laughed. "It ought to be the other way about. A ducal information booklet, perhaps. Do you know that people are supposed to call me Lady Robert now? Did you ever hear anything so ridiculous?"

"It's just a form of address," said her companion.

"Yes, Georgina, you grew up among the nobility, and it seems quite natural to you. I did not." Flora turned one hand palm upward. "And so it does not." She snorted. "Lady Robert, as if I had no identity of my own. No name even."

"What does Lord Robert think?" Verity wondered.

"Robert," Flora corrected. "You may call him Robert. I so decree. For all the host of brothers."

"Even Hightower?" asked Georgina dubiously.

"Well." Flora hesitated. "Yes, of course. Nathaniel won't mind."

"It's not that he'd *mind*."

"No." Flora shrugged, then nodded. "It just doesn't seem quite right, I agree." She turned back to Verity. "Hightower's the oldest, you know, and heir to the duke. He has a sort of…natural dignity."

"So does Violet," said Georgina.

"Yes. His wife," Flora informed Verity.

There were so many of them. It was difficult to keep track. "Do you feel part of the family?" Verity asked them.

"Yes, indeed," said Georgina. "The duke and duchess have been more than kind."

But Flora made a face. "I worried, once upon a time, about acceptance. Now I struggle to keep my head above the…tribal waters."

"You say the oddest things," Georgina replied without judgment.

"I'm known for it," Flora answered. "And if you knew what I was *thinking*…" She wiggled her dark eyebrows.

"You'll put Verity off us."

"I don't think I will." Flora surveyed Verity. "I was impressed when we visited the school together. Verity seems level-headed and intelligent and charitable."

"Randolph chose her," said Georgina. "Sebastian says he's most discerning of them all. So she must have all kinds of good qualities."

"I'm right here listening to you," said Verity. She appreciated compliments, but it was strange to be talked about so frankly. She also felt that life was suddenly going very fast. Yesterday, she'd been plain Miss Sinclair, with a reasonable number of familiar connections. Now she was being propelled into another family—large, complicated, and inquisitive.

"Here's the prettiest sight in the ballroom," said a deep voice above them.

Verity looked up. The Gresham brothers had arrived, three tall, broad-shouldered men. They were quite a sight, standing together—blue-eyed, auburn-haired, very handsome. Verity rose along with her companions.

Sebastian held out a hand. "My dance," he said to Georgina. "At long last." He took her fingers possessively.

"Would you do me the honor?" Robert said to Verity, with a perfect bow. She accepted, and they moved to join the set that was forming. Randolph came behind them with Flora.

"So you and Randolph have progressed from singing to matrimony," said Robert as they moved down the line in the country dance.

The wives had trusted in Randolph's choice, Verity thought. Robert was another matter; she could hear it in his voice.

"You do sing sweetly together," he added.

"Have you been assigned to evaluate me?" Verity asked.

"I've taken it upon myself," he replied.

It seemed the entire Gresham clan spoke freely. Verity found that both refreshing and disconcerting. How far was too far?

"Randolph is a splendid fellow, you know. I should like to see him happy."

"And you don't think I'll make him so?"

"He's offered for you, and he usually knows what he's doing. I just don't get the sense..."

"What sense?" Verity asked when he trailed off.

"The one I got with my other brothers."

"The one? I fear I don't understand." Verity felt insulted, and suddenly sad. "Is it some sort of arcane perception?"

"I don't mean to offend you, Miss Sinclair."

"Indeed, *Robert*. I was informed that I should call you Robert, now that we are to be one big happy family."

"That sounds like Flora."

"Flora, yes. *Not* Lady Robert."

He smiled briefly. "I see that I *have* offended you. I beg your pardon. I'm not often clumsy."

"Really?" Verity was furious, and not entirely certain why.

"You're a bit like Flora, aren't you?"

"I don't know her well enough to judge," Verity replied through clenched teeth.

"That's a good sign," her partner said, seemingly to himself. "Isn't it?"

"I have no opinion on the matter."

"But is Randolph like me?" He seemed to have abandoned conversation for inane musing.

"No," said Verity. "He's quite lucid."

Robert looked at her. He appeared much struck, but he said only, "Ah."

And then the dance, and the joust, were over.

# Sixteen

The following morning, Randolph woke early. He'd dreamed of something he couldn't quite remember, only that it had been disturbing. As he dressed, he wondered if it had to do with the fact that he longed to see Verity, and yet didn't look forward to their conversation. Would all end between them as it had begun—with her rejection of a country cleric?

After breakfast, restless, he got out his lute and strummed the strings. He hadn't practiced in a long while. He settled to try the tune that still ran in his head but never came out quite right.

After a few minutes, he was interrupted by a knock at the door. "Yes?" he called, a little irritated.

The door opened. Harris stood in the corridor in her somber black. This was unusual. His mother's superior lady's maid never sought him out. "Her Grace is ill," she said.

"Mama?"

"She's been ailing for some days. She wouldn't say so, or let me send for the doctor. But her condition has become serious. And the duke is out." Harris looked reproachful.

Randolph rose, setting the instrument aside. "I'll come see her."

"It would be better to send for the doctor," Harris repeated.

Worried now, Randolph followed her to his mother's room. The duchess lay in bed, unprecedented at this time of day. She was deathly pale. Sweat beaded the hair at her temples. She plucked at the coverlet as if it offended her. "You told Randolph, Harris?" she said. "Against my express orders?" She sounded peevish. Mama was never peevish. "I want to get up," she added. But when she tried to sit, she wasn't able. She fell back on the sheets as if half fainting.

A bolt of fear shot through Randolph. He'd never seen his mother really ill. Every other thought went out of his head. "I'll send for Papa," he told Harris, and rushed off to do so.

"And the doctor," Harris called after him.

"Yes."

The duke arrived first, but Dr. Loughton was practically on his heels. The latter, a wise and sensible man of sixty who'd treated the family for years, went up at once to examine the patient. When he came down later, he wore a grave expression. "I'm afraid this is quite serious. It appears to be typhoid fever."

Randolph watched his father take in the news. He looked like a man who'd sustained a sudden, stunning blow. His own expression must be similar, Randolph thought, because that was exactly how he felt.

"Miss Harris tells me that the duchess has been

feeling poorly for several days. Her weakness, headache, and fever are characteristic of the disease."

"She told me she was tired," said the duke. "She hates fusses."

"As I know well," replied the doctor, offering a brief, understanding smile.

"Tell us what to do."

"She needs to rest. Not to 'stop lazing about and get on with things.'"

Randolph could hear his mother saying these words.

"I'll see to it."

"Miss Harris says she hasn't wanted to eat, but she must keep up her strength. Broth and soft foods. Barley water. Lemonade, whatever she will take. I'll send over something for the headache." He looked at them. And saw two men struggling with shock, Randolph thought.

"Nurses," said his father.

Dr. Loughton nodded. "Miss Harris is determined to care for her, and I've given her detailed written instructions. But she'll require help. I can recommend someone."

"I think we'll have plenty of volunteers," the duke responded with an odd sort of proud pain.

A strange desperate fear surged through Randolph. "I'll sit with her!" He ignored the doctor's startled glance. "You must let me sit with her, Papa!"

"Of course, Randolph."

His easy agreement quieted Randolph. As did a brush of memory, explaining why he felt terrified even though it didn't banish the feeling.

"I should warn you." Dr. Loughton hesitated.

"Yes?"

His father's voice was tight with anxiety. A stranger wouldn't notice, but Randolph heard it plainly.

"Please tell us everything," the duke added.

"She'll get worse before she's any better," the physician replied. "The fever will go up and down, perhaps with a cough and bodily pains. It's very likely that she'll become delirious."

"But Mama will recover," Randolph blurted out. "She's very strong. We'll care for her, and she'll recover."

"I have every hope that she will." Dr. Loughton paused, then added, "This disease commonly lasts for weeks and is singularly exhausting."

The duke turned away, as if he didn't want them to see his face. "Thank you, doctor," he said.

"I'll call twice a day," the man replied. "Morning and afternoon. And whenever else you need me, of course. You need only send word."

Randolph's father nodded. Dr. Loughton took his leave.

"I must go to her," the duke said. Now that their visitor was gone, fear was clear in his tone. "You'll notify your brothers?"

Randolph suppressed his own worries in the face of his father's obvious pain. "Of course, Papa."

Rushing down to the library, glad to have a task, Randolph wrote brief notes to Robert and Sebastian. There was no need to go on and on; they'd call at once to hear the rest. His letters to Alan and Nathaniel and James—as if the latter could hear anytime soon—were a bit longer. But what was there to say, after all? Except that Mama, the center around which their family revolved, was very ill, and might not be herself for some time. Some limited time, Randolph thought fiercely as he finished the last letter. He'd take care of her. They all would. And then she'd recover, and the world would right itself again.

---

Verity was puzzled, then a bit irritated, when Randolph didn't call as he'd promised. She waited all morning for him to arrive, or send a note of explanation at the least. She was afire with impatience to dispense with the archbishop problem. But Randolph never came. She nearly wrote to *him*, but then she remembered that he'd mentioned planning to attend the Garnetts' party. She'd find him, and his explanation, there tonight.

But she didn't. Verity fumed, until she noticed that none of the Gresham family was present. Which was odd. One or another of them had graced every large event she'd attended in London. She said as much to Olivia.

"You haven't heard?" Olivia replied with raised eyebrows.

"Heard what?"

"I'm surprised. Aren't you practically a member of the family now?"

Olivia so enjoyed knowing more than other people, Verity thought. And then stringing out the story until her listener was panting over her. "Please tell me."

Her friend relented. "The duchess is very ill."

"Oh no."

"On her deathbed, some say. Foaming and raving." Olivia's voice held a hint of relish.

"What?" This picture shocked Verity to the core. "I saw her only a few days ago. She seemed perfectly well."

Olivia shrugged. "Well, you know how people exaggerate."

"But this is… Tell me the truth of it, Olivia!"

"Truth? You expect me to sort through a load of tittle-tattle? You're in a better position to do that yourself."

"Of course, I must go and inquire," Verity murmured. She would have rushed out immediately if it hadn't been so late.

"You can get all the details," Olivia said. "Then we'll know the *truth*." Her tone and expression mocked the final word.

Verity had lost all interest in the party.

"Oh look, there's Miss Reynolds," Olivia said. "All on her own. I wonder how she wangled this invitation."

Not really hearing, Verity wondered why Randolph hadn't informed her about the duchess.

"Let's go and speak to her," Olivia continued. "We can ask her where she found her *amusing* little dress."

"I have to go." Verity looked around for her mother, spotted her, and walked away. She didn't hear Olivia's offended huff.

The Sinclair ladies called at Langford House at the earliest suitable hour the next morning. At first, it seemed the footman would turn them away. But when Verity explained that she was Lord Randolph's fiancée, they were admitted and taken up to the drawing room.

Randolph came in a few minutes later. The change in him in such a short time was startling. He looked haggard. "I'm sorry," he said before he sat down. "I said I'd call. I forgot. I should have written you. Too. I suppose I'm not accustomed to being engaged."

His voice caught on the last word. He didn't sound at all like himself. He more collapsed than sat on the sofa beside her.

"When Sebastian and Robert arrived, I pushed the rest of the letters off onto Robert," he went on disjointedly. "He thought of some others." Randolph made a vague gesture. "I wasn't thinking. Things have been in disarray here."

"How is she?" asked Verity quietly.

He shook his head. "Feverish and vague and very restless. She keeps wanting to get up, but she hasn't the strength. Which makes her fretful. It's rather… dreadful to see."

"I'm so sorry."

Randolph went on as if he hadn't heard. "Mama likes to be active, you know. I think of her in motion. Papa will sit and read for hours, but Mama is always rushing to finish some task, or go out riding or… It's difficult to keep her still. Even when she can hardly move." His voice caught on the last sentence. He bent his head.

Verity wanted to take him in her arms. Her mother murmured some words of comfort.

"Music soothes her," he went on. "I used to… I had the pianoforte moved upstairs so I could play for her, but I find I can't." He held up his hands; they shook visibly. "I'm useless. I keep having to get up and make certain she's still breathing."

Verity took one of his hands and held it. From the state he was in, she feared the duchess really was dying. She caught his restless gaze. "Let me play for her. I should so like to help."

"You?" Randolph seemed to really see her for the first time this morning. "Verity."

"I'm here," she said.

His fingers tightened on her hand. "You could play for her," he echoed, as if his mind was moving more slowly than usual.

"I could."

"You wouldn't have to go into her room."

Before she could assure him that she wasn't worried about this, her mother spoke up. "Verity isn't afraid of sickrooms. We often visit ailing parishioners at home."

Feeling a surge of love and pride, Verity nodded. "Yes, we do. I can take a turn at nursing."

"Hannah's here. And Harris. And Flora. She never learned to play though."

Verity didn't recognize two of these names. But it didn't matter. "Then I shall," she said.

For a moment, he clung to her like a lifeline. Then he led her and her mother upstairs without further discussion.

Verity found that the pianoforte from the music room had been moved to the bedchamber across the hall from the duchess's. With both doors open, the sound would carry easily.

She removed her gloves and bonnet and pelisse, leaving them on the bed. Her mother did the same and settled in a chair in the corner. Verity sat down at the instrument, thought over the pieces she knew by heart, and started to play. Randolph stood beside her. She was glad to see his tense expression ease a bit.

There was a spate of garbled words from across the corridor. Randolph stiffened and went out. Verity played. When one composition ended, she moved smoothly into another. She'd played for more than an hour when her mother said, "I must send word. I have an appointment to go shopping with Lucy Doran."

"You should go, Mama," replied Verity.

"I don't like to leave you alone." Her mother fidgeted. "Though there seems nothing for me to do. I gladly would."

"I know. But there doesn't seem to be anything for you to do. And I'm fine here."

"Well, I suppose it's all right." Her mother rose to retrieve her bonnet. "I hate feeling useless. It drives me distracted." She put on her pelisse and gloves. "You *will* send word at once if you or the Greshams need me for anything."

"I will."

With a nod, her mother departed.

Randolph returned a little while later. "The music seems to be calming her. Thank God." He grimaced. "Mama thought it was me playing. Even though I was standing right beside her. I told her it was you, but I'm not sure she understood." He paced as Verity's fingers moved through a Haydn sonata. "If only there was something I could *do*!" he exclaimed.

"You could have someone bring up the sheet music from the music room," Verity replied without missing a note. "I'll run out of pieces I've memorized soon."

"Of course!" He practically ran from the room.

In ten minutes Randolph was back, his arms full. A footman followed with more pages. Randolph looked around, hesitated, then dumped the music on the bed, gesturing for the servant to do likewise. Piles of paper fanned out on the coverlet. As the footman went out, Randolph gazed at them.

"If you could sort it," Verity suggested. "And pick out your mother's favorite pieces."

"Yes, yes." He bent over the music, shuffling the pages. "Can you play a piece at first sight?"

"Pretty well." Actually, Verity was proud of her skill at this. But she knew Randolph's attention was elsewhere. It was no time for a discussion of musical methods. Or anything else. She wondered how he functioned in his parish if he had such a strong reaction to illness. Of course, things were different when the patient was family, but his state still seemed extreme.

He'd laid out several selections within her reach when there was a cry from across the hall. Randolph dropped what he was doing and rushed out. Verity played on.

Time passed. Verity grew tired, but she was also carried away by the notes and harmonies she produced. She fell into an oddly distant state and scarcely noticed when a maid came in with branches of candles and lit them. Flora looked in a bit later and thanked her. "The music sounds lovely in the sickroom," she said. "Soft and haunting. It helps bring the duchess back when her mind…wanders."

"She's very bad?" Verity asked.

Flora sighed. She looked tired. "Her fever is high. Today, she's been delirious most of the time. The doctor says that's to be expected with typhoid. I've seen it before."

"Typhoid." That was dreadfully serious. "But she'll get better?"

Flora started to answer, but bit off her words when Randolph came in. "You must rest," he said to Verity. "You've been going for hours. Your hands will cramp. And you must have some dinner."

"I'm fine."

"He's right," said Flora. "We'll be no use if we exhaust ourselves. I'm going down to eat. Come with me."

Verity's eyes were on Randolph's face. "In a moment."

With an understanding nod, Flora went out.

Verity stopped playing. The silence felt profound, a little ominous, after the continuous stream of music. Her hands were stiff. She flexed them.

"You see?" said Randolph. But there was no force behind the words.

"It's true, I must rest a bit." She was hungry, Verity realized. She'd eaten nothing since breakfast. "But I'll come back afterward."

"We can't ask you to—"

"You didn't ask. I offered," she interrupted. "What we should do, as I can't play constantly, is decide which times are best for the duchess. To help her the most."

He brightened a little at this concrete suggestion. "The trouble is, the nights are the hardest. Mama has bad dreams. She wakes not knowing where she is or who we are."

"Then I will play for her at night."

"How can you?"

"I'll stay here at Langford House, like Flora."

"You would?"

She nodded. She liked and admired the Duchess of Langford. But even more, she wanted to ease the pain in Randolph's expression.

"Verity." He sank to his knees as if stricken by a sudden weakness and put his hands over his face. She thought he shuddered. "I've been through this before, you see. And it...didn't end well."

Verity thought of people she knew who'd succumbed to a sudden raging fever. It happened in Chester, and must occur much more often among the miasmas of London. She pulled his hands free and held them, then met his anguished gaze. "She's getting the best of care. I'm sure all will be well."

He stared as if he was searching for assurance in her eyes. Then he slumped farther and rested his head in her lap.

It was daunting to see a man who'd always been so balanced, so smoothly in charge, look lost and afraid. She stroked his auburn hair. Her hand trembled with the intensity of her wish to comfort him.

"I'm glad you're here," he said, his voice muffled by her skirts. "Thank you."

"I'm happy to help." Though true, the words were insufficient.

After an indeterminate time, Randolph straightened. Kneeling beside her on the floor, he said, "The music helps me, too. Like a soothing hand. But to be able to talk freely, to have someone... That's even better."

Verity's throat grew thick with tears. She leaned forward and kissed him softly.

This wasn't the exploratory kiss of Carleton House, or the passionate kisses of Quinn's cottage. It wasn't the impulsive caress indulged in the lighted garden. This touch, though lighter, was of another order entirely. A wordless pledge, an open acknowledgment, it felt more like their singing, a soul connection. When Verity drew back, she was trembling.

Randolph smiled at her so sweetly that it made her heart ache with delight. He rose and held out a hand. "Come. I must take care of you, too. You require dinner."

Verity took his hand and rose. They stood face-to-face. He pulled her to him, and they rested together. Desire whispered up Verity's spine, a simmering promise for the future. She was sorry when he let her go. "Come," he repeated. "I hereby enlist you in our conspiracy to make Papa eat."

Hand in hand, they went downstairs. Randolph walked into the dining room first, and when she followed, Verity stopped short. She hadn't realized that there were five Gresham brothers at Langford House now. They stood protectively around their father, forming a breathtaking picture of masculine beauty.

Flora caught her eye. She nodded and smiled as if she was well aware of what Verity was thinking.

Randolph introduced her to Alan and Nathaniel. The latter had just arrived and was still in riding dress. As they all moved to the table, Robert mentioned that their wives hadn't accompanied them because one had a new baby at home and the other was about to give birth. Fleetingly, Verity remembered that she'd been angry with Robert the last time they spoke. That emotion seemed long ago and trivial. While soup was placed before them, Sebastian wondered where on the high seas James might be by this time and when their letter might reach him.

Verity had expected a dour mood at the dinner table. She'd imagined they'd all be worried and distracted, and she'd meant to find ways to raise their spirits. She'd often done as much when she and her parents visited bereaved families. Not bereaved, she corrected immediately. And wouldn't be, she prayed.

Instead she found a group as determined as she was to support one another. They said heartening things, offered special dishes to those nearby, and kept their expressions hopeful. Except when they cast anxious sidelong looks at the duke, Verity noticed. She wasn't well acquainted with this impressive gentleman, but even she could see the change in him. His body seemed to have shrunk inside his immaculate clothing. His face was blank. Even when he responded to his sons' remarks, he wasn't really there behind his blue eyes. He ate mechanically, as if fulfilling an onerous duty. Verity felt like an intruder whenever she looked at him.

A servant was sent for Verity's things, with a note explaining the new plan to her mother. Verity was braced for objections, but her valise arrived with a sympathetic note from her parent. Mama had even thought to include some sheet music that Verity had brought with her to London.

Verity unpacked in the bedchamber where she

played. It was both economical and sensible to use the same room. She could nap and rise and play in the night as others slept, and then lie down again. Randolph searched out more of the duchess's favorite pieces, and as the house settled into nocturnal silence, Verity sat down to play them. The first notes rang strangely in the hushed house, even though she was playing quietly. But only a few bars in, she fell into a familiar peace. Music had been her joy and solace, her celebration and consolation, for most of her life. She was glad to offer it up as a healing gift, grateful that she had the ability. Let it do some good, she thought as her fingers moved over the keys. Let it truly help.

In the days that followed, Verity's life took on a dreamlike routine. The outer world receded. She had no idea, and no interest in, what was happening beyond the walls of Langford House. There could be nothing more important than pulling the duchess through this crisis. The London season, and even her mother's visits, seemed part of another existence. Here was only music, and Randolph, who often sat near her as if she was a hearth fire and he desperately needed warmth.

She was playing Mozart in the depth of the night when she heard raised voices from the duchess's room. She paused, listened. Repeated, the cry sounded like a call for help. Verity rose and went to see.

Across the hall, Flora was struggling with the duchess, who was pushing and clawing, seeming determined to get out of bed. "Help me," said Flora.

Verity hurried forward. "Where is the nurse?"

"She went down to the kitchen for more broth. Catch her other side."

Verity moved around the bed and did so. The duchess's flailing arm was unexpectedly strong. It took both Verity's hands to still it.

"Let me go!" cried the older woman, writhing and grimacing. "It is unjust to keep me imprisoned here! I've done nothing wrong."

"Her fever is high all the time now," Flora murmured, gripping the duchess's other arm. "She doesn't know us."

The duchess looked shockingly changed. Her face was sunken, so that the fine bones stood out, and nearly as white as her nightdress. Her blue eyes were wild and vacant. Her beautiful hair escaped a thick braid in untidy tendrils.

"Your Grace," said Flora. "Adele. It's all right. You're home in your own bed. You're ill. You must rest."

"Harpies!" came the reply. "Swooping and screeching and ripping at me with your black talons. It hurts!" She drew up her knees and hunched as if to curl into a ball. The movement set off a cough that racked the older woman's too-slender frame.

Verity met Flora's eyes across the bed. Tears welled in them.

"It's all right," Flora said again. "I know it hurts. You're ill. Lie back now."

Between coughs, the duchess began to moan.

"See if you can give her some barley water," Flora murmured.

Verity let go of the duchess's arm and picked up a glass from the side table. But their patient turned her head away when Verity tried to put it to her lips. She began to cry, and Verity couldn't help weeping along with her.

"It's all right," said Flora, choking back her own tears. She repeated that over and over, and after what seemed like an eternity, the duchess subsided. She fell back on the pillows as if exhausted, but then began picking at the bedclothes. "This is my opal brooch," she said, holding up an imaginary object. "Arthur gave it to me when we were young, but he's abandoned me now in this vile prison. He vowed for better or worse, you know, but he's gone away."

"He was just here," Flora replied. "He wants to stay with you always, but he has to sleep a bit. He'll be back soon."

The duchess's hand dropped. Her eyes closed. She looked desolate, and it tore at Verity's heart.

"She'll be quiet for a while now," Flora whispered. "These…episodes wear her out."

"To see her this way." Verity blinked back her tears. Flora nodded.

The duke appeared in the doorway. He was still dressed in the clothes from dinner, and it was obvious he hadn't slept. He looked wretched. "I felt she needed me," he said. He came in, sat beside the bed, and took his wife's hand. She showed no reaction. The fear in his face was so stark that Verity took a step backward.

"It's very kind of you to play for her," the duke said without looking around. "For us all."

"I'm happy to, sir."

"You have all you need?"

"Yes."

Verity didn't think he heard her. He held the duchess's hand as if it was his whole world, and he could think of nothing else. Verity backed away. Flora moved with her into the corridor. "She's always calmer when he's there," she said. "Even when she appears insensible."

"He loves her so," Verity murmured.

Flora nodded. "I wanted that kind of love. I was so happy when I found it. I didn't quite realize the danger of that kind of pain."

The nurse returned carrying a pot of broth on a tray. With a funny feeling in the pit of her stomach, Verity went back to the pianoforte.

# Seventeen

Randolph tossed and muttered in his bed, fighting a nightmare that seemed to have gone on forever. His mother lay dying, and he was desperate to reach her. In a corridor whose walls moved in and out like an infernal bellows, he ran toward her room—on and on and on. But he couldn't get there. Each time he seemed close, the floor steepened, and he stumbled and clawed and slipped backward. Over and over, he found himself back where he'd started. He was helpless, and time was running out. Unless he could defeat these hellish obstacles, she was doomed.

And then, suddenly, he was at her doorway. She was right inside, wondering that he hadn't come to see her. He could hear her asking why he'd abandoned her, and it drove him nearly mad. But the opening was blocked by a great shadowy figure, arms held out to catch him. Randolph pushed and punched and shouted. After what seemed an eternity, he knocked the creature aside and fell into the chamber.

To find that she was gone. Mama lay perfectly still, hands crossed on her chest, her face waxen and empty.

It was too late. He hadn't been able to do anything; he hadn't been there for the end. Randolph collapsed to his knees by her bed. And then he was looking at Rosalie's face as he'd seen her in her coffin, a doll with all her warm animation stripped away, lost to any farewells he might have made. Desolation ripped at him and pulled him down.

Randolph struggled awake with a gasp, sweating and wild. He panted. For a moment, he didn't know where he was or when it was. Then reality seeped back to him. His mother *was* dying. No, she was only ill. She would *not* die!

He shoved back the twisted bedclothes, stood, and jerked on his dressing gown. Barefoot, he lurched down the hall to his mother's room, still half in the dream. There, by a dim light, he saw his mother, pale and breathing with some difficulty, but not still and dead. He picked up her hand from the coverlet. It was clammy but not cold.

"Randolph?" His father sat on the other side of the bed, shadowed, holding her other hand.

"How is she?" Randolph asked.

"The same."

Tragedy couldn't happen with his father present, or so some young part of Randolph had always thought. Papa's face said that might not be true. An unbearable idea. He backed away from it.

Randolph heard music. He went toward the music. Still disoriented, trying to shake off the dream, he entered the room where Verity played the pianoforte. She looked up, startled, then stiffened and half rose. "What's happened? You look dreadful. Is the duchess…?"

He'd reached a place of refuge; in his dazed state, that was all Randolph knew. "I dreamed she died," he murmured. "Just like Rosalie. I dreamed Mama was dying, and I couldn't get to her room. They wouldn't let me see her, speak to her, tell her I loved her. They kept me out."

"Who are they? Who is Rosalie?"

Randolph scarcely heard her. "A simple inflammation of the lungs, that's what all the doctors said. But it got worse and worse. And they wouldn't let me in her room. We hadn't even had time to announce our engagement, and that foul disease came along and killed her." His fists clenched at his sides.

"Killed who?" Verity asked.

"Rosalie." Randolph felt a reminiscent brush of crushing grief. He began to pace. How small this room was! "Her parents thought it improper for me to be in her bedchamber. Improper! As if I would…as if it mattered by that time. We were to be married, and I wasn't allowed to sit with her! I should have been by her side as she faded out of the world. They were cruel, barbarous! I wouldn't stand for it now. I wouldn't be some obedient *boy*, subsisting on secondhand news and relayed messages. She died without me." And there was the agony again. "If Mama slipped away, and I couldn't reach her…" He put his hands to his head.

"Didn't you look in on your mother just now?" Verity said.

"Yes."

"And she's alive."

"Yes. Yes, she is."

"And no one stopped you."

Letting his hands drop, Randolph shook his head.

"She was a bit better today. Flora said so."

"Did she? Was she?" Randolph blinked and finally came more fully awake.

"The doctor agreed. The duchess took a whole bowl of broth, and she spoke to your papa. She knew him."

Randolph took a deep breath.

"And you can sit with her whenever you like," Verity added. "No one will keep you from her."

"No." Randolph relaxed into a combination of relief and gratitude. How comforting she was. "I shouldn't have come rushing in here half awake. I beg your pardon. Sometimes a nightmare can seem more real than life."

Verity nodded. She sat on the bench before the pianoforte, looking at him. Her blue-green eyes seemed doubtful. Well, of course she was shaken. It was the middle of the night, and he'd burst in on her practically raving. What exactly had he said? The whole incident was fading now, as dreams did on waking. "I'm sorry to have disturbed you."

"You were very upset." It seemed half a question.

"I was." He gave her a rueful smile. "Thank you for listening to me. I don't normally have nightmares."

"These are difficult circumstances."

Randolph only nodded. He didn't want to speak of his mother's illness again. And he wanted to forget the dream. "I'll see you tomorrow." Walking back to his bedchamber, he decided he wouldn't try to sleep any more. Sleep was treacherous. He'd get out the lute.

Verity sat on after Randolph was gone, puzzling over his disjointed confidences. Randolph had been engaged before. Why had he never mentioned this? Why had no one else told her? There was never any shortage of busybodies to share such information. People couldn't resist. "Rosalie," she murmured. Who was this Rosalie who'd died? Randolph had spoken as if she knew, when he must know she didn't. Verity felt a brush of...humiliation?

She began to play again. The music soothed her as well as the others.

A previous engagement didn't matter, of course. It had obviously been some time ago, and Rosalie was gone. Nothing to do with her. But there'd been such anguish in Randolph's face and voice when he spoke of Rosalie. It had sounded as if his feelings were very much alive. Granted, his nightmare had been about his mother. Still.

Verity wasn't jealous. She would not be jealous. She was...unsettled. A situation that she'd regarded in one way was suddenly different. It was like turning and discovering that the ground dropped away a few feet behind your back. There was a moment of dizzy realignment. She'd begun to feel part of the Gresham family, and now she discovered that they'd been keeping secrets from her. Unless they all thought she knew. Which brought her back around to wondering why Randolph had never mentioned this significant piece of information.

She'd ask him, as soon as things were more settled at Langford House. The duchess was getting better, so it wouldn't be much longer. As the crisis began to wane, Verity was more and more conscious of the great many things she and Randolph had to talk about.

The next morning, Verity found herself alone in the breakfast room with Sebastian. Since they took turns sitting with the duchess, no one in the family was keeping regular hours. One never knew who would turn up where, except when they all gathered at dinner.

Oddly, despite his bulk and martial bearing, Sebastian was the most approachable of Randolph's brothers. Or so it seemed to Verity. There always seemed to be a spark of sympathy in his blue eyes. She knew he liked plain speaking, and practiced it himself. So when he smiled a good morning, she made a snap decision and said, "I didn't realize Randolph had been engaged before."

Sebastian stopped loading his plate and gazed at her. "What's that?"

"To Rosalie?"

"Rosalie who?"

Verity passed over this missing piece of information and tried again. "When he was younger."

Sebastian frowned. "How much younger?"

She didn't know that either. "So sad that she died."

"Died? I never heard anything about this. Rosalie, you say?" He shook his head. "Why don't I know?"

Verity wondered if she'd made a mistake. No, Randolph had said *engaged*. He'd said they were to be married. She remembered then that he'd said they never had a chance to announce it. Had he conducted a clandestine courtship? Why? If he had, she'd just exposed the fact, she realized.

"Mama would know," Sebastian said. "Whatever it is. She knows everything." His face shifted, and Verity easily followed his thoughts. The duchess was the font of knowledge except when she was very ill and delirious.

"I may have misunderstood," Verity said. She didn't want to reveal Randolph's secrets, except to herself.

Her large leonine companion examined her. "Randolph seems very fond of you," he said.

The kindness in his tone and the lukewarm nature of the phrase shook Verity. She remembered the emotion vibrating in Randolph's voice last night. She saw again the duke holding the duchess's hand as if it was his only lifeline. The comparison disturbed her.

The turning point came the following night. After another day when the duchess tossed and muttered in her bed, her fever broke in the wee hours, and she fell into a deep natural sleep. Verity didn't hear the news until the doctor confirmed the nurse's opinion when he visited in the morning. "The crisis is past," he told the family group hovering in the hallway. "From now on, the disease will ebb. Her Grace must still take care to eat and rest, of course."

"As if I can do anything but rest," came a hoarse, thready voice from the room. "I've never been so weak in my life."

They rushed to surround the bed. The duchess looked back at them, recognition and intelligence in her eyes once again. She was gaunt and pale, but she smiled. The duke took her hand, turning his back on the rest of them, his head bent.

Randolph understood; his father's feelings were overwhelming. He couldn't let anyone but Mama see.

Randolph sent up silent thanks, in the wake of all the prayers he'd made through his mother's illness. His heart swelled with joy and gratitude, and he saw the same sentiments in the faces of his family. Tears ran down Flora's face; Robert pulled her closer to his side. Nathaniel swallowed and blinked even as he smiled.

Randolph caught Verity's eye. How splendid she'd been through this dreadful time! He tried to put his appreciation into a smile. Sebastian's fist tapped his shoulder, and Randolph turned to meet his brother's grin. The room, and Sebastian in particular, buzzed with celebratory energy. Randolph could tell that even Alan wanted to leap and laugh.

"No rowdy games in the house," the duchess murmured, clearly aware of the bubbling mood.

All the Greshams burst out laughing. "Not even a tug of war in the gallery?" asked Robert in a cajoling voice from their youth.

"Or sliding down the waxed floor," added Sebastian in similar coaxing tones. "Just a race. No flying cricket balls involved."

Their father choked. Randolph couldn't tell if it was a suppressed laugh or a stifled sob. He found he didn't wish to know.

"Only ruined stockings," the duchess answered. "No, not even leapfrog."

Randolph felt like leaping. Normality had been restored after a terrifying interval. Except that Mama looked so very tired.

Dr. Loughton seemed mystified. "Her Grace needs quiet," he said. "I must suggest fewer visitors at one time." He made a herding motion.

As the duke sat down beside the bed, Randolph followed the rest of them out. He saw his father bury his face in the coverlet and his mother rest her hand in his hair. His throat grew tight. If Papa had lost her…but he hadn't. They hadn't. After a period of recuperation, Mama would be the center around which they all revolved once again. With that reassurance, exhaustion hit Randolph like a roundhouse blow. When had he last slept more than a couple of hours? He was dazed with fatigue. He headed back to bed.

Dinner that night was loud. The released tension came flooding out in mock disputes and lively stories. "Remember that Christmas joust we staged in the upper gallery?" Sebastian said. "We were meant to be the flower of chivalry."

"You brought horses into the house?" asked Flora.

"No, no, we three eldest were the steeds." He indicated Nathaniel and Randolph. "We put the younger ones on our shoulders. I got Alan, who had no proper grip on his lance at all."

"I was four," said Alan. "Or so you tell me. I don't remember this one."

"You had Alan because you were the tallest," said Nathaniel.

"We had to handicap the lists," Sebastian agreed. "Nathaniel took James, and Randolph had Robert."

"Who kicked me on the nose," Randolph observed. "It hurt like blazes."

"Excitement of the moment," said Robert. "And we won, didn't we?"

"The final score was never satisfactorily resolved," said Nathaniel.

His eyes twinkled, but Verity noticed that his chin had come up.

"I don't believe I heard about this exploit," said the duke. He looked much better, Verity thought. An improved appetite would soon restore him completely.

"Because we stole cues from the billiard room for our lances," Nathaniel said.

"What?" The older man put down his wineglass. "You might have put someone's eye out. Good lord, how did all six of you survive to adulthood?"

His oldest son nodded. "Now that I am about to be a parent myself, I shudder to think of it."

"The rule was a touch to the chest," muttered Sebastian. "No one was poking at eyes."

"I should hope not," said his father. "But there are such things as accidents."

"Well, we promise never to do it again, Papa," said Robert, his eyes glinting with mischief. "You know best."

"Doubt I could carry Alan for long these days," said Sebastian, half seriously.

The table dissolved in laughter. Sebastian took it good-naturedly.

"I don't know how the duchess did it," Flora said to Verity a little later. The ladies had decided to stay with the festivities in the dining room rather than leave the gentlemen to their port. But people had shifted their seats, and they were now side by side. "Six boys! Every time I think of it, I'm in awe."

Verity nodded. "At least they're more subdued now that they're grown up."

"You think so?" replied Flora with raised eyebrows. "They stranded Nathaniel with nothing but a moth-eaten wolfskin to wear on his wedding day."

"I beg your pardon?"

"You well may. But you heard me correctly."

"Where did they find a wolfskin?"

"This is your first question?" Flora asked with a smile. "Rather than why?"

Verity smiled back. "The reasons…unfolded in my mind. I assumed it was the sort of idiotic prank that men play on one another. The details were the puzzle." Verity looked down the table. It was difficult, and then too easy, to imagine the heir in nothing but a tattered scrap of fur. Yet he was such a dignified, reserved man. "Nathaniel?"

Flora nodded. "I know. My point is, the six glorious Greshams haven't abandoned the habits of their youth. And they have greater ingenuity now, and resources. I took steps to make sure my wedding included no…surprises."

The more she knew Flora, the more she liked her, Verity thought. "How?"

Flora ticked off points with her fingers. "I gave them no warning. I sent Robert for a special license ahead of time, and I made arrangements with the local clergyman when we were all down at Langford for Christmas. One morning, I had my mother gather them up." Flora smirked. "Even though Mama is the kindest person—she's spending three months with her sister right now so that Robert and I can have our house to ourselves—she has a fierce reputation. She… overawed the brothers when they were young, and the effects linger."

"So you had no special gown or wedding breakfast?" Verity wasn't certain she'd have liked that.

"Of course we did. The duchess knew all about it."

"Sebastian said she knows everything about the family," Verity remembered.

Flora nodded. "So I'm just dropping a friendly word in your ear. Take care to manage your own wedding day. Especially as Randolph is a churchman. You wouldn't want the bishop, or whoever officiates, to come upon him naked and draped in flowers on the altar, or something."

Verity choked on shocked laughter. The image was all too vivid, and tempting. But her father's friend the Bishop of Chester would not be amused. As for the *embarrassed* Archbishop of Canterbury, it didn't bear thinking of. "They'd never do that."

"I've learned not to try to predict what they will or won't do. It's easier to limit their scope."

Verity tried to picture her wedding to Randolph. The intimacy they'd shared on the daybed seemed so long ago. They *had* been alone together here, but the duchess's illness had loomed more starkly than any chaperone. And now there was, or wasn't, Rosalie. The future seemed uncertain.

At the other end of the table, an argument erupted over some other past contest. The brothers turned to the duke to referee, and he seemed to enjoy it. The Gresham family wasn't just suitable and eminent, Verity thought. They were fun. Any woman would be glad to join them.

"I shall go home tomorrow," Nathaniel said when the dispute died down. "Thank God I have good news for Violet. She's been so worried." He looked concerned, and Verity remembered that their first child was due soon. "I'm sorry Mama won't be able to come and be with her," he added.

"She will be very sorry, too," the duke said. "But she won't be strong enough." His tone brooked no argument.

"I know."

Violet's own mother wasn't mentioned; Verity didn't know why, though the others seemed to. A new family was an undiscovered country.

"I'll ride with you partway," Alan said.

She'd have to go soon as well, Verity thought. The critical need for music was past. She'd find an opportunity to corner Randolph first, however, and thrash everything out.

A footman came in. "I'm sorry, Your Grace. There's a gentleman who insists—"

Before he could finish, a shorter figure walked in on his heels. "Yes, I beg your pardon," the man said. "I'm sorry to interrupt your meal. But I've come to fetch my daughter."

"Papa," said Verity, rising from her chair.

Randolph stood quickly. The newcomer resembled Verity in the shape of his face and the color of his eyes and hair, though the bright hue of the latter was muted by gray. Mr. Sinclair was a bit pudgy. Randolph and his brothers towered over him, but he had a strong presence nonetheless.

"Get your hat," he said to Verity. "We must go."

"Is something wrong?" she replied.

"Several things. We will discuss them elsewhere."

He looked stern, Randolph thought, and not particularly happy to be here.

"Is Mama all right?" said Verity worriedly.

"Quite all right."

"Won't you have a glass of wine with us?" asked the duke. "Or perhaps, have you eaten?"

"I require nothing, thank you."

Recovering from the surprise of his entry, Randolph stepped forward to greet Verity's father. His response was perfunctory, and the look he gave Randolph was depressingly familiar. The higher up in the church a man was, the more common the censorious gaze.

Verity moved to his side. "Lord Randolph and I are engaged, Papa."

"So I have heard. From a number of people. Though not from my wife and daughter, for some reason." His tone implied that he knew the reason, and deplored it.

"I meant to write to you, but then the duchess fell ill."

"So I was also informed. I was very sorry to hear it."

"She's better," said Randolph. "She's turned the corner." He would never tire of saying it.

"Splendid," the visitor replied. "You've no further need for Verity's…services then."

He made her help sound wrong, or inappropriate at the least.

"She's been wonderful," the duke said. "A real blessing to our family."

The phrase was not one his father usually employed. He was trying to turn Mr. Sinclair up sweet, Randolph thought. A touching but probably futile attempt. But to his surprise, it appeared to have an effect. Mr. Sinclair smiled and said, "As she is to ours."

"Won't you join us in a celebratory glass?" the duke repeated.

He didn't specify the celebration. He'd have the fellow toasting their match in a moment, Randolph thought. But he once again was mistaken.

"I'm afraid we must go. Verity."

"Why?" she asked, her chin high.

Mr. Sinclair sighed. "I'd rather speak of this later, at home."

"Chester? I'm not going to Chester."

"Verity. I made my position clear in my letter to you. We must step back and consider your future carefully."

Even as his heart sank, Randolph felt his family gather itself around him. Robert and Alan moved to stand just behind him. On the other side of the table, Sebastian braced as if for a charge. Nathaniel and his father stepped closer to their visitor, the epitome of dignity and power.

"We've watched over Verity very carefully," said Flora. Randolph hadn't realized that she could sound as high-nosed and imposing as her ferocious mother.

"My future is settled," Verity declared. "As far as my engagement goes, that is."

"Is there some problem?" asked Randolph's father.

Mr. Sinclair sighed again. But he didn't look cowed. "I protest at being forced to speak in this way. But I do not approve of the match."

Surprise showed in expressions around the room.

"You have an objection to my son?" Randolph's father asked, every inch a duke all at once.

"Not personally, exactly," Mr. Sinclair answered. "I'm sure he's a pleasant enough young man. But his judgment appears to be flawed. I will say no more on that score. Except that I won't wed my daughter to a man who has spoiled his prospects and is doomed to a meaningless position on the sidelines of his profession."

"Papa!"

"Randolph?" exclaimed Sebastian at the same moment. "Are you sure you have the right man? Haven't mistaken him for someone else?"

"Surely this is an exaggeration of the circumstances?" the duke said.

His temper rising, Randolph watched his brothers try to puzzle out the situation. No one looked surprised at their father's superior knowledge. Papa generally knew what was what.

Mr. Sinclair was shaking his head. "With respect, Your Grace, you aren't privy to the inner workings of the church."

"He ought to have changed out of the white," Randolph said. "If he hadn't been hurrying to go, he'd have—"

"Weak men blame others for their failings," the older man interrupted, as if stating an invariable truth. Randolph suppressed a paradoxical desire to shake some charity into him. "Come, Verity. We're going now," Mr. Sinclair added.

"What if I won't? You can't make me."

Randolph had never heard his intended sound

so rebellious, or so young. Her expression warmed his heart.

"You intend to make your home here?" was the dry reply.

"You would be welcome to stay with us," said Flora.

"I'm sure the gossips will find that curious."

He wasn't threatening, Randolph acknowledged. Spreading tales was obviously beneath Mr. Sinclair. The tittle-tattle would happen on its own.

Verity stood very straight, her hands in fists at her sides, her magnificent bosom rising and falling rapidly. She looked like Boudica facing down the Roman invaders. "Very well, I'll go with you," she said finally. "I have a good deal to say to you. I won't change my mind, however." She marched from the room.

Her father followed. The duke went with him. He meant to give Mr. Sinclair the most ceremonious of farewells, Randolph realized. He doubted it would matter.

"What was that about?" asked Sebastian. "I didn't quite get it."

"You are not alone," answered Robert. "Randolph?"

All his brothers looked at him.

"I wish Georgina was here," Sebastian said. "She'd explain it."

"I'm not sure even she could do so," replied Nathaniel. "Shall I postpone my departure for a few days, Randolph?"

"There's no need for that. Please don't." If—when—he told his brothers the story of the archbishop and the ram, they'd fall about laughing, Randolph thought. Even Nathaniel. At first. And he wouldn't blame them. At this moment, however, it was hard to see the humor in his situation.

# Eighteen

Seething, Verity endured the short ride back to her lodgings. Protests wanted to burst out of her, but she wouldn't begin in a hack. She intended to prevail, and that meant no useless rants.

Up until now, Verity's rebellions had been silent and secret. Her longing for adventure and a life far different from her parents' steady round had manifested through books and quiet practice and her plan for London. She hadn't indulged in fruitless complaints or grand pronouncements. But she was done with discretion now. She was going to fight for what she wanted, and she wanted Randolph.

How gratifying it would be, she thought, to snatch up a sword, as he'd done at Rochford's, and slash her way through obstacles. Such violent physical activity must be a great relief to the feelings. Not that she'd actually wound anyone. But to astonish and terrify—that would be splendid. As soon as matters were set straight, she'd ask Randolph to teach her fencing. The idea took fire in her mind. His lessons would be delightful in so many ways.

Verity remembered the duchess's remark about finding adventures all around her. Fencing with Randolph should qualify. And other activities—with Randolph. Squashing her father's objections was another example, she supposed, though far less appealing.

"You know, Verity, your welfare is always my foremost consideration," said her father.

She knew that he thought so. And she had contrary arguments. Which he would hear when she was ready. He gave her an uneasy sidelong glance. Good!

The cab pulled up before the house. Verity got out and knocked as her father paid the driver. The landlady's maid admitted them, and they walked up the stairs side by side. But not together, Verity thought.

Their set of rooms seemed quiet and unpopulated after her stay at Langford House. Mama had made their London dwelling as much like her quiet spot in Chester as she could. However, the version of her mother waiting for them was not that bookish lady. "So!" she said, standing as they walked in. Her eyes snapped with anger. "Here is my dear family, who conspired to keep me in the dark."

"There was no conspiracy," said Verity's father.

Not a good tack to take, Verity thought.

Mama pointed at him, a vulgar gesture that was unlike her. "*You* had concerns that you chose to keep from me when we came down to London." She swiveled to point at Verity. "*You* were told of them and said nothing." She turned back. "As to *why* Verity was informed and I was not, that is a mystery."

"I trusted her to behave properly, and I saw no reason—"

"No *reason*!"

Papa really was botching this, Verity thought. Had he never noticed how that slightly pompous tone always irritated Mama? Didn't he see how her lips had tightened? Verity left him to it. Her task might be easier if they were at odds. Perhaps she could play them off against each other. That was a calculation she'd never made before. The Sinclair household avoided disputes. Indeed, any displays of strong emotion were characterized as vulgar and lower class. Verity realized she was glad to see her parents aflame.

"No *reason* to tell me, or consult me," her mother continued. "Thank you very much."

"The story isn't fit for female ears," her father attempted. He didn't *whine*, Verity thought. It was more of an aggrieved grumble.

"Bosh!"

"Molly!"

She couldn't be distracted by this new version of her parents, fascinating as it was. She had things to accomplish. "Enough!" said Verity. "Just tell me, now, what Randolph did to the Archbishop of Canterbury."

"He didn't do it himself," replied her father, looking shocked.

"Whoever did it, whatever it was, I will know. At once."

"It's improper," he murmured.

"Stephen!" said her mother.

Verity pulled off her bonnet and threw it on a side table. It bounced and fell off the other side. The gesture was a mild relief. She did the same with her pelisse, purposely crumpling it before she threw.

"Embarrassing, improper, scandalous… I don't care. Tell me or I'll go up to Canterbury and ask the archbishop myself." She'd rather like to do that, she realized. She longed for action.

"What has that man done to you, Verity?" replied her father. "You were so sweet and mild before you became embroiled with him."

"I was silent, Papa. That's not the same as sweet. And those days are over." Did her mother look approving? Did she have an ally? "Tell us the story," Verity finished.

Her father gave a low grumble, like an angry bear. He paced, then sat on the sofa. "It happened up North."

"In Randolph's parish in Northumberland?" Verity asked when it seemed her father wouldn't go on.

"Right. At a Christmas pageant."

"The archbishop attended?" Verity prompted. It was odd for the chief prelate to be so far from home at that time of year, but she wasn't going to distract her father with questions.

"He was in the area. Some favor for a noble family, I believe."

"And so, at the pageant."

Her father spoke in a rush. "Some irreverent jokester had put a ram in the manger instead of a lamb. And the creature assaulted the archbishop."

"That's it?" Verity had imagined so much worse—quite wild scandals in fact. She was actually disappointed.

"Knocked him down?" said her mother, as if she was thinking something similar.

"No." Papa sighed, looking resigned. "The ram mistook His Grace's white vestments for a ewe. He was bent over, speaking to a child, I believe. And the ram...addressed himself to the archbishop's...hindquarters." Under the stares of his wife and daughter, he added, "There. I've told you. Let us not speak of it again."

Verity's mother choked. On a laugh? Verity wasn't sure. She'd figure it out, as soon as she could stop thinking of rams she'd seen among the flocks near Chester. And the high-nosed archbishop. "So, well, of course they pulled the ram off."

"Eventually," said her father. "But the incident was not only deeply humiliating, it was dangerous."

"And *not* Randolph's fault," Verity said. "He didn't bring in the ram. I'm sure he knew nothing about it. It's unfair to blame him for the stupid prank of a parishioner."

"When he learned the archbishop would be attending, he should have checked every element of the arrangements," her father said. "*I* would have. And discovered the ram, too. And gotten rid of it well ahead of time." There was no doubt in his voice.

"Even when you were in your first parish?"

"At any time."

Silently, Verity admitted that he was probably right. Papa was a stickler for detail. "It was just a silly accident," she tried.

"Which became a scurrilous jest. You don't know what it's like to stand before a congregation and preach to them, Verity. If a churchman is to help people, he must be listened to and heeded. And for that, he requires respect. Not sniggering whispers behind dirty hands."

Verity could see how fervently Papa believed this. The archbishop must feel it far more keenly. She might have argued that a hearty laugh over the ram, even telling the story on himself, could have dissipated the effect. But she didn't think the point would weigh with Papa. Anyway, it was too late for that. "This was years ago, wasn't it? What about forgiveness?"

"I'm sure the archbishop has forgiven Lord Randolph."

"But not forgotten, eh?" said Verity's mother.

"I would say, rather, that His Grace formed a judgment of Lord Randolph's character and feels that he's not a person to trust with heavy responsibilities."

"You mean he'll never allow Randolph to advance in the church," Verity said. Having lived in a cathedral close for much of her youth, she knew that the church hierarchy encompassed all the emotions seen among the laity. There were politics. Revenge was not unknown, despite the scriptures.

Papa acknowledged her point with a nod. "So you see why he isn't the husband for you."

Verity had so much to say about this that words crowded her tongue and stopped it.

And then her father startled her by adding, "I'm well aware that you don't want to spend your life in a country parish, Verity, or even a provincial deanery."

"You are?"

"My dear girl, what demure miss spends all her free time buried in Cook's voyages, or throwing kitchen knives at a defenseless log?"

"I didn't think you noticed."

"When we had to call on the knife sharpener every month?" Her mother looked amused. "But Stephen, has anyone tried to fix this? Lord Randolph is the son of a duke."

"I'm sure he's done what he can. And failed, demonstrably."

But had he? Verity wondered. She needed to find out.

"Couldn't you speak to the archbishop?" her mother added. "You have a respected position."

"I have it because I know when to intervene and when to keep out of a matter."

"You won't then?" Verity asked.

"I'm not acquainted with the young man. I can't vouch for him."

"Even if I tell you he's a truly admirable person?"

"I can see that he's earned your regard. But this is a decision for your whole life, Verity. And you are choosing the very thing you wished to escape. There are many other estimable young men in London."

He was right, and completely wrong. "You think if...*when* I marry Randolph, it will reduce your credit with the archbishop," Verity accused.

Her father drew himself up. "No such thing!"

But Verity glimpsed a hint of guilt in his eyes. Before she could mention it, or decide it was kinder not to, the housemaid came in. "Miss Townsend," she announced.

"She's called each day to see how things go on," Verity's mother murmured. "The Townsends invited me to dinner, too."

Verity was touched, and a bit surprised, to hear it.

"You're home again," Olivia exclaimed when she entered. "Splendid."

"The duchess is much better."

"That's splendid, too." She plumped down on the sofa.

Verity introduced her father. Olivia gave him a brilliant smile. "You can't think how I've missed your company, Verity," she went on. She seemed perfectly sincere. "You will come with me to the Randalls' rout party?"

It was only half a question. Verity agreed before either of her parents could speak. She needed to get out and talk to Randolph. And others perhaps; she had to think and make a list.

"Oh good." Olivia chattered on about all that had happened since Verity entered what she insisted upon calling *seclusion* at Langford House. After a bit, though, she appeared to sense the fraught atmosphere among the Sinclairs. Dropping curious looks and airy farewells, she took her leave.

"A vivacious young lady," said Verity's father when she was gone. "Townsend. Is she the daughter of Mr. Peter Townsend? The one who endowed all the new windows at Saint Anselm's?"

"He might have. He's quite rich," Verity said.

"Doesn't *he* have a son?" was the plaintive reply.

"He's some sort of merchant," said Verity's mother.

"Hoity-toity. Your grand relative the Duke of Rutland didn't think a great deal of me when we met."

Verity blinked. She'd never heard of this before.

"The party tonight," her father continued. "Are you likely to meet Lord Randolph there?"

"I hope so!"

"Perhaps it would be better not to go then. Until matters are—"

"They are settled," Verity interrupted. "And I promised Olivia." She was going, if she had to climb out her bedroom window.

"Well, you are not to—"

"What?" It was rude to break in, but Verity was wild with impatience. "All the world knows I'm engaged to Randolph."

"That is very awkward."

And was going to become much more so before they were done, Verity thought.

---

That evening, rejoining the festivities of the season, Verity found the party a bit…repetitive. She felt as if she'd returned from another country and found that society had changed. It wasn't the endless round of variety and excitement she'd imagined when she'd begged to come to town. And thought she'd found when she arrived. That seemed so long ago now.

Many people approached her to ask about the duchess's illness, and some of them seemed genuinely concerned. Others treated her recovery like another bit of gossip, collected to fill time at a morning call. Verity wondered if these latter individuals would have spoken in the same curious tones if Her Grace had died. And then she was shocked at herself. Fortunately, Olivia pulled her away from this languid question and out of her unsettling reflections.

"I'm so glad you're back," her friend said. "I've had *no one* to talk to."

Verity gestured at the chattering crowd.

"No one interesting," Olivia amended.

"I don't know how interesting I am tonight." Verity could think of nothing but Randolph and when she might talk to him.

"You've worn yourself out nursing your almost mother-in-law," said Olivia. "How tedious it must have been."

"I wasn't really nursing. Mostly, I—"

"Listen, I've heard the most delicious on-dit," Olivia interrupted. "Charles Wrentham has challenged Mr. Rochford to a duel."

"What?"

Olivia nodded, her eyes sparkling.

"Why? Isn't dueling illegal?"

"Yes." Olivia waved this consideration aside. "As to why, I believe he might have heard some garbled story about a young lady visiting Rochford's house. Alone. In the evening."

Verity's blood seemed to freeze in her veins. "Olivia, you didn't!"

"You know I didn't. Quite improper." She giggled.

"I *mean*, you didn't tell Mr. Wrentham that it was Frances." Too late, Verity realized that her phrasing implied a young lady *had* visited, and she knew about it.

"Of course not. I'm not so inept. Or untruthful." Olivia practically wriggled with glee. "I was angry at the time, not to go. But this is so much better."

"You *arranged* for Mr. Wrentham to hear the tale. The lie."

"I may have let fall a bit of encouragement, here and there," was the airy reply.

"And if they kill each other?" Verity asked. Her mind was still awhirl.

"Nonsense. How stuffy you're being. One of them will nick the other with a sword point, and that will be that."

"How do you know it's to be swords?" A memory of Randolph slashing at Rochford rose vividly in her mind.

Olivia looked sly. "I've been cultivating Mr. Wrentham's second. Lord Carrick. I met him at Salbridge in the autumn. A very *dramatic* young man." She laughed. "Isn't it exciting?"

"It's dreadful, Olivia. You must speak to someone, this Carrick perhaps. Tell the truth and stop the duel from happening."

"Are you mad? I'm going to find out where they're meeting and sneak out to watch. Lord Carrick will tell me where, eventually."

"Then I'll have to do it," Verity replied. She didn't like the idea. She was barely acquainted with Mr. Wrentham, but from what she'd seen he wasn't one to listen. As for Mr. Rochford, if he'd been challenged, perhaps insulted, he wouldn't draw back. Indeed, he was probably as thrilled as Olivia at the outing.

"I'll never forgive you if you do," Olivia declared. Her eyes snapped with annoyance. "Why would you ruin all the fun? *And* expose me to scandal."

"I wouldn't mention you."

"Indeed? What *truth* would you share then?"

That was the crucial question. Verity wondered if

she'd be obliged to confess her own visit to Rochford. "When is this duel?"

"I shan't tell you. Indeed I'm sorry now that I mentioned it at all."

"Olivia, you must see that this isn't—"

"I *see* that you've become a grandiose Gresham before you're even married," Olivia said.

"I'm not grandiose. Neither are they."

"Oh, Verity," Olivia answered with exaggerated patience. "It's just wit."

"Wit is striking because it's so true. That wasn't."

"How priggish you've become." Her expression hardened. "So you insist on being serious, I see. Very well. *Seriously*, it isn't wise to cross me, Verity. If you interfere with my amusements, I'll make certain you regret it." She walked away.

Verity stood alone in the noisy room and considered adventures. It was easier to read about them than to participate, she acknowledged. Books told of slogging through leech-ridden swamps, subsisting on maggot-infested ship's biscuit, and fighting off hostile man and beast, yes. But one could read right over those bits and on to the triumphs. Also, the narrators hadn't paid nearly enough heed to the human element, she thought resentfully. It seemed to Verity that *people* complicated everything one tried to do. Not that she was giving up. She scanned the room. She wanted Randolph—to tell him, to consult with him. Which was a good sign, wasn't it?

She didn't see him. Lord Robert was standing on the other side of the chamber, however. Verity walked over to him. "Good evening."

He greeted her more gravely than usual.

Verity had no time for subtleties. "Is Randolph coming tonight?"

"If he'd imagined you'd be here, I'm sure he would have," Lord Robert said. "I believe he thought you'd be locked away in a tower or some such thing."

"This isn't a fairy tale," she replied. She saw the irony—that she should be the prosaic one—and dismissed it. "Will you give him a message for me?" This was better than trying to send a note under her father's eye.

"Of course." Lord Robert looked amenable, and curious.

"Tell him I know about the ram."

"The… Did you say *ram*?"

"Yes."

"As in a male sheep?"

So he didn't know about Randolph's problem with the archbishop, Verity concluded. Well, *she* wasn't going to tell him. "Yes. And I must talk to him as soon as possible."

"About the ram?"

"Among other things. Quite a few other things."

"I'm sure he'll call on you first thing."

"That won't work." Papa would hover. "Tell him to meet me in the park outside Gunter's, where we had the ices, at eleven."

"At your service," replied Lord Robert dryly. "Is there a secret password?"

"Matters are snarled enough without sarcasm," Verity said.

"So they are." He hesitated, then added, "Randolph takes things hard. He's always been that way."

Verity liked Randolph's family. Very much. But Lord Robert could be just a bit irritating. "Things like an engagement?"

"That seems to be good for him."

Verity thought of repeating *seems* in a caustic tone. But it was always wise—intellectually frugal—to use the opportunities you were given. "What about the other time?"

"I beg your pardon?"

"The other engagement," she said.

Lord Robert gazed at her, one auburn brow raised. "Whose?" He looked only inquiring, a bit confused.

She might as well make the final throw, Verity decided. "Rosalie's?"

He cocked his head as if reviewing a store of information. "I don't believe I know any young lady named Rosalie. Is she a friend of yours?"

There was no trace of deception in his face. So he was no help. Verity shifted impatiently, wondering if this evening would ever end.

The crowd of chattering guests shifted, and she saw Georgina and Emma through a gap. Lord Sebastian's wife was as beautiful as ever, but Emma looked positively radiant. Verity had never seen her appear so happy.

"Interesting," Lord Robert said.

"What?"

"Lady Emma's new glow. We must go and investigate."

"You notice such things?" So how could he have missed his brother's youthful attachment?

"A pink of the ton knows all," replied Lord Robert

lightly. "It is part of our...compelling appeal. So I have to make sure that I do."

"Know all?"

"Precisely."

"But no one can, can they? *All* is far too big." They moved toward the Stane ladies.

"Very perceptive, Miss Sinclair. A great deal of it is sleight of hand. Or sleight of mind, I should say." He seemed to be amusing himself. "Switch ideas so adroitly that people don't even notice they've been diverted. Better yet, make them laugh."

Emma did when they joined her, without any ploy from the famous Pink. "I'm going to marry Mr. Lionel Packenham," she told Verity. "He called this morning and made an offer. It was the most romantic thing."

"Ah," said Lord Robert. "Splendid." Having discovered the cause of Emma's glow, he fell into conversation with Georgina. They moved away a little.

Mr. Packenham was the gentleman Olivia had characterized as a wet fish, Verity remembered. The one with such a perfect pedigree and pile of money that he didn't "require a chin." She could picture him. He wasn't handsome, but he had a shy, pleasant smile. "I'm not well acquainted with Mr. Packenham."

Emma nodded. "He doesn't push himself forward. Or foist his opinions on people who aren't the least interested."

This seemed a curious encomium for a bridegroom.

"Indeed, he doesn't *have* a head full of opinions," Emma added.

"And you like that about him?" Verity asked.

"Excessively. He's very kind and...peaceful." She

blinked and nodded. "We are agreed that we shall have a calm, regular life. I will set my own routines. And no one will get me into trouble when I don't even want to do the thing," she finished fiercely.

Verity had never seen Emma so vehement.

"Lionel thinks I'm perfect," she went on. "He said so. He doesn't dismiss me as a less pretty version of Georgina, or stupider and less lively than Hilda. He hasn't even *met* Hilda." She said it triumphantly.

"Of course you aren't those things."

"I'll get up each morning knowing just what will happen," Emma said. "My household will be quiet and ordered and *soothing*."

"You don't think that will be a bit boring?" Verity couldn't help but ask.

"Not in the least! It sounds like…heaven."

And probably a pipe dream, Verity thought. But there was no reason to spoil her friend's mood.

"Also, Lionel is not particularly fond of dogs." Emma spoke as if this was a precious virtue. "Did you know that my mama has twenty-three pugs? She breeds them. We shall have *no* canines, of any kind. Lionel's not interested in history either. Not at all. He would never make a child of his memorize some moldy old saga! He was shocked at the idea that I had to do so. And he thinks, very rightly, that creatures like badgers should be left to gamekeepers."

Rather bewildered, Verity realized that Emma's glow was partly smug satisfaction. She was pleased with herself, with her purposeful acquisition of Mr. Packenham. Verity tried to picture dire encounters between her friend and ravening badgers. Her imagination failed. You never knew about people, she thought. Even the quiet individuals had stories lurking beneath their placid surfaces, and unexpected passions. "I wish you very happy," she said.

"I intend to be. You and Randolph must come and visit us in Somerset. You won't want to bring a dog, will you?"

Unlike Emma, she had no clear picture of her future, Verity thought. It had veered into uncharted territory. "I hadn't thought about it."

"Well, you should," Emma said. "If you want things to be as you wish, you have to think about it. Not just dogs, I mean. Everything."

From an unexpected source came wise advice.

# Nineteen

RANDOLPH SAT IN HIS ROOM HOLDING THE LUTE, BUT not playing. Exhaustion was at the root of this lethargy, he thought. He hadn't slept well for many days. When he was more rested, he'd see what needed to be done. He ought to climb into bed right now in fact, even though it wasn't yet ten. Would he rest any better tonight though? At a knock on the door, he looked up. "Yes?"

His father entered. "Will you come down to the library for a bit?"

Randolph rose and put the instrument aside. "Am I in trouble?"

"Of course not."

He joined his father, and they walked together down the stairs. "When we were called to the library as boys, it usually meant a scold."

"Not in this case" was the reply, accompanied by a rueful smile.

"I usually deserved it," Randolph added. "Or some brother or other did."

In the library, they sat in facing armchairs.

The duke poured glasses of wine and handed one to Randolph. "I thought we might discuss the recent…development."

Irrationally, Randolph felt as he had after some youthful transgression. "I suppose I ought to have expected Mr. Sinclair's objection," he said.

"It's difficult to anticipate idiotic behavior." The duke sipped his wine, deep red in the candlelight. "Unless one is an idiot. Which of course you are not."

Randolph smiled, as he was meant to. But he couldn't agree. "He's right about my position, Papa. My chances of advancement in the church are poor. And Verity doesn't want to spend her life buried in a country parish. It was the very first thing she said to me." Despite everything, he remembered the encounter fondly.

"Her wishes are important to you," the duke said.

"Yes. Naturally." An odd question from a man so devoted to his wife's happiness, Randolph thought.

"I ask only because…if someone wanted an excuse to end an engagement—"

Randolph nearly leaped to his feet. "I do not!"

"Good." His father nodded. "That's settled then. What do you intend to do?"

The fog of exhaustion rolled back in after Randolph's momentary bolt of rebellion. "Call on Mr. Sinclair, I suppose. Perhaps I can talk him 'round. I must say he seemed immoveable—like a type I've met before."

"Rather fond of his own opinions?" put in the duke. "Not susceptible to persuasion?"

Randolph nodded. "But I'll think of something. Whatever I have to do to keep Verity." His mind offered up a flash of memory—clanging saber blades as he beat at Rochford. So gratifying, and impossible.

"I wonder if I might be of help?" asked his father.

An old longing for Papa to make things right warred with Randolph's need for independence. He knew all his brothers felt the conflict. They'd discussed it. At the root was a fierce desire to make their parents proud. "We've always wanted to stand on our own feet."

"You rarely ask me to put my oar in," the older man agreed.

"And *I* would be the one who does," answered Randolph, humiliated. "The one who takes things too hard, who has to be coddled, who can't succeed on his own."

The duke sat up straighter. "My dear boy." He put down his glass and leaned forward to place a light hand on Randolph's knee. "Don't be daft."

"You always told us to take responsibility for our actions," Randolph pointed out.

His father sat back. "I did. When you were children, forming your characters. And look how well you've *all* done. But that never meant you had to stand alone. What more could I ask than to help my sons?"

Randolph's throat tightened. He swallowed to clear it.

"And I've aided your brothers on a number of occasions."

"Really? Which? How?"

The duke smiled appreciatively. "My lips are sealed in that regard. As they will be about your affairs."

"Of course." Still, Randolph's mind bubbled with surmise. Who had it been? James, before he sailed off across the world? Alan had had some dealings with the Prince Regent last year and might well have needed Papa's counsel. Surely not Robert. Or Nathaniel; the heir to the duke was a paragon.

"Shall we take stock?" said his father. His amused look suggested that he knew exactly what Randolph was thinking. "How shall we show Miss Sinclair's father that he's wrong?"

Randolph came back down to Earth with a metaphorical bump. "That's the trouble. He isn't."

"I might argue, but never mind. If you were...reconciled with the archbishop, Mr. Sinclair could have no further objections." The duke's expression grew haughty on the final word, as if he still couldn't quite believe any man would object to a son of his. "What have you done so far, on that front?"

Trying not to feel discouraged, Randolph said, "I apologized, of course. At the time and in a letter afterward."

"This had no effect?"

"I received a chilly response, from the archbishop's secretary."

"A snub then."

Randolph nodded. "I worked very hard to do a good job in my parish."

"And did so, I have no doubt."

"The congregation seemed pleased. My bishop sent a commendatory letter about our support for the poor."

"Did you send a copy to Canterbury?"

"I asked the bishop's offices to do so. I thought it would have a greater effect coming from there."

"And did it?"

"None at all," said Randolph.

"One wouldn't expect our chief prelate to be vindictive," his father mused.

"I don't think that's it. More like...whenever I come to his attention, his mind shies away and moves to something else."

"I see. Did you make progress reports? Listing all your successes?"

"No." He'd given up at some point, Randolph realized. He'd liked his parish duties, and he didn't really enjoy remembering the ram either.

"Or enlist friends in the church to sing your praises?"

"No." He should have thought of that. Who could he have asked?

"You're not really a politician, are you?" the duke asked with an understanding smile.

Humiliation hovered over Randolph again, suggesting his brothers would have done better in his situation. Well, no, Sebastian and Robert would have fallen down laughing at the ram. They wouldn't have been able to stop themselves. James, too, probably. Alan would have been more interested in scientific observation of the phenomenon than in placating the archbishop. Randolph perked up. Nathaniel would have done better. He couldn't deny that. But to come second to Nathaniel—not bad. "I did get a new appointment in Derbyshire. I've been wanting to move south, and I thought that was a sign of, er, redemption."

"Perhaps it was. Does Miss Sinclair know about your new parish?"

Randolph nodded.

"I'm sure she'll inform her father then. She looked like a young lady with arguments ready when they left."

That was a cheering thought.

"Shall I make some inquiries about the archbishop?" asked his father.

"What sort of inquiries?"

"Discreet ones."

"I haven't quite gotten over the belief that you can fix anything," Randolph observed.

"Untrue, I fear."

Still, Randolph felt vastly better. Experience said that Papa could do a great deal. There was no more astute ally.

"Together, we can do much though."

"Thank you, Papa."

The duke stood. He rested a hand on Randolph's shoulder. "You should get some sleep."

"So should you."

"We can all rest now." And with that he went to say good night to his providentially well wife.

"What's going on?" she asked when he entered her bedchamber.

"I'm not sure what you—"

"I know there's something," she interrupted. She made an uncharacteristically languid gesture. "I can feel it in the air."

"You need to rest."

"Tell me, and I will."

Giving in, the duke recounted Mr. Sinclair's visit.

"Not approve of Randolph?" she said when he was done. "The cheek!"

Outrage had brought some color back into her face, at least.

"I wonder if he's told Verity about the ram?" she added.

"He said he hadn't had time. He would have been wise to tell her."

"Wise," the duchess repeated thoughtfully. "Has he been wise? I'm not sure what to think about this match."

"You had doubts about Nathaniel's at first," the duke pointed out.

"True. And then Violet...bloomed."

"Like her namesake in the spring," the duke replied with a smile. "You fretted over Robert, too."

"He and Flora spent so much time sniping at each other."

"As they still do. Though I wouldn't call it sniping, precisely. Jousting, perhaps."

"Why do they enjoy it so, I wonder?"

"There's no accounting for tastes. You also questioned Alan's choice, as I recall."

"The very first of our sons to marry." The duchess smiled. "How I could have thought Ariel an adventuress."

"Or James's Kawena a—"

"Yes, yes, you've made your point," she said. "I worried about all of them. Needlessly, as it turned out."

"I would never say that. But it seems we can trust our sons to find their way to happiness."

"None of the others suffered a disappointment like Randolph's. Has he told her about *that*, I wonder?"

"It seems to me that they've done very little talking." They exchanged a warmly amused glance before the duke added. "So he and Miss Sinclair have a good deal to discuss."

"Oh lud, what a conversation. I wonder how it will go."

"I think a…challenging conversation will be quite good for Randolph." The duke saw that he'd surprised his wife, which was curiously satisfying. It seemed he did indeed know a few things about their sons that she didn't.

The duchess sank back on her pillows with a sigh.

"This has tired you out."

"I'm so weary of being tired," she responded fretfully. "How am I to watch over my family when I can't get out of bed? If I were to call on the Sinclairs…"

"Leave it to me," he said.

"*You're* going to call?"

"Not that. But something."

"What will you do?"

"That remains to be seen."

Her worries masterfully assuaged, the duchess relaxed into a doze.

---

Randolph waited for Verity in the park outside Gunter's, under a blustery and threatening sky. He'd slept much better after his talk with his father, and he was ready for action. He was also more than ready to see his betrothed. In a strange way, it seemed an age since they'd met. The days of his mother's illness had run together in an unreal blur, life in abeyance. Now they could move ahead.

She was late. He refused to worry. Her father might

try to prevent her from seeing him, but she wasn't eighteen. And he wasn't a boy who would stand for that sort of interference this time. Still, it was a great relief when he saw her approaching. He felt a smile spread over his face as he walked toward her. He took her hand and kissed it.

She smiled back at him, but looked preoccupied. "We have some problems," she said.

"I intend to call and talk to your father. I'm sure I can convince—"

"There's Papa," Verity agreed. She made a checkmark in the air with one of her gloved fingers. "Then there's a duel we must prevent," she added, miming another. "And there's Rosalie."

Randolph gaped. "What duel?"

"Let's walk. We can go over to Hyde Park."

Randolph would rather have sat down. "The weather's not right," he said. "It's going to rain."

"I need to move," Verity replied in a tone that was almost militant. She grasped his arm and pulled him along at a rapid pace. The wind whipped her skirts around their knees and tried to snatch their hats.

Randolph chose the most sheltered streets, and once at the park, he headed for a path bounded by hedges. The place was nearly empty. Only a few riders braved the gusts. The treetops twisted and swayed.

The wind was a little less on the path. Their headgear seemed safe for the moment, though puffs still made Verity's cloak billow. "What duel?" he repeated then.

Verity nodded. "We should take matters one by one. It's probably good to get the duel out of the way."

"It usually is," replied Randolph dryly. "What are you talking about, Verity?"

"It's Olivia's fault. She's...obsessed with tormenting Mr. Wrentham. And Miss Reynolds."

"I don't understand."

"That's because it's completely nonsensical. Which doesn't mean it isn't serious."

The wind swooped down and caught Randolph's hat brim. He only just saved it from flying away. "Let's go back to Gunter's," he said. They could find shelter there without the complications of family. Surely there would be a nook where they could talk privately. "I'll buy you another strawberry ice."

Verity stopped short and looked at him. "You remember the flavor I had?"

"Of course."

She gazed up at him, her blue-green eyes limpid with emotion. There was no one about. Randolph bent and kissed her.

It was a tender kiss, full of promise. That promise moved toward fulfillment. Randolph revised his plan. They couldn't do this at Gunter's.

Verity drew back a little. Her breath came out on a sigh. "Why must everything be so complicated?"

"Is it really?" No one could stop them from marrying, Randolph thought. Family support was preferable, of course. But surely Verity's father would come 'round eventually.

"Olivia has somehow...connived to make Mr. Wrentham believe that Miss Reynolds visited Mr. Rochford's house. Alone, in the evening."

Randolph took a moment to untangle the names.

"Ah."

"Olivia had her invitation from Rochford, you see, which put the idea in her head. I have no idea how she managed the rest."

"I do see." He saw that they didn't want people thinking about young ladies visiting Rochford. Perhaps investigating. "Wrentham issued a challenge?"

Randolph shook his head. "Sort of thing he would do, the clunch. Just draws more attention to the matter."

Verity nodded. They'd reached the end of the sheltered path, and the wind tugged at her bonnet. Randolph turned them around to walk between the hedges again. He didn't like the state of the sky.

"You'll have to stop them," said Verity. She'd regretfully decided that this part must be up to Randolph. No gentleman would talk to her about a duel, stupidly. And she didn't want to press Olivia for details. Her friend was too clever; she'd be suspicious. "As I understand these matters, you can speak to Mr. Wrentham's second. His name is Lord Carrick."

"Oh lud, not Carrick," said Randolph.

"You know him?" This ought to be good, but it seemed it wasn't.

"I met him at Salbridge in the autumn. He'll make a whole Cheltenham tragedy of the meeting. He's probably hired an orchestra."

Verity frowned. Had she heard him correctly? And was that a distant rumble of thunder? "Orchestra?"

"He likes staging dramas. He was behind a play they put on at the house party. Quite a memorable performance, as it turned out." His smile faded. "I'll never dissuade Carrick from participating in such a scene."

"A duel, with real swords, is not a play."

"I'm well aware."

Their eyes met in a shared memory of the bout at Rochford's. "Well, at least you know him."

"And Wrentham, and Rochford. Have no fear, I'll find a way. There'll be no tattling about late-night visits."

"Good. Now, as for Papa." That was thunder, Verity concluded. But it sounded far away. "He told me about the archbishop's ram."

Randolph's resolute expression became startled, then amused. "Don't let him hear you put it that way."

"I only wish he could. I'm all out of patience with the man."

"You don't think I was careless?"

"It was a silly accident! Years ago, according to Papa."

"Three years."

"Then it is past time for the archbishop to forget about it."

"You are a gem among women," said Randolph.

Verity felt a tremor of pride. "I thought of asking my mother to intercede with the Duke of Rutland. She and the archbishop are both related to him."

"You think he'd help?"

"I'm not well acquainted with him myself, but what harm could it do to ask?"

"A good deal, possibly." Randolph grimaced. "If the duke hasn't heard the story, then approaching him would simply spread it farther."

"Ah. And make the archbishop angrier," Verity said. "I see."

"My father is looking into the matter. I expect he'll come up with something. He always does."

Verity could easily believe this. It was a great relief. "So that leaves only Rosalie," she said in the teeth of a rush of damp wind.

Randolph looked down at her profile. Her tone had changed. "I mentioned Rosalie after that dream, didn't I? I wasn't sure, afterward, precisely what I'd said."

"You did."

"Are you angry?" She sounded terse.

"I'm curious why you hadn't told me you were engaged before."

Still, her tone suggested something sharper. "I would have."

"And yet you didn't."

"I've scarcely thought about Rosalie for years." Which was mostly true, Randolph thought. Recent events had brought his former love back into his consciousness. "And there's scarcely been time. I don't know a great deal about your life."

"We have plenty of time now," she said crisply.

A gust of wind buffeted them. Randolph grabbed his hat again. They didn't actually have much time. Rain was undoubtedly imminent. But he could see she didn't want to hear about that. Best to speak quickly and get her home before it started. "Just after I was ordained, I came down to London for a visit," he began. "I met Rosalie Delacourt at a concert."

"Did you sing with her?" Verity interrupted.

"No." Randolph searched his memory for music they'd shared, and found none. Their time had been so brief. "We were…drawn to each other at once. We became engaged."

"You offered for her, you mean."

"That is the customary procedure." He wasn't an idiot. He didn't tell her how very pretty Rosalie had been, how elfin and delicate. He didn't say he'd thought himself head over heels in love. "And then she fell ill. A virulent fever. And in a matter of weeks, she died." He still felt sadness. That was natural. But it didn't rip at him as it had then.

"Her family wouldn't let you see her," Verity commented.

"I wasn't allowed in her room," he agreed with an inner prick of resentment.

"That must have been terrible."

He gave a curt nod. "It was also six years ago," he finished. "All over long ago. Truly, Verity."

"It didn't sound over when you spoke of her that night."

"Nonsense. Of course it is."

"You seemed anguished," Verity said.

"I was half out of my mind with fear for Mama."

"And Rosalie."

"The dream muddled them up. They do that, you know. Think of the odd dreams you've had. A nightmare is irrational."

"Yes." She didn't sound convinced. "Tell me more about Rosalie."

"There's little else to tell." This seemed a chancy line of conversation.

"What was it like the first moment you met?"

The memory unfolded in Randolph's mind, and he

was briefly caught up by it. "We talked and talked and found we agreed on every important point."

"Every single one? How extraordinary. Are you positive? Or did you talk and she listen?"

She sounded rather tart. Her blue-green eyes bored into Randolph. "What?"

"And did she actually agree? Or did she nod and smile and praise you whenever you made a statement?"

Randolph was taken aback. "You didn't know her."

"I didn't," Verity said. "So very likely I'm being unfair. Tell me one of her opinions with which you agreed."

"What?" he said again. That clap of thunder was louder. They needed to get moving.

"You said you agreed on every important point. I'm interested in one of Rosalie's points."

Randolph tried to remember an occasion when Rosalie had expressed a strong opinion. Such as the determination of his current companion on *their* first meeting—never to marry a country clergyman. He couldn't come up with one. "She was very young," he said. "Her mind would have developed over time."

"I'm sure it would have," answered Verity. "And such development would have promoted idyllic happiness."

She sounded very much like Randolph's dry inner voice, which so often spoke wisdom, however sharp or unwelcome. Perhaps he had set Rosalie up on a pedestal, Randolph thought. Or rather, he'd idealized their story. The truth was, he hadn't really known her. There'd been no time.

Verity was perfectly right, he acknowledged. Rosalie hadn't expressed opinions or done anything in particular. She'd admired him, and that had been enough for his younger self. He'd been a little smug, cocky, stuffed full of fresh learning and great plans. A pretty girl who was eager to praise them was the summit of his desire. There was no telling where their lives would have gone. Very likely Rosalie would have tired of listening, at some point, if her death hadn't destroyed all their possibilities. She'd been a human girl, not a paragon. He would always remember her affectionately, but…

He didn't want a wife who simply listened and agreed, Randolph realized. Not any more—if he ever really had. He wanted a partner full of ideas and passions, who occasionally interrupted him and quite often made him think. Even when he didn't really want to. He wanted someone who contributed to plans for their future, rather than accepting whatever he suggested. He wanted a woman who set him afire with longing. In short, he wanted Verity Sinclair. He loved her as he'd never loved Rosalie, with a man's clear-eyed understanding and wholehearted intensity.

He hadn't said so when he offered. He hadn't understood the depth of his feelings then. He needed to tell her. It was becoming a familiar impulse, the need to tell Verity, to hear what she thought.

"I've made you sad," she said, sounding rather melancholy herself. "I beg your pardon. Of course I know nothing about it." She looked at the ground.

He'd barely even kissed Rosalie, Randolph thought. There'd been a few stolen embraces after their engagement was settled, but those had been nothing like the flash of passion with Verity by the pianoforte, or the ecstasy at Quinn's cottage. And to compare such things was caddish, and he wouldn't do it. He didn't have to. He knew where his priorities lay.

"I'm not usually waspish," said Verity. "I suppose I was...am jealous." She sighed. "How dispiriting."

"I don't think of Rosalie," Randolph repeated. "She's gone. My mind is full of—"

"And yet, what does Shakespeare say? Her 'eternal summer shall not fade.'"

She touched some truth in that—a wispy, nostalgic principle. "For the callow youth I was, perhaps. But as you guessed, that boy thought more of himself than any other. What he called love..." Randolph shrugged. "I don't quite recognize it now. Not since I've become acquainted with you. It's much more... expansive, isn't it? Fiery and challenging and informative and rather all-encompassing, really."

"Love?" murmured Verity.

"I'm not sure why it took me so long to see that I love you with all my heart."

She stared at him. She blinked and swallowed. "I was thinking *exactly* the same thing," she said, wonderment in her voice.

He smiled down at her, joy unfolding many layered inside him. "Well. That's good then."

"Oh, Randolph." She threw herself into his arms.

Jubilantly, he caught her. And here was yet another sort of kiss—this one free and exulting, a promise sealed. How many more were waiting to be discovered? He couldn't wait to find out.

The crack of thunder over their heads seemed a proper punctuation—and much too close. He had to step back. "We need to go. The storm is nearly upon us."

Verity nodded. Hand in hand, they hurried back toward the gate. They were barely halfway there when, with a blinding flash and a splintering crack, lightning struck a tree not twenty feet away. Randolph moved quicker than thought, an arm around Verity's waist, pulling her tight against him. He took a long step and then another. Even as the thunder assaulted them, shaking the very air, he got them behind a stone plinth.

A heavy section of the tree, split off by the lightning, thudded to the ground near where they'd been standing. Branches speared through on either side of the statue above their heads. He held her. She was trembling. He expected he was, too. It was difficult to tell over the beating of his heart.

The skies let loose then, a deluge, pounding on their hats and shoulders, soaking them instantly. Randolph bent his head and held on. Verity clung to him. The fallen half-tree hissed and sputtered.

"I've n-never been so close to a lightning strike," Verity said, her lips inches from his ear.

"Nor I." Water streamed down his coat, her cloak. It dripped off his hat brim onto her neck. "What a fool I was. I knew it was going to rain."

Verity laughed.

When he peered down at her, she laughed harder. He could feel her body shaking with mirth now.

"A nervous reaction," she gasped. "An excess of—"

She dissolved in laughter.

Randolph couldn't help smiling. And then laughing as well. *Rain* was a massive understatement. This was a fluid barrage. A pummeling to follow the volley by tree. It was like standing under a waterfall. His hat was slowly drooping down over his skull. Her bonnet was disintegrating over her bright hair. But they were all right—pressed deliciously together, laughing like lunatics.

Then Verity said, "I suppose we should go on before we catch a chill."

The phrase froze Randolph's blood. The laugher died in his throat. "Come. I must get you home." He guided her back to the path. "I'll find a cab."

Verity picked up her sodden skirts. He kept his arm around her. They rushed together through the rain to the park gate.

Randolph had to step into the street to stop a hansom cab. "Ye'll soak the seats," the driver objected, hunched under a hooded cloak. "No one else'll want to ride."

"You have a blanket," Randolph said. He could see it from where he stood. "We'll spread it out and sit on it." He'd rather have put it over Verity, but getting the ride was more important.

"Well—"

"And I'll give you a guinea extra."

This won the driver over. Randolph hastily unfolded the blanket and helped Verity into the vehicle. He gave the man the address and joined her. She nestled against him. "You're cold," he said.

"So are you." She slipped her arms around him and rested her head on his chest.

Randolph forgot the chill. Indeed, he was much warmer. He had a sudden flash of the two of them, in this cozy position, over and over down the years to come, right into old age. The idea touched him to the heart.

In a few minutes, the cab pulled up before the door of Verity's lodgings, and Randolph handed her down. "You must go home," she said when the maid opened the door and began exclaiming over their bedraggled state. "And get out of those clothes."

If only they could do so together, Randolph thought. He'd be more than happy to help her out of that wet gown and set of stays, and untie her laces as he had at Quinn's cottage. He could almost feel the cloth under his fingers. But that was impossible. For now. *Soon, soon.* He bowed and climbed back into the cab.

# Twenty

At Langford House, Randolph squelched up to his bedchamber and changed into dry clothes. He went out again immediately, into the abating rain, and paid a visit to Angelo's. Wrentham wasn't at the fencing academy. Randolph hadn't really expected him to be. But there were rumors of a duel floating about the place, as Randolph had anticipated. Here and at the clubs, that sort of gossip would be rife. No one seemed to have specifics, at least. Not yet. He was able to procure Charles Wrentham's London address, but no word of Carrick. Going on to White's, he discovered that the latter had lodgings in Duke Street.

Randolph went directly there, impatient with the obstacles being thrown up before him. He wanted to marry; Verity wanted the same. Why must things be so complicated?

Lord Carrick was not at home. Nor was Mr. Wrentham when Randolph tried at his rooms a little later. It was vastly frustrating. Fierce in his desire to have Verity, Randolph wanted to shake sense into both of them until this idiotic idea of a duel rattled out their ears. And then do the same to the ram-obsessed Archbishop of Canterbury.

Which would be conduct unbecoming to his profession, Randolph thought as he turned for home. Of course he'd never *do* it. But he could *imagine* how satisfying it might feel.

Back at home, he found that his mother had heard about the sodden pile of clothing he'd left on his bedroom hearth. She made an unusual fuss about his soaking and insisted he wrap up in a blanket and drink hot tea at her side before an early bedtime. The entire household had developed a sensitivity about chills. Randolph would have objected, if he hadn't already sent a note to Verity to make certain she was unaffected by their drenching.

The next morning, Randolph was up betimes and in Duke Street right after breakfast. He sent up his card at Lord Carrick's lodgings and was asked upstairs. Fortunately, as a churchman, he was used to calling on near strangers, not that a parson was wanted in this case.

Carrick was as Randolph remembered him, a handsome young man—not tall but well-set-up, with regular features and reddish hair nearly the color of Robert's. His ivy-green eyes looked mystified just now. "We met at Salbridge last autumn," Randolph reminded him. "When I came over to see my brother Robert."

"Oh yes." It wasn't clear that Carrick remembered Randolph.

"And your play."

Carrick stiffened. His eyebrows drew together.

Shouldn't have mentioned the play, Randolph acknowledged silently. Not the way it had turned out.

Chatting was no good—too many potential pitfalls. "There's no sense beating about the bush," he said. "I came to talk to you about the duel."

"Ah." Carrick's expression cleared. "You want to attend? I'm afraid I can't accommodate you. It's becoming rather a crowd. Which won't do at such an occasion, you know." He smiled.

Randolph's spirits sank. Carrick's excitement and enthusiasm and heedlessness were all in that smile. He wasn't going to be helpful. "It *is* being talked about. No one's sharing the cause, I hope."

Carrick looked haughty. "The honor of a young lady is involved. Of course the reason will not be divulged."

Which pretty much guaranteed it would be, Randolph thought. And who used a word like *divulged* in normal conversation?

"There's a good deal of speculation of course," Carrick added. "But naturally my lips are sealed." He was the picture of smug satisfaction.

Rochford trailed a string of dalliances, Randolph thought. There was no reason for anyone to think of Verity, or associate her with any of the parties to the duel. But people would be chattering and trying to dig up dirt. Randolph didn't trust Rochford's valet to resist bribery. And there was Miss Reynolds to think of, too. No one seemed to be considering her. Who else knew the details of this ridiculous dispute? "How did the challenge go down?" he asked, pretending to be the sort of fellow who relished such details.

"It was at Easton's," replied Carrick, naming one of London's gaming hells. "Rochford was playing vingt-et-un. Devilish high stakes, too. Charles found him there and issued his challenge, complete with a glove. He said Rochford looked dumbfounded to be brought to book. I must say, I never would have thought it of Miss… But no more on that score." He put his finger to his lips, his eyes dancing.

Yes, the whole rigmarole would be out before long, Randolph thought. Carrick put a good story above all else; he wouldn't be able to resist. They scarcely knew each other, and he'd nearly let Miss Reynolds's name slip. How must he speak to his cronies? Randolph felt a flash of irritation—at Carrick and his smirks, at Miss Olivia Townsend. Sneaking mischief and malice could do more damage than outright attack. He'd seen it before. But it did no good to get angry. "I called to ask you to quash the meeting," he said without much hope. "Won't you urge Wrentham to call it off?"

"Why would I do that?" Carrick seemed genuinely perplexed.

"Dueling is never wise," Randolph tried. "Beyond the danger, it simply draws more attention to the… cause. People who knew nothing about it start trying to guess."

Carrick shrugged. Clearly Miss Reynolds's reputation was of little interest to him. "You're a clergyman, aren't you? I forgot. I suppose you have to be a wet blanket."

Rather than a childish care-for-nobody, Randolph thought, fuming. "Dueling is illegal," he pointed out.

"You wouldn't lay information?" Carrick glared at him. "You may be a parson, but you're also the son of a duke. You wouldn't peach on us."

Were they schoolboys talking of stolen cakes? But Randolph didn't want to involve the magistrates. That would spread the story even further.

He gave up on Carrick. He would try Wrentham himself next, though after their encounter at Angelo's, Randolph had little hope that hotheaded young man would listen. Perhaps Rochford? It was more difficult for the challenged man to draw back, especially with two idiots like Carrick and Wrentham likely to crow and call him a coward. Still, he would try. He looked for a hack.

~

At that same moment, Verity was being admitted to Langford House to inquire about the duchess's progress. She'd chosen a time when her parents were out and told the servants only that she had an errand to do. The landlady's footman who accompanied her through the streets wasn't privy to her father's objections. And if she should encounter Randolph and spend some time alone with him, who would know? Verity hugged their last conversation to her chest, where it hummed like a favorite love song. It was a moment that would always be the most cherished of her collection.

There was no sign of her betrothed when she arrived, however, and for now, she was the only visitor. The duchess was propped up on a stack of pillows eating a nourishing egg custard. "You look better," said Verity as she sat down beside the bed.

"I must have looked positively ghastly before then," the older woman replied with a smile.

Verity remembered the duchess's terrible delirium. She thrust the picture away.

"I'm very happy to *be* better," the duchess continued. "And grateful. But I've discovered the unique frustration of being more than ready to get up while unable to do so." She examined Verity. "And how are you?"

Verity felt her smile broaden until it was more like a grin. She couldn't help it. She wanted to shout her happiness from the rooftops. "I'm quite well."

"You look it." The duchess put her empty dish aside. "Brighter than I've ever seen you. Did you and Randolph have a good talk?"

"You know about that?" Verity was surprised. And then she wasn't. Randolph's parents seemed to specialize in omniscience.

"His father thought it was in the wind."

"Well, we did." The phrase *love you with all my heart* echoed in Verity's brain. She was still grinning, she realized.

The older woman examined her face. Verity felt she was being weighed by a compassionate but demanding intellect. What was the duchess looking for? "So you know about—"

"The archbishop and the ram," Verity answered.

"Heavens, it sounds like an Aesop's fable." The duchess waited.

"And Rosalie. Why was she such a secret?" Verity's curiosity stirred. "Sebastian doesn't know about her. Nor Robert. I asked them."

"Did you?" The older woman shrugged. "Not a secret really. Randolph simply enjoyed keeping the matter private."

"You knew the whole time though."

"I did."

"Randolph thinks you know everything."

"It's a useful illusion for a mother of six boys." The duchess paused, then said, "You don't care that Randolph was engaged before?"

"Of course. Who wouldn't?"

"A young lady marrying for position or convenience or convention."

Verity flushed. Fleetingly, she feared that Randolph had told the duchess about their indiscretion at Quinn's cottage. But in the next instant she was certain he hadn't. "I'm not doing that." The duchess was watching her. It felt like a test, and an opportunity. Verity spoke in a rush. "I love him so much!"

The reaction was gratifying. The older woman slowly smiled at Verity, a warm, delighted smile. "That makes all easier, and occasionally harder."

"All?"

"You haven't asked for my advice," the duchess said slowly.

"Yes, I have. Now."

She laughed. "Well, I will tell you this: not talking openly can ruin a marriage. Or a family. I've seen numerous examples during my life."

"What if the other person won't talk?" Verity asked, interested.

"That is…unfortunate. But as we're speaking of Randolph, I don't think you need to worry. He's the most introspective and…sensitive of my sons."

Tears suddenly burned in Verity's eyes.

"The two of you haven't had much time for

confidences, have you? I'm afraid my illness got in the way. But the unspoken isn't unheard."

"I can see where Randolph gets his oracular tendency."

The duchess laughed again, but added, "I believe unsaid words pile up and push people farther and farther apart. Until, eventually, they become a wall. The forms of life may look the same, but inside all is…distance."

It was a chilling thought. "What you're suggesting sounds rather difficult," Verity commented.

"Oh yes." The duchess raised one eyebrow, just like Lord Robert.

"So I must talk openly, and endure whatever I hear in return. Without saying anything unforgiveable."

"I wouldn't choose the word *endure*." The duchess shook her head. "We all say silly things when we're angry or wounded. A good marriage includes quite a few apologies and a large helping of forgiveness."

"You argue with the duke?"

"Of course. Does this surprise you?"

"You seem so well suited."

"We're strong-willed people with marked moods and opinions. Why would we always agree?"

Verity took this in with considerable relief.

"I want to say again how kind you were to play for me, for us all," the duchess added.

Verity wondered at the abrupt change in tone until a deeper voice said, "Allow me to add my thanks." The duke stood in the doorway. "It was such a kindness. And hard work, I know." He came in and sat on the other side of the bed, taking the duchess's hand.

"I was happy to help." Verity noticed that the duchess looked tired. She'd taken up a good deal of her time. And the air of the room was different now that her husband was present. "I should go," Verity said, rising. The duke and duchess's farewells were warm, but they didn't urge her to stay.

"I'm rather curious to attend a *ton* party," said Verity's father as the family walked into a crowded reception room on Friday evening. "It's been years since I did so, and not often then."

Verity looked around the busy chamber and felt only impatience. Did all adventures have these sagging, frustrating parts where nothing seemed to *happen*? To ask the question was to confirm it, she supposed. Their lack of progress was just maddening. She almost felt she'd rather be dangling from a crumbling cliff face or fighting crocodiles.

Olivia joined them. "There's to be another phrenology exhibition tonight," she said. "I suppose Herr Grossmann's appointments have fallen off, and he's here to drum up more business."

"Indeed," replied Verity's father. "I'm curious to see this fellow. You wrote me about him, Molly."

Verity's mother nodded. "He had a session with Mr. Rochford at one of our first outings, didn't he, Verity? It seems so long ago now."

Excessive politeness had fallen back over the

Sinclair household like an outmoded cloak. It made Verity want to race around the room like a maddened cat, clawing draperies and knocking over vases.

"What do you think of Herr Grossmann's system?" Olivia asked.

Verity's father made a face. "Phrenology is like saying our lives are written in the palms of our hands, or that a person is hot-tempered if she has red hair."

Verity resisted raising a hand to her hair.

"There he is," her mother added.

They all turned to see Herr Grossmann coming in. The plump German gentleman wore his customary frock coat and narrow trousers, his beard bushy below shrewd blue eyes. His gangly young assistant was with him. Michael, Verity recalled. The lad's black hair and pale skin was a marked contrast to his employer. Herr Grossmann offered the crowd a bow and moved on. "He's to set up in one of the side parlors," Olivia said. "We should go and watch. We may not see Herr Grossmann again."

"Why not?" asked Verity.

"The fad for phrenology is fading. Which is too bad. It gives one so many opportunities for raillery."

The four of them followed others into the parlor. As before, Herr Grossmann's cranial diagram sat on an easel. A scatter of gilt chairs stood before it. Verity looked at the image of a man's bare head in profile, and the sections marked out *hope*, *combativeness*, *self-esteem*, *parental love*, *acquisitiveness*, *benevolence*. Herr Grossmann positioned himself beside the single chair next to it. Michael went to stand at the side with his notepad and pencil.

"Oh yes," said Olivia. She darted away.

In a moment she was back with Charles Wrentham, tugging at his arm. She practically dragged him to the chair. His protests were quiet, but obvious.

"Nonsense," said Olivia. "Here, Herr Grossmann. Your first subject of the evening." She gave Mr. Wrentham a shove. He almost tripped. Staggering, he grabbed the back of the chair.

"Very good," said the German. He grasped Mr. Wrentham's elbow and executed a neat twist to seat him. Before the young man could protest further, Grossmann had his fingers in his hair. Mr. Wrentham's jaw tightened.

"I've heard Mr. Wrentham is a dab hand with a sword," said Olivia.

"Olivia!" Verity hissed.

"Hmm," said Herr Grossmann, shifting his fingertips. "I find a marked tendency toward combativeness."

Verity wondered. It seemed that a truly combative man would have fought Olivia off. Or, if he wouldn't contend with a woman, he'd have repulsed the phrenologist.

"The bump of firmness is pronounced," the German continued. He addressed his audience. "This can indicate stubbornness, or it may simply signal a tenacious temperament." His assistant scribbled in his notebook.

"This gentleman is somewhat lacking in eventuality," Herr Grossmann continued. "That is the area of the factual memory. It can also be referred to as the historical faculty."

"Ha!" said a female voice behind Verity. She turned to find that Frances Reynolds had entered behind her. "He can't remember what really happened, you mean."

Verity thought that Charles Wrentham growled. She wasn't close enough to be certain. As Miss Reynolds moved away, Verity felt a pang of guilt. She'd known Olivia was going too far with those two. She'd done nothing to stop Olivia, and now they were all very nearly in the soup. Perhaps she deserved it. But Miss Reynolds didn't. And then Verity had an idea.

The Duke of Langford appeared at her side, and Verity suppressed a start. "Good evening," he said. "What do you think of this system?" He indicated Herr Grossmann.

Verity stole shamelessly from her father. "It's rather like palm reading, isn't it? I don't think it's so easy to discover people's characters."

"I've observed that good palm readers are experts at a kind of Socratic dialogue."

Verity had once felt, talking to the duchess, that she was being evaluated. She had that sense again now. "They ask the questions that give them the information they need to…prognosticate?"

"Exactly." He looked approving.

"I can see how that would work. But Herr Grossmann doesn't ask questions."

"No. I wonder if he has spies?"

"Spies?"

"I haven't paid much attention to the craze for having one's skull examined," the duke went on. "But I suppose a clever man could gather information and gossip in advance, and use them to formulate his *findings*."

"He prefers that his clients make appointments,"

Verity observed. She looked at Michael. Might he be more than a passive recorder? And bribe taker, of course. "But he didn't know who would present themselves tonight."

"True. And research would take him only so far. Beyond that, we remain mysteries to each other."

Verity looked up at him, curious. "Even after many years of...close acquaintanceship?"

He met her gaze. The duke's blue eyes were so like Randolph's in shape and color, and yet so different in their depths. "The mathematicians have a word," he replied. "*Asymptotic*. It describes a thing that approaches another, closer and closer, but never finally reaches it."

"*Asymptotic*," repeated Verity.

"People are like that, I think. We may understand a great deal about someone, but never all. There are always surprises."

This sounded right, Verity thought. As this man so often did. "Which is the fun of life," she concluded.

He smiled at her, and Verity's breath caught. The Duke of Langford's wholehearted smile was blindingly charming. It subsumed the smiles of all his handsome sons, and surpassed them. "You're very welcome to our family, you know," he said. "And we will make sure you get to join us."

Verity found she couldn't speak. She coughed to remind her throat of its proper function. "Th-thank you."

Olivia appeared at Verity's side. "Will you try Herr Grossmann, Your Grace? He's ready for another...subject."

"I believe you almost said *victim*, Miss Townsend."

"I would never be so clumsy."

"Wouldn't you? Ah, there's Conyingham. If you young ladies will excuse me." He gave them an exquisite half bow and walked away.

Olivia watched him go. "You know those tiresome old men who leer at one and say, 'If only I were thirty years younger'?"

"Yes?" replied Verity.

"Well, if only *he* was."

Verity laughed.

They walked together back into the main room. Verity saw Emma deep in conversation with her future husband. They looked happy, and quite unaware of the crowd surrounding them. Then she noticed Frances Reynolds standing against the wall not far away. She was pretending not to look at Charles Wrentham, talking fiercely with a group of friends on the opposite side of the room. The duchess's advice came back to Verity like a branch of candles carried into a dark room. If there'd ever been a pair who needed some plain speaking, it was these two.

Verity searched the busy room. Where was Randolph? She needed Randolph. She finally had a plan.

"Where are you going?" Olivia asked.

"To fix things," Verity replied as she walked away.

# Twenty-one

Half an hour later, following his fiancée's explicit instructions, Randolph caught up with Charles Wrentham in another of the reception rooms. He was moving toward the front door, which wouldn't do. "Heard you had your head examined," Randolph said.

Wrentham snorted. "The fellow's a charlatan. *Eventuality*. What sort of tripe is that?"

"I need to speak to you," said Randolph.

"I'm sorry, it's not convenient." Wrentham lowered his voice. "I'm not going to talk any more about the duel. I told you. I'm carrying through. There's no other choice." He sounded more resigned than pugnacious.

"Not about that," said Randolph. "Something else. Just a few minutes of conversation." He herded Wrentham toward the designated location.

"No. I don't wish to be rude, but I'm leaving. I have an urgent appointment with a bottle of brandy."

"It will still be there if you're a few minutes late," replied Randolph dryly. He didn't understand what Miss Reynolds saw in this young man. But then he didn't know her either. And they'd looked all lovey-dovey when they acted together in the play at Salbridge, he remembered.

"Let me be!" exclaimed Wrentham.

They'd reached a corridor, and there was no one nearby to hear. What was more interesting was that Randolph had caught a despairing note in his companion's tone. Mr. Wrentham was not happy. Why? Randolph steered him left rather than right toward the front entry as he asked, "Is something wrong?"

The younger man bared his teeth and shook a fist. Then his shoulders slumped and his expression shifted from anger into tragedy. "Nothing whatsoever. Except that I can't do anything right," he said. "Everything I try goes ludicrously wrong!"

With a light touch on Wrentham's shoulder, Randolph guided him into the small back parlor that was his goal. Fortunately, it was empty. Still.

"I made a fool of myself over cards at Salbridge," Wrentham continued, seeming not to notice his surroundings. His words came faster, a spate suddenly released. "And now here in London I don't send flowers when I should have. And whose bouquet was it, anyway? I have my suspicions there! Then I'm accused of not turning up for meetings I know nothing about. As if I'd ever leave a lady standing alone. Well, I ask you!"

He looked at Randolph, dark eyes snapping.

"'Course you wouldn't," Randolph replied.

"You can damn well be sure I wouldn't! And then I'm twitted with being timid and dull. Wouldn't dare ride my horse backward through the park, would I? Well, I showed her! Only it wasn't her, seemingly. If

I ever get my hands on the person who sent that message...but that's nothing to the news that she'd been taken in by Rochford, of all men."

He clenched his fists again. Randolph could see that it was no use suggesting this idea was as false as the others he'd listed. Wrentham wasn't listening.

"Lured her with a pack of lies, I expect. Or threw her into a hack and dragged her to his house." He nodded as if this idea was more appealing to him. "I wanted to kill him. I *shall* kill him! He may be a very devil with a rapier, but I'm not so bad myself. Well, you can attest to that."

He glared again. Randolph bit back comments on Wrentham's wild fencing style. Rochford could carve the young man up like a Sunday roast, if he decided to be an idiot.

Wrentham fell onto a sofa, sullen. "And then I'll flee to France and never see my home again and everyone will be sorry."

Where was Verity? Randolph wondered. Another minute and he'd be telling Wrentham he was acting like a schoolboy. He didn't think that was what she had in mind.

Verity was in a nearby room. She'd finally tracked down Frances Reynolds, sitting half hidden by a clump of greenery. "There you are," she said. "Come along."

"Where?"

"With me." She took the younger girl's arm and urged her up and across the room.

"Where?" repeated Miss Reynolds. "What are you doing? We scarcely know each other. Actually, we don't know each other *at all*."

"Something important," Verity replied. She had to slow several times to acknowledge polite greetings, but at last they reached the door and the corridor outside.

There, Miss Reynolds rebelled. She pulled her arm away and stopped. "I won't move another inch until you tell me what's going on," she said.

Verity admired her spirit, even as she wondered where it had been these last few weeks. "An adventure," she said.

"An—"

She hadn't included herself in the plan, Verity realized. That wasn't right. "And a chance to set things straight. With Mr. Wrentham." If Miss Reynolds refused the opportunity, she'd have to let her go.

Speculation followed surprise on the girl's pretty face. She frowned, considered, then gave one nod and followed Verity into the small parlor they'd picked out.

Randolph stood by the door. Mr. Wrentham was sprawled on a sofa looking petulant. He jumped up as they entered and exclaimed, "Miss Reynolds!"

Verity could see why he'd excelled at amateur theatrics. As they'd planned, Randolph moved to shield the entrance and keep everyone else out. Verity took a station in the center of the chamber. "So," she said.

It was all very well to recommend open and frank discussion, Verity thought. The duchess had made it sound like a calm, rational exchange of views leading to perfect understanding. Or perhaps that's what Verity had heard. Now she realized that conflicting feelings would pop up. Probably with yelling. This sort of talk most likely required skill or practice, or both. Which she didn't actually have.

Well, someone had to start. "Right," she said. "Here's the thing. Those flowers? Mr. Wrentham didn't send them. That trick with the horse? Frances had nothing to do with it." Verity hoped to avoid naming Olivia. "I've discovered they were pranks played on you. Both. As was the missed meeting at the museum. Deplorable, unamusing jokes."

"Was Callaghan behind them?" demanded Mr. Wrentham.

Verity didn't know a Callaghan. She avoided distraction. "No."

"And how did *you* find out?"

She evaded that question as well. "My point is... you mustn't let them stand in the way of the strong attachment you obviously feel for each other."

"That doesn't explain Rochford," Mr. Wrentham said. He glowered at Miss Reynolds.

"Who is Rochford?" the latter asked.

"Feigning ignorance won't help you. Everyone's heard you went to visit him. At his house. Alone."

Randolph very much hoped that everyone hadn't yet heard. He started to object.

Miss Reynolds spoke first. "Well then, *everyone* has got the wrong end of the stick." She looked humiliated but resolute. "I don't know a Rochford, and I have certainly never visited him. As if I would do such a thing! How dare you suggest it?"

"False rumor," Verity said. "Another prank."

"Prank!" Wrentham turned on her. "You will tell me who's behind this...persecution. *At once.* And by God, I'll make them eat their filthy, lying—"

"Charles," said Miss Reynolds.

He looked around. His gaze encountered the girl's bright-red face. "Oh, the deuce," he said in a very different tone. "Don't look like that, Frances. I can't bear it."

"Did you hear what Miss Sinclair said? It was a hoax. All these misunderstandings. Someone was playing mean tricks on us."

"Which they will pay for!"

"Is that the important thing? Is that what you wish to talk to me about?"

Miss Reynolds appeared to have a knack for open discussion, Verity noted.

"Have you nothing else to say to me?" she added, blinking back tears.

"No, Frances, dash it. Don't cry. You know I love you. Have since the play."

"Do I?" She swallowed. "You said you didn't even remember how it was in Salbridge."

"Well, I was angry. And I'm an idiot." Wrentham let out a great sigh and shook his head. "Things just seem to pile up and drive me distracted. I couldn't get any of them right. Will you marry me anyway? Even though I'm a complete bungler? Say you will."

Miss Reynolds examined him. "You really mean it?"

"Never meant anything more." He took her hand and gazed down into her eyes.

"Well, then I will. I've been *trying to* for months."

He laughed and kissed her hand.

"There. That wasn't so very difficult, was it?" asked Verity.

The finally united couple turned to stare at her.

"You must get along great guns with Lady Robert," said Mr. Wrentham.

It took Verity a moment to realize that he meant Flora. "I do," she answered.

"I must say the Greshams are better men than I." He looked at Randolph. "Can't see the appeal of a managing woman myself."

"Charles," said Frances.

"Right. Doesn't matter. Not my problem."

"I'm in the habit of speaking my mind," Frances added.

"Not the same. You're adorable."

Frances gave her intended a brilliant smile.

"Small matter of the challenge," Randolph put in.

"What challenge?" Miss Reynolds looked from him to Wrentham, brightly inquisitive.

"Never mind," Wrentham told her. "I'll withdraw it tomorrow," he said to Randolph.

"What challenge?" Miss Reynolds repeated.

"Tell you later," Wrentham replied. He gazed at Randolph. And Verity.

The fellow was waiting for them to leave the room and give him some privacy, Randolph thought. Which seemed a cheat. They'd fixed his romantic problem; they should get the reward of hearing how he talked himself out of that one. Or better yet, have this parlor to themselves for a bit. But they weren't going to; he could see that.

"So that's done," said Verity out in the corridor. "On to the archbishop."

"You are a marvel," said Randolph.

"I had some help from your mother."

He wasn't the least surprised.

A chattering group came out of a room along the hall. He wanted to say how much he loved her. It was nearly unbearable that he couldn't take her in his arms when he felt he'd waited a long age of the world to find her. But the group surrounded them. It included friends who pulled them along. Their solitude was at an end.

Later that night, rattling around in his bedchamber, too restless to sleep, Randolph came upon his lute in the wardrobe. He took it out, sat down, and opened the case. As he strummed a few chords, his fingers moved automatically to pick out the maddeningly elusive tune he'd been trying to master for months. It lay haunting, poignant at the back of his mind, like a peak he could see but never reach.

He played the first notes. That sounded right at last. He added the next bit. *Yes!* He hadn't been able to get that fingering on the strings the last time he'd tried. He started over at the beginning, breath held. And after all this time, he heard the song that had come to him in an odd sort of vision ring out into the air. Anxious, he tried it again. *Yes!* He had it now. Because of the love in his heart, he decided. He'd had to know real love to play this song.

Randolph exulted. Here was a sign. All would be well. He'd make Verity happy. He played the melody again. He sang the words. He'd really gotten it! He fell into a pleasure of harmonies and variations. Soon he forgot all else in the lovely sound.

# Twenty-two

The duke found Randolph at breakfast the next morning and sat down to join him. "I've had a thought," he said.

Randolph came alert. His father's thoughts were always worth hearing.

"But first, a few questions," he added. "Your mother told me that Miss Sinclair has dreams of traveling the world. Having adventures." He smiled. "You, on the other hand, are a rather settled person."

"Because of my profession," Randolph replied. "I've always envied James a bit, but a church can't sail away like a ship, and my work is important to me." He longed to give Verity everything she wanted, yet he had his ambitions, too. "I'd planned to make a difference through the church. I do. Though in a smaller way than I'd hoped."

"So you're not averse to traveling, if you could continue your ministry at the same time?"

"Not at all. What do you have in mind? Not missionary work. I wouldn't care for that."

The duke merely shook his head. He looked as if

he was filing information away. "Is Miss Sinclair on good terms with the archbishop? I'm not sure of her exact connection."

"He's her mother's second cousin." He and Verity had discussed this when they'd wondered again if her mother could intervene. "They haven't often met. He gave her a prayer book when she was six."

His father nodded again. "Well, unless you object, I believe I will go over to Lambeth and call on His Grace."

"To intercede for me." While a younger part of Randolph felt relieved, another didn't like the idea of pushing his problems off on his parent.

"I wouldn't put it that way. To feel out the situation, perhaps. See what possibilities may be open. Unless you'd rather I didn't, of course."

Randolph wavered. And then he realized that he wanted to talk to Verity about this plan first. Her opinions were always cogent, and he thought better when he thrashed a matter out with her. "Can I tell you this afternoon?"

"Of course." The duke rose. Randolph was relieved to see that he didn't look at all offended. "Whenever you like. I shan't do anything without your say-so."

He went out, and a few minutes later Randolph followed.

A great part of the season was people pairing up, Verity thought as she sat alone in their rented drawing room. Emma was certain she'd gotten just the mate she wanted, and for all Verity knew, she was right.

Frances Reynolds had come to town with her sights set on a particular gentleman, and now she had him.

Verity looked down at her original London plan, with the items she'd ticked off weeks ago and those that remained. She'd made inquiries about the Derbyshire town where Randolph was newly posted. He'd called it pleasant, not the least bit countrified, but she couldn't quite agree. Ashbourne seemed picturesque; several coaching roads came together at the center, but it was far from a metropolis. Life there would be like the one she'd grown up with and had been determined to leave behind. The rectory would resemble her childhood home. She would make some friends and do good works. It wasn't what she'd dreamed. However, she would have Randolph.

Randolph would provide tempestuous, passionate elements that had not featured in her placid childhood. And if her experience so far was any measure, life with him would be an adventure in itself. Perhaps it would do. She suppressed a sigh. Of course it would! She loved him.

As if her thoughts had called him, Randolph walked in. "I told the maid she needn't announce me. This is a stealthy visit."

Verity folded up her plan and set it aside. "Mama took Papa to see the circulating library." She stood up and walked into his arms.

They welcomed her joyfully. So did his lips. They belonged together, Verity thought; all would just have to be well.

A delightful, enflaming time passed in kisses.

"I hope your mother finds something wonderful to

read, and that it takes her an hour or more," Randolph murmured in her ear.

Verity laughed breathlessly. She ran her hands over his ribs, deploring the shirt and waistcoat that kept her from touching his skin. Randolph murmured his approval.

At last, regretfully, he stepped back. "I don't suppose we could just elope? I could get a special license."

"The Archbishop of Canterbury grants special licenses," Verity pointed out.

"Ah...yes. Dash it." He let out a frustrated breath. "I've come to talk to you about him. My father offered to go to Lambeth Palace."

Verity stood straighter, transfixed by this news. "To talk him 'round?"

"My father said he had a suggestion." Randolph frowned. "But I'm not a boy, running to Papa with a skinned knee."

He was sensitive in this regard. She knew that. But they couldn't reject such a powerful ally. Verity thought quickly. "He should go," she said. "And we must go with him."

"We?"

The duchess's principle of clear and open discussion had worked with Mr. Wrentham. There had been a few bumps, true, but they'd won through. Verity felt bold and mighty. "We'll all talk to him," she said. "I can remind him of our relationship. Of course. That's better than having Mama do it."

"I don't know what else I can say to him," Randolph replied. He sounded resentful. "I've apologized. Repeatedly, and thoroughly."

"Oh well, you can just stand by, looking penitent and stalwart. Perhaps I'll weep a little?" She framed the scene in her mind—the influential duke, the sad young relative. Tears were too much, she decided.

Randolph gazed at her as if surprised. "I don't know," he repeated.

The three of them left at midmorning the following day in one of the duke's carriages. Verity had told her parents she was going to see Olivia and left a note to be found in case she should be missed. But there was no reason she should be, she thought. The archbishop's residence was on the south side of the Thames, only a few miles from Mayfair. They'd be there and back in no time, if all went well. Indeed, it seemed so simple now, with the duke on their side.

From the coach window, Randolph watched the passing scene. He was a bit worried that they hadn't sent ahead to make an appointment. His companions had decreed that it would be better to surprise their quarry. And when he'd tried to argue that the archbishop didn't care for surprises, he'd been overruled. The combination of Papa and Verity was irresistible.

All too soon, they arrived at the palace. At the entry, the duke handed over his card. "I've brought along a young relative of the archbishop's," he said, indicating Verity. "Miss Sinclair. And my son."

"The archbishop is extremely busy," said the clerical gatekeeper.

"I'm sorry. It's rather important."

Papa didn't sound the least sorry, Randolph

thought. He also noted that his own first name hadn't been mentioned.

After a few minutes dithering, they were admitted into the presence of Archbishop Charles Manners-Sutton, who was a few years older than Papa, smooth-faced and aristocratic. He greeted the duke cordially. Randolph hung back behind his tall father. "Your wife has been in our prayers," said the archbishop.

"Thank you, she's much better."

The archbishop nodded as if taking credit.

"I'm sure you remember your cousin, Miss Sinclair."

"Of course."

"She's recently betrothed to my son Randolph."

Forced to come forward, Randolph offered a graceful, and he hoped humble, bow. "Your Grace. I'm glad to see you well."

The archbishop's eyes widened. "Ah. You."

"Shall we sit down?" said the duke. Verity didn't wait for an invitation. She walked over and sat on a small sofa. She gave their host a melting smile.

"Does your father know you're here?" he asked.

"Of course not. He follows your lead in every way."

Both the words and her tone appeared to startle him considerably. Randolph's doubts flared.

The rest of them sat.

"I thought you might be pondering a wedding gift for your young relative," the duke said.

The archbishop looked at him as if he was speaking an unknown language.

"She's very keen on travel, you know."

Verity picked up his cue as if they'd planned the

whole exchange, when Randolph knew for a fact they hadn't. "Oh yes, it's been my lifetime ambition to see the world."

"And so when I heard that you were about to appoint a roving envoy to look into needs of the church abroad..."

Papa let the sentence trail off. Randolph watched Verity's eyes light up as she assimilated the implications. He watched the archbishop's eyes narrow with calculation. The man didn't like being manipulated, naturally, but Randolph could almost see him thinking that such an appointment would get Randolph, and the story of the ram, out of England for an indefinite period. Perhaps forever, Randolph thought a little uneasily. It was a fascinating opportunity, though he'd miss having a congregation of his own.

"An interesting possibility," the archbishop answered. "I'll consider it."

"Liverpool was telling me about the position," the duke replied. His tone, and his mention of the leader of the English government, indicated that thinking about it wasn't good enough. "He seemed to think that such a man would need connections and a talent for diplomacy."

"Diplomacy?" repeated their host irascibly.

"Someone who wouldn't dream of repeating awkward stories, even when they're quite amusing."

The two elders locked gazes. The air seemed to crackle with tension. Randolph had to resist grinding his teeth. He met Verity's bright gaze and took the risk of hope. The silence stretched and stretched until he could scarcely breathe.

"Very well," said the archbishop at last.

The duke gave him a charming smile. "You won't be sorry. Randolph will do an exemplary job for you. He has many talents, and he's eager to do so."

Randolph caught the cue this time. He nodded. And didn't smile.

"And he'll be so well trained for wider responsibilities in the church when he returns."

This was a step too far. Randolph could tell from his superior's face. He'd give no further guarantees. But seeing Verity's glowing expression, Randolph didn't care. They could meet up with James and travel with them a bit, he thought. And they'd see so many marvelous things. He was actually quite interested in the far-flung outposts of the church and how they got on.

His father rose. "Thank you," he said. "I'm very grateful."

As they took their leave, Randolph saw the archbishop calculating how best to use the gratitude of a duke.

"That went rather well," the latter said as they climbed back into the carriage.

"Splendidly!" cried Verity. "You do think so, don't you, Randolph?"

He nodded. As usual, his father had known best.

# Epilogue

The entire Gresham clan was present at St. George's in Hanover Square just two weeks later, filling one side of the church while members of Verity's family sat on the other. The archbishop himself had suggested a special license for Randolph's wedding, not so much granting it as thrusting it upon them. Now that the appointment had been made, he seemed eager to get his new envoy out of the country as quickly as possible. Verity's hastily assembled wedding clothes had been sewn with an eye to the heat of the tropics. Her intense delight in this had been one of the high points of Randolph's recent days.

Verity's father presided at the ceremony, wholly reconciled now that the archbishop had shown signs of his favor. No one told Mr. Sinclair how the appointment had been achieved. And he didn't ask, which suggested he had a good bit of diplomatic talent himself.

Alan stood up with Randolph, having drawn the long straw in a contest suggested by Robert, after Randolph confessed himself unable to choose a best man from among his brothers. The youngest of them did his part with assurance, even though his gaze kept straying to his new son, held by the lovely Ariel in the front row. Next to her, Nathaniel hovered over his wife Violet, due to deliver very soon.

The wedding breakfast was held at Langford House, since the ceremony had taken place so far from the Sinclair home. The duchess was up and about again, with limits, and had been pleased to give Mrs. Sinclair free rein in organizing the event. The crowd filled a great reception room, chattering and browsing the lavish buffet.

When the time seemed right, Randolph slipped away to fetch his lute. Then he stood before them all with his new wife beside him. Together, they sang the song that had come to him in a kind of dream, apparently for this moment precisely. That was what Verity had said, anyway, when he told her the story and taught her the tune.

*More than honey, the words you speak are sweet,*
*Honest and wise, nobly and wittily said.*
*Yours are the beauties of Camiola complete,*
*Of Iseult the blond and Morgana the fairy maid.*
*If Blanchefleur should be added to the group,*
*Your loveliness would tower above each head.*
*Beneath your brows five beautiful things repose:*
*Love and a fire and a flame, the lily, the rose.*

They let the harmonies twine and soar. Variations emerged unexpectedly, chiming sweet in a minor key. What one began, the other caught and embroidered.

Their voices were perfect complements; their artistic instincts beautifully matched. This was what their life would be like, Randolph thought, as the ancient words vibrated in his chest. Thrilling. Reciprocal. A marvelous edifice built together, not all easily, but with delight.

There were tears here and there in the crowd when the last notes died away. The duke and duchess had twined hands.

"I got him the lute," Randolph heard Sebastian explaining.

"I beg your pardon," Nathaniel replied. "You taxed me with finding it."

Sebastian grinned. "Oh well, Randolph wouldn't know the song if it wasn't for us, would he, Georgina?"

His wife nodded, smiling with wet eyes.

"Have you nothing to add?" Flora asked Robert. "There must be some way that you made all this possible."

Robert shook his head. "I'm speechless. I only wish I'd found such a gift to give to you."

Flora had to blink quickly then.

Verity leaned close to Randolph. "Do you think one can burst with happiness?" she asked.

"You'd better not," he teased. "I have a great many plans for later."

"I might need help with my laces," she murmured in his ear.

"My fingers are yours to command. Always."

They might have stood gazing into each other's eyes forever. But one of Verity's somewhat tipsy cousins offered a toast. "To Lord and Lady Randolph."

The others echoed him and sipped champagne.

"Lady Randolph." Verity tried the new title on her tongue, a little dubious.

"It'll sound well on accounts of your travels," Randolph suggested. "Sell more books."

Verity's answering smile was all he could desire, for the moment.

Read on for a peek at
Book 1 in Jane Ashford's
brand-new Lovelorn Lords series
*The Loveless Lord*
Available August 2018 from
Sourcebooks Casablanca

As Benjamin Romilly, fifth Baron Furness, walked down Regent Street toward Pall Mall, tendrils of icy fog beaded on his greatcoat and brushed his face like ghostly fingertips. The rawness of the March evening matched his mood: cheerless and bleak. He couldn't wait to leave London and return to his Somerset home. He'd come up on business—annoyingly unavoidable—not for the supposed pleasures of society. His jaw tightened. Those who complained that town was empty at this time of year were idiots. Even though walkers were few in the bitter weather, he could feel the pressure of people in the buildings around him—chattering, laughing. As if there was anything funny about life. It grated like the scrape of fingernails across a child's slate.

Some invitations couldn't be refused, however, and tonight's dinner was one. His uncle Macklin was the head of his family and a greatly respected figure. Indeed, Benjamin felt a bit like an errant child being called on the carpet, though he could imagine no reason for the feeling. He didn't see his uncle often. Well, lately he didn't see anyone unless he had to. He walked faster. He was running late. He'd had trouble dragging himself out of his hotel.

He turned onto Piccadilly and was instantly aware

of several figures clustered in the recessed entry of a building on the right, as if the light from the tall windows could warm them. Ladybirds, not footpads, Benjamin recognized, even as a feminine voice called out, "Hello, dearie." One of them moved farther into the strip of illumination that stretched from the window, her appearance confirming his judgment.

Benjamin strode on. She hurried over to walk beside him. "A fine fella like you shouldn't be alone on a cold night," the woman said. "Look at the shoulders on him," she called to her colleagues. "And a leg like a regular Adonis."

"No, thank you," said Benjamin.

She ignored him. "Such a grim look for a handsome lad. Come along, and I'll put a smile on your face, dearie. You can believe I know how." She put one hand on his sleeve to slow him and gestured suggestively with the other.

"I'm not interested." Paint couldn't hide the fact that she was raddled and skinny. Gooseflesh mottled her nearly bare breasts, on display for her customers. She must be freezing, Benjamin thought. And desperate, to be out on a night like this one. He pulled out all the coins he had in his pocket. Shaking off her hand, he pushed them into it. "Here. Take this."

She quickly fingered them. "Ooh, you can get whatever you want for this, dearie. Some things you haven't even dreamed of, mayhap."

"Nothing." Benjamin waved her off and moved on. Some plights could be eased by money, he thought. There was a crumb of satisfaction in the idea, when so much misery was intractable.

"Think you're so grand," the woman screeched after him. "Shoving your leavings at me like a lord to a peasant."

Benjamin didn't bother feeling aggrieved. It was just the way of the world. Things went wrong. Good intentions got you precisely nowhere. And he didn't blame her for resenting the position she'd found herself in. He pulled his woolen scarf tighter about his neck and trudged on.

Stepping into the warmth and conviviality of White's was like moving into a different world. The rich wood paneling and golden candlelight of the gentlemen's club replaced the icy fog. There was a buzz of conversation and clink of glasses from both sides of the entryway. Savory smells rode the air, promising a first-rate meal.

Surrendering his coat and hat to a servitor, Benjamin was directed to a private corner of the dining room, where he found his uncle standing like a society hostess receiving visitors.

Arthur Shelton, Earl of Macklin, was nearly twenty years Benjamin's senior, but he hardly looked it. The sandy hair they shared showed no gray. His tall figure remained muscular and upright. His square-jawed, broad-browed face—which Benjamin's was said to echo—showed few lines, and those seemed scored by good humor. Benjamin shook his mother's brother's hand and tried to appear glad to be in company.

"Allow me to introduce my other guests," his uncle said, turning to the table behind him.

Benjamin hadn't realized there was to be a party. If he'd known, he wouldn't have come, he thought.

And then he was merely bewildered as he surveyed the three other men who comprised it. He didn't know them, and he was surprised that his uncle did. They all appeared closer to his own age than his uncle's near half century.

"This is Daniel Frith, Viscount Whitfield," his uncle continued, indicating the fellow on the left.

Only medium height, but he looked very strong, Benjamin observed. Brown hair and eyes and a snub nose that might have been commonplace but for the energy that seemed to crackle off him.

"Sir Roger Berwick," said his uncle, nodding to the man in the center of the trio.

This one was more Benjamin's height. He was thinner, however, with reddish hair and choleric blue eyes.

"And Peter Rathbone, Baron Compton," said their host.

Clearly the youngest of them, Benjamin thought. Not much past twenty, he'd wager, and nervous looking. Compton had black hair, hazel eyes, and long fingers that tapped uneasily on his flanks.

"Gentlemen, this is my nephew, Benjamin Romilly, Baron Furness, the last of our group. And now that the proprieties are satisfied, I hope we can be much less formal."

They stood gazing at each other. Everyone but his uncle looked mystified, Benjamin thought. *He* felt as if he'd strayed into one of those dreams where you show up for an examination all unprepared.

"Sit down," said his uncle, gesturing at their waiting table. As they obeyed, he signaled for wine to be poured. "They have a fine roast beef this evening. As when do they not at White's? We'll begin with soup, though, on a raw night like this." The waiter returned his nod and went off to fetch it.

The hot broth was welcome, and the wine was good, of course. Conversation was another matter. Whitfield commented on the vile weather, and the rest of them agreed that it was a filthy night. Compton praised the claret, and then looked uneasy, as if he'd been presumptuous. The rest merely nodded. After a bit, Sir Roger scowled. Benjamin thought he was going to ask what the deuce was going on—hoped someone would, and soon—but then Sir Roger took more wine instead. All their glasses were emptied and refilled promptly.

It wasn't simply good manners or English reticence, Benjamin concluded. Uncle Arthur's innate authority and air of command was affecting these strangers just as they did his family. One simply didn't demand what the hell Uncle Arthur thought he was doing.

Steaming plates were put before them. Eating reduced the necessity of talking. Benjamin addressed his beef and roast potatoes with what might have appeared to be enthusiasm. The sooner he finished, the sooner he could excuse himself from this awkward occasion, he thought. He was about halfway through when his uncle spoke. "No doubt you're wondering why I've invited you—the four of you—this evening, when we aren't really acquainted."

Knives and forks went still. All eyes turned to the host, with varying degrees of curiosity and relief.

"You have something in common," he went on. "*We* do." He looked around the table. "Death."

Astonishment, and denial, crossed the others' faces.

The older man nodded at Benjamin. "My nephew's wife died in childbirth four years ago. He mourns her still."

In one queasy instant, Benjamin was flooded with rage and despair. The food roiled dangerously in his stomach. How dared his uncle speak of this before strangers? Or anyone? All Benjamin asked was that people let him be. Little enough, surely? His eyes burned into his uncle's quite similar blue-gray gaze. Benjamin saw sympathy there, and something more. Determination? He gritted his teeth and looked away. What did it matter? The pall of sadness that had enveloped him since Alice's death fell back into place. He made a dismissive gesture. No doubt his tablemates cared as little for his history as he did for theirs.

Uncle Arthur turned to the man on his left. "Frith's parents were killed in a shipwreck eight months ago on their way back from India," he continued.

The stocky viscount looked startled, then impatient. "Quite so. A dreadful accident. Storm drove them onto a reef." He looked around the table and shrugged. "What can one do? These things happen."

Benjamin dismissed him as an unfeeling clod even as his attention was transfixed by his uncle's next bit of information.

"Sir Roger lost his wife to a virulent fever a year ago."

"I didn't *lose* her," this gentleman exclaimed, his thin face reddening with anger. "She was dashed well *killed* by an incompetent physician, and my neighbor, who insisted they ride out into a downpour."

He looked furious. Benjamin searched for sadness

in his expression and couldn't find it. Rather, he looked like a man who'd suffered an intolerable insult.

"And Compton's sister died while she was visiting a friend, just six months ago," his uncle finished.

The youngest man at the table flinched as if he'd taken a blow. "She was barely seventeen," he murmured. "My ward as well as sister." He put his head in his hands. "I ought to have gone with her. I was invited. If only I'd gone. I wouldn't have allowed her to take that cliff path. I would have—"

"I've been widowed for ten years," interrupted their host gently. "I know what it's like to lose a beloved person quite suddenly. And I know there must be a period of adjustment afterward. People don't talk about the time it takes—different for everyone, I imagine—and how one copes." He looked around the table again. "I was aware of Benjamin's bereavement, naturally, since he is my nephew."

Benjamin cringed. He could simply rise and walk out, he thought. No one could stop him. Uncle Arthur might be offended, but he deserved it for arranging this…intolerable intrusion.

"Then, seemingly at random, I heard of your cases, and it occurred to me that I might be able to help."

Benjamin noted his companions' varying reactions: angry, puzzled, dismissive. No one, not even his formidable uncle, could make him speak if he didn't wish to, and he didn't.

"What help is there for death?" said Sir Roger. "And which of us asked for your aid? *I* certainly didn't." He glared around the table as if searching for someone to blame.

"Waste of time to dwell on such stuff," said Frith. "No point, eh?"

Compton sighed like a man who despaired of absolution.

"Grief is insidious, almost palpable, and as variable as humankind," said their host. "No one who hasn't experienced a sudden loss can understand. A black coat and a few platitudes are nothing."

"Are you accusing us of insincerity, sir?" demanded Sir Roger. He was flushed with anger, clearly a short-tempered fellow.

"Not at all. I'm offering you the fruits of experience and years of contemplation."

"Thrusting them on us, whether we will or no," replied Sir Roger. "Tantamount to an ambush, this so-called dinner."

"Nothing wrong with the food," said Frith, his tone placating. He earned a ferocious scowl from Sir Roger, which he ignored. "Best claret I've had this year."

Benjamin grew conscious of a tiny, barely perceptible, desire to laugh. The impulse startled him.

"Well, well," said his uncle. "Who knows? If I've made a mistake, I'll gladly apologize. Indeed, I beg your pardon for springing my idea on you with no preparation. Will you, nonetheless, allow me to tell the story of my grieving, as I had hoped to do?"

Such was the power of his personality that none of the younger men refused. Even Sir Roger merely glared at his half-eaten meal.

"And afterward, should you wish to do the same, I'll gladly hear it," said Benjamin's uncle. He smiled.

Uncle Arthur had always had the most engaging

smile, Benjamin thought. He suddenly recalled a day twenty years past, when his young uncle had caught him slipping a frog between a bullying cousin's bedsheets. That day, Uncle Arthur's grin had quirked with shared mischief. Tonight, his expression showed kindness and sympathy and the focus of a keen intellect. Impossible to resist, really.

In the end, Benjamin found the talk that evening surprisingly gripping. Grief had more guises than he'd realized, and there was a crumb of comfort in knowing that other men labored under its yoke. Not that it made the least difference after the goodbyes had been said and the reality of his solitary life descended upon him once more. Reality remained, as it had these last years, bleak.

# One

Benjamin rode over the last low ridge and drew rein to look down on his home. It was a vast relief to be back, far from the incessant noise of London. The mellow red brick of the house, twined with ivy, the pointed gables and ranks of leaded windows, were as familiar as his own face in the mirror. Furness Hall had been the seat of his family for two hundred years, built when the first baron received his title from King James. The place was a pleasing balance of grand and comfortable, Benjamin thought. And Somerset's mild climate kept the lawn and shrubberies green all winter, though the trees were bare. Not one stray leaf marred the sweep of sod before the front door, he saw approvingly. The hedges were neat and square—a picture of tranquility. A man could be still with his thoughts here, and he longed for nothing else.

He left his horse at the stables and entered the house to a welcome hush. Everything was just as he wished it in his home, with no demands and no surprises. He'd heard a neighbor claim, when he thought Benjamin couldn't hear, that Furness Hall had gone gloomy since its mistress died. He could not have cared less about the fellow's opinion. What did he know of grief? Or anything else for that matter? He was obviously a dolt.

A shrill shout broke the silence as Benjamin turned toward the library, followed by pounding footsteps. A small figure erupted from the back of the entry hall. "The lord's home," cried the small boy.

Benjamin cringed. Four-year-old Geoffrey was a whirlwind of disruptive energy. He never seemed to speak below a shout, and he was forever beating on pans or capering about waving sticks like a demented imp.

"The lord's home," shouted the boy again, skidding to a stop before Benjamin and staring up at him. His red-gold hair flopped over his brow. He shoved it back with a grubby hand.

Benjamin's jaw tightened. His small son's face was so like Alice's—it was uncannily painful. In a bloody terror of death and birth, he'd traded beloved female features for an erratic miniature copy. He could tell himself it wasn't Geoffrey's fault that his mother had died bringing him into the world. He *knew* it wasn't. But that didn't make it any easier to look at him.

A nursery maid came running, put her hands on Geoffrey's shoulders, and urged him away. Staring back over his shoulder, the boy went. His deep blue eyes reproduced Alice's in color and shape, but she'd never gazed at Benjamin so pugnaciously. Of course she hadn't. She'd been all loving support and gentle approbation. But she was gone.

Benjamin headed for his library. If he had peace and quiet, he could manage the blow that fate had dealt him. Was that so much to ask? He didn't think so.

Shutting the door behind him, he sat in his customary place before the fire. Alice's portrait looked down at him—her lush figure in a simple white gown, that glory of red-gold hair, great celestial blue eyes, lips parted as if she was just about to speak to him. He'd forgotten that he'd thought the portrait idealized when it was first finished. Now it was his image of paradise lost. He no longer imagined—as he had all through the first year after her death—that he heard her voice in the next room, a few tantalizing feet away, or that he would come upon her around a corner. She was gone. But he could gaze at her image and lose himself in memory.

Three days later, a post chaise pulled up before Furness Hall, uninvited and wholly unexpected. No one visited here now. One of the postilions jumped down and rapped on the front door while the other held the team. A young woman emerged from the carriage and marched up as the door opened. She slipped past the startled maid and planted herself by the stairs inside, grasping the newel post like a ship dropping anchor. "I am Jean Saunders," she said. "Alice's cousin. I'm here to see Geoffrey. At once, please."

"G-geoffrey, miss?"

The visitor gave a sharp nod. "My…relative. Alice's son."

"He's just a little lad."

"I'm well aware. Please take me to him." When the servant hesitated, she added, "Unless you prefer that I search the house."

Goggle-eyed, the maid shook her head. "I'll have to ask his lordship."

Miss Saunders sighed and began pulling off her gloves. "I suppose you will." She untied the strings of her bonnet. "Well? Do so."

The maid hurried away. Miss Saunders removed her hat, revealing a wild tumble of glossy brown curls. Then she bit her bottom lip, looking far less sure of herself than she'd sounded, and put it back on. When footsteps approached from the back of the hall, she stood straighter and composed her features.

"Who the deuce are you?" asked the tall, frowning gentleman who followed the housemaid into the entryway.

Unquestionably handsome, Jean thought. He had the sort of broad-browed, square-jawed face one saw on the tombs of Crusaders. Sandy hair, blue-gray eyes with dark lashes, which might have been attractive if they hadn't held a hard glitter. "I am Alice's cousin," Jean repeated.

"Cousin?" He said the word as if it had no obvious meaning.

"Well, second cousin, but that hardly matters. I'm here for Geoffrey."

"*For* him? He's four years old."

"I'm well aware. As I am also aware that he is being shamefully neglected."

"I beg your pardon?" Benjamin put ice into his tone. The accusation was outrageous, as was showing up at his home, without any warning, to make it.

"I don't think I can grant it to you," his unwanted visitor replied. "You might try asking your son for forgiveness."

She spoke with contempt. The idea was ridiculous, but there was no mistaking her tone. Benjamin examined the intruder in one raking glance. She looked a bit younger than his own age of thirty. Slender, of medium height, with untidy brown hair and dark eyes, and an aquiline nose, she didn't resemble Alice in the least.

"I've come to take Geoffrey to his grandparents," she added. "Alice's parents. He deserves a proper home."

"His home is here."

"Really? A house where his dead mother's portrait is kept as some sort of macabre shrine? Where he calls his father 'the lord'? Where he is shunted aside and ignored?"

Benjamin felt as if he'd missed a step in the dark. Put that way, Geoffrey's situation did sound dire. But that wasn't the whole of the truth! He'd made certain the boy received the best of care. "How do you know anything—"

"People have sent reports, to let his grandparents know how he's treated."

"What *people*?" There could be no such people. The house had lost a servant or two in recent years, but there'd been no visitors. He didn't want visitors, particularly the repellent one who stood before him.

"I notice you don't deny that Geoffrey is mistreated," she replied.

Rage ripped through Benjamin. "My son is *treated* splendidly. He is fed and clothed and…and being taught his letters." Of course he must be, though he was scarcely of an age for schooling. Perhaps he ought to know a bit more about the details of Geoffrey's existence, Benjamin thought, but that didn't mean the boy was *mistreated*.

Two postilions entered with a valise. "Leave that on the coach," Benjamin commanded. "Miss...won't be staying." He couldn't remember the dratted girl's name.

"It doesn't matter," she said. "Take it back. I'm only here to fetch Geoffrey."

"Never in a thousand years," said Benjamin.

"What do you care? You hardly speak to him. They say you can't bear to look at him."

"They. Who the devil are *they*?"

"Those with Geoffrey's best interests at heart. And no sympathy for a cold, neglectful father."

"Get out of my house!" he roared.

Instead, she came closer. "No. I won't stand by and see a child harmed."

"How...how dare you? No one lays a hand on him." Benjamin was certain of that much, at least. He'd given precise orders about the level of discipline allowed in the nursery.

"Precisely," replied his infuriating visitor. "He lives a life devoid of affection or approval. It's a disgrace."

Benjamin found he was too angry to speak.

"Please go and get Geoffrey," the intruder said to the hovering maid.

"No," Benjamin managed. He found his voice again. "On no account." His hand swept the air. "Go away," he added. The maid hurried out—someone who obeyed him, at least. Though Benjamin had no doubt that word was spreading through the house, and the rest of his staff was rushing to listen at keyholes.

"Would you prefer that I report you to the local magistrate?" his outrageous visitor asked. "That would be Lord Hallerton, would it not? I inquired in advance."

She scowled at him, immobile, intolerably offensive. Benjamin clenched his fists at his sides to keep from shaking her. While he was certain that any magistrate in the country would side with him over the fate of his son, he didn't care to give the neighborhood a scandal. It seemed that spiteful tongues were already wagging. Who were the blasted gossips spreading lies about him to Alice's parents? The tittle-tattle over this female's insane accusations would be even worse.

The two of them stood toe-to-toe, glaring at each other. Her eyes were not simply brown, Benjamin observed. There was a coppery sparkle in their depths. The top of her head was scarcely above his shoulder. He could easily scoop her up and toss her back into the post chaise. The trouble was, he didn't think she'd stay there. Or, she'd drive off to Hallerton's place and spread her ludicrous dirt.

The air crackled with tension. Benjamin could hear his unwanted guest breathing. The postilion, who had put down the valise and was observing the confrontation, eyed him. Would he wade in if Benjamin tried to eject his unwelcome visitor? He had a vision of an escalating brawl raging through his peaceful home; actually, it would be a relief to punch someone.

Into the charged silence came the sound of another carriage—hoofbeats nearing, slowing; the jingle of a harness; the click of a vehicle's door opening and closing. What further hell could this be? Benjamin had long ago stopped exchanging visits with his neighbors. None would dare drop in on him.

When his uncle Arthur strolled through the still-open front door, Benjamin decided he must be dreaming. It was the only explanation. His life was a carefully orchestrated routine, hedged 'round with safeguards. This scattershot of inexplicable incidents was the stuff of nightmares. Now if he could just wake up.

His uncle stopped on the threshold and surveyed the scene with raised eyebrows. "Hello, Benjamin. And Miss…Saunders, is it not?"

"You *know* her?" Benjamin exclaimed.

"I believe we've met at the Phillipsons' house," the earl replied.

The intruder inclined her head in stiff acknowledgment.

Benjamin could believe it. His lost wife's parents were a fixture of the *haut ton*. Entertaining was their obsession. One met everyone in their lavish town house, a positive beehive of hospitality. Indeed, now he came to think of it, he was surprised they'd spared a thought for Geoffrey. Small, grubby boys had no place in their glittering lives. "And do you know why she's here?" he demanded, reminded of his grievance.

"How could I?" replied his uncle.

Too agitated to notice that this wasn't precisely an answer, Benjamin pointed at the intruder. "*She* wants to take Geoffrey away from me."

"Take him away?"

"To his grandparents," Miss Saunders said. "Where he will be loved, and happy. Rather than shunted aside like an unwanted poor relation."

Benjamin choked on a surge of intense feelings too jumbled to sort out. "I will not endure any more of these insults. Get out of my house!"

"No. *I* will not stand by and see a child hurt," she retorted.

"You have no idea what you're talking about."

"*You* have no idea—"

"Perhaps we should go into the parlor," the older man interrupted, gracefully indicating an adjoining room. "We could sit and discuss matters. Perhaps some refreshment?"

"No!" Benjamin wasn't going to offer food and drink to a harpy who accused him of neglecting his son. Nor to a seldom seen relative who betrayed him by siding with the enemy, however illustrious he might be. "There's nothing to discuss, Uncle Arthur. I can't imagine why you suggest it. Or why you're here, in fact. I want both of you out of my home this—"

"Yaah!" With this bloodcurdling shriek, Geoffrey shot through the door at the back of the entry hall. Clad in only a tattered rag knotted at the waist, his small figure was smeared with red. For a horrified moment, Benjamin thought the swirls were blood. Then he realized it was paint running down the length of his small arms and legs. Shrieking and brandishing a tomahawk, the boy ran at Miss Saunders. He grabbed her skirts with his free hand, leaving red streaks on the cloth, and made chopping motions with the weapon he held. Fending him off, she scooted backward.

In two long steps, Benjamin reached his small son, grasped his wrist, and immobilized the tomahawk—real and quite sharp. Benjamin recognized it from a display shelf upstairs.

Geoffrey jerked and twisted in his grip, his skin slippery with paint. "Let go! I'm a red Indian on the warpath." He kicked at Benjamin's shins. As his small feet were bare, it didn't hurt. His red-gold hair was clotted with paint too, Benjamin noted. There were a couple of feathers—probably chicken—stuck in the mess.

His son began to climb, as if Benjamin was a tree or a ladder. Paint rubbed off on his breeches, his coat. Because of the tomahawk, Benjamin couldn't let go of the boy's wrist. He grabbed for him with his other hand.

Geoffrey lunged, caught the ball of Benjamin's thumb between his teeth, and bit down. "Ow!" Benjamin lost his grip. Geoffrey thudded to the floor, frighteningly close to the blade he held. But he was up at once, unscathed. The rag he was wearing fell off. Geoffrey capered about stark naked, waving the tomahawk and whooping. A drop of blood welled from Benjamin's thumb and dropped onto his waistcoat.

The immensely dignified Earl of Macklin knelt, bringing his head down to Geoffrey's level. "Which tribe do you belong to?" he asked him.

The boy paused to examine Benjamin's uncle. Benjamin edged around to grab him from behind. But it was no good. Geoffrey spotted the maneuver and raised his weapon.

Arthur waved him back. "Your ax is from the Algonquian tribe, I believe," he said to Geoffrey.

The boy blinked his celestial blue eyes. "You know about red Indians?"

"Your grandfather was very interested in them.

He showed me his collections and told me stories he'd gathered."

Benjamin wondered when his father had had an opportunity to share his fascination with artifacts from the Americas with Uncle Arthur. He didn't remember any such sessions. Perhaps when he was away at school?

"Grandfather," repeated Geoffrey. He said the word as if he'd never heard it before. A pang of emotion went through Benjamin. Gritting his teeth, he pulled out his handkerchief and tied it around his bleeding thumb.

"Your father's father," added the earl, nodding at Benjamin.

Geoffrey turned to look. There was something unsettling in his blue gaze, Benjamin thought. Not accusation precisely; rather a speculation far beyond his years. And nothing at all like the gentle inquiry characteristic of his dead mother.

A gangling lad in worn clothing erupted from the rear doorway through which Geoffrey had come and skidded to a halt beside the boy. "You said if I reached down the paint, you'd stay in the schoolroom," the new lad said. "Where's your *clothes*?"

"No," said Geoffrey. He was holding the tomahawk down at his side as if to conceal it, Benjamin noticed.

"You gave me your word," argued the newcomer. He was a dark-haired boy of perhaps fourteen, with hands and feet that promised greater height and sleeves that exposed his wrists. Benjamin had no idea who he was.

"Didn't!" declared Geoffrey. "Never said it." The little ax came up in automatic defense.

"Where did you get that?" cried the older lad, clearly horrified.

Geoffrey laughed. He danced in a circle, waving the tomahawk.

In a move that looked well practiced, the youth stepped forward, snapped out a blanket from under his arm, threw it over Geoffrey, and quickly wrapped him up like an unwieldy package. Picking up the squirming bundle, he attempted a bow. "Beg pardon, your lordship," he said, backing toward the rear of the house. Muffled shouts of protest mixed with laughter came from the woolen folds. They faded as the door closed behind the young duo.

Silence fell over the entryway. Benjamin's uncle stood up. The postilion was staring like a spectator at a peep show. Miss Saunders brushed at the drying paint on her skirts. She looked shaken. "You allow Geoffrey to play with…hatchets," she accused.

"That thing was on a shelf ten feet up," Benjamin said. He was pretty sure that was the spot. "In a locked room. I'm certain it's locked." Wasn't it always? "I've no notion how he got it."

"Precisely. You know nothing about your own son! Who can tell what other dangers surround him? I'm surprised he hasn't been killed."

"Nonsense."

"And was that…rustic youngster your idea of a proper caretaker?"

Unable to supply any information about this person, and aware that appreciation of his ability to truss up a wriggling miscreant would not be well received, Benjamin ground his teeth.

"I must take Geoffrey to the Phillipsons at once," his unwanted visitor added.

"Drag him into your post chaise and rattle off together?" asked Uncle Arthur amiably.

Benjamin nearly growled at him. Then he noticed Miss Saunders's expression. The prospect of sharing a carriage with his naked, paint-smeared, ax-wielding son clearly daunted her. He could almost enjoy that. Indeed, if he hadn't been defending his home from invasion, he might have laughed at the scene just past. Before taking steps to see that it never recurred, of course.

"It seems to me that we need a bit of time to consider the situation," his uncle added. "I know I would appreciate a chance to get acquainted with my great-nephew." This latter sentiment seemed perfectly sincere.

Miss Saunders muttered something. The word *savage* might have been included.

"I won't have her in my house!" Benjamin said.

"I've no wish to stay with a monster of selfishness!"

But in the end, the earl somehow persuaded them. Benjamin was never sure, afterward, how he'd come to agree. Was it simply easier? Had he been that desperate to escape his two unwanted guests and shut himself in the library again? And why had he promised to review his son's educational program with these near strangers? It was none of their business. And he was not afraid of what he might discover. Absolutely not. Even though he had no idea what it might be. Finally alone again, he sank into his familiar chair and put his head in his hands.

Upstairs, Jean Saunders sat on the bed in her allotted chamber, hands folded in her lap, jaw tight, and contemplated a rescue mission gone seriously awry. Her plan had been simple, efficient. She would swoop in, collect Geoffrey, and be gone. She should be on her way back to London by now. Her cousin Alice's husband had been portrayed as so deeply sunk in mourning that he didn't care what happened in his household. Hadn't he? Where had she gotten that notion? She'd expected to face a drooping, defeated fellow who might well welcome a relief from responsibility, not a gimlet-eyed crusader blazing with outrage. How could people have characterized that... masterful man as broken by grief? His eyes had practically burned through her. He'd pounced like a jungle cat to restrain his rampaging son.

Jean let out a long—not entirely unappreciative—breath at the memory. Still, the gossip about his lordship's shameful neglect of Geoffrey was clearly on the mark. The boy was like some sort of wild animal. If he'd landed a blow with that hatchet... Folding her arms across her chest, Jean realized that she'd expected Geoffrey to be a cherubic child, like the smiling illustrations on top of a chocolate box. She'd envisioned him in a little blue suit with a lace collar, dimpled and pink, putting his arms around her neck and softly thanking her for rescuing him. She'd thought to take his little hand and lead him off to happiness. Nothing could be more unlike the reality of a prancing imp painted red, shrieking, and bent on mayhem. The maniacal glee in his eyes!

She let her arms fall to her sides and sat straighter, gathering her tattered resolution. It wasn't Geoffrey's fault that he hadn't been taught manners, or any vestige of civilized behavior, apparently. That was the point, wasn't it? He deserved far better. He must be guided and nurtured. She'd come here to save him, and she was going to do so. Hadn't she'd nagged the Phillipsons half to death to make them offer refuge to their grandson? If Baron Furness found out the whole plan was her idea, and that Geoffrey's grandparents were far from enthusiastic… Well, he could hardly be angrier than he was now.

Jean gripped the coverlet with both hands. He'd been furious. Standing up to him had been like confronting a force of nature. Perhaps he cared about his child after all? She'd be glad of that, naturally. Yet he hadn't been affectionate with Geoffrey. And the boy had bitten him! What sort of bond was that?

No, Jean was all too familiar with neglectful parents. Geoffrey needed a new home. Probably her host was worried about his reputation, and resented being exposed and thwarted. An old adage floated into Jean's mind. *Like father, like son.* Did Geoffrey get his wild ways from his parent? A shiver passed through her. With a grimace, she banished it. She'd vowed never to be afraid again, and one blustering baron wasn't going to cow her. Still less a four-year-old child.

The streaks of red paint on her gown caught Jean's eye. She'd had to promise the Phillipsons that she'd take care of establishing their grandson once he was in London, seeing that he had the proper attendants. They were far too busy to bother with a child. It had seemed a trivial condition at the time, with her righteous indignation in full flood. Jean's chocolate box vision wavered into her mind again, immediately replaced by the naked, whooping reality. But Geoffrey would improve with gentle guidance and plenty of affection. Wouldn't he? Quite quickly? Jean had no brothers or sisters. Indeed, she'd never had much to do with children of any stripe. Had she made a mistake?

No. Jean pushed off the bed and stood up like a soldier reporting for duty. She knew what it was like to be a miserable child. Memories of cold, dark silence rushed over her, setting her heart pounding and making her mouth dry. With practiced determination, she shoved them away. She'd come here to do the right thing. She would fight, and she would prevail.

# *Two*

Arthur slipped his arms into the evening coat his valet was holding for him and waited while Clayton smoothed it over his shoulders. The mirror told him that they had achieved his customary understated elegance. "What word among the household?" he asked. "What do they say about young Geoffrey?"

Clayton looked thoughtful. The man had been with the earl for more than twenty years, and Arthur valued his canny insights as much as his personal services. "Opinions vary, my lord, depending on how close the person is to the young heir. Concerning the incident today, the general suspicion is that Master Geoffrey was playing a prank. He does not habitually run about the house clad in a tea towel, I gather."

"That tomahawk was no toy," Arthur pointed out.

Clayton nodded. "Yet he didn't actually strike anyone, I understand. Even under, er, provocation. He's said to be an intelligent child. Apparently, he can read."

"What, at four years old?" The earl was impressed. "Who taught him, I wonder?"

"People were reluctant to discuss the exact arrangements of the nursery with an outsider," Clayton said. "Particularly after the housekeeper entered the kitchen."

"Hmm."

"Yes, my lord. The head gardener is of the opinion that the boy disguises what he can and can't do and is devious in bargaining for what he wants."

"At his age?" Arthur replied. "That would be precocious indeed."

"The junior kitchen maid believes he is possessed by the devil."

Arthur laughed. His valet didn't, but his eyes showed amusement. "It sounds as if he might become a son for a father to be proud of."

# *About the Author*

Jane Ashford discovered Georgette Heyer in junior high school and was captivated by the glittering world and witty language of Regency England. That delight was part of what led her to study English literature and travel widely in Britain and Europe. She has written historical and contemporary romances, and her books have been published in Sweden, Italy, England, Denmark, France, Russia, Latvia, the Czech Republic, Slovakia, and Spain, as well as the United States. Jane has been nominated for a Career Achievement Award by *RT Book Reviews*. Born in Ohio, she is now somewhat nomadic. Find her on the web at janeashford.com and on Facebook. If you're interested in receiving her monthly newsletter, you can subscribe at eepurl.com/cd-O7r.